CRAIG HALLORAN

ZOMBIE IMPACT

Zombie Impact Series:

Apocalyptic Zombie Thriller

Books 1-3

Copyright February 2011 by Craig Halloran

Revised 2021

TWO-TEN BOOK PRESS

P.O. Box 4215, Charleston, WV 25364

Amazon Edition

ISBN Paperback: 978-1-941208-10-6

ISBN Ebook: 978-0-9827799-2-7

Information about this author and his other works available at:

WWW.CRAIGHALLORAN.COM

Publishers Note:

This book is a work of fiction. Names, characters, places, and incidents either are the product of the author's imagination or are used fictitiously, and any resemblance to the actual persons, living or dead, events, or locales is entirely coincidental.

❀ Created with Vellum

CRAIG HALLORAN

ZOMBIE
DAY CARE

BEWARE OF
ZOMBIES

BOOK 1

1

LOCATION UNKNOWN

HE SHUFFLED DESPERATELY over the hillside. Sweat soaked his face and clothes. His hair was matted and coated with dirt. He looked over his shoulder, gasped, and pushed forward. His elbows and knees were scraped and caked with dried blood. His jeans and shirt were in tatters. He clutched at the stitch in his side as he jogged into the bright sun lowering over the horizon. He could make out a small town miles ahead. *I can do it.*

He felt like he was in summer football practice, pushing his body to its limits, quivering from exhaustion. This training was different. This time, if he stopped, he was dead. He hadn't liked football practice; he'd hated it ... they all had. He remembered the smoking scowl of his least-favorite coach shouting behind his back, "Move it, whale tail!"

He was a cumbersome teenager back then, stuck on the team's interior line. He was good at standing in people's way, so he got the start. It didn't hurt that he was big either, except today being bigger was far from better. He would have done anything to be a little guy who could run like the wind. He ran the best he could, long heavy strides turning into a pathetic jog.

His big belly groaned with hunger and fear. He didn't know how far he had run. He remembered his last meal though. Yesterday morning. It was fast food, Taco Bell and Mountain Dew, eight dollars' worth. His concern subsided for a moment, but a loud moan not so far behind him jolted his nerves. Fear gave his legs new strength. His feet ached and burned with each heavy step as he pushed on. He took a quick glance over his shoulder. Something was back there, trudging after him. He heard another moan.

The world had turned upside down. Zombies were real. They were taking over. It didn't all start in some small town, either. No, it was a meltdown in major cities. The outbreak spread like fire, New York to Beijing to Moscow. Zombies cropped up everywhere and flipped the world into turmoil. He and his friends and family headed for the hills. The hills were alive. They all fought hard after the surprise. He watched his loved ones get afflicted and devoured. They came for him, but he manned the higher ground. He blew their brains out, all of them except one. He ran out of ammo and made a dash for his car. He drove away until he ran out of gas, just a few miles from where he left.

He dozed off, feeling safe and exhausted, in the middle of nowhere. He laid his head back just for a second, listening to the madness on the satellite radio. *America has fallen! Russia has fallen! The Middle East has fallen!* He fell asleep ....

His eyes snapped open. A shuffle of dirt caught his ear. He wiped the drool from his mouth. The rear-view mirror showed nothing. His heart raced. Something was out there. A flicker of movement caught his eye in the side-view mirror. He jerked out of the way just as a hand clutched for his neck. He scrambled through the passenger side door and fell outside.

The zombie was there, moaning at him. It came around the hood of the car. He moved the opposite way. *Now what?* It wasn't fast, but it just came steadily for him, like a stubborn child. He thought of Duck-Duck-Goose. *Why did I think of that?* Around and around they went.

He was uncertain of what to do. *Just don't let it catch you.* His only option was to run into the town that was miles away. Maybe more zombies waited there, anywhere, everywhere ... there was no choice.

He slipped around to the driver's side of his car, reached in the window, and popped his trunk. He was faster than the zombie, that much was certain. He couldn't run forever though. As it pursued him around the car, he circled back to the trunk and reached in. He fumbled around, eyes never leaving the creature. He found a handle and pulled it forth. A small sense of security filled his body as he wielded a big wooden softball bat. It was a gift he had bought for his girlfriend.

"This is messed up," he muttered.

He stepped around the car again and bashed in the back passenger window. Still the zombie came, quicker than before it seemed. He made another round to the smashed window and reached inside, cutting his arm on the jagged glass. *Idiot!* The zombie came faster now. He grabbed his backpack as his blood dripped down his arm. *Screw it!* He slung the pack over his shoulder. He hoped everything was in there. *Be prepared.*

He squeezed the handle in both hands. *I gotta do this now!* The zombie came on as he backpedaled.

"Please don't make me do this. Just go away!" he said, waving the big bat.

Still it came, moaning. He looked at the bloody gash on its shoulder. A man-sized bite of flesh was gone, as well as part of its dangling arm. The rest of the zombie was perfect. It was tall, full-figured, and dressed in a football jersey and tight jean shorts. He blinked hard. He could see the painted nails that once scratched his back and belly. Black was her color. Now she came for him, unsteady, black-eyed and slack-jawed. Blue veins rose along her once soft and sensual skin. He couldn't believe he had to bash in the brains ... of his girlfriend.

"No!" he screamed, hoisting the bat high.

Still she came. He swore he could see a smile on her crossed mouth. Jeanine always had a smirk. He blinked hard again. It was something he always remembered. Deep down inside he still loved her, or it. He had been ready to propose, but the world began to end. Still she came, chin down, shuffling his way. He wanted to hug her. His instincts screamed to kill her. Everyone else he knew was dead. He couldn't do it. He felt a lump in his throat rise as he let out a sob. *I can't*. He screamed, snatched up his backpack, and ran.

He had been running ever since. Night was coming, and the tiny town was getting closer. He tried to remember Jeanine the way she used to be, but could not. He was huffing along, fighting for breath as he tried to reach the town. He gave another look back and there she came, step after determined step. He could swear she was getting faster. She used to be faster than him anyway. He never minded running behind her before, but now he had to stay ahead to stay alive. It was a discomforting memory for Nate McDaniel.

2

Nate was walking as fast as he could, often looking back over his shoulder. His zombie girlfriend was nowhere to be seen. The sun was dipping into the dusk as he made his way into the town. Pear trees and flower beds were planted along the streets. There were no stoplights, just signs and well-defined crosswalks. The polluted sounds of human interaction were vacant. He followed the railroad tracks across a rusting iron bridge above a wide stream. He was cautious. Zombies could be anywhere. He hoped there were none.

He cupped his hands to his mouth but then lowered them. Maybe yelling wasn't such a good idea. Nate didn't want to alert the unknown. He knew better. He was starving now, and his stomach hadn't stopped growling for miles. He was exhausted. He never remembered being so tired. His feet were aching and burning like fire. He had to find food. There had to be something left in this town. As he finished crossing the bridge, he looked back again. Nothing was there. He saw a black bird perched on a power line above, then something snapped and he lurched forward.

"Damn!" he shouted.

Blinding pain shot over his shin and up through his knee. His leg was wedged between two rotted railroad ties. His jeans and skin were torn just below the kneecap. He was bleeding and held fast. He tried pulling his hurt knee up.

"Ugh!"

It didn't help that he was over two hundred and fifty pounds. He was dead weight, and the effort jammed his leg further down.

"No—No—No! Lord no!"

He closed his eyes and took a breath. The lowering sun went dark as a cloud passed. He felt the shade on his face. Somewhere a crow squawked and flapped away. He opened his eyes and looked back. He watched the black bird dart over the head of a figure. It was her. *Already!* She was coming his way. His chin dipped into his chest.

"Come on, Jeanine!" he yelled, knocking his bat into the bridge.

His heart was sinking. He was stuck, and she was going to eat him. His stomach coiled into a knot. His will to survive was not the strongest, but his desire not to be eaten alive was something else. Deep inside, fear consumed him. He pushed on the rotting boards. They groaned under the desperate power of his supple muscles. He strained in agony as she approached step by step, stumbling over the rotting ties.

Fall! Fall off the bridge, dammit!

She came on, unfettered by her missteps, crossing the bridge only a dozen paces away.

How does she move so fast?

Nate couldn't comprehend how the slow-going figure stayed at his heels like a bloodhound. He thought of the story of the tortoise and the hare. He used to love that story.

He ripped his leg free with a scream. A torn slab of flesh and jeans was hanging down his leg. Thick splinters were burning deep under his skin. He saw muscle, or was it? *Don't look, idiot!* Tears watered down his paunchy face as he struggled to his feet. He saw a necklace hanging from her neck. He bought her that on her birthday ... a gold crucifix. *Why couldn't she be a vampire?* She was almost to him. He ran on in a desperate limp despite the pain building inside his leg.

He needed a car, a truck, anything with wheels. *A bike!* He was parched. His body was already pushed beyond its limits. All of those tennis lessons never prepared him for this. Had anything? He looked down at his knee. His jeans were soaked. A dark patch of material was sticking to his leg, and his shoe was bloody. His body became weak at the sight of all the blood. It's why medical school was never an option.

The sign of a small convenience store was in the distance. He forced himself forward. It seemed to take forever. He looked back, and she wasn't there. He kept moving, holding his stomach because he felt so sick. He made it to the glass doors and tugged on the handle. It was locked.

"No!" he cried.

He pulled again and again, looking for someone inside. The shelves were half full, but there were no signs of people. Wiping the burning sweat from his eyes, he surveyed the parking lot and leaned back on the door.

"What the — !"

He fell inside the doors with a thud. As he looked up in bewilderment, he noticed the words on the door: PUSH and PULL. A smile crossed his haggard face. He shoved the door closed and looked for a latch.

"Come on," he mumbled. "Come on!"

It was a key-only lock. He screamed again. He hustled over to the register and rummaged his bloodstained fingers through the shelves. He checked the counter. *Nothing!*

He pounded on the counter as he shouted, "Damn! Damn! Damn!"

He knew she would arrive at any second. What now? He tried something new.

Whack! Whack! Whack! He busted open the register with the bat.

He jerked open the drawer and found a key in one of the change bins. He snatched it and limped over to the door. There she was, passing the gas pumps. *Almost here!* He stuck the key in the lock, but it didn't fit. The key slipped through his fingers and clattered on the floor tiles.

"Shit!"

He grabbed the key and tried sticking it back in the keyhole. It didn't fit. *No!* He turned the key over, and it slipped inside. Something slammed into the door. She was pushing from the other side of the glass, moaning at him. He shoved back, wedging his foot against a store shelf. He turned the lock, but the door was no longer shut. She was pushing him back inside. She was stronger than a man.

"No!" he screamed. He lowered his shoulder and knocked the door hard, shuffling her backward.

Clatch!

He got it. "Thank God!"

He slunk down on the glass doors with a gasp of relief. He couldn't move. His leg was throbbing, and he didn't have the strength to stand. His breathing was loud, and he could feel sweat dripping off of his nose as he closed his eyes.

Wham!

Her fist busted into the glass, leaving a spiderweb mark. He rolled away, eyes wide. How much energy did he have left?

I can't do this.

"Go away!" he screamed. "Go away!"

3

NATE TORE HIS JEANS OFF JUST BELOW THE KNEE. THE BLOODY GASH made him sick, and he spit up bile. He rummaged through the shelves and found some gauze, antiseptic, and medical tape. He closed his eyes as he placed the loose flap of skin back over his shin and knee. His eyes watered as he sprayed on the antiseptic. He pounded at the floor, biting his lip. He wrapped it with gauze and taped it off. Jeanine pounded and moaned on the other side of the glass. The whole building seemed to shake with every blow.

He found an elastic bandage, and his bloody hands wrapped it around his knee. The blood no longer soaked his bandages, but he still felt ill. He ripped off the top of a bottle of ibuprofen and limped over to the glass cooler doors. He found a twenty-ounce bottle of Mountain Dew and pulled it out. He twisted off the yellow cap and read the inside.

"Better luck next time," he read as he flicked it away.

He took a handful of pills and washed them down with the green liquid. It was lukewarm, but he still sucked the entire bottle down like ice water. It was delicious all the same, and his stomach churned again. *I'd do anything for a burrito.* He tore into a box of snack cakes, washing them down with another bottle of the soft drink. He looked over at Jeanine, wiping his mouth on his sleeve, watching her continue to claw at the door. *I have to be dreaming. I can't believe I was gonna marry that.*

The sky was turning black as the sun dipped and a blanket of gray clouds began to roll in. He heard the soothing sound of rain-drops landing on the metal roof above.

"Now it starts to rain," he said as he sat down in front of the foun-tain drink machines across from the entrance door.

He sipped on his bottle, watching her bang and scratch at the doors. Her breasts jiggled underneath the black and gold jersey, and he thought of all those blissful mornings with her. *I'm sick. She's getting ready to eat me, and I can only think about her tits.* Her face was a maul of horror. Her hair seemed to be drying out. Blue veins had begun to swell under her tanned skin. Nate wanted to pinch himself, but the effort wasn't in him.

Nate closed his eyes and tried to remember Jeanine from back when. They had been together for years, and she wasn't something he deserved. She had been a good person, but he had been bad. Not bad in the good sense, but rather bad in the pathetic, character-lack-ing, "me first" sense. He was spoiled and brainy, a bit of a slob who ate too much, played video games, collected comics, and watched too many movies. *What a winner.* But he also had a golden tongue that tickled a woman's ear with all those words they liked to hear: I want you. I need you. I love you. They never meant a thing to him, until he met her. Jeanine was different.

She liked him for her own reasons, ones he never understood. They only had a few things in common; one of them was softball. He had the big bat, and she liked it. They both were competitive and smart ... maybe she liked that, he thought. He had the brains that got you a full scholarship anywhere, and missing classes still got him straight A's. It was the only thing he was better at than Jeanine. *That and video games.* Whatever the connection was they had, it was special, and he loved her every single day. Now she was gone, her haggard face etched forever in his nightmares.

Nate peered around the convenience store. Where was everyone?

People from many afflicted cities such as his fled the zombies that pursued them, that much he knew. He didn't see any dead bodies though. Whoever owned the store picked up and ran, hoping to return one day. He pulled the bat along his side and took off his backpack. Unzipping it, he reached inside. He pulled out his phone charger. He patted his pants pocket. His phone was still there. He squeezed it out and turned it on.

The display showed thirty percent battery life and no signal bars.

"Great," he said under his breath. He moved it around in the air, and a small green bar appeared. He dialed 9-1-1. It was busy. He waited, and Jeanine's raps on the door were in a steady cadence now. Her moans continued, like a dying hound's, and the glass and metal doors shook over and over. He covered his ears. *She never moaned that much with me.* He dialed again. Busy. He tried again. Busy — Busy — Busy. He fought the urge to sling the phone down, sighing aloud.

He stared at her long and hard. He had no choice. He had to kill her. He studied the softball bat he bought for her. It seemed like a crude way to go. He noticed the lighter fluid stacked by some bags of charcoal near the door. *Maybe I should set her on fire.* The smell would be disgusting, and there had to be a more humane way to kill her. It was the bat or nothing. At least he could bury her body then.

As darkness fell and the heavier rains came, his taut body softened. The loud rain began to drown out her moans. It relieved him. He took another sip as his eyes fell closed. He was fast asleep as she still pounded away.

4

Nate gasped. A violent spasm awoke him from his deep slumber. His skin was cold and clammy. Sunlight from the storefront windows bathed his face and body. He rubbed his bleary eyes as his heart thundered in his chest. The double glass doors were still intact. Jeanine was still there, too.

Her head was now sticking through the glass, and her jaw clutched open and closed. It made him think of a glass stockade, but crueler. The only thing keeping her from pushing through was the tiny wires holding the safety glass intact. Nate grimaced. He could see the glass cutting into her neck. She made no effort to force her way back out, only forward. She was stuck, but the moaning continued.

"I can't take it anymore!" he yelled.

He got up, growling. He noticed his leg was swollen and purple from the knee down. He grabbed a plastic bottle of Mountain Dew and limped over to face her. As he came closer, her mouth snapped open and closed like a cow chewing its cud.

"Sorry, baby, I know you hate this stuff," he said, shoving the bottle, cap first, into her mouth.

If Jeanine had a flaw, it was talking too much. He fantasized about doing this many times before. She hissed in and out of her nose, as her wide mouth was filled with the green bottle, which was over halfway in. He stepped back, eyes looking about. An eerie sensation of peace fell over him. The moaning was gone.

She crunched down on the bottle that was stuck in her mouth. Green carbonation squirted into the air. Shaking her head back and forth, the bottle remained. He limped over and grabbed the bat.

This is it. Got to do it!

He looked into her dark, long-lashed eyes and knew nobody was home. There was no other way. It was her or him. *Until death do us part.*

As he approached, he could see her perfect white teeth biting deep into the bottle. It pinched inward, and her eyes widened as she sucked on the bottle.

"What the hell?"

She seemed to be drinking it. Green fluid dripped down her chin and gashed neck. He could hear a wheezing and sucking sound coming from her. The bottle began to empty, and it started to collapse as if it were squeezed by a hand. The bottle fell and rattled on the tiled floor. He looked at her, the bottle, then back at her. He approached with the bat raised high. Her listless face was silent. He watched as she struggled to pull her head free, her eyes catching his, passing him over as if he wasn't there. The hunger and aggression were gone. She was just stuck inside the glass, trapped like an animal, not knowing what to do.

"Now what?" he said, setting down the bat.

He waited minute after minute. The store was becoming hotter as the sun rose further. It was past noon, and it must have been a hundred degrees inside. There wasn't a window to open. He had to pee, and he headed for a bathroom in the back. His ears and mind were monitoring any signs of danger.

"Ah!" he said as he began to pee.

It was the most relief he had felt in forever. He walked back out and there she was, moving very little, a defeated creature. He felt bad for her all of a sudden. Did the soft drink cure her? What was going on? He took over another bottle and twisted off the lid. Her black eyes glimmered up at him. Her arms pressed the glass from the other side as the jagged edges had her neck still caught. Nate poured some to her lips. She didn't try to bite, but licked her lips with her blackening tongue. The liquid ran down through a hole in her neck.

"Ugh!" he said, stepping away and spitting.

Her eyes were fixed on the bottle now. He had to get out of there though, as the sweltering heat was too much. The key was still in the lock. He crouched down and slid over to it. He reached up, unlocked it, and slid back away. She pushed the door in, and she pulled it back out. It was in slow motion as she went in and out, back and forth, legs shuffling over the sweep. It reminded him of a cartoon and a revolving door. He stuffed some pop bottles in his backpack, along with some candy, nuts, and protein bars.

Here we go. He mustered his courage, and as she backed out again, he shoved himself past her. He was free. *Yes!* He hid behind the gas pumps and waited. She kept moving back and forth. He checked his smartphone. One green bar showed with twenty percent battery power remaining. *Just get a car and go!*

He walked around the building. No cars. There wasn't a single one to be seen. He saw the backyards of tiny houses nearby with sheds on many lawns. *There has to be a bike in there.* He limped into one fenced yard. It had a decent-sized storage barn in the back. He straddled the rail, and he fell onto the other side.

"Ow!"

The barn was padlocked. He knocked the lock off after several swings with the bat. He jerked open the doors, and a pair of Schwinn mountain bikes hung in the back.

"Yes!" he said, pumping his fist. "Thank you Jesus!"

He lifted one bike down and got on. The pedaling was excruciating as he wobbled at first, but he was fine; he was moving. When he rounded the convenience store, Jeanine wasn't there.

"Shit!"

He tried turning his head every direction at once, but she was gone. Fear filled him from head to toe as he listened for her. Nothing but the wind was with him, and very little of that.

He pushed off and pedaled around the store three times. He looked up and down the roads. All he saw were small houses and buildings, lined up side by side, with overgrown lawns. Something crept up through his spine as he stepped back in front of the store. A large chunk of broken glass was crumpled on the ground. His heart jumped as he heard rustling coming from the inside, and that's when he saw her. She was wandering the aisles and knocking things onto the floor.

"Jeanine!" he yelled. No response.

He backed away, still straddling the bike. *Now what?* He got off the bike and walked inside. He poured more soda into a large cup and set it on the ground. She lumbered towards the cup and kicked it over, spilling the contents onto the floor. She kneeled to the ground and licked it up like a dog, every bit, giving Nate a disturbing feeling. *I can't believe this.* He wanted to cry. She grabbed the cup and tried to eat it. Nate had a crazy idea.

He poured a path of the soda along the floor and outside. He set the bottle at the end of the path. She lapped it up as she crawled on her hands and knees. He took out his smartphone and recorded her.

He held the phone high in the air. He got two green signal bars. He uploaded the file on YouTube: "ZOMBIES LIKE MOUNTAIN DEW! MUST WATCH!"

He posted a tweet: "MOUNTAIN DEW WILL STOP THE ZOMBIES!"

His smartphone died.

5

A DOG WAS BARKING SOMEWHERE, FOLLOWED BY MORE BARKS AND howls. Nate hadn't heard them before. Now they seemed to come from everywhere. Even cats were darting across the abandoned streets.

He left Jeanine behind at the store. As he pedaled around the small town, he noticed a Sheriff's detachment and came to a stop. He dismounted the mountain bike and limped to the door. It was open.

"Hello?" he said, waiting. He clutched his bat as he stepped inside.

It was a small red brick building with a teller window inside. *This is where they pay taxes and fines, I bet.* A small, enclosed waiting room with three hard plastic chairs was illuminated by glass-block windows. Another heavy-duty door waited before him.

He pressed his ear to the steel door and closed his eyes. He heard nothing. He turned the knob, but it was locked. He kicked at the door, but it didn't give in. It just made his leg hurt even more. He grabbed one of the chairs and tossed it through the teller window with a loud crash, shattering glass all over the floor.

He sat up on the counter, careful of the glass, and slid to the other side. There were a couple of offices in the back that he searched around. He looked in a small break room with a table, chair, fridge, and coffee pot. He checked the phone on one of the desks. There was a dial tone. He called 9-1-1. It was busy again. He slammed the handset to the ground, saying, "Damn!"

He headed down a dimly lit hallway. A pair of small holding cells were each big enough for a few people. Handcuffs and keys hung from the wall. He clenched his fists and shook them. *This is good.* The shotgun rack was empty. *That's bad.* He stepped inside the jail cell and pulled a soda from his backpack. He twisted off the cap, sat down on a metal cot anchored to the wall, and took a long drink. He took another swallow, set the bottle down, and closed his eyes. He thought about his next step. Maybe he could find power in the town somewhere. He froze with fear as he heard the sound of scraping glass.

His heart was racing on the inside. Someone or something must have heard him break the glass door. He exited the small cell with his bat gripped in two white-knuckled hands. Something was following him. The sound of the crunching glass ate at his soul. Was it another zombie? Would he dare to peer through the small square window in the door he tried to kick in earlier? He wiped the sweat from his eyebrows. *Here goes.*

He peeked and screamed, "Gah!" He dropped his bat and clutched his chest.

It was Jeanine's face pressed into the window. *How did she get here so fast!?* He heard more scraping of glass as she dragged herself over the counter. He couldn't move. He looked down at the bat. *Grab it, idiot!* It seemed as if he was in slow motion as he picked it up and began to backpedal deeper into the corridor. He felt the cold cinderblock wall on his back ... a dead end. *Sonuvabitch!* Only one other cell remained. He heard her coming, and saw her long gashed leg cross into the light. Her head poked around the corner, followed by the rest of her body. She slowly came his way.

"No, Jeanine! Please stop!" he cried, stepping inside the barred door.

He began to pull the door inward the further she came. He felt like a coward now. He had a weapon, but he couldn't use it. Not on her. And what would happen if he didn't kill her ... she would eat him.

"I won't be eaten! I won't be eaten!"

She was passing the first cell, and he could hear her say, "Num-Num. Num-Num."

He could not make out her drooping face. She was a creepy silhouette of a woman with a dipping shoulder and a dangling arm. For someone that moved so slowly, things seemed to be happening awfully fast. Nate realized he hadn't grabbed the keys. If he locked himself in the holding cell, he would starve. He could see the keys hanging on the wall at the beginning of the corridor. *Idiot!* Now Nate wasn't sure which fate would be worse, being eaten or starving to death. *Why me?*

He shouted at the top of his lungs.

"Why me!"

Jeanine shuffled closer his way as Nate pulled the barred door further inward. Jeanine stopped, turned, and entered the other cell. He stood transfixed as she looked through him. *Huh?* The light from the small window in the back of the jail cell displayed the scene as she reached over for his soda bottle sitting on the cot. He couldn't feel his legs as he watched her pick it up. *Shut the door, idiot!*

He didn't remember what happened next; fear and adrenaline wiped out his thoughts. Something slammed shut with a loud bang. He had her trapped inside. She didn't seem to notice a thing.

"Num-Num ...."

6

THE OTHER SIDE OF THE PHONE LINE RANG AGAIN AND AGAIN. IF IT wasn't ringing, it was a busy signal. Everything in the town was dead except for the phone lines. Nate sat in a recliner, propping up his aching leg. A dead television screen sat before him. A breeze billowed through the sheer curtains in the small home he occupied near the jail. Days had passed since he had locked Jeanine in the cell. He wanted to leave the town, but couldn't. He was too scared, and his leg wasn't getting better.

He loosened the bandages around his knee. *That's bad.* The gash was infected, swelling his leg. His gout had flared up, making things worse. His bare foot was fat like a pillow. He shut the recliner, grimacing at the jolt, and slipped on a red flip-flop he had taken from the convenience store. He grunted as he stood. Using the bat as a cane, he hobbled over to the front door, opening it into the rising morning sun.

The sounds of birds chirping filled the air.

"Huh."

No dogs lay at the door. The bowl of food he set out was empty.

"Time to feed my girlfriend, I guess," he said, hobbling back down the street.

The bat echoed off the concrete sidewalk as he went. He had never felt so alone and trapped. Things had been perfect a few months ago. There had been a good job waiting for him once he finished his master's. He had a fine-looking wife lined up, too. Now she was a zombie, along with the rest of the world. He wondered if he was the last man on earth and if he'd ever have Taco Bell again.

He had patched his leg up the best that he could, but the pain was a constant reminder that his purgatory wasn't over yet. *What did I do to deserve this?* He didn't have it in him to search for more medicine, and the town pharmacy was bare. Despair addled his brain as horrors lived in his sleep. He searched for a vehicle, but all he had was a bike. He couldn't bend his leg now, and he could barely stand the pain. His entire purpose was to feed Jeanine her Mountain Dew and hope somebody from the living swung by on a golden chariot. Anything would do.

The sheriff's depot was in sight just a couple blocks away. It would take forever to get there. He was looking inside the window of a bank, thinking he could rob it. There was a pawn store too, but no guns and no ammo. He moved on. *Why am I doing this?* He tried to think of things he didn't like about Jeanine. Being a zombie was the main thing, that and beating him at foosball. Her snorting laugh was annoying, but her giggles were cute.

"This time I'm gonna do it. I can do it. I can kill her. I'll — kill — it!"

He tried to think of the last thing he killed. His face was a knot of concentration. *I killed a squirrel with a pellet gun once. Oh ...*

"Yeah, I killed zombies." Those zombies had been friends and family. He could see their ghoulish faces coming after him. He had killed them ... so why couldn't he kill Jeanine? Maybe it was because the bat seemed like such an inhumane device. It was also a symbol of the best times they had together on the softball field. He kept moving and began to sob. For all he knew, the last one he would ever love was inside the building. He sighed just before he walked inside.

He entered the front door, stepping over the broken glass. The crackling underfoot stirred the hairs on his back. He didn't hear anything as he closed his eyes. He pictured Jeanine inside the cell as she had always been. He saw her standing there, a smiling tomboy with freckles and a nice body for a tall girl. If God had a woman in mind for him, it was Jeanine.

He exhaled and stepped inside the dim corridor. He made his way down the hall, breathing heavily. He wiped the sweat from his face with his shirt. There she stood, in the middle of the cell, facing the sunlit window in the back. Her dark hair flowed down over her neck. Her jean shorts were riding up inside her full rear. *Is that cellulite?* He shook his head. Her shadowed figure seemed perfect. His heart pounded. *Can it be?*

"Jeanine," he whispered.

The figure turned in slow motion. Her gored shoulder and dangling arm stopped his heart. The sunken black eyes were like deep wells, and the drooping jaw seemed to hang near the floor. *No–No–No!* It was all the same, only the day had changed. He looked down at the floor and all he could hear was a raspy breathing sound. A half-filled bowl of green soda lay on the floor. *That's interesting.*

The bowl was filled when he left yesterday. Another full bottle sat on the cot. *She didn't drink much.* Lost in thought, he didn't notice she crept up to the bars.

"Num-Num."

He leaped back, almost falling to the floor. A fresh burst of pain lanced through his foot and leg. It was killing him.

"Geez Jeanine, you scared the shit out of me!" he yelled back, swinging the bat into the bars.

"Num-Num."

"Go get your num-num! Dumb! Dumb!" *Oh, that's funny. Idiot!*

Her face was lost like an abandoned child's. The glassy black eyes were widened, without understanding. She backed away from the bars and began to kneel at the bowl. As Nate watched in disgust, something pricked at his ears. He moved back down the hall.

There was a different sound in the distance. He heard dogs barking from somewhere as he tilted his neck and shut his eyes. He looked back at his girlfriend, who was making loud lapping and slurping sounds. He headed toward the front door and stopped again. The sound grew louder and more distinct in his ears. Whatever it was, it was coming his way. A burst of energy empowered him.

He made his way into the bright sun and looked above. The noise seemed to be coming from the sun itself. He shaded his eyes with his hand and looked around. Louder and louder, the sound came. He saw a black speck appear in the sky. It got bigger with each passing second. He loved Vietnam movies, and he knew that sound. *Is that a helicopter?*

"I can't believe it's a freaking helicopter!" he yelled as he hopped up and down, crossing his arms and bat high in the air. He was frantic with joy. It soared over his head, bringing a whoosh of air, almost knocking him to the ground. He could see heads peering down at him from two hundred feet above.

"Come down! Come down!" he shouted.

The helicopter looked like an enormous bird of prey. It rounded over the town a couple more times and lowered itself to the street.

... THUWMP! THUWMP! THUWMP! THUWMP! THUWMP! THUWMP! THUWMP! THUWMP! THUWMP! THUWMP! THUWMP! THUWMP! ...

The noise was music to his ears. It might as well have been angels who came out of it, once it landed. It was people, people in uniform, and Nate couldn't believe his eyes. An impeccable man in a blue Air Force uniform with silver stars on his shoulder shouted over the roaring helicopter.

"Are you Nate McDaniel?"

"Yes!" he screamed.

"Are you sure?" the man said, yelling in his ear, his hand on Nate's shoulder.

Nate fumbled for his wallet in his back pocket and pulled it out to show the man. The officer tipped up his sunglasses and gave it a good look. The man slapped him on the shoulder; a broad smile was on his face as he gave a thumbs-up to the men behind him. The soldiers in camouflage returned the signal.

The man yelled back in his ear, saying, "Guess what, Nate?"

"What!"

"You're a hero!"

"I am?" he yelled, feeling confused. "Why?" He read the man's name tag. *Dotson.*

"Son"—the officer grasped his shoulders tight—"you sent the tweet that saved the world!"

"I did?"

The officer nodded and began looking around. "Say, where's that zombie?"

"What?"

"The zombie!"

"Inside there," he pointed back towards the sheriff's office. General Dotson pointed to his men. Two soldiers with M-16's headed inside, followed by a smaller man in black with a mustache, dark glasses, and a shotgun. Nate shook his head. Something was going on.

"Hey — what are they doing?'

The general pulled at his arm, ordering him, "Stay here, son!"

Nate jerked his arm away and ran back toward the building. *Jeanine!* Every step felt like a nail was being driven in his leg as he ran inside. He rounded into the hallway and faced a rifle barrel lowered into his chest. He kept going. Jeanine's face was pressed to the bars. The wiry man in black had the shotgun pointed in her face.

"NOOOO!" Nate screamed.

KA-BOOM!

He watched as her body fell lifeless onto the cell floor. He sunk to his knees, gawping. Two hard-faced soldiers grabbed him under his arms and dragged him back outside. He couldn't feel a thing. The wiry man with the shotgun lit up a cigarette as he walked by.

Nate said, "Th-that was my girlfriend." He could see his reflection in the man's dark glasses. He could make out two beady eyes as well.

The man leered at him, and with a deep southern accent said, "*Was,* is the key word, son."

7

GUTHRIE, WEST VIRGINIA

THE ROAD WOUND UPWARD, across a picturesque landscape of turning leaves and tall pines. The morning dew and lifting fog coated the grassy grounds along the way. The minivan with balding tires accelerated, screeching up the hill. The radio commercials droned on between breaks of blathering talk-radio hosts. It was another big day, the annual celebration of the day Nate McDaniel saved the world.

The van screeched as a small buck came into view, leaping away from the honk.

"Stupid deer," the driver muttered as he stepped on the gas. He hated this road. It was an unkempt disaster of potholes and mud. He could never keep the van clean, even during the dry summers. Why should he care? It was a company car. He had brought his cherry-red muscle machine up once, his first day, and busted a rim. He hated the dreadful hill ever since.

Mile after mile, he suffered the gushing praise about Nate McDaniel, the man who saved the world. *With Mountain Dew or whatever.* He had roomed with Nate in college, the two of them had even pledged in the same fraternity. They had good times and a few bad. He squeezed the wheel. His roommate never cracked a book or went to class. Nate was bright, lucky, and lazy. He always hated that about Nate, the ne'er-do-well. There was something else he didn't like either. Nate was a notorious liar who led a charmed life.

Here it comes, here it comes! A smooth spot of blacktop flattened up ahead, with several bumps rising in the road. He jammed on the gas.

"Yah-hooooo!" he cheered as the muffler dragged sparks over the exhilarating bumps and clanked the cargo in the back. It gave him a rush. He braked hard, entering a hairpin turn, and shot back up the hill, straddling a snapping turtle in the road. *The next one won't be so lucky.* Something on the radio caught his ear.

"Up next hour, Nate McDaniel will be joining us, celebrating the sixth-year anniversary of when he saved the world," the speakers blared.

He switched it off, shaking his head. *That son-of-a-bitch couldn't save a cat from a tree with a ladder and a fireman.* Of course, having Nate as a friend had its benefits. It had been this same old roommate, the aspiring biologist and doctor of bullshit, turned savior of the world, that called and offered him his current assignment ... and the pay was great. He allowed himself a smile as he thought about his 401k.

He hadn't seen his old roommate since college. It seemed like a lifetime ago. The private college hosted lots of academic challenges and a few interesting women. Nate somehow landed the goddess of the geeks in Jeanine. He never understood that relationship – or what happened to her six years ago, for that matter. *Charmed life.*

He approached a weathered, fenced-in structure. Fallen leaves covered the ground and rooftops of the old government building. Moss and ivy decorated the walls and gutters. It was early in the morning on the hilltop, but it might as well have been night. High trees choked out most of the sunlight like jagged curtains.

He passed a blue sign on the road with gold letters: GUTHRIE FACILITY/WEST VIRGINIA. It wasn't his favorite place in the world. His van's brakes squeaked as he pulled alongside a weathered guard shack. An older man in mirrored sunglasses stepped out alongside his car. The guard wore a starched green uniform, and a shotgun was slung over his shoulder. He rolled down his window.

"Evening, John," he said, sticking his head out the window with a faint smile.

The man strolled around the car with agonizing slowness, checking his decals and looking in the windows. Another guard half the man's size appeared, shirt half-tucked over a pot belly. The smaller guard began running a long bomb-detecting device under the van's frame. *Every single time.*

The guard stepped stooped beside his window. The man's weathered face had a whimsical look, and his big calloused hands clutched the driver's window edge. His big head, full of thick white and gray hair, peered in the back of the van and withdrew. A toothpick jutted under John's mustache, and a frown crossed his face.

"State yer business, civilian," John said in a voice as country as a coal-burning stove.

He cleared his throat. "I've come to kidnap the princess."

The man's eyes widened as he gasped and said, "You best get a nicer chariot, Sir Lancer Lots. Ain't no princess going nowhere with you in this thing." John kicked the door. "Maybe you should settle for Fergie over here." He jutted his thumb toward the dumpy little guard.

He looked over and saw it was John's grandson, in a uniform sewn by his wife. The boy was about ten, heavy, with his chubby face scrunched up in a sneer. *It looks like the boy still has some pit bull in him.* He knew little Ferguson wasn't fond of working with his grandpa. It was that time of the year when mommy and daddy unloaded the boy while they committed consensual adultery.

"Hi Ferguson," he said with a wave that drew the boy's tongue. *You have no resemblance to your father.*

John the guard asked in his usual cheerful voice, "So what's new, Henry. Did you enjoy your time off?"

"Sure, John, the cruise was wonderful, even with all the work, rain, and lack of sunshine," Henry replied.

"That's too bad. Did you get me any taffy? I don't see any," John said, wringing his hands, licking his mustache.

"I didn't think you could have taffy. Remember what it did to your dentures the last time."

John's smile was bright white, "My teeth are just fine. Now, give me some taffy, or you ain't going in."

Henry opened the center console and pulled out the splashy box and handed it over. The boy bounced on his toes by the van's side. John inspected the box as a look of satisfaction crossed his face.

"You're alright, Henry. I'll let you in I guess."

"Gee thanks, I can't wait. Anyone in there I should know about?" he said, bringing the van in gear.

John rubbed the side of his face.

"Nah ... it's just the usual suspects. I keep thinking there is something I need to tell you. You'd think if something new happened, I'd remember. It's just the same faces every day. Well, if I remember, I'll give you a ring," John said, giving him a salute as he stepped inside the guard shack.

Henry watched the man press something that made a loud buzz, and the gate slid open, shaking and rattling over the ground. He waved back as he pulled through. He heard John holler from behind as the gate began to close.

"It's your brother! Your brother's in there!"

A chill went down his spine. *What!?*

8

THE FLUORESCENT LIGHTING HUMMED ABOVE AS DETERMINED footsteps echoed down the corridor. The old facility was built like a block limestone prison and smelled like bleach. The shining elevator door waited ahead, a red light shining like a beacon above it.

Holding a box in his hands, Henry rose up on his toes and brushed the scanner with his back pocket. Nothing happened. He set down the box, pulled out his wallet from the back of his pants, and slapped it to the scanner. Nothing happened. Shaking his head, he pulled out the magnetic security card and tried again. The red light switched to green as he snatched up the box and got inside.

Up he went, coming to a stop after only one floor. The doors parted and he stepped into a lobby. An abandoned receptionist desk greeted him. The surrounding offices and cubicles were without life or light. *Good.* He hated the small talk, especially with the handful of people he worked with in the dreary place. A scent of coffee hung in the air. *I hope it's fresh. I wonder who is here?*

He headed toward the back, stepped inside his office, and set the box on his desk next to a picture of him, his brother, dad, and mom. Looking around, he noticed things were out of place and his fridge was cracked open. He looked inside.

"Jimmy!"

His drinks were gone, every last one of them. He thought about his younger brother and the problems he caused. During college, when the zombies came, Jimmy had gone into mental decline. Jimmy was only a year younger, and seemed to take all his frustrations out on him. Jimmy's issues were only a nuisance at first; however, the past couple of years, the issues had become quite problematic. And now, Jimmy was back, causing Henry to simmer within. *Why can't we get rid of him?* Henry had no idea what he'd done to deserve a brother like his.

There was a rustle of clothes behind him, and he twisted around. Nothing was there. He stepped into the hallway. Somewhere in the room, fingernails were tapping on a desk or countertop. The office area wasn't big enough for twenty workers, but he still had trouble locating the sounds. He squinted, scanning the room. *Who in the world?*

He felt his chest pocket and remembered his glasses were still in the mini-van. He had plenty of trouble seeing without them, and it made him uneasy. An office chair groaned from inside one of the cubicles. Turning his head, he backed up on his tiptoes, looking over the partition walls. A ghost-like voice whispered from somewhere close inside the room.

"Oh Henry ..."

Oh my!

"Oh Henry," someone said again, closer than before.

He headed toward the source, step by step. He jumped out in front of a secluded cubicle.

"Gotcha!"

A black flat-screen monitor greeted him.

"Huh?" he said, scratching his head.

He started to turn around as claws dug into his side, driving him into the ground. A woman whispered as she chewed on his earlobe.

"Oh Henry! Oh Henry!"

It began to tickle now, as he burst out in laughter. He couldn't catch his breath as he tried to fight the soft belligerent figure accosting him.

"Stop!" he cried. "Stop!" He saw a thick tussle of brown hair as he shoved her back into the desk.

"Ouch!" she cried, bumping her head.

He gasped. "I'm sorry!" he said, reaching over, but she bounded onto his chest, tickling him again.

"You're gonna pay now, Henry! Henry!"

He strained, trying to defend himself. She was groping him all over now. The tickles began to subside and turn into something else. They both were out of breath when he got his first good look at her. Her pretty round face had an alluring grin. Underneath an open lab coat, her buxom figure was enshrined in lacy maroon lingerie and high black heels. Her heavy breasts wanted to burst out of her bra.

"Miss me?" she said as she straddled him, pinning his arms back behind his head. Her perfume was vitalizing. He was conquered.

"Words could never describe my longing for you?"

She slammed his hands back again.

"Is that a *yes* or *no*?"

"Yes, Tori! Yes! Now get off me before someone comes."

She wiggled her hips on his.

"I'm pretty sure you don't want that ... Oh Henry." Her voice was like honey. She was right, but he was chicken.

She looked around.

"No one's coming. It's just me and you."

She winked at him.

He tried to squirm, but she squeezed his wrists. Her voice was like poison. "Did you cheat on me?"

Oh no! Not this again. "No, never!" He hadn't, either. "Of course I want you, but my creepy brother is here," he whined, "and—"

She sealed his mouth shut with a powerful kiss and began sucking on his tongue. She nibbled and licked his ear. "They're in the basement, so just relax and let me take care of you," she whispered. He did. Tossing off her lab coat, she unbuckled his belt along with his pants. As she jerked his pants down below his knees, the elevator chimed.

"Crap!" he said, wiggling away.

"What are you doing?"

He tried to whisper as he said, "Didn't you hear that — it's the elevator!"

"You're being paranoid."

She leaned onto his shoulders, her fragrant hair covering his face. Grabbing her shoulders, he pushed her off and fixed his clothes. Tori sat back, biting her lip and blowing the hair from her face. More lights came on above them, and her face lit up. They looked at each other and scrambled.

He stood up, peeking over the low wall of the cubicle as she looked for her lab coat. They heard someone very close by, sucking the bottom fluid from a cup with a straw. He couldn't see anyone though. He needed his glasses. Several silent seconds passed as he motioned for her to stay put as he headed into the office, looking around. *Who in the—*

Tori shrieked as he jerked around just in time to see her crouched behind a chair. Goosebumps were all over her half-naked figure. A lanky man with a crooked ball cap and watery eyes hung over the partition wall. The man was laughing, shrill and creepy.

"Nice outfit, Tori. How'd you know that's what I like," Jimmy said in a disturbing voice while dangling her lab coat.

Tori darted behind Henry, clutching his waist. "Go away, you pervert!" she yelled.

Tori hated Jimmy. He hated Jimmy. Everyone hated Jimmy.

His brother climbed over the wall and sauntered over, pulling up his baggy pants and straightening his grungy lab coat. "So, my prodigal brother returns."

"That would be you, Jimmy," Henry said, snatching Tori's lab coat.

Jimmy was a twenty-something two-time college dropout who had failed to socially connect beyond middle school. He was smart, cunning, and weasel-eyed. Henry couldn't stand the sight of him. *Why are you here?*

"What are you doing here, Jimmy? I thought you were gone for good."

Tori began moving away toward the elevator, heels clopping on the floor.

"Bye, Tori," Jimmy said, chuckling as she flipped him the finger. Jimmy wiped his nose on his sleeve. "Pops said he needed some help, so here I am. I've taken over since you were gone."

9

A LARGE GOLD AND BLUE CERAMIC COFFEE MUG SAT STEAMING ON THE break table. A black LCD TV hung from the wall, showing an aerial view of zombies being herded into a road-sized tunnel. The view panned backward, exposing hundreds, growing to thousands, of morbid men and women inside miles of chain-link fence. Security officers guarded the perimeter and forced the hapless people inside the tunnel.

Another video clip showed a billow of black smoke from a burning dump truck. The gray and white ash remains of the zombies were spilled onto the blacktop. More security forces cleared the area, but they weren't quick enough to get all the renegade footage. It was a scene from what happened in the years after Nate McDaniel saved the world.

Someone was tapping a spoon on their coffee mug in the room.
Tink. Tink. Tink.Tink.

Henry blocked it out, focusing on the scene above. Nate McDaniel's charming face appeared on the screen, again. Nate was busy recalling the events of his heroic situation to the television hosts that treated him like the President.

"Bugs ya, don't it," said a voice that crawled under his skin.

"You know me, don't you," he said.

Jimmy took a sip from his mug and jerked back. "Ow! Damn coffee's hot!"

Really, idiot! "Why do you even bother? You never drink it." Henry was shaking his head as he pointed the remote, turning up the volume.

His brother made another annoying sniff from his nose. It must have been the hundredth time in ten minutes. His mere presence made the walls close in, and the sound of his condescending voice made it worse. "Just trying to be like my big bro."

"Great. You are doing such a fine job, too." Sitting back on the break table, he studied the picture on the screen.

Jimmy started again. "Well—"

"Sssh!" He pointed his finger at the television.

Nate McDaniel was on the screen, tall and stylish, between two leggy reporters. *Nice, Nate.* Nate looked as sharp as he'd ever been. A gold cross was displayed around his neck. *He's got makeup on.* Henry listened to the conversation on the television ...

"So, Mr. McDaniel, or should I say 'the man who saved the world,' how does that scene make you feel?" the short-haired blond reporter asked.

"Please, call me Nate."

"Okay, Nate. Take us back. Six years ago you sent a message that saved the world. Three years ago you began another quest — saving zombies. Tell us about that."

"Well, Julie, it's like this. What I discovered wasn't a cure, as people say. Rather, the caffeine and sugar combinations only suppressed zombie people's appetites for flesh and brains."

The hungry-eyed woman hung on his every word.

"We still need to find a cure so the zombie people can live normal lives in the world, just like the rest of us. That is why I helped found the World Humanitarian Society."

A tan, long-haired brunette asked the next question. "First, Nate, I want to thank you. You saved millions, possibly billions of lives, and you seem to be on a noble quest to save even more." She was shaking her head. "You are amazing."

He was grinning.

"Thanks, Christy. But I don't deserve all the credit."

"Sure you don't," she added, squeezing his knee, drawing a look of disdain from her co-reporter.

"Tell us about the World Humanitarian Society, Nate," the blonde interjected, casting a quick glare at her counterpart.

"Oh, sure."

He began rubbing his hands on his thighs when the camera zoomed in for a close-up.

"Well, like many of you, I also lost a lot of people I loved to zombieism. When I, I mean we, discovered a way to subdue their aggressiveness, we also learned there were other issues we needed to deal with as well."

The reporters sat engrossed.

Fiddling with his cross, he continued, "Because the zombie people were so despised, we quickly began their incineration. And that clip"—he motioned in the air—"was one of our methods of paying them back for what they did to us. But after time, when the threat subsided, people like you and I started to wonder if our families were truly lost. People began trying to find their loved ones, wanting to bring them home, find a cure, and have resolution ... even reconciliation."

"It certainly was an unforeseen blessing, don't you think?" Julie the blonde asked.

Nate shifted in his seat as he replied, "Absolutely. So many questions worldwide arose. Taxes, assets, debt, family, custody? Who was in charge of all of these decisions? Families? Governments? The zombies ... er ... zombie people?"

Christy the brunette added, "I remember going through all of this. It was horrifying. We had no idea where my brother and his wife were, and we got stuck with their children. I didn't know anything about parenting," she said with a shrug.

"So ... the World Humanitarian Society stepped up, and with the blessing of the United States and the United Nations, they were able to

facilitate the process of bringing order to the lives of the families and the zombie people. But—their main mission is to find a cure."

Julie patted his knee.

"And we know you'll find one, Nate."

"Nate, do you think the remaining z-people will get to vote?" Christy asked.

"Only if they're Democrats," he said with a subtle smile, causing a burst of unnatural laughter from both women.

"Tell us about your fiancé," the brunette asked. Nate kissed his cross....

HENRY SHUT THE TELEVISION OFF, tossing the remote on the table. *Ludicrous!* Nate was lying: the sweaty palms and flickering eyes. He knew the story coming next. How he tried to save Jeanine from the zombies, and how they were trying to find a cure for her ... somewhere.

"What do you think about all of that, Jimmy?"

His brother was stooped over, head inside the fridge, saying, "I love Nate, man. He saved the world. Woo Hoo!" Jimmy raised his arms high in the air. "I wish I was him. I'd be banging those two reporters right now."

Jimmy began humping the table, spilling Henry's coffee.

"Imbecile!" Henry snatched his cup from the table as the hot liquid stung his hand and almost spilled on the floor.

Jimmy stopped in motion, eyes frozen, then shouted, "I'm Nate McDaniel, baby, I saved the world!" His brother started banging the table, using his fists like tom-tom mallets.

"What is wrong with you? Every day you have to jerk off! You create havoc! You leave a mess! You leave—you come back. Over and over again, like a rabid flea."

Henry set his coffee down and rolled his sleeves up as he rounded the table.

Jimmy hoisted his fists up. "Let's go, bro!"

Henry caught his brother by the wrist and bent it downward, forcing Jimmy to his knees.

"Ow! That's cheatin'! Let go!" Jimmy cried.

He wouldn't. He wanted to break it. The look in Jimmy's distraught face gave Henry satisfaction. He fought the urge to kick in his ribs.

"You stay away from me and everyone—especially Tori! If I catch you leering at her again, I'll break your hands—got it?" He cranked the pressure up one more time.

"Yes," his brother said, writhing to the floor.

He let him go. How many times had they fought like this? He bailed his brother out time after time. Everyone did. That was part of the problem. Violence wasn't his style, but he was more than just a run-of-the-mill scientist. He'd been a formidable ballplayer and runner in his day, too. Jimmy was nothing of the sort, just a pathetic life on legs.

Henry headed down the hall and scanned the elevator pad with his card. He stepped inside, and he could hear his brother laughing and sniffing. His brother was a risk, a dangerous one, and he was back. There was only one way his brother could have gotten back in. It was time to check in with his dad. *Don't forget your glasses.*

10

THE ELEVATOR CHIMED AS THE THIRD-FLOOR BUTTON LIT AND THE STEEL doors slid open. Thirty feet down a hospital-white corridor was another open room and entryway. The elevator doors began to close behind him as he started ahead. He noticed he was shaking as he stopped inside the entryway.

He stood inside the small square room and rubbed his shoulders. The facility was always cold. A set of lab coats lay on a shelf along the wall, and he slipped one on over his navy oxford shirt and beige dress pants. Another set of stainless-steel doors awaited him. Above the door, a red beacon loomed. He always wondered if, more than just a color, it was a warning.

On the white wall beside him, he saw a plaque that read: *W.H.S., Guthrie WV Unit, Certification III.* He pushed his glasses up the bridge of his nose and wondered if he should have grabbed anything else from the van. Beside the plaque was another rack filled with shotguns with synthetic black stocks. The sight of them gave him little reassurance compared to the days they kept armed guards at every door. Now there was less than a skeleton crew, one inside and John on the outside. *I wish they would finish that other elevator. Here we go.*

When he swiped his magnetic card, the green light flared, and he watched the silver doors yawn wide. He walked out into a vibrant room only the most creative minds could have imagined. The sight was always unsettling, unnatural and impossible. The kaleidoscopic colors were intense and overwhelming. His chest tightened, and a cold sweat overcame him as he balled his fists.

Inhale your sanity. Exhale the madness. Welcome back to Zombie Day Care.

Small children's bodies were in slow motion, sputtering inside a rainbow room full of giant stuffed toys and radiant beanbag chairs. The bright clothes the children wore were in stark contrast to their olive-gray skin and thinning hair. Near the middle of the room, a boy, about five years old, fell down a slide. A slack-jawed girl, maybe seven, stood in front of a large screen, staring at an episode of *Mister Giggle Pants*. Another little boy. wearing a red-and-white-striped shirt, was chewing the popcorn from the inside of a beanbag chair.

The words "num-num" slowly escaped their gothic little lips, like a heartbeat. The sound of soothing classical music did little to block out the eye-jolting assault on Henry's senses. Henry watched a little girl in a pink dress, still with much of her blond hair, walking on a treadmill at an agonizing pace. He looked at the machine's timer: sixteen hours and thirty-five minutes. *She must have just started.*

He looked up, searching for people in lab coats working along the platforms and catwalks surrounding the room from above. No one was there. He walked deeper into the playroom, careful to avoid the children. He watched one child in a bright yellow Juicy Fruit shirt yawn widely. He steered clear of that one, as the sight of its gray teeth tingled his fingertips. *They're still dangerous.* But few of the others in the lab shared Henry's sentiments.

A voice shouted from above, "Hey, Sam Becket's back! Welcome back, Dr. Becket!"

There was a smattering of applause coming from somewhere on the catwalk above.

Shielding his eyes from the bright lights overhead, he yelled back, "I'm not Dr. Becket ... quit saying that."

"You look like him though," the same voice said.

"No, I don't. I have black hair and glasses." Henry pointed to his rectangular spectacles.

He watched a heavyset man traverse over the catwalks with loud footsteps to stand over him.

"You sound like him."

Shaking his head, he pleaded, "I don't *sound* like him either. Can we please stop doing this?"

The man above was a few years older than he, with thick black hair, an unkempt beard, and meaty arms like sailor.

"Not until you say it," the man said in a determined voice.

"Say what?" He knew what.

The man was nodding his head, hairy arms folded over his belly, saying, "You know what."

It seemed as if every eye was on him now, but he couldn't tell from the lights. A little zombie child approached, causing him to step further away.

"We're waiting," the man said with his arms outstretched.

He held his finger up, and the man above pressed his arms out while leaning forward on the rail, saying, "Make sure we all can hear it."

He put his hands on his hips and said, "Oh crap!"

"Yes!" Rudy shouted. "Yes—you nailed it!"

Polite applause from another pair of unseen hands erupted inside the room. The man above him began climbing down a tunnel ladder. The husky man dropped to the ground, stumbled, and fell face-first into a bright green beanbag. Jumping up, the man jogged over and gave him a hug.

"I'm glad you're back, Sam ... I mean Henry!"

"Okay, okay Rudy, enough."

He squirmed away, looking around as another zombie boy walked away.

"You act like I've been gone all year."

As Rudy stepped back, Henry could see the weathered Quantum Leap T-Shirt inside his lab coat. His friend must have everything the show ever made. Henry had even bought him one of those shirts for Christmas.

A thrill was in Rudy's voice as he talked. "Man! I–am–glad–you–are–back! It's never the same around here when you're gone. It's like a morgue."

"It is a morgue."

"Good one, Bawk. Anyway, when your brother showed up right after you left—"

"Wait a minute." He grabbed Rudy by the shoulder. "When? *Right after I left?*"

Rudy turned a little pale, averted his stare, and said, "The next day."

He's been here for two weeks. How? Why didn't anyone say something? Tori? Rudy?

"Why didn't anyone tell me?" He was angry.

"Man, you sound just like him."

"Who? Jimmy?"

"No dude, Scott Bakula."

He rolled his eyes and grabbed his dumpy friend again. "Why didn't you guys tell me?"

The blustering man's eyes widened when he brushed his hands away and said, "Because we knew it would upset you, and we didn't want to ruin your vacation."

"Rudy,"—his voice was rising— "there are things more important than my vacation, and that would be the safety of all these people." Rudy's head was down. Henry felt something brush along his side, causing him to half jump away. He exhaled; it was Tori.

"You mad at me too, lover?" Her voice was as sweet as honey.

"Yes!" he said as he straightened his glasses, climbed inside the steel ladder tube, and huffed up the rungs.

Rudy was pointing at Tori as he mouthed the words *I told you he'd be mad.* The two followed him as Rudy tried to prompt Tori to go first, but she pushed him along ahead of her.

"Almost," he said, snapping his fingers.

The catwalks crossed over a platform constituting the outer rim of the daycare. The entire layout made him feel as if he were on the set of an eighties spy movie. Computers and monitors were displayed along the walls and behind partitions. Some other familiar heads popped up and sank back down behind their stations. It was the usual lukewarm reception at best. Watching zombies all day for a living did little for social development. *Where's Dad?*

Spying another set of doors along the wall, he headed for it with determination. *I bet he's in there.* More footsteps came from behind him, clamoring over the metal walkway. A warm, delicate hand caught up with his, slowing him down.

He pulled away, but it held him tight.

"Let go, Tori. I've got to see him."

She barred his way with her body, chest out, hands on hips.

"Don't be mad. Settle down, we've got something to show you." She pressed closer. "Just give us a minute."

Two heads of black hair were peeping over their monitors, with grins resting below.

Rudy's heavy hand slapped his butt saying, "Come on, Bawk, you gotta see this!"

He couldn't imagine it was anything good, but their voices were filled with excitement. Tori's suggestive smile subdued his sense of dread, and Rudy's wild expression raised his brows.

"Okay, but can we drop the Quantum Leap bit? I don't look like him."

She grabbed his chin. "But you do sound like him ... it's very sexy."

"Man, if you looked like him, you'd have it all," his friend was saying, pulling at the picture on his shirt.

"I'm better looking than that guy."

Tori was fingering a lock of his hair when she said, "It's okay, lover, nobody looks better than a movie star."

He slumped a bit as she pulled him down the platform. A small overlook extended out and above a smaller multicolored room below. A thickset boy, almost five feet tall, walked around the room at alarming speed for a zombie. A crop of medium brown hair hung down over its sunken eyes. The boy rushed around on brick-heavy feet, elbows and knees stiff as boards as he rammed into a padded wall, fell to the floor, picked itself up, and rushed about again.

"What the hell!" Henry said, pulling his glasses up and glaring at Tori, then Rudy. "How did this happen, Rudy?"

"I don't know, I'm not a biologist. I'm just a watcher and recorder. GS-16, dude." Rudy waived his ID that was pinned to his white coat in Henry's face. "Now check this out."

Henry knew full well that Rudy did know, he just didn't want the credit for it.

Rudy pulled a red rubber ball from a black canister and hurled it upside the zombie child's head, bringing forth a grunt. It turned and chased after the ball. Henry's breath stopped as it picked the ball up. *This can't be.* An uncomfortable thrill raised all his hairs from head to toe. The slack-jawed face below showed mild curiosity before its face contorted. The ball began to bulge while the child squeezed it as a bear would. It was grunting, trying to dig its clipped nails deep into the rubber. Neither the ball nor the zombie yielded.

"He'll play with that ball for hours, unless he bites it." Rudy was enamored by the scene, while Henry went over and grabbed Tori by her wrists.

"How long?" he said with disbelief.

"About a week," she said in a nervous voice. "Your dad told us just to observe. That's all we've done. It'll be alright, Henry. Relax. We're getting closer to a cure."

There is no cure. There is no good in this. Why! Why! Why!

He could never understand how, after just a few years, people seemed to forget the zombies were within days, maybe hours, of wiping out the human race. Instead of destroying the menace, they wanted to cure it. It was insanity. There was no good to be had in zombies, no matter who they used to be. No one listened to him these days. At least no one important did, anyway.

"Watch this! Watch this!" Rudy yelled, almost falling over the railing.

The grayish child bit into the rubber, teeth tearing it like a piece of chicken. The ball deflated along with Henry's excitement. Another chill went down his spine as long-dead images arose in his head.

"Are there any others?"

"No," Tori and Rudy both replied.

"Good. Where is my dad?" he demanded, looking at the doors to the micro-lab. Instead, they pointed below, meaning the basement. Henry knew he had to put a stop to this. Before it was too late.

11

A WALL OF MONITORS DISPLAYED THE INTERIOR ACTIVITY OF THE facility, inside and out. Many of them were without a picture, showing only a black screen or a green error message. Fingers tapped into a keyboard as the remaining views above switched back and forth.

The rest of the room was dark, featuring a low electronic hum and empty office chairs. Three security stations were there, but only one was occupied. There was a set of lockers, a small table, some cobwebs, and a refrigerator. Along the wall was a half-empty gun rack below a gray locker labeled AMMO. The dust was more modern than the equipment, but it would do. This facility was only a satellite agency, one of many, diminishing in funds and employees.

Guthrie was an old government building -- a place no one cared to remember. When the zombie infestation was curbed and the World Humanitarian Society was created, there was a dire need for zombie care. Guthrie was an abandoned West Virginia state facility that was easier to conceal than modify. It was one of the first of its kind. The politicians in Washington, D.C. who had zombie family members were the first to hide the ones they loved, rather than incinerate them. The children were considered the least dangerous among the afflicted, so they were taken in first.

The first couple of years, many of the powerful slipped unnoticed up the swerving hill to visit Guthrie. However, the change in the seasons brought changes in offices, and those visiting privileges were revoked. None of them seemed to care though; there was no fervor about it. The zombie children were none the wiser. If their families had stopped caring, it was never missed by their kids. The funding was. Guthrie was on its last legs, a metal tomb decaying in the hills, soon to be taken by the greenery and forgotten.

Candy wrappers and crushed beer cans lay scattered on a black desktop, along with a credit card. A jittery hand began dicing up lines of white powder. A crisp green bill was rolled up. One by one the lines disappeared from the desk into the green tube in long heavy sniffs. *It's not crack, but I still like it.* Jimmy sat back, wringing his nose as he opened his eyes in observation. Things became perfect, crystal clear. He was ready for anything now, his brother be damned.

Jimmy had a mission, a secret one that no one but he knew about. They paid him, fed his need, and promised there would be more. The government men were fools; he would have done it for free. The drugs were more than enough to see everyone suffer.

His shaking hands and dirty fingers became busy opening computer files and rebooting black screens. *This will be awesome!* He powered up digital recorders beneath the monitors, bringing the sounds of more whirs and whines.

He spun around a few times, humming a demented tune. Jimmy flopped back down in his chair, his gaze transfixed on some figures on a particular screen. Jimmy observed Henry, Rudy, and Tori standing in wonder at the sight of Louie in the kid cave. Anger rose inside him as he watched his brother's commanding presence control his stooges. His brother was a tall, lean figure with jet-black hair and soft features. Henry's vivacious girlfriend seemed spellbound by his words.

Jimmy didn't know why he hated his brother, he just did. The pair used to be inseparable. In high school, Jimmy realized he wasn't what his brother was — refined, athletic, and sociable. People made Jimmy uncomfortable. People were cruel, and they didn't understand him. He tried to fit in, but he just didn't. They teased him. As smart as he was, no matter what he tried, he still lived in Henry's shadow.

Jealousy consumed him for years. Then the zombies came, and his bad habits became worse. He never realized it was the drugs that rattled his mind and embellished his delusions. The little devils of his conscience always suggested Henry stood in his way to raging success. He no longer recollected they had been best friends at one time. They used to hunt, fish, and crack game codes days on end. Even after high school, they were still at it. When the zombies came, their violent struggle for survival managed to put an end to all of that. Somehow it was all Henry's fault in his mind.

Henry. Henry. Henry. Sometimes he was torn between love and hate, but not for long. His plan should have taken place already, but it proved more difficult than he anticipated. He pounded his fist over and over again on the desk. Henry's look of concern troubled him. *He's always worried about something.* Henry never let him have the kind of fun he wanted. Henry never trusted him, and he would be hard-pressed to succeed with the protector around. He almost had what he wanted now. *He can't stop me now. It will be too late.*

He didn't notice he was shaking and sweating as he watched his brother leave the screen. Tori and Henry were arguing when Tori stormed away. Jimmy began laughing under his breath, a wicked one, followed by another deep sniff. He wiped his sleeve along his nose, thinking about what he had to do next.

Clicking his mouse, he opened folders, one by one, until he came to a folder reading TORIHOT. Inside it were several tori.wav files beckoning to be opened. Launching number 17, he became excited. There she was, splendid as a daisy working at her desk, breasts heaving inside her tight black dress. *You'll be mine soon, baby doll.* He leaned back and unzipped his pants.

12

WASHINGTON DC

NATE MCDANIEL HAD TROUBLE SLEEPING. It was the time of year where the interviews and the past wore his mind down. Saving mankind had its benefits: fame, fortune, and a never-ending line of willing companionship, but none of it cleared his conscience. The truth was something with little meaning to him back then, but now he had become obsessed with it.

An eighty-inch TV showed a variety of pictures as he lounged on his soft leather sectional. News, sports, Facebook, Twitter, and other sites were active, along with the voices from ESPN radio. A wireless keyboard sat in his robed lap, and a half-empty glass of orange juice sweated on the lamp table at his side. A soft figure huddled in the corner of the sectional, snoring softly. She was dark-haired and wearing lime-colored lingerie. He couldn't recall her name. *Julie? Christy? Danielle?* She was a talk-show anchor, one of the best. If the audience only knew what a freak she was.

He laid a cotton blanket over her. She rustled. *Oh no.* She settled back down, continuing to snore. *Good.* It was time to obsess on the truth again as he began to learn what guilt was. Jeanine entered his thoughts a lot this time of year. No therapy could remove the image of her hapless face being splattered across the tiny jail cell. The ringing blast of the shotgun woke him up in a cold sweat countless nights. *That little man in black.* He hated him.

The killer's uncompassionate viperous face haunted his thoughts. Fate entwined him with that man, who could be seen in the background of many interviews he caught on the web. He never got his name, but he was there, armored in dark glasses and a chiseled expression. He took a sip of juice as he reviewed the headlines on the plasma screen.

WHS CLOSE TO ZOMBIE PEOPLE CURE

ZOMBIE PEOPLE TAKE OVER VILLAGE IN SOUTH AFRICA

SOUTH BEACH WOMAN CLAIMS ZOMBIE PERSON IMPREGNATED HER

GOVERNMENT OFFERS NO EXPLANATION TO ZOMBIE DISAPPEARANCE

MAN CHARGED WITH HATE CRIME FOR KILLING ZOMBIE WOMAN

ZOMBIE VACCINE TESTED IN AUSTRALIA

MYSTERIOUS ZOMBIE CARE DEATHS IN ATLANTA RAISE QUESTIONS

Every day he did more research, contacting a few sources under anonymous profiles. The list of conspiracy theories had grown for years, but now it had begun to dwindle. A few of them began to make sense. There was one big question no one asked anymore: *Where did the zombies come from?* It bothered him day and night.

He was now the poster boy for the World Humanitarian Society, but that was all. He was given a script and told to stick to it. Jeanine, according to his handlers, was his inspiration for finding a cure. They had convinced him to go along with this by giving him the firm impression he had no choice. He played along just like he always did. He even lied to her family about how it all ended. He was a coward, but he was no longer used to it.

He got up, ignoring the biting pain in his stiff knee, and pulled some curtains back. The sunlight began to fill the room with a soft glare. It was Saturday, his date's day off. *Christy. That's it.* He cast another glance the woman's way, but she hadn't moved. He gave a sigh of relief and limped from the living room in his Washington, D.C. condominium. A loud space tune jingled from the kitchen. Pain stabbed him below the knee as he bolted over and snatched at his smartphone. He missed, and it dropped with a loud thump into the metal sink, still ringing. He got a hold of it and answered in a soft voice, "Hello."

The voice was blaring on the other side.

"Good morning, sir, how are you feeling?"

He held his hand over the phone while looking over at Christy.

He tiptoed back to his bedroom.

"I'm fine. Why are you calling, Harry?"

"Just making sure you survived your big day. You and Christy made plenty of headlines last night."

He sat down on his bed, face drawn tight. "What? She was in a limo the whole time. She met me here. No one could have seen." He didn't see anything in the papers, but he hadn't been checking the tabloids either.

"Take it easy, son, I'm just pulling your leg. Glad to hear you are alright. I'll let you get back to your day. Have a good one."

The line went dead. Nate's face was blank as he stared at the phone.

Every day, at any hour, Harry or some other underling of the WHS would call. There was never a day without them. He hated it. They always seemed to know what he was doing. Rubbing his knee, he got up, checked his blinds, and scoured the ceilings and doorways. He ran his soft hands along the mirrors and door frames. It was a habit. Despite all of his precautions, they still knew who was with him.

Inside the bathroom, he brushed his teeth, gargled, and spit. He stared in the mirror, rubbed his grizzled face, and squeezed some blackheads on his nose. He combed his curly brown hair with his fingers and smiled at himself. *Not feeling it today.*

The day after his global celebration was usually filled with relief and relaxation. All of the planning and interviews from being *the man who saved the world* were done. He was still filled with anxiety, however. Someone sent him a link to one of his profile accounts. It led to another series of videos, articles, and speculation ... and they made sense.

He hung his white terrycloth robe behind the bathroom door, slipped out of his Darkslayer pajama pants, and got in the shower. The hot water drilled deep into his hairy chest, steaming the bathroom glass.

"Ah," he said as he worked up a soapy lather.

He slipped at the sound of a rubbing squeak that came from the other side of the shower glass. He tried to rinse the soap from his eyes, only to open them to a burning sensation. *What in the ....* A figure began to appear in the moisture of the glass. It started with an "*S*" and ended with an "*X*."A perfect figure with a heart-shaped ass stepped inside.

"Good morning." Christy's voice was hotter than the water.

He watched the water soak her hair and cascade down her body.

"It certainly is," he said.

While Christy erased all his anxiety, another figure moved about the condominium. The cries and moans from inside the shower brought a smile to the man's crooked lips. The man made out the word on the shower door, nodded, and walked away.

Minutes later, Nate stepped from the shower and got the impression someone else had been there. On the floor, an imprint of a shoe appeared on the wet tile, but Christy stepped right through it. He noticed nothing else strange.

"What's wrong?" she said, staring up into his eyes and wrapping her hands around his neck.

He tossed her onto his bed, ignoring the twinge in his knee. "Nothing, baby."

13

GUTHRIE, WV

"GRANDPA," said little Ferguson as his pudgy thumbs worked his Gameboy, "... are you ever going to tell me what's inside there?"

John's grandson asked that question often over the years. The ten-year-old boy had been coming to work with him, once or twice a year, since he was six. John wasn't one to tell a lie or make open assumptions. He just scratched the back of his neck while gazing upward into the dim midday sky. What kind of story would he concoct this time around?

"Well, Grandpa?"

A brisk wind was rustling the turning leaves, and the surrounding pines began to bend. He poured the last of his coffee from his battered metal thermos. He took a sip of the lukewarm substance, thinking about the daunting building inside the rattling fence.

The air felt cold in his lungs as he struggled to find the right words.

"Fergie, sometimes yer just better off not knowing. Besides, I can't really say for sure, and maybe that's the best for both of us."

He rubbed the boy's head with his rough hand.

"And I figure if the Lord wanted us to know, we'd know. I do know this; there are some good people in there, so I just assume good things must be going on."

His grandson's head never came up, nose down in his video game. A few moments passed before John took another long swig of coffee.

Ferguson made a flat remark. "The kids at school say there are zombies in there."

He choked in mid-swallow and began to cough.

"You all right, Grandpa?"

A small hand was pounding on his back. John took another slug of coffee and began clearing his throat. He pulled his mirrored sunglasses from his weathered eyes.

"Who on earth told you that?"

"Teddy Knox ... Jasmine Starks ... Russell and his dad ... lots of kids say it."

He honestly had no idea if zombies were in there, but he suspected it. The truth was, there had never been a zombie within a hundred miles of the place as far as he knew. But something about this facility never settled right with him. It was remodeled no long after they got the creatures under control. He'd worked there when it was a state-owned building, then the federal government took over, followed by the WHS. Sometimes people just knew things in small towns.

Everyone knew there were zombie cares all over, and where many of them were, but not all. For top-secret reasons, certain situations were only "need to know" by those who knew. He'd waved many a dignitary through the gates from time to time, but he still did not know. He didn't want to, either.

John's voice was playful as he said, "Now, what makes you think they have any idea what's in here? They're just pulling your leg, trying to scare you."

His grandson growled as a deflating chime came from his game, and the boy snapped it shut.

"It says so on the Internet. They showed me a website."

"Did it scare you?"

Heck, the sound of thunder scared the boy, and he couldn't imagine him not being scared of zombies.

"Yeah ... but I'm not scared anymore."

"Why not?" John was curious.

"I'm never scared when I'm with you, Grandpa."

John's mild eyes began to tear up as he gave his grandson a warm hug.

He studied the facility. Green beacons shone around the lower entrance and all along the fence. Well, they had. Now, many of the beacons were blacked out. *This place is going all to heck.* He could have sworn some of those lights flickered as the sun dipped below the tree-tops, shadowing the outer gate in darkness. He couldn't shake the cold. *This shift won't end soon enough.*

14

Red. Green. Red. Green. The basement was indistinct from the rest of the facility, cold and impersonal. More florescent-lit corridors led from the elevator to a stairwell. As he made his way down the spiraling steps, an uneasy feeling set in again. Working upstairs was uncomfortable, but downstairs was downright claustrophobic. A red beacon awaited him at the bottom. It was time to get some answers. He sucked in his breath and scanned his card to open the metal doors.

The room looked like a forensics lab, lit in a pale yellow glow. A pair of autopsy tables kept two small bodies at rest. Chlorine, vinegar, and other pungent smells filled his nose. A large black man was pulling green-and-white-striped papers from a loud printer. The man quickly tore each sheet off and studied the results, pushing up his thick-framed glasses.

Henry could hear the man mutter *uh –huh* sounds under his breath. He watched as two big hands crumpled the large papers into a tight ball. The big man spun and shot the wad of paper over the autopsy tables. The ball of paper landed with a bang inside a metal trash bin in the corner.

"That's a three!" the man shouted in a deep voice, arms high and fingers almost touching the high ceiling. Henry began a mild round of applause, and the man lurched at the sound.

"Well, look who's back," the big man said, arms wide as he approached.

Oh no. He felt the man's arms wrap around him, pinning his arms as if he were a child. His feet left the ground for a long moment, and his back cracked before he felt the hard floor again. Henry straightened his glasses.

"Do you always have to do that?"

"Of course ... you're my boy," the man said, smiling. It was hard to resist Stanley's charm. The man was always positive, his face wizened and cheerful, and he had a soothing and powerful voice. Henry's anger had subsided, but not to the point he would not vent his concerns. As ingenious a scientist Stanley was, he still had his flaws.

"Dad, why on earth is Jimmy back here?" he said, raising his voice. "What are you giving to the zombies? Is what I saw with Louie the result of the XT serum?"

Henry approached the man and looked up into his eyes, but Stanley turned away, shuffling papers on a desk.

"Don't worry about it, Son ... you're always so serious. Come over here; we had a breakthrough while you were gone."

Stanley draped his arm over Henry's shoulders and shoved him along between the autopsy tables. Two girls in pink-and-white-striped sweat suits were strapped down. Their faces were ashen, eyes sunk, skin dry and grey. Black pupils rolled all over without a flicker of knowledge. Their hands and feet flinched from time to time. He expected some moans, but they were silent.

Careful to keep his distance from the edge, Henry stayed at the foot end of the tables.

"What is this? They aren't moving."

"They're dying," Stanley said in a sobering voice.

The words sent a jolt through his body.

"What happened? How do you know?" Henry said, studying the two girls.

His dad leaned against one of the tables and lit a cigarette.

"Well, one day they just stopped moving." Stanley snapped his fingers. "They stood for days before they fell down."

"Aren't Jill and Jean the oldest here?" he said, circling the metal tables and taking a closer look. He pulled an ophthalmoscope from his pocket and flashed a beam of light in Jean's eyes. The girl's pupils didn't shrink, which wasn't normal.

"Yep, but they were also afflicted earlier as well. These are the senator's grand-girls. They've been in other facilities before."

Henry was still finishing college when all of this happened. The senator's family had made many visits, unlike the rest. Now that the senator was out of office, his contact with the girls had been lost. The family had signed off on the girls and ceremoniously buried their memory. Henry suspected the senator's influence had funded Guthrie, and now those funds were diminishing.

If other daycares had zombies dying, he had not heard. If longevity was an issue, this might be the first case. It felt good knowing these creatures would eventually die. It gave him hope.

"How long have they been like this?"

"About a week," Stanley said as he pointed the red dot of a thermal scanner at Jill. "Seventy-five degrees. It was eighty when I brought them down here. I am guessing when it hits room temperature, they're done."

"Then what?" Henry felt a strange pang of sympathy.

"Then, *the up and ups* said to cremate them."

The zombie girls were each hooked to a pulse and blood pressure monitor. The digital pulse figure was between fifteen and twenty beats per minute, compared to the usual forty to fifty beats per minute. The blood pressure readout was blank.

As his father blew smoke into the air, a hum and whir sounded and the wispy vapor was sucked into a vent above. The sound stopped. Stanley looked up, blew more smoke, and the sound returned, taking away the smoke, but the fans kept going.

"So, is the cremation chamber working?"

"Sure, that's where all the garbage goes."

It was a fitting end to the zombies. As far as he was concerned, they never should have stopped the genocidal disintegration. The zombies weren't people; they were flesh-eating life takers, the bottom of the food chain. He saw it firsthand, and it still horrified him. If there was anything he could do to stop them, he would. But the WHS wouldn't allow it. He kept those thoughts to himself.

He was deep in contemplation when he felt something brush against his lab coat. He let out a cry of alarm when he turned.

"Mom!"

She didn't reply. He backed up, facing her. Her curly red hair was in contrast to the metallic environment surrounding her. She was as tall as he, dressed in tight blue jeans and a brown wool turtleneck sweater. His nerves were on edge from the unexpected sight. It had been a long time since he had seen her. She opened her mouth to speak.

"Num-Num. Num-Num."

His heart collapsed in his chest. Her resemblance to the real thing had caught him off guard. She followed him around the table as he backed away, giving her a closer inspection. *She has a wig on!* Her clothes, painted nails, and makeup increased the illusion of a real woman. Her cracked and sunken eyes, slack jaw, and pasty hands reminded him she was still a zombie.

"What did you do?" he said, voice cracking. He was freaking out. She almost looked like someone he once loved. He fought an instinctive urge to hug her. "Why is she here running loose?"

"Henry … settle down," Stanley said in a reassuring voice. "She's as sweet as a kitty cat. Just look at her. She's still got that something, makes those jeans look just right … just like the first time I saw her."

He couldn't hide his bewildered look.

"That's sick, Dad!"

"No, Son, that's love."

Stanley walked over and stroked her cheek.

"Num-Num."

It pained Henry's ears to hear his mother say that.

If he hadn't been certain before, he was now: Guthrie was his least favorite place in the world. His mother, Linda, wasn't home in West

Virginia when the zombie outbreak came. She was at a teaching seminar in Houston, Texas. She had been one among tens of thousands of victims. It was a miracle when they found her days before her scheduled cremation. They had no idea where to look after months of searching. A news camera, of all the dumb luck, caught her face on the evening news at a controversial location in North Dakota. Stanley fought like a man possessed to get her back, but it was Henry who called in a favor, to Nate McDaniel.

Henry's irritation returned.

"Is that why Jimmy is back? If Mom dies, is he going to be a pallbearer?"

His palms and fingers fanned out, beckoning for an answer. His mom gave up on his brother long ago, but Stanley just never understood. Stanley gave Jimmy too many second chances.

Stanley shrugged and moved away from the argument, saying, "He's family. He should have a chance to say good-bye. I never got that chance with my mom or dad. You don't understand. Just let it be; it will be over soon."

The sad look in Stanley's eyes told the rest. Henry watched Stanley give his mother a kiss on the cheek.

Stanley changed gears and said, "Are you and Tori still getting on well? She's a fine-looking lady. She reminds me of your mother."

Not this again. Please not this again. It was too late, as Stanley had begun the story of how he met his mother. Meanwhile, his mother walked away, bumping over and over again into a bookcase.

"I remember the first time I saw your mother. It was my first day as the assistant basketball coach at the middle school. Linda was coaching the cheerleaders. I never saw hair like that on a woman before ..."

"Hey Stan—" But Henry knew it was too late to stop him from talking.

"... I was down, and so was she. Your dad had just left her and you two boys. He went to Vegas to be a comedian, and lucky for me, he never made it back."

Henry buried his hands in his face. Telling the story kept Stanley from the reality he couldn't handle. Henry let his stepfather go on, knowing Stanley wouldn't stop now anyway. *Please don't talk about the honeymoon.*

"... Both my knees were shot from college ball, but Linda talked me into trying some classes. I told her if she went out with me, I would take classes. I loved playing ball, but if I'd never blown my legs out, I never would have realized what I could do."

Stanley tapped his head with his long finger.

"I ended up with a scholarship — in biology," Stanley said with a wry smile. "Man, a scholarship in basketball and biology. My mom would've died if she ever knew. I'd almost forgotten how much I liked science when I was a boy. Mom bought me my first chemistry set."

Henry could recount the story word for word if he had to. Still, he played along, mindful of his mother lumbering through the lab. It took about fifteen minutes of intermittent nods and *uh-huh's* before Stanley finished. The big man sat down at a metal desk chair and rubbed his knees as he watched his zombie wife. The exhausted expression on Stanley's round face stirred sympathy in Henry's chest.

Henry hated to say it, but he felt compelled. "You can't bring back the dead, Dad."

Stanley's voice was solemn when he said, "Christ did."

"Yes, but he was God."

"The apostles did."

Stanley flicked a long ash on the floor.

"Dad," his voice was soft as he patted his stepfather's big shoulders, "you have to let this go. You look tired. How long has it been since you ate?"

"I'm okay. It's only been a few hours. Tori always brings me something down."

There was a long moment of silence between the two as the exhaust fans kicked off. Only the sound of Linda's shuffling feet remained.

"Okay. Let's go back to Jimmy and the XT Serum. Jimmy has to go —now! Remember the last time? Do you remember what my sick brother did to Jill and Jean?" he said, making a frantic motion towards the zombie twins strapped to the tables.

Jimmy did disturbing things to the girls, things Henry couldn't bring himself to speak of. Jimmy was a self-absorbed little minion who'd do anything for a laugh or a thrill. No one ever understood Jimmy's sick sense of humor.

His father was nodding; his face was in his hands as he said, "I know, I know." Stanley whispered, "... I'll ask him to leave tomorrow."

"Try now! Or I'll do it."

"You can do it."

Some satisfaction filled him up. Getting rid of Jimmy would be the very next thing Henry would do.

"Now, what is going on with Louie upstairs? Is that the XT Serum?"

Stanley nodded. "I knew I should have waited."

Life started to fill Stanley's voice as he sat up. "Take a look at this." Stanley got up with a heavy groan and headed over to a computer screen.

Henry followed him and saw MRI head scans on the flat screens. One was cold: black, blue, and gray. The other screen had flares of orange, green, and red above the brain stem. He studied the data on the screen.

"This was three days ago?"

His stepfather was nodding.

"Who ... Jill and Jean?"

Stanley pointed and said, "This one is Jean."

"But I thought they were dying."

"Well, as such, I thought they would be better subjects. I did both. Same results."

It was significant. Brain activity on a zombie was almost non-existent, but here there was something. As a scientist, Henry couldn't control his excitement. This was a big deal. All of these years in the facility had been spent dealing with children. Their brains were more apt to learn and absorb information. They relied more on instincts and had a stronger survival mode. Zombie children reacted to stimuli more often than adults. Their minds hadn't been polluted and their brain cells were still an incubator of growth. The zombie children shed the most light for hope of a cure.

"So how come they are still dying?" he asked with avid curiosity.

"There is only so much XT, and it was a small dose at that. It lasted a day. The girls ... began walking again."

He pulled on his dad's shoulder and said, "Does anyone else know?"

"Nah, I kept them down here." Stanley's smile widened. "Think about it, Son, with this breakthrough we can get back our funding. Maybe get a huge promotion."

"What about Louie? Is he on it?"

"One dose, every other day. Look at his brain pattern."

Stanley toggled between the screens and opened another file. One-fourth of the subject's brain above the lower stem was a rainbow of color.

"Wow!"

They clasped each other's shoulders. Things were getting better.

But someone else did know. The cameras above had caught it all. He had been watching all along. Jimmy knew everything, and a gold mine would soon be his.

15

HER TUMMY GRUMBLED AS SHE ENTERED THE BREAK ROOM. ALL OF THE excitement from Henry's return flustered her. Bathed in the white refrigerator light, Tori rummaged through the shelves. Pulling out a box of pizza, she grabbed a roll of paper towels from the break-room countertop. Opening the box, she let out a disappointed moan. *Hawaiian? ...Oh, there's a piece of sausage.* She stuffed it in her mouth, chewing with a shrug. *What the heck.*

"Girl's got to eat," she muttered, placing three slices on a plate inside the microwave and hitting the PIZZA button. As happy as she was that Henry was back, she felt blue. So much had happened while he was gone, and she hadn't told him. Rudy and Stanley told her it would ruin his trip, but not telling him seemed to have ruined it all anyway. She wished she could have just gone with him on the cruise, something she had never taken before. Oh, what she would do for him on the open sea. His kind eyes and handsome face soothed her soul like no other man; even his serious demeanor didn't dissuade her efforts.

"Henry needs us, girls," she said, hoisting her bra straps as she produced a jar of nail polish.

She checked her teeth on the rectangular mirror she had taped inside of a cabinet door and shot herself a wink. She pulled out a chair, took a seat, and began re-painting her long black nails. She had just finished applying the last coat when the microwave chimed. She got up, took out the steaming pizza, and tossed it onto the table. The strong smell of the pizza caused her stomach to groan again.

The room was quiet as she turned her back to the doorway and reached back inside the fridge. She felt eyes were burning on her lower back. Someone was there. She looked back over her shoulder hoping to see Henry, but only a black television monitor greeted her concerned glare. Back inside the fridge, two liters of leftover birthday soda were all she had to choose from. The one that read "diet" got the honor. She froze before she pulled the bottle free. Her nerves were on edge, and all she could hear was the refrigerator's hum.

"Who's there!" she yelled, turning with the bottle held before her like a club.

The room was empty. Her made-up eyes darted back and forth. She stepped into the doorway and peeked outside into the main office. The cubicles and office were dark where the overhead fluorescent lights were only on in part. She liked the dark, but not today. Along the outside of the break room, she began flipping on more switches, and the office became as bright as could be.

Sighing, she sat back down and said, "That's better."

Eating her pizza, she checked out a copy of USA Magazine. Nate McDaniel was on the cover, and she wondered if she would get to meet him. Henry had told her a few interesting things about him. She found that man fascinating, but not as good looking as she hoped. Coughing on a big bite of pizza, she took several big drinks of the soda.

"Damn!" Still coughing as she went to the sink, she began drinking from the spigot. Something was stuck in her windpipe, and she was hacking hard. It flustered her, but she got it washed down.

"Whew, that was scary."

She felt a pair of hands on her hips.

"Ah Henry, my hero, you came to save the day."

Turning to face him, she recoiled in horror, shoving Jimmy's leering face away.

"Son of a bitch!"

She rounded the other side of the table. Men had pawed at her since she was thirteen, and she had learned to handle them, but this man gave her the willies.

"Ah come on, Tori, it ain't like you don't want me," he said, followed by a heavy sniff. "Remember that time we went to the movies?"

The ball cap was twisted on his head, half covering his long grubby hair. She could see the dandruff flakes on the shoulders of his sports jersey. He looked her up and down, brown eyes wild with lust. The strong odor of alcohol mixed with sweat replaced her hunger with nausea. Jimmy's face had turned from good looking, like his brother, to an unkempt miscreant no one wanted to know. Long ago, she had gone to the movies with him in school, and she had been naughty. Now, she felt as if all of those sins had caught up with her. Her knees were locked as he made his way between her and the door.

"Go away, Jimmy," she managed to let it out. "That was a long time ago. I don't even remember it." She did remember it, however; now it came back to haunt her.

"Well I sure do," he said on his approach.

He reached out and grabbed her cheeks in one big hand and squeezed them. She couldn't believe she wasn't moving. Some strange power kept her still. Something kept her near, something dangerous. His breath was on her neck, and she felt him inhale her. He was like a snake when he whispered in her ear.

"Henry ain't got nothing on me girlie, and you know it."

Something inside her snapped. Her weakened will turned to iron as anger replaced her weakness. She launched her knee into his crotch. He groaned aloud as he sank to the floor, cursing.

"You bitch! You bitch! You bitch!"

She didn't hear a word as she ran away as fast as her legs would go. Tears were streaming down her cheeks as she entered the elevator. She felt exposed and worthless. She couldn't tell Henry; he wouldn't understand. She just had to keep it inside and pray Jimmy left soon. Or died.

She wanted out of this place, but didn't know where to go. The elevator opened into the parking garage, and she ran for her car, shutting herself inside, hoping no one would miss her. It was a long time before she settled down. She was crying so loud that she almost didn't hear the elevator open. She crouched deeper into the backseat of her car and buried her head. She heard footsteps shuffling over the gravel close by, and she couldn't remember if she had locked the door.

16

HE SAW COLORS AND HEARD SOUNDS THAT WERE FAMILIAR. THERE WERE shapes and people, some moving and others not. Everything was new whenever he opened his eyes. A hunger and curiosity burned inside, but he didn't know what that was. Confusion and fear overwhelmed his senses, but it was all normal as far as he could comprehend.

A soft wall barricaded his path somewhere else. He moved along its side, tripping over plastic objects he didn't know were there. He fell, got up, and fell again. He didn't remember how many times he had done this. He didn't remember how many times he did anything. Things would go black and turn to color again. Every place he awoke was in different shades. Yellow, blue, and gray surfaces coated his eyes.

Something sharp jabbed him, but he felt no pain. More of those familiar-looking things stared down on him. There were balls of many colors, filled with lines, triangles, circles, and other shapes. Somehow, he knew them, but most times they scared him.

Abandonment, loneliness, and despair were emotions he did not remember. Flashes of other figures intermingled with his thoughts. He smelled things that made him hunger, and his mouth watered.

His bleak existence had no meaning, not to him. He traveled up
something and slipped down it. A thrilling sensation overcame him.
He wanted that again but didn't know how. Something smacked him
in the head. It was round and red. He picked it up and said, "Numma-
numma."

17

SHE WAS STILL THERE, LYING LIKE A BABY SHEEP IN A MEADOW. THE plush mattress cushioned her curled-up figure, snuggled in Nate McDaniel's silken sheets. No sound, no matter how abrupt, stirred her excellent figure. She was exhausted, but not from him, as he would like to think, but rather by her demanding job with the media. He sat at her side, admiring the woman he had just scored. Being the most famous man in the world had its advantages, but he knew he worthy of none. Sighing, he covered up her naked figure and walked stiff-legged from the bedroom.

Shaking his head, he said, "I hate it when this happens."

She's still here. He couldn't stand that. She was one of *those.* A woman who wanted to hang around, pick his brain, or have a nice dinner in town. More press, more pictures, maybe a wedding ... he understood the road she was on. He'd been trying to get off the celebrity highway for years, but it wasn't possible.

The seclusion of his high-rise condominium kept most wanton predators at bay. It was his three-thousand-square-foot man cave. The starlets of his world came and went as he saw fit. This was his anti-matrimony lair. No girls allowed ... for long.

He descended a short set of stairs into a den overlooking downtown DC. Nate's study was plenty big, with custom mahogany cabinets, marble countertops, and an oversized minibar. Closing the door behind him, he grabbed a Gobster energy drink from the fridge. Pulling back the tab, he glanced over the can. *Caffeine and sugar... the nectar of the zombies.* He let out a quick laugh; after all, it was his dumb luck that made the discovery. It seemed that two of his favorite ingredients were the zombies' as well. He felt an unsettling in his stomach and so he set the can down.

He watched the busy city streets below. The streams of people, as small as ants, seemed to be on the move as the rain began to splatter his window. He could never crush the thought that all of those people might have been zombies, should have been zombies, if not for him. Now, he wanted to be ready if it happened again.

The only good coming from the zombies was dismemberment of global terrorism. The Middle East was inflicted at the outset and their losses were reported heavier than most. Leaders of the tightly-knit networks all but disappeared, either from death or zombieism, as most speculated. Many differences were settled, as people all over the world seemed to understand that there were bigger problems to be addressed ... like extinction.

Sitting down in a comfortable leather desk chair, he checked some accounts, read messages, and texted a few that had dangled in his thoughts for days. He felt as if there were a thousand things he needed to do, but that wasn't the case. A thirty-six-inch monitor was suspended before him. He spent about ten more minutes hammering at the keys, chugging down the rest of his energy drink. *Crap.* It was past noon, and he had a needy woman to contend with.

Snatching another drink, he looked down into the rain. DC was a foreign place to him. A large city that left him trapped. He never felt lost, however, because someone would find him. Something always plagued him though. Why was there no zombie outbreak in D.C.? One in fifty people abroad had turned, yet a much smaller fraction in the nation's capital was afflicted. No senators, congressmen, joint chiefs, or Supreme Court Justices crossed the undead path. The conspiracy theories should have abounded, but they did not. It was a theory only a few others he knew still talked about.

He was tapping his finger on the side of the black and blue can. He had been digging and thought he found something worthwhile, but there was no one to tell. *I wonder what Henry will think.* Most of his friends and family were gone, and he never seemed to have time to make new ones. Henry Bawkula was about the only one he ever contacted over the years. Henry he could trust, but he knew his college friend wouldn't feel the same about him. *Not after Jeanine.*

As he continued his search, he came to believe something big was going on. He was a liar, and he knew a liar when he heard one, and those who proclaimed him a hero were the worst liars by far. He used to lie to stay out of trouble, but they lied for power. He was caught in the middle. He wanted to disappear.

He dragged himself over, slumped down in his cloth sectional, and began playing the latest Darkslayer RPG game on his monitor. *Ah yes, my favorite escape from reality, smash-mouth fantasy.* He had spent over an hour chopping down monsters with a massive battle axe when the power went off. The overcast sky provided gray light in an otherwise black room. It was dead quiet, other than the beating rain. He stepped from his study and looked down at the black furniture silhouettes in his living room. His knee began to ache again as he looked outside at the other buildings whose lights were still on.

A weird feeling overcame him. *What was that!?* Something shifted in the shadows, he was sure of it.

"Christy?" he whispered. There was no reply. "Christy?"

He waited on the landing, squinting. Fear filtered inside him as he stepped down the stairs. He began to relax as the edges of his furniture became clear, and he began to recognize the layout in the dim light.

He banged his knee on the edge of an antique buffet. *OW!*

He stubbed his toe on a couch leg. "Dammit!" His eyes began to water as he hobbled towards his bedroom.

He felt stupid as he sipped more fluid from his canister.

I don't even have a flashlight. Or match—Or candle—Stupid!

There never had been a need. He pushed the cracked bedroom door open. The heavy curtains had remained closed, and the room was as black as a coal mine. He knew his way around and made it over to Christy's side. He ran his hand along the small of her back and caressed her hair. He shook her body a bit.

"Hey," he said softly.

She didn't respond.

"Hey!" he whispered in her ear. "Wake up!"

He ran his hand down her back, over her rump, and up again. She didn't stir. He jostled her hair. Nothing happened. He felt something wet on his hand. He held it to his face.

What the hell is this? It was dark, sticky, and warm. He shook her hard, panic coursing through him, but she didn't move.

"Christy! Christy! Wake up, baby! Wake—*ulp!*"

Something seized him from behind, strangling his neck and squeezing his throat. He felt as if a bear had a hold on him as he tried to scream, but his tongue did not move. *Help! Help! Dear God, help me!* A sharp needle sunk deep into his neck, injecting a fluid that burned like fire. His body went numb as he felt himself fall helpless onto his bed.

18

"WHAT HAPPENED!? WHAT HAPPENED!?"

Henry was almost yelling. The distraught look on her sweet face unsettled him. They had been going at it for over fifteen minutes. Sitting on the car hood, arms folded, she kept her head buried in her chest. He knew how stubborn she could be. They'd been on-again, off-again over the years, and this was a big reason why. She wouldn't talk about some things to him. She stuffed things deep inside, unwilling to share her past. This was another one of those times.

He asked her again, cheeks reddening more by the second.

"Was it Jimmy? Did he say something perverted to you?"

She shook her head back and forth, choking at the sound of the name.

"Come on ... tell me what is wrong, you're driving me crazy," he said, immediately wishing he had not let those words out.

"What!" she said, raising her voice and head, mascara running from her eyes. *"I'm driving you crazy!?"* She slipped off the hood of her car.

Oh no, here we go. Henry stepped away.

"You leave me here—for two weeks—with these—perverts! Your

sick bastard of a brother shows up and ogles me like a webcam slut ... and you think I'm crazy!"

He was being driven further backward. Tori's fingernails poked into his chest as her voice echoed off the concrete walls of the garage. There was nothing he could do now. Stanley warned him about these Italian women, and it wasn't as cute as it used to be.

"I'm sorry," he said as he slipped on some gravel, shielding himself with his hands. He never would have thought worrying about the feelings of a woman would make him want to crawl in a hole. Moments like this made him miss being a bachelor. He wanted to know what was wrong, however, so he stood his ground. He had to do something fast. In a quick gentle motion, he caught her up in his arms and squeezed.

"What are you doing—let go!" she demanded, trying to pound his chest.

He didn't though, holding her tight, hoping she wouldn't knee him in the gonads as she had done once before.

"Forgive me. You don't have to tell me anything."

His words softened her body, and he could feel her pull close. Tori wrapped her arms behind his back. The smell of her exotic perfume, coupled with her warm body, aroused his senses. Things were beginning to feel better, as his and her longing were beginning to be intertwined by the rush of emotion and adrenaline. He wanted her now, and he felt she needed him. Her sobbing turned into low passionate whimpers as her hot lips pressed into his neck.

The sound of the garage elevator opening interrupted his thoughts, and he pulled away. Someone was rushing his way. He pushed Tori behind him.

"Is everything okay?" It was Rudy. His chubby face was flushed red.

"What do you mean, 'is everything okay?'" Henry asked.

"Well,"— the hairy man stopped to catch his breath—"... it was like you guys both disappeared. I've been trying to find you for the past twenty minutes."

"Did you call my cell phone?"

"Yes!" Rudy retorted, pointing at Henry's waist.

Reaching down, he realized his phone case was empty on his belt, and a quick pat-down of his clothes revealed he was without the mobile device.

"Oh ... sorry."

He wasn't embarrassed, however. Tori was still hugging him tight from the side. Rudy was giving her a funny look.

"Hey, were you guys about to get busy?" Rudy asked, wiggling his hips.

"No!" she said.

Henry intervened. "She's just upset"—he felt her arms tighten around his waist—"... that I've been gone so long." He did the best he could on the fly.

His friend was rubbing his messy beard.

"Ah ... so you *weren't* getting busy. I get it." Rudy winked and said, "Brown chicken, brown cow."

Henry stood there gawking at his friend whose mind had wandered somewhere else. As the awkward moment passed, he asked again, "Now, why did you need to get a hold of me?"

Rudy seemed confused, as if he'd just woken up, and finally said, "Uh ..." His eyes lit up. "Oh shit, that's right. Louie is missing, man. Louie is frickin' missing!"

Tori let out a sharp gasp beside him. He couldn't believe his ears. It wasn't possible. There were security cameras everywhere, and every precaution was taken. His thoughts went to Jimmy, and another chill went down his spine.

"What! What do you mean? He can't be missing! It's not possible—"

"Man, I'm telling you, he's gone. Weege and I have been looking for almost an hour."

"An hour! Why didn't you tell me sooner?" he yelled, as he rushed back toward the elevator.

Idiots. All of them. Trusting Jimmy. He wanted to kill somebody as he hammered at the only button outside the elevator.

"Tori, you stay here," he shouted.

"Hell no, I'm going in."

He grabbed her. "No, you're going home."

She jerked away from him. "Don't tell me no, mister, I've got a job here, too." She glared at Rudy, who turned away from her angry stare. "I'm sure it's not going to be that big a problem."

He'd rather face a zombie than her wrath again, so he let it go. "Where's Ralph? Is he looking?"

"No, he left an hour ago, sick as a dog. He puked something awful," Rudy said with a sour look on his face.

Henry didn't see Ralph's car. He looked up at the elevator light. It was red. He kicked the door.

"You got to use your card, man, the button don't work," Rudy said, scanning his card. Nothing happened.

Henry tried his and Tori hers. Nothing happened.

Something wasn't right. He had to get in there. His dad and Weege were in certain danger. They all were.

19

Washington, DC

EVERYTHING inside of Nate McDaniel was screaming for help. His life was rushing through his thoughts. Those last moments with Jeanine, good and bad, resurfaced more than anything. That's what they say happens when you're about to die. You think about what you loved most.

He knew there were at least two people in the room; one was the big one who had turned him over like a rag doll, the other he wasn't sure. The lights had come back on, and he could hear thunder cracking in his ears. He couldn't move at all. He could see his assailant better now, broad and ugly faced, flat nosed, a grin of yellowed teeth, wearing a tailored blue suit. The man's powerful hands clutched at his clothes, sitting him upright like a mannequin on the bed's edge.

His neck was sideways, looking at the other figure. *You're the son of a bitch who shot Jeanine!* The same man stood in front of him, small, clad in black, a short mustache, and the dark countenance of a killer.

The little man's southern accent was heavy as he spoke. "Well, asshole that saved the world ... look what you done gone and got yourself into. You killed yer girlfriend and killed yerself."

WHAT!? Nate tried to shake his head but couldn't.

The man's face was inches from his, and Nate could see his own watery eyes in the man's dark sunglasses. The man's breath was pure tobacco, and he could see the man's jutting lower lip.

"Now, why would the jackass that saved the world do something like that?"

He could feel his hair being pulled back as his head was being shaken for him. *I didn't kill anybody! I'm not killing myself! Please don't kill me!*

His head was let go as the little man stepped away and sat in a chair in front of him. He wanted to scream. He wanted to cry so bad, beg for his life or anything, but he couldn't do either.

His captor continued, "You see, boy, you did save the world, and that pissed a lot of people off. I think you know who I'm talking about. You know that den of world leaders that patted you on the back and gave you a bunch of bullshit accommodations ..."

Nate thought he blinked, but he wasn't sure.

"... Yep, you might look dumb, but I knew you weren't. I tried to tell them. We should have killed you the day we found you, but they needed someone to make them look good. Stupid politicians ..."

What are you talking about? I didn't do anything! Oh God—please don't let him kill me!

"... and sure, rich jerkoffs like you get bored sometimes and start getting too nosy. The last thing we need, or the World Humanitarian Society rather, is the man who saved the world pronouncing conspiracy theories ..."

The man was straddling the kitchen chair, as casual as if he'd been conversing with his best friend. He watched as the little man spit dark juice into his favorite coffee cup.

"You couldn't be happy, like a fattened calf, could ya, boy. All the money, fame, glory and poontang couldn't satisfy your quest for why things happened. Things people don't give a shit about anymore. No

—you had to lump yourself in with all the other nutcases out there, and figure out where the zombies came from."

The man pinched his fingers almost together, inches from his face.

"You got this close," the man said in a dry hiss.

Nate could see the other, big man cross his path and begin moving something on the bed behind him. A bottle of something rattled near his ears. There were sirens somewhere, as well as other sounds intermingling with the heavy rain and rolling thunder.

What is happening? Dude, I don't know that much. I can't prove anything. Please don't kill me! You don't have to kill me!

He saw the seated man pull out a pistol, automatic and nickel-plated. The gun looked like a shiny club in the man's small hand. He envisioned Jeanine's head blowing open like a bloody watermelon again. *Please not me! Please not me! Dear God, please not me!*

"Yeah boy, it's time to tie up the loose ends."

The small man stood up and pulled the slide on his weapon.

Shick–tick!

Nate could see the man twist a silencer onto the gun barrel as his adversary stepped out of sight. *Where is he! Where is he! I don't want to die like this.* He wondered what would happen after he died. He hoped the stories he heard as a boy about Jesus were true. He had nothing else to hope for. He remembered Jeanine's cross on his neck. *Jesus save me.* He didn't want to die. *Please forgive me for all the things I did and did not do.* He could feel his heart sinking.

Something cold was being pressed into his right hand. It was steel. His body was being turned around on the bed. He saw some pictures of friends and family on the dresser tops. There were pills he hadn't seen before there, too. There was white powder in a small bag by his mirror. He caught a good look at himself as his repositioners took a pause. The big man, who was missing some teeth, was grinning above him as Nate stared in the mirror. He was pasty, slack-jawed, and pathetic. His pupils were wide and glossy, like a zombie's. The wiry southerner stuck another needle in his arm.

"This is so they think you took all those drugs we scattered about."

There was a slapping on his shoulder as they panned him around. A gold-plated can of Mountain Dew was on his nightstand. *All this, over that!* He was facing his pillowed headboard now. He saw Christy's frozen stare. A thick patch of blood soaked the sheets behind her back. His arm was raised before him, a gun in his grasp. *No! Please no! How can you be so cruel! This can't be real! I didn't do anything! I saved the world!*

"Be thankful, son, you could have died a zombie. Heh. Heh."

20

GUTHRIE, **WV**

HIS INVINCIBILITY COMPLEX had taken over. Every devious plan had worked so far. Spinning around in the security desk chair, Jimmy shouted at the top of his lungs.

"I'm the next Nate McDaniel! I'm the King! The world is mine!" He let out a high-pitched *"WOOOOOO"* like a rock star.

The monitors provided humorous activity as he watched his brother pound on the elevator door inside the garage. *Thinks he's so smart. We'll see.* His stepfather Stanley, still in the basement lab, was oblivious to the chaos as he attempted to waltz with Jimmy's undead mother. *Scratch him, Mom! Bite him!* He hated Stanley as much as the rest, but mainly because of his brother. His stepfather had always been good to him. They'd had good times fishing and playing ball, but he didn't remember those days anymore.

Jimmy was now consumed with the bankroll he would get when he turned over the XT Serum. But that wouldn't happen until his secret employers had some proof it worked. That was where Louie came in.

Jimmy started laughing as he watched Weege pulling at the thick mop of black hair on his head, screaming at the monitors

Tsk–Tsk, Weege! You should have paid closer attention. Instead, the frail little geek from Dubai chose to jam on his smartphone, play games, and come to the aid of his ailing counterpart Ronald. Ronald was a cautious master of many things, except his diet. *The world's greatest Big Chug fan, down at last.* Squeezing eye drops into Ronald's drink had sent the man running to the toilet and then all the way home.

His mind seemed to grasp the entire understanding of the universe as he sucked down another can of light beer. Crushing it in his hands, he cut himself.

"Damn!"

He laughed like a hyena. It had all been so easy. Ronald's leaving allowed him to shut down the elevator, just long enough to switch Louie into another cell. Weege never suspected he had run a separate loop over his security feed until it was too late. Meanwhile, the zombie boy was safe in an adjacent cell they thought was empty, because of another bogus video feed. Rudy was too lazy to physically go and check, relying on the video cameras instead. Jimmy orchestrated all of this from inside the small security room.

He watched the zombie boy Louie on another screen. The boy was wound up like a kitten, ready to pounce on a ball of yarn. The hefty gray boy circled his cell at an alarming speed. *He looks like Frankenstein on crack.* Jimmy giggled to himself. Now there was only one more thing left to do. Let the little monster loose. He checked the screen monitoring the garage. *You ready, brother big shot? How about you, stupid slut and sloppy boy?* He hated them all. He couldn't wait to see them suffer. Still, he wanted to savor it.

The sound of Metal Maiden's song "Run from the Hills" began playing in his pocket, causing him to lurch. He got out his phone, dropped it, cursed, and then answered it.

"Hello," he said in a voice as dull as a spoon. He snorted heavily, his glassy eyes intent on the words coming from another side.

"The live feed is down, JB III. We need to see some data. A storm's hitting your area, so the boss wants it all done now. Execute the plan. Get the data on tapes. Lock it down and get the serum. No one leaves alive but you."

He felt cold for a moment, shifting in his seat. He swallowed hard as he said, "Uh ... yes, sir. Uh ... did you say no one?"

"That's right, boy. You want to save the world—you got to make some choices. Can you do it?" The voice on the other end was harsh, unfamiliar, maybe foreign.

"Yes ... Yes sir."

"Good, son. Execute within the hour." *Click.*

He saw all their faces on the screens again and swallowed. He didn't want them all to go, just two.

They don't like me. They judge me. All of them. Screw 'em all. Now it's my time.

The hard surfaces in the security room closed in on him, and he felt surrounded by darkness. He snorted heavily again and snorted in another white line.

I can do this. I'm gonna be the next Nate McDaniel.

He typed away at his computer and watched as the elevator opened in the parking garage. The stunned group stepped inside, but not before Henry looked back at the garage camera. He could swear his brother could see him. *Screw you, Henry!*

21

THE TRIP BACK THROUGH THE HALLWAYS AND SLIDING STEEL DOORS WAS agonizing. *Red. Green. Red. Green.* A wild zombie was on the loose, and fear festered inside all their bellies as they passed from room to room. Henry had no idea what to expect. Rudy stepped on one of his heels again. He shoved the man in front of him. His concerns for his father were heavy, and as far as he understood his friend's blathering, Stanley didn't know. He had a shotgun now, but no ammo. *Jimmy.* Shells were in short supply, but there were always some in the weapons locker.

"We Got the Heat" began ringing on Rudy's phone as they stood in the secure corridor just outside of the zombie playroom.

"It's Weege," Rudy said. "What's going on, man? Did you find the little zombie turd yet?"

He held the phone up, speaker on. Weege's foreign dialect was crystal clear and full of excitement.

"I got him! He's in another cell!"

They all looked at one another in relief, except Henry.

"How'd he get in another cell, Weege?"

"I don't know. My computer froze up, and I noticed I was on a repeating video feed. It had to be Jimmy screwing around again. Just like the last time. He's — a — bastard!"

That Jimmy was. Last time he forgot to feed the zombies, and two people almost died. Jimmy said it was an accident, but Henry knew it wasn't. Maybe it was drugs, maybe it was intentional, but it was time for Jimmy to go.

"Weege, its Henry. Are you sure that Louie is locked up?"

"Yes, I can see it on the screen. He's a busy little monkey, but he isn't going anywhere."

He could feel Tori's nails digging into his side.

"Have you checked the cages?"

There was a pause. "No — I'm not going down there."

"Why not? We have to be sure."

"You go. It's not in my job description."

Rudy butted in and said, "You're a stand-up guy, Weege."

"I'm alive. I'm staying alive like disco, baby. This episode is freaking me out. I can't believe what happened today!"

The sound in Weege's voice seemed to allude to something else, but Henry wasn't sure.

"What do you mean?"

"A ... just come up here. You need to see for yourself."

"Why?" Tori said.

"It's better that way."

Tori scanned her security pass, and the door slid open. A zombie was standing nearby, and she let out a screech. The small child didn't notice, as it shuffled back in the rainbow room, mumbling "num-num." Henry took a quick head count and saw all the children except Louie. *All here, good.* The vivid colors, cartoon screens, and classical music were amplified, making him feel as if he were inside a carnival's madhouse. They crept inside, wary of the zombie children whose sunken faces stared on and past them like shadows.

Climbing up the ladder tubes, Rudy had the pleasure of going up last, behind Tori. His tongue hung out like a wild man. She hadn't noticed.

"Mother of mercy," he muttered underneath her high heels.

Traipsing over the catwalks, they converged on Weege's station. The excited man was in his thirties, with big brown eyes and a teenager's face and build. A thin goatee patch was under his chin. He was sweating and motioning for them to come closer.

"Look! Look! Look!" he cried, pointing to his computer screen.

Henry expected to see a zombie doing cartwheels, but it wasn't what he expected at all. It was an Internet news site headline. His heart sank as he read it. "Man Who Saved the World Found Dead! Murder! Suicide!" He murmured over the details.

"NATE McDANIEL WAS FOUND *dead inside his DC condominium at 12:45 EST today. Inside sources say that Christy Backwater from FNN News was found dead inside the penthouse as well. A pistol and casings were found at Mr. McDaniel's bedside. The two had last been seen leaving together from her TV studio. The nature of the relationship was not known, but the evidence of drugs, including sex-enhancing stimulants, suggests an elitist booty call gone bad.*"

HENRY FINISHED the rest to himself. He could feel Tori hugging and sobbing at his side and Rudy patting his back. They didn't know Nate. But he knew this couldn't have happened like the news said. His old friend was too smart for that. He looked up and saw Weege pointing a smartphone his way. "What are you doing?"

"I wanted to capture the look on your faces when you saw the news. Very interesting. See — look!"

He held out the picture of their frozen expressions: mouths wide, brows high, and shock growing on each face.

"Why don't you make a poster too, moron," Tori said. "I'm sorry, baby," she said, rubbing Henry's back.

He hadn't heard from Nate in months, other than the occasional text. He never understood what Nate McDaniel went through, but he felt worse than he ever would have imagined somehow. None of

Nate's interviews seemed genuine or honest. It all had to be scripted. Maybe he had more to say and someone stopped it.

"Man, Christy Backwater is dead? She was hot! That's terrible man." Rudy was sitting down and watching live newscasts while munching on Weege's nacho-cheese chips. "Best legs I'd ever seen."

Tori smacked him in the head.

"Not better than yours ... of course ... Tori."

"She's dead, idiot — show some respect!"

"Sorry."

Henry sat down at another station, his face lined with concern. He hated this place, the zombies and everything. The most popular man in the world was dead. He needed to tell his dad. *Crap.* What about Jimmy and Louie? He'd forgotten all about that.

"Where's my phone? Where's my phone?" He looked at his friends, who were now crammed around Weege's monitor, fighting for position. Henry headed to his station, and there it was, sitting on the desk. A few new text messages were there. *Tori. Tori. Tori. Nate 1215?* The message from Nate contained only a string of letters: CPWWSZH.

It didn't make any sense, but he suspected it was a warning. Jumbles were something they played in college, each trying to top the other. They also used it for other things. It was their own language they created for themselves and some others. If it was indeed serious, he knew he might be in danger.

"What is it, lover?" Tori said in his ear.

He looked at her, saying, "I got a message from Nate this morning. It might be a warning. It might be why he was killed." He didn't know why he was telling her this, but now didn't seem like a time for secrets. Too many changes in the status quo were abounding around him. His mind raced to lock it down. This couldn't all be randomly happening on the same day. There had to be a reason.

Her voice was excited. "What does it say?"

He showed her the phone.

"What does that mean?"

"I don't know yet, but I'll figure it out."

"Let's ask Weege. He might know — he's a freak like that."

He was firm as he pulled her back, saying, "No—keep this between us, Tori. I'll get it. I need them to focus on the next step."

He could see concern growing on her sweet face. He knew she trusted him and would do anything for him, but her tongue slipped from time to time.

"What is the next step?" she whispered.

"It's time to lock up the zombies. There has been a breach, and I need to tell Dad."

"Just call him."

"We tried." Rudy had sauntered over. "You know he won't answer. He never does. As for the breach, he won't report it. He's too afraid they'll shut us down."

He spoke up, "Okay, Weege, get over here." They all gathered. "Let's lock up the rest of the zombies. We need to gather Dad and Jimmy. I have a bad feeling this place isn't safe. I'm going to check on Louie. Weege, monitor the floors ..."

Henry looked around.

"Is anyone else here?"

"It's after five, dude, the rest have rolled. It's just the night shift," Rudy said.

"Okay then, you and Tori go down there and latch the cages."

His friends gave him a funny look.

"Okay, I'll go with you. You don't know how to lock them without the security cards. I'll show you. Let's go."

Their footfalls rushed over the platform, across the catwalk, and down the ladders. He hated this. Herding the zombies was dangerous because they were stubborn. This was what he needed Ronald for. The burly man would bundle up, round up the children, and toss them in. It wasn't something the rest of them usually had to do.

A simple scratch from a zombie would garner a feverish reaction, but their bites were fatal. There wasn't anything you could do. He could see the worry on their faces as they donned heavy cotton beige suits and thick padded gloves. There were over a dozen cells along the outer wall, like ones you would see in an animal shelter but much larger and more secure. Tori opened several of them, side by side. Each hatch had a red light.

Here we go. "You ready, Rudy?"

"Yeh, who are we getting first?"

"Peggy. She's the easiest."

They surrounded a gaunt little girl who was dressed in a Halloween outfit and appeared to be about five years old. The child stood before a large flat-screen television that showed nerdy little kids singing and playing instruments.

"On three, Rudy!" he shouted through a mesh-faced protective mask. His heart was pounding. He'd never done this before. "One ... Two ... Three!"

Each man locked his hands around the girl's wrists and stretched her arms taut. He could feel her little arms pulling back, strong like a small animal, but not strong enough. Her fingers clutched as they dragged her toward the cell, but she wasn't fighting. They had her inside, let her go, and each rushed back out. Tori scanned the door lock. It turned from red to green. Henry was relieved.

"Here's how you do the double lock," he said with a muffled voice.

There was a small concealed handle at the top of the silver cage, like one used to open or close an old window. He spun it around until it clicked.

"You got it, gorgeous!" Tori said.

"I got it, baby!" He winked inside his mask.

"I'm sweating my ass off, and I'm still single. Can we get this over with, you two love turds?" Rudy exclaimed.

"Okay, Rudy, okay. Tori, be sure to double-lock those other cages too; we don't want the rest accidentally getting out."

One by one, using the same tactic, they got the other zombie kids inside. The zombies resisted with only the chronic "Num-Num" phrase. Oh, to have a muzzle on them, Henry thought. He'd do anything to never hear those words again. It took about thirty minutes with little Mike, because he wouldn't let go of the jungle gym. The little boy in Quantum Leap pajamas, provided by Rudy, had been clutching the yellow-coated play set for hours. Henry considered cutting off the boy's fingers, but a screwdriver managed to pry them off.

"Ah ... that sucked," he said as they all took off their masks and anti-zombie suits.

Everyone's hair was matted and wet. Rudy was soaked head to toe in sweat, but the sight of Tori in damp jeans and a V-neck T-shirt made him sweat more. It made both men gawk. Her eyes enlarged when she looked their way, and she made a dash for her lab coat.

"Man, you are one lucky dude. She is smoking."

The comment didn't bother him as it felt good for a change, having a woman like that.

"Hey! Hey, guys!" It was Weege shouting from above in alarm. "Hey!"

They all walked over and looked up at him. Weege's dark face was ashen.

Henry yelled up, a smile on his face, "What is it, Weege? Did the Pope die too?"

"No! No! It's Louie! He's gone again!"

22

"NATE MCDANIEL IS DEAD?" JIMMY SAID WITH A HYSTERICAL LAUGH. He never would have known if he hadn't been watching all the commotion at Weege's station. Looks of alarm and surprise caught his fancy as he zoomed in another camera to see more. He watched from above the scene. The expressions on their faces excited his flesh. Their suffering brought him joy. He knew his time had come, and it was his turn to be the most famous man in the world.

He checked his recordings on the screens from the security room, and they were all in order. The monitors were saving every image and clip for his purpose. He knew the live feed might go. It happened from time-to-time, so he made a backup recording. The remote area created havoc on communications when the wind and rain came. He could see his stepfather Stanley singing to the undead girls inside the biolab. As far as he could tell, they weren't going anywhere.

Jimmy rubbed his nose, snorted, and looked for his brother Henry. *Go ahead, brain child. Go put up the zombies. I've got a surprise for you.*

He Googled Nate McDaniel's and Christy Backwater's faces on his smartphone. He touched her face on the screen. "Oh yeah, babes like you will soon be mine."

He finished off another can of beer and pulled up the action in Louie's cell. He bit his dirty fingernails while twisting his ball cap around before he entered a code. His foot was tapping as he waited. Jimmy had not only helped Stanley give Louie the XT Serum, but he also had been starving the boy. The lack of zombie dew that kept the children docile would build Louie's hunger for flesh and brains. He saw to it Louie missed his doses. The XT serum sped up the boy's metabolism, as well as other things. That's what his employers told him to do. That is what he did.

Jimmy looked at another camera feed; he could see them in the zombie suits, jerking the little minions into their holes. He loved doing that. He hated the rotten little fiends. His life could have been perfect if not for them. They took his life, his friends and family, in a single day, all but Henry and Stanley, the ones he despised most. That was when the world of madness consumed him and crushed his soul. He couldn't cope with all the changes. He survived the only way he could, like a rodent feeding on others. He considered suicide, but he didn't want to leave this miserable world for the next. Those were his thoughts back when, but he didn't remember them anymore, as many memories were a clump of fried brain cells. He just wanted to feel great all the time. He wanted to be the next Nate McDaniel.

He could see them in the kiddy zoo now, and he knew they were talking about him. *Stop talking about me. I might show mercy.* He pressed RETURN on the keyboard.

"Bye-bye, douche bags!"

23

A FAMILIAR SOUND FILLED HIS HEAD. HE TURNED TO FACE IT. AN opening stood before him, and he couldn't help but pass through. Many colors and objects were beside him, behind him, and below him. Everything was spinning, moving, and stopping. There was blackness, and there was the light. Something was shuffling below him and humming above him. He heard sounds before him and said, "Numma–Numma."

Louie didn't understand where he was or what he was doing. He ran his hands over the cold metal walls of the daycare. He could hear voices, but he didn't understand. He smelled things, but didn't know what that meant. He needed something, but he didn't know what it was. He had to find it. Everything was blurry though. The shapes seemed to make sense, but the bright colors annoyed him. Somewhere nearby was what he needed. Instinct pressed him that way, as more objects rushed past him. The sounds of voices became louder, and he stopped moving. The hunger was building inside of him as he moved toward the sound. It was food he wanted, and it was near. He just didn't know what the food was.

Louie didn't know what the loud words meant, but they frightened him.

Someone shouted, "Sound the alarm, Weege!"

24

IT HAD BEEN ONE OF THOSE DAYS THAT LASTED A LOT LONGER THAN normal. The midday sun had long passed, and the dark clouds above were filled with rolling thunder. The heavy breeze was such that John had closed the guard shack door. His feet ached from all the standing, and his butt was sore from all the sitting. Over an hour had gone by without a word between him and his grandson. The boy was intent with his video games, and not much for conversation.

"Is that battery ever gonna die, Fergie?

The boy looked up, rubbing his puffy brown eyes, and said, "I've got more batteries. There's a plug-in here too."

"Oh ... Wanna play some cards?"

"No."

Shrugging, John pulled a card deck out from a top desk drawer. The guard shack was accommodating. It had an air conditioner filled with icy air and a toasty heater as well. A back-up diesel generator was outside, but he had never used it. There was a beige push-button phone sitting on the counter, but it only made calls inside the facility. He had never used it before, either, and didn't know anyone who had.

He dealt out a hand of solitaire with his blue and white drugstore cards. He hadn't won in weeks, but maybe this would be his lucky day ... but he didn't feel lucky. He felt like a man in the forest tracking a bear, waiting for the big beast to show up at any second. He wiped the dampness from his forehead. *Why am I sweating?*

Sprinkles of rain came and went with an occasional rumble of thunder. Somewhere in the distance, he swore he heard a tree fall.

"Hey Fergie, why don't you help me out with these cards? You were always good at this."

The boy looked up, his freckled cheeks smudged with snack-cake fudge.

Messy boy.

The boy replied, "Do I have to? I'm comfortable."

He sighed. "Suit yourself."

After a couple of rounds of solitaire passed with failure, he shuffled the deck again and dealt a new set on the counter. He kept thinking about what a long day it had been as he looked outside, stroking his mustache.

His stomach was growling. He opened the door and inhaled some fresh air. The cold drizzle was refreshing on his face. The facility was quiet as always. He hoped someone would come out. It had been a while since Ronald left without having said a word, green as a toad. *Poor fella, never seen him look worse, and he looks bad enough to begin with.*

Taking his glasses off, he squinted at the facility. The green lights spread on the fence posts had turned red. About then, a fierce wind picked up, forcing him back inside, and he closed the door with a loud smack, causing the boy to lurch from his seat.

"Ferguson, did you see those lights turn red?"

"Uh-huh."

"Well, how long ago did that happen?"

There was a pause.

"Fergie! How long?" he almost shouted as a chill rushed through his veins.

The boy took the time to check his watch and said, "Maybe forty minutes."

John felt all of his muscles tighten between his shoulder blades. "Forty minutes!"

He didn't know what to do. Those lights had never come on before. He grabbed the telephone. It rang and kept ringing. He left it off the hook. A sudden gust rocked the shack, and the wind began to howl like banshees.

The boy had a stunned look and fear in his eyes. The boy dropped his game as he cried out, "Grandpa!"

John rushed over and put his arms around the boy. The child was shaking and clutching at his clothes.

"Come on, Fergie, let's get in the truck." The boy didn't want to go anywhere, not letting go of his legs. The wind was so loud he couldn't hear his own voice. He tried to pick the boy up.

"Fergie, let me go!" he hollered.

He was nervous now, feeling trapped inside the shack as the heavy rain began beating down on the metal roof like rocks. If he didn't get moving, they might be in for a long night. It hurt him to do so as he hoisted the boy up into his arms, tearing the muscles in his aged back. Somehow, he slung a hundred pounds of dead weight over his shoulder and stepped into the unexpected maelstrom.

The rain soaked him the second he stepped outside, splashing him like a thousand tiny waves. The winds roared in his ears, and he could see where a large pine had fallen onto the fence. He fought through the wind and could hear the boy's terrified screams in his ears. He forced his way through the chaos and fumbled for the handle on his truck door. He opened it and blockaded himself inside the door as the boy crawled inside like a frightened rabbit. He jumped inside the cabin as the wind slammed the door behind him.

"Sweet Mary!" he said, wiping his soaked face with his hand. "Where did that come from?"

"Take me home, Grandpa! Take me home!" the boy urged, crawling under the glove box.

He was going to do just that, but he hesitated. The sheets of rain came, and he could see the red lights flickering against the facility. He figured they would need help, but he wasn't going in. He'd just make a call from down the road. He didn't want to leave anyone hanging, either. What if they needed help? A blinding flash dazzled his vision as lightning struck the ground between the fence and the facility. It scared him to death. The boy was screaming.

"We're going, boy! We're gone!"

He fired the big white truck up with a roar as classic country blared from the speakers. He couldn't see much of anything, but he knew the road. He backed up, fishtailing the truck around and taking off. He didn't get too carried away moving down the road, but in his rear-view mirror, he thought he saw a tree fall on his guard shack. *That was too close!* Every harrowing minute he felt safer the further he went. The storm seemed to worsen as he winded down the hill. He stopped the truck.

"Grandpa, what are you doing?"

He wanted to go back; it was the right thing to do. He grabbed his grandson's shaking leg and gave the situation serious thought. It came down to a choice between life or death. *Get Fergie home or his grandma will kill me.*

"Screw that mess!" he said as he jumped on the gas.

"Grandpa ..."

"Yes, Fergie?"

"I don't want to work with you anymore," the boy said as they headed down the hill.

"That's okay, can't say I'd blame you."

He was worried about the people inside. They should be safe, but he would probably be fired for leaving. If there were zombies in there, he hoped they didn't make it out. He'd have to let somebody know, but it would have to wait. He was going home. Family comes first.

The roads were covered with rising water when he reached the bottom of the hill and turned on the main road. A wave of water on the windshield that was followed by another giant splash blinded his sight. A small convoy of black vans and SUV's raced past him, the likes he had not seen in a long time. He couldn't say for sure, but he had a pretty good guess where they were headed. *That's odd.* Maybe those folks inside didn't need his help after all. Maybe things were worse than he imagined. Maybe he was wrong. He muttered a prayer.

25

INSIDE THE FACILITY, THE LIGHTS WERE FLICKERING LIKE HUMMINGBIRD wings, sending shivers of fear down everyone's spine. In the back of his mind, Henry fully expected the hyperactive zombie child to charge from underneath a pile of toys at any moment. He spun slowly around, with his head on a swivel, as his friends did the same.

"Where is he, Weege!?" he yelled.

A frantic figure raced over the catwalk and leaned over the guard rail, aghast.

"I don't know, he could be anywhere. Hurry—get up here."

Rudy and Tori looked over at him with frightened eyes.

"Go up there and help him. I have to tell Dad and find Jimmy."

She grabbed his arm.

"You have to come up—until we find him! He has to be in here, there's nowhere he can go." Her voice was shaking, and her hand trembled as she said it. "This is bad, I can feel it. We have to stick together. Don't go!" she urged.

He took her in his arms, and he didn't want to go anywhere. He was torn. If something happened to his brother, he could live with that, but not his stepdad. No, Stanley wouldn't be ready for the unexpected.

"I've got to go. I love you!"

He gave her a long hard kiss. He could feel her warm tears on his cheek, and when he looked back in her eyes, he could see how frightened she was. He didn't want to leave her.

"Now get up there you two!"

Rudy was already up the ladder shoot as he pushed her along. She went up with heavy sobs. He ran over to the cages and checked that all of the children were secured. Each quick glance confirmed they were safe.

The playroom was a long oval, almost four thousand square feet. The cages ran along the back walls of the odd arena. One of those cages should have housed Louie, and it was on the other side.

He put on his suit and mask, then took the mask back off. It blocked too much of his peripheral vision. *This suit better work.* He passed by the locked cages, expecting something to lunge at him any second. Another shotgun was racked along the wall; he pulled it off and checked the chamber. It was empty, and the ammo box was nowhere to be found. He pulled one shell from his lab-coat pocket. It was buckshot, a joke from John the guard long ago. The old man told him it would bring him luck. But would it kill a zombie? *Better than nothing.*

He moved fast along the inner perimeter until he approached cage 17, where Louie was last seen. He stopped, loaded the shotgun, and leveled it at his hips. *Here we go.* He was burning up inside, sweat soaking his suit inside and out.

He jumped in front of the cage door, but nothing was there. He felt relief, but only for a moment. He had begun to back toward the center of the room when he noticed something. The light to the security-room door was green. It was open, just enough for a boy to squeeze through. *Crap.* He could see white light spilling from the crack, and he knew what he had to do. He hoped he would find a trapped zombie in there.

He scanned his badge and a negative beep sounded, so he peeked inside. The fluorescent lights inside were flickering, causing a strobe effect. He was sure nothing was in there, but at the other end, the

elevator was open, like the mouth of a black tunnel. A red light glimmered above the entrance. He sucked in his breath and squeezed
between the doors, wedging himself in between them. He was
halfway through when the light turned red. *Oh no!* He was stuck. He
felt a sharp pain as the door pinched his shoulder. The pressure was
building. If Louie showed up now, it was over; he was trapped. Was
this something Jimmy had done? Was his brother capable of murder?
He pushed on the edge of the door, but it wouldn't give.

With a grunt of desperate determination, he pushed with all of
his might. The door budged enough for him to force his body
through. He flexed his shoulder. It wasn't dislocated, but it felt like it.
He found little relief when he realized he was alone in the corridor.
He noticed the light above the door was green again, and the crack
was still there. It was odd.

He headed toward the elevator shaft. *What am I going to do?* Step-
by-step, he walked toward the elevator, shotgun ready. The closer he
got, the more he could see of the dim outline of the elevator. The
flickering lights made him feel like there was movement all around
him. His heart was beating in his ears. Within ten feet, the image
inside became clearer. He stepped inside. The elevator was empty.

The buttons inside weren't lit as he pressed them a dozen times. It
didn't make sense to him. There was power in the building, and the
generators would be humming if there wasn't, but he didn't hear
them, and he usually could tell the difference. He started to worry.
What if the power went out? They had been through storms before,
but not with a zombie on the loose. What if lightning struck a generator or a tree fell on it? Everything was going wrong today, and dread
sunk in deeper. Where was Louie? Where was Jimmy, and what
about Stanley? Second thoughts surged in his mind; they should have
stayed together. *Tori was right. I better head back.*

As he made his way back to the cracked door, he heard Tori's
bloodcurdling scream from the other side. He ran for the opening,
but the door slid closed and the light turned red.

"NOOOOOO!" he screamed, but nobody heard.

26

BETWEEN HEAVY SNORTS WERE JOSTLING FLINCHES AS THE THUNDER rattled his core. The monitors were clear before him as he had arranged backup power. Jimmy was smarter than everybody, and he knew it. He felt like the demi-god of a black dungeon, with the lives of others balancing on his whims. Now he was distracted, trying to reconnect the encrypted live feed to his associates. The live feed was still broken by the storm. It wasn't going to happen, so he had to resort to plan C, for he had forgotten B, and A was fading in his memory.

Now, enthralled with his own power, he turned Louie loose to feast on his former friends. He felt the excitement, like the first time he was in a brothel, when he saw the looks on their distraught faces. He watched as his brother wiped sweat from his brow, agonizing over what to do next. He was laughing as if he hosted a horror film festival, fingers clasped together under his chin.

"Henry the zombie. Henry the zombie," he repeated in a childish tune. "Oh Henry, I am sorry I have to blow your head off! But this is how I save the world!"

He couldn't help himself; it was all coming together so well.

There was another problem, and paranoia set in as he remembered he had to get his stepfather's serum. The data he needed wasn't on the main server. No, his stepfather was too old-fashioned. It was on Stanley's non-networked computer, at an isolated work station, passcode-protected and all. He had to get that data. Stanley wasn't going anywhere. His movements suggested there was nothing to worry about.

"Good Stan, just keep working like a fool."

Tori and Rudy were climbing the stair chutes like frightened chickens while Henry played the hero with an unloaded shotgun. *What an idiot!* Checking his monitors, Jimmy tried to locate Louie, dying to see the boy take a bite out of any of them, allowing him to record the show.

"Ah, there you are, chunky."

There was an unlit alcove used for storing stuffed toys and other cuddly things. The boy was hunched over, pulling the stuffing from the inside of a massive light-blue teddy bear. Louie was in husky jeans, tennis shoes, and a blue-striped shirt. The boy's brown hair was hanging down over half his face, while his chubby hands jammed white clumps of synthetic material in his mouth.

"You're eating the wrong thing, stupid!" Jimmy shouted, poking the computer screen.

He watched a little longer, until his brother's movements caught his eye. Maybe his brother did have shotgun shells after all? Maybe Jimmy had missed some of them? He was certain he got them all. Or had he? Even so, he knew he could outsmart his brother. He cackled again.

Accessing the security and elevator door systems, he cracked open the main entrance to the romper room. His knees were bouncing up and down as he sat biting his nails. He watched with jovial clarity, zooming in on his brother's stern expression.

"Come on. Come on, little wabbit."

His brother peered through the door and began to inch through. He hit a key, closing the door.

Jimmy jumped up with elation,

"Yes! I got you—you bastard!"

He couldn't believe it had been so easy. They were hamsters in his cage, and he ruled their world. A loud crash of thunder shook his bones, followed by a brilliant flash of white on the monitors, causing him to drop his beer can.

"Dammit!"

He looked at the outside monitors, but the wind and rain blocked his view of anything worth noticing. He had to get moving. He looked back at the screen and watched Henry force himself through.

"What!?"

His trap had failed, but that was temporary.

He followed his brother's movements, heading towards and away from the elevator. As Henry made his way back to the playroom, Jimmy saw something else happening. He closed the door just in time to see his running brother scream. There was another crack of thunder. Jimmy realized he couldn't watch. He had to get moving.

He stood inside the security room, which worked as a panic room of sorts. Inside it, he could safely execute his wicked intentions without anyone knowing. It used to be that three guards monitored the facility at all times, but now there was only one, lying on the floor dead as a stone. The guard was laughing and joking with Jimmy one moment, and shot with a taser the next. He hadn't moved since. The old man with crystal-blue eyes and invigorating stories couldn't handle the final thrill. His heart gave out. Jimmy, as shocked as he was, laughed like a hyena at the thought. Now he bent down and took the dead fellow's .357 magnum. *This looks easy enough.* He aimed the gun at the old guard's head, pulled the trigger, and moved on.

The security room was in the basement, isolated like a bunker in the ground. A corridor went left and right as he exited. The left took him to the main elevator down to Stanley's lab. On the right was an emergency exit door, rarely used, and unknown to most. It was there he would make his glorious exit. He walked down the hall to the small lobby by the elevator, took the spiral stairs down, turned up the adjacent corridor, and entered his stepfather's lab.

"Working hard, Stan?" he said.

Stan looked up with worry and surprise on his face.

"Uh ... yeah, Son, you know me, I'm always working hard." His stepfather stood up tall and walked toward him. "I've been meaning to talk to you anyway, I'm glad you're here," Stanley said with his usual warm smile.

It took Jimmy off guard, and he slackened his grip on the pistol hidden inside the back of his pants. He saw his mother wandering toward him, bringing a sour look on his face.

"Let me guess, you and Mom are having a baby?"

Stanley's face darkened, and his tone changed from a gentle creek to a crashing wave.

"You need to show some respect you little —"

"Little what, Pops?"

"I've done all I can for you, but even my patience is limited. You can say what you want to me, or about me"—Stanley was towering over him, making him cringe—"but don't talk about your mother like that. Dead or alive!"

Jimmy wanted to crawl in a hole at that moment and began to have second thoughts. *What am I doing? What do I do? Why am I here?* Something reminded him of Nate McDaniel. *Oh yeah!* The evil twinkle in his eye returned as fast as it had left, and Stanley stepped back with a look of uncertainty.

"Oh, I agree, Stan." His voice was like a slithering snake. He snorted, wiping his nose on his sleeve. "As a matter of fact, I was just coming down to say good-bye. I have another job lined up. What do you think about that?"

Stanley was backing away as he spoke, looking for something.

"Oh ... well, that's great, Son."

"I need a favor though," he said, stepping toward the autopsy table and glancing at the twins with a seedy smirk. "I need a reference."

"Sure, Son, anything, let me type you up a letter."

"Great, Stan, and while you are doing that, whip me up all the paperwork for the XT Serum. I'll be needing that too."

Stanley turned as if someone had just been shot only to see the barrel of a gun lowered at his belly.

"N-n-now—put that away, J-J-Jimmy."

Jimmy took a step forward saying, "Don't you mean 'Son'?"

"S-s-son."

"Give me the serum or I'll put you away—and don't call me Son!" he said, placing his other hand on the gun and pulling back the hammer with a click.

Stanley fidgeted in front of him, eyes fearful and darting.

"What do you want, Son—excuse me—Jimmy?"

"Fire up that computer—put it all on here, and give me the serum," he said, pulling out a jump drive. Stanley didn't move. Jimmy knew that Stanley kept all of the information on his own personal computer.

"Now!"

Stanley flinched and sat in defeat before his computer. Sweat was rolling down his crinkled forehead as he wiped his mouth and tried to log in. The shaking was so bad Stanley had trouble finding the keys.

"Hurry up!" he screamed into Stanley's ear.

Stanley held his hands up and said, "Okay, I'm in. Here it is." Stanley looked back over his shoulder and shrugged.

"Load it on here."

"Come on, Jimmy, don't do this. It's for all of us. That's why I brought you back"—the man stood up—"... to celebrate."

He wanted to believe. He knew Stanley didn't lie. Stanley had been good to him. Something jostled him from behind.

BANG!

Jimmy screamed. He had squeezed the trigger as his mom's cold hands gripped his head and neck. He tore away, dropping the gun to the floor and running away. He saw his mother standing there, listless, with his hat and some hair in her hand. Stanley was kneeling before her, grasping his bloody belly, eyes filled with shock.

"Dad!" he cried, but he didn't know what to do.

He watched as Stanley clutched the waist of his late wife and looked up into her gaunt face.

Stanley was saying, "Though I walk in the shadow of the valley of death I shall fear no..." He died there, hands sliding down her legs, as her hand came down and stroked his head before she walked away.

Jimmy stood huffing in the corner, bewildered. It took almost a minute before he was able to move. Slowly, the power of greed gave him the strength to move. Stepping over his stepfather, he downloaded all the files from that workstation as he snatched the jump drive. He slid open the glass doors of the refrigerator. Two glass bottles with cork tops were almost filled with a milky blue liquid marked XT. He found a black traveling case nearby with a syringe and needles stuffed in black foam inserts. Empty gaps were cut out the size of the bottles, and he placed the serums inside, snapping the case closed. He checked his pocket and felt the jump drive. Now he had the serum in hand. He was worried as he looked around when he saw the gun lying on the floor by Stan. He snatched it up. He had it all.

"Yes!"

He looked over and saw his mom bumping between the autopsy tables.

"Bye, Mom, next time I come back I'll have the cure."

Now it was time for him to finish off the rest.

27

THE Y WERE ALL TRANSFIXED AT THEIR INDIVIDUAL WORKSTATIONS ABOVE the daycare room. Everything was quiet as they clicked back and forth, trying to find images of the floor below them. Tori was more pressed to keep tabs on Henry. *Where is he? What's wrong?* Her monitor didn't show anything, just the same picture of the playroom below, free of lumbering children. She wasn't the smartest girl in town, but she understood how to operate a computer. What twenty-something didn't know how to these days? It was a second language if anything.

"You guys find anything?" she said, her voice trembling. She was picking at her lips between clicks on her mouse.

Rudy and Weege both answered, "No!"

Rudy added, "I don't know about you, but I don't think Louie is in there."

"He has to be! Find him or *you're* going down there," she said, shaking her fist.

"I'm not online! I don't have Internet!" a shrill voice said, like the sky was falling. The computers and cameras had been screwy ever since they got back up to the observation level. It was frustrating everybody.

"Chillax, Weege!" she snapped.

The flickering screens and shaking walls seemed to pitch from the winds, rain, and thunder outside. She banged her mouse on the counter and decided to take a walk and look over the rail. There was nothing, just annoying cartoons and plastic toys. She wanted to cry but tried to be strong for Henry. She closed her eyes and sobbed, thinking of their first date. Someone tugged at her arm.

"Let go, Rudy, now's not the time," she said, jerking her arm away. The cold grip held her fast as she turned to face him.

"What the He—AAAAAH!"

Louie held her wrist with an iron grip that she couldn't tear free. Louie was a bearish boy, slightly fish-eyed, round-faced, and with a mouth full of cracked gray teeth.

"Numma! Numma!"

Her legs sagged. Others were screaming as well. She screamed again, ringing her own eardrums at the creepy sight of him.

The boy nipped her finger, let go, and began to trot off in a funny way, holding his ears and cringing. Rudy chased after the boy with an umbrella, roaring like a neutered lion. The closer Rudy got, the more Louie slowed down. The boy turned back towards him, still backing away.

"Numma! Numma!"

The boy backed over a ladder hole and fell through.

Tori was still screaming in the background.

"It scratched me! It bit me!"

Rudy slammed a lid down over the ladder hole and latched it shut. "It can climb. That damn thing can climb! Weege, I'll lock the lids—you get her to the medical bay—now!"

She was bawling as she looked at the bloody gash that tore the skin on her hand. There was a deep bite mark on her index finger, dripping blood.

"I don't want to be a zombie!"

Her tiny friend was pulling her along, and she felt helpless in his grasp. Weege shoved her into a white room along the back wall that looked like a dentist's office with an oversized circular saw.

"No, no, no, Weege! I can't do it!"

"Take off your lab coat!" Weege yelled like an angry cartoon character.

She clutched at it, shaking her head.

"Now, woman—or you will be a zombie!" he said in an urgent accent. "Now, dammit!"

She did it, and as soon as it fell to the floor, he tied a knot of medical tubing above her bicep. She couldn't believe what was happening. Her hand turned cold and numb. She couldn't help but cry. Her hand was pasty and white, lifeless as fallen leaves, while everything above her wrist began to burn. She saw Weege punch a green button on the circular saw, and it whirled into action. She was crying uncontrollably now, thoughts filled with despair and Henry.

"I don't want to lose my arm, Weege," she pleaded.

"There is no time for drama, close your eyes and shut up!" he said, putting a wooden rod inside her mouth.

She clamped down, tears and mascara mixing into lines and running down her cheeks. He positioned her arm beneath the spinning blade. She wanted to die, be shot, anything but this.

"I don't want to do this."

"Say your prayers!"

She didn't even notice he covered the exposed appendage with a blanket. He jammed a needle in her shoulder, shooting something that burned like fire inside.

"On three!"

She bit down hard, praying. *God, don't let this happen!* She was whimpering, lip trembling.

"One!"

He pulled down on the handle with all his might.

SLICE!

"Aaaagh!" Her head was exploding when she blacked out and slumped in the chair.

.   .   .

WHEN SHE WOKE UP, her arm felt like it was burning. She was strapped to the dentist's chair and saw Weege wearing green goggles, wielding a blow torch. The stench of burnt hair and skin wafted into her nostrils as she writhed in agonizing pain.

Now her own fury was unleashed as she tried to speak.

"What the fah—"

Another needle plunged into her skin, and the room turned dark as she passed out again.

Rudy stood there, shaking his head in despair, as Weege finished cauterizing the wound. She lay still on the table like a discarded whore, makeup smeared and soaked with sweat and blood. Her chest rose up and down as he studied her dismembered arm. The flesh was pink above the cut and the rest of her looked fine. He stroked her wet hair from her eyes. *This must be the hottest one-armed chick ever.*

The surgery was finished. She was alive and well, but he could take no chances. The two men left her strapped in the room and secured the door. Louie was still trying to push his way up through the ladder hatch from below.

"Watch this," Rudy said as he stood beside the portal. When he screamed, the zombie boy cringed.

Weege pulled up his goggles.

"Hmmm ... I've never seen a zombie do that before. Do you think XT Serum works?"

"I don't know, but we're trapped up here unless help comes."

Weege looked worried.

"What if Tori ... you know ... starts to become a zombie?"

He shook his head, saying, "Then we better get some zombie dew."

The zombie boy's head and his mallet hands were banging underneath the latch, shaking the catwalk. They checked their phone signals, and no bars showed. They fidgeted, paced, and sweated while waiting, still looking for Henry.

"Numma! Numma! Numma! Numma!" continued to throb in their ears.

28

BACK IN THE SECURITY ROOM, JIMMY SLUNG A CHAIR INTO THE WALL AND kicked the old guard's corpse, screaming aloud. They were all alive inside the zombie arena. He blinked and tried to figure out why Louie had not bitten them, or at least torn them to bits.

"They should be zombies by now!"

But they weren't. He saw Henry, still trapped in the corridor, pacing while pulling his thick black hair in clenched fists. Tori was harnessed to a table, now missing an arm and out cold. *Good.* The other pair he hated fumbled at their computer stations, shouting back and forth, while Louie tried to press through the metal hatch onto the catwalk. Jimmy wondered if he could release those doors, but he couldn't. He punched the monitor and screamed again. His knuckles bled, and he sucked on them as he thought.

He cradled the black case holding the serum to his chest. *I just got to leave and get paid.*

"The videos! I need the videos!"

He checked the DVR recorders, but there wasn't anything significant on them. No one had been turned, and no one was dead but Stan. He couldn't let it all end there when he was so close. He had to see them all come to an end. He couldn't leave them around to steal his glory. He had the serum and the notes. He had them all trapped. One by one he pressed the keys and watched his brother in the corridor.

"Let's see how this treats you, Henry? It's dinnertime, Louie."

29

Helplessness crushed his will. Henry heard his girl screaming, and he could only imagine the worst. They were all doomed, trapped inside with a monster boy. He hurt his other shoulder trying to knock the door aside. He struck it with the butt of his shotgun, denting the shining surface a dozen times.

"Tori! Tori! Tori!" he yelled, his voice full of agony.

He was hoarse, throat dry and spirit broken. Jimmy had done this; he had no doubt. He had two options: wait for a miracle or head for the office. He went inside the elevator and began to pop the hatch in the ceiling.

He could hear the thunder and the beating rain above his ears. A ladder led to the roof where another pair of elevator doors was closed. He had an idea; he could get outside and try to get help. There was a problem—what if he couldn't get the door open? Jimmy would have secured it just the same as the rest. He hopped back down inside the elevator, landing hard on his ankle and rolling to the floor.

"Ow!"

It hurt, but he got up despite the agony. He'd had plenty of ankle sprains before. He tried walking if off. *Circulate the blood. Don't get stiff.*

What about Stanley, Tori, and the rest? He had to help them, or why had he even come back?

He headed toward the security door and pressed his wet ear on the cold metal. He didn't hear a thing. He took out his security card.

"Why not?"

In a limp motion, he pressed it over the pad. The door slid back open. He stood gawking as a wave of cold air mixed in with his sweaty zombie-proof suit. He looked all around, head turning in all directions. He knew something was out there. He grabbed the shotgun, which was propped along the wall, and stepped outside. Nothing, not a sound could be heard, except the humorous sounds of the TV and symphony music.

He scanned his card, allowing the door to close back, but he wedged the shotgun lengthwise on the sweep. The doorway remained two feet open. He walked into the room, eyes darting and every step more painful than the one before.

"Henry! Henry!" someone was yelling from above. "He's over there—in the ladder shoot. He's in the ladder shoot!"

He could see Rudy's frantic hands motioning across the catwalks. A meaty figure was scrunched inside the metal ladder tube. He saw its head turn, freezing his blood. The boy's nostrils flared. In an urgent move, it began climbing down the ladder and fell onto the floor.

It can climb! Panic raced through Henry's body.

No one knew what to do, as if all their thoughts became stuck in a snowbank. Someone's mind thawed in time as Louie began coming his way.

"Get up a ladder chute!" It was Weege's shrill voice shouting.

There were several ladder chutes along the walls; he bolted for the closest one. Rudy was running over the top, trying to guess where he was going. The boy was coming his way in a stiff trot, elbows locked and mouth clutching. It sent a jolt of adrenaline through his body. Henry was faster, running at full speed, oblivious to his swollen ankle and trying to distance himself further from the boy. He leaped over a set of massive toy blocks the boy crashed through. *It's fast! Shit! It doesn't look fast!*

Running created little comfort space. He needed more time to get in the tube. He was exhausted and in a heavy sweat-soaked suit. It occurred to him too late that the suit was slowing him down. *Crap!* He circled around the edges of the room, but every time he got too far away the boy would cut across the middle. His lungs were burning, and he was slowing down. He had to go for it. He made another half lap, dashed below one of the tubes, and began climbing up. He made it up the first few rungs when his gloved hands slipped. He began to fall, but his foot caught on a rung. Pain lanced through his ankle. Looking down, he saw Louie's clutching mouth and green eyes peering hungrily up his way. Rudy and Weege were screaming for him to move.

Fighting his way up the rungs, he hit the top and pounded away at the locked hatch.

"Open up! Open up! I'm trapped in here!"

He had never felt fear like this. Louie fumbled on the rungs below, lips and jaws smacking, eager to have a bite of him. Henry wasn't sure the suit would stop him from being torn to pieces if Louie got to him. The snap of the latch resounded from above, and the hatch was pulled open with Rudy looking at him eye to eye.

"It's about—*urk!*"

Something powerful was pulling Henry down. His arm got caught in the rungs, which pinched him underneath his armpit. Rudy was trying to pull him up, his bearded face filled with red cheeks and wrought with panic. He could feel the boy's hands crushing his ankle in a mighty grip, then something clamped down on his toe like a bear trap. He screamed in agony, drawing a high-pitched frightened-pig squeal from his friend above. The child's grip and jaws released his toe as Louie fell hard onto the matted floor. Henry didn't look down; he was out of the chute and on the catwalk. Rudy slammed down the door and latched it shut.

He mustered quick breaths as he struggled to pull off his suit.

"Get it off me! I've got to see!"

Rudy stood there, beet-faced, with snot running down his nose. Henry thought he was choking. Rudy pulled out an inhaler and sucked in some white misty air. Now Weege was at his side, helping him jerk off the suit. Henry pulled off his socks and checked his foot and ankles. There were red impressions on his ankle and his toes were bruised, maybe broken, but the skin wasn't broken.

"Whew!" he said, looking around. "Where's Tori!?"

30

As Jimmy sat there, he couldn't believe they were all okay, after all his planning. He guzzled another beer as he watched all of them escape certain death. He knew he had them trapped, but for how long. The sight of his brother's face made him angrier by the second. The rest of the crew, trapped inside, were just as bad, always plotting, scheming and wanting to take away his glory.

His words were almost incoherent.

"You shall not have it."

He needed to leave. He prepared another line of cocaine. Another idea was certain to blossom; they always did.

He could see them trying to figure a way out, pointing and thinking out loud. The little man from India's face was a knot of concern, while the fat guy looked like his brain was starving for ice cream. Henry pranced back and forth, the calm inside the storm, pulling them all together to plot against him. He would not let that happen.

He took a heavy snort.

"The glory shall be mine."

He rubbed his reddened nose, noticing a trickle of blood coming down over his lips. "Hate it when that happens."

He needed a plan, a decision ... he just had to relax. His mind was a jumbled mess; it failed to yield the clarity he needed to find a direction and make a choice.

He imagined them escaping the facility, being on the news and taking his spotlight. He would be locked up, behind bars, and his brother would be branded the next man who saved the world. All he had to do was kill them all, leave, take the serum and footage to his conspirators, and get paid a handsome fee. That wasn't enough; he wanted more. But that was never discussed; it was only what he wanted. He wanted to be the next Nate McDaniel, and that wouldn't happen while his brother lived. Now his strength was returning, and the sweat of alcohol began to seep from his pores like fumes of clean ideas. Opening his bloodshot eyes, he watched the men on the screens. His now-brilliant mind hatched another devious plan. Another fit of theatrical laughter passed as he prepared for his next move. His voice was dry as ice as he said, "Yee-hah."

31

"Sentient," he whispered.

Henry brushed his bangs from his glasses as he watched the footage on the monitor. Weege was fidgeting at his side, while Rudy kept pressing his index finger on the screen.

"Stop touching my screen, dammit," Weege said, smacking the hairy-knuckled hand. "I hate it when you do that. Why do you do that?"

Rudy became defensive. "Do you think that really matters *now*— whether or not I touch your screen—when a zombie is about to come up here and eat your fragment of a brain?"

"Okay, cut it out you two. We need to plan, not bicker."

They weren't getting anywhere fast. He'd seen Tori strapped and stabilized to a table, and it slammed into his soul. She didn't deserve this; no one did. He felt responsible for it all; he always did. Her expression was peaceful as he held her soft face in his hands, apologizing over and over again. He sobbed inside the madness, trying to remember why he had ever gotten into all of this. His girlfriend had one arm, and he supposed if Stanley could still love his undead wife, he could love a one-armed woman. His dad and brother were another concern. He had no idea where they might be. There was no doubt Jimmy had caused all of this. And small surprise, either.

He looked again at Nate McDaniel's text. CPWWSZH. *WHS* ... *World Humanitarian Society? Z ... Zombie?* He remembered a link Nate had texted moons ago. He scrolled back and opened it up. He broke out in a cold sweat.

"Can't be," he murmured.

He had skimmed the article. He always did that much, but he had neglected to give it any serious thought. Now, with the death of his friend, things seemed to be more... realistic. Inside the article were the other three letters, WPC. *It can't be, can it? WPC ... World Population Control.* It would explain why China was one of the first nations to fall. Nate had prevented it from going much further. *Wow!* Henry chose to keep that information to himself and move on.

The cracking thunder, driving rain, and howling winds did little to cover the sound of Louie hammering at the hatch and moaning, "Numma! Numma! Numma!"

The boy's voice and pounding fists became stronger by the minute. At any moment he was certain the boy would burst through and life would end.

The facility had been poorly designed, without considering the needs of the staff. They had to rely on cell phones and an old intercom phone system to communicate among the various offices. It was a fifty-year-old government building with modern technology jammed inside, and nothing ever worked the way it should have. Getting people inside to fix it was nearly impossible, and for the most part, out of the question. They were supposed to add an elevator and a fire escape leading to the top observation room, but the funding ran out first. They were supposed to do lots of things, but it never happened. The facility wasn't designed to be a secret lab for housing zombies. They were forced to make do with what they had.

The phone rang and rang on the other end every time he tried to contact Stanley in the lab. His stepdad almost never answered the phone, though. He said he never heard it; his mind was always busy.

Deep inside, Henry felt something wrong had happened below, but he held out hope.

The failure of both cell phone and landline service squashed the chance of anyone coming to help them. Possible flooding at the bottom of the hills would make things worse if anyone did come. No, they were forgotten for the time being, left to fend for themselves.

"Guys, we have to get out of here. I have a plan," Henry said as they gathered around.

"Well, what is it? "Rudy asked.

"We need to trap Louie, like the others. We'll use the dog snares."

The little man objected, hands flailing in the air, saying, "We need to kill him and get the hell out of here! How is a doggy thing going to help?"

Rudy rolled his eyes.

"See those poles over there?" Henry pointed at the wall on the other side. "They are what dog catchers use for rabid dogs. They have a noose you flip over the neck to snare them. It's real easy."

Rudy was shaking his bushy head, saying, "Henry, he's awful strong. I don't think we can hold him. He about busted that hatch off the hinges. We should try to kill him, it's the only way."

Henry wanted that more than anything, the truth be told, but he believed killing a child, even an undead child, was wrong. Now that Louie had just shown a radical transformation in behavior, the death of another zombie child was even harder to justify. If sound scared Louie, could he feel pain, too? The scientist inside him had to find out. He had to know. Was Stanley that close to curing the zombies, or was this something else?

"No, we can't kill him. Not now. He's just a zombie, we can outsmart him. Rudy, suit up. We're going down."

His friend's chin dropped into his chest with a heavy sigh.

Little Weege grabbed him by his lab coat.

"I have an idea! Maybe we just need more zombie dew?"

They all looked at each other, Rudy's eyes holding the most interest, staring at him for the chance.

"Hmmm," Henry said, rubbing his chin. "Maybe he hasn't been fed, maybe Jimmy starved him. Do we have any?"

Rudy's voice was flat.

"It's all downstairs."

They all looked down over the rail as if it were an abyss. Rudy snapped his fingers.

"Wait a minute," he said, running over to Ralph's station. He picked up his red sixty-four-ounce Big Chug cup and said, "It's still got over half a tank. Maybe more ..." He shook another half dozen empty cups sitting on the desk. "Nope, these are all gone."

Henry took the sixty-four-ounce cup and folded its waxy top closed. Standing by the rail of the catwalk, he leaned over the ladder chute, eyeing the floor twenty feet below. The catwalk was shaking beneath his feet as Louie pounded away. He held the cup over the rail as his friends tried to guide his aim.

"A little further," Rudy said.

"Back to the left," said Weege.

"No—up to the right."

He glared at them, took simple aim, and dropped it.

Plop!

The cup landed flush on its bottom, and they could see liquid splashing up and out, dripping down the cup's side. The top had flipped open, but it was still upright.

"Great shot, Bawk!" Rudy said.

Now they waited, and the pounding still came, second after second, minute after ... it stopped. Something was climbing back down the ladder, and they saw Louie fall to the ground with a thud. The boy was on his knees, sniffing the air.

"Wow, he's sniffing." Henry felt an odd sense of delight.

The boy began licking the drops off the colorful mat, and he snatched up the cup. Louie opened his mouth wide like a bass fish, bringing a gasp from his audience, then stuffed the cup inside and chomped down with a squish. Henry could hear his heart thumping inside his chest. They all shouted as Louie began walking around a good bit slower than before, his hunger apparently satisfied.

"Yeah, Louie!" Rudy said.

"Don't get too excited. We don't know how long this will last," Henry said. "Wake up Tori. We have to get out of here. I'm going for more dew," he said.

"I'm going too." He felt a delicate hand on his shoulder. It was Weege.

"Thanks, Weege, but I've seen you run." He patted the man on the head. "A one-legged zombie could catch you."

They all let out an awkward laugh, but the room felt empty.

"Watch my back," he said, heading across the catwalks. As he opened another hatch, his heart raced. He was almost to the bottom when he realized he had forgotten his zombie-proof suit. *Crap!* He moved dropped, forgetting his swollen ankle and busted toes, falling to the floor.

"Ow!" he cried, momentarily forgetting where he was.

He staggered up, turning around. He didn't see or hear the zombie boy. He crept toward the storage room, opened the door, and headed inside. He grabbed a few bottles of the zombie dew from the shelves and twisted off a few caps. He grabbed a small bowl. *I've just got to lure him into a cell, and we can get out of here.*

"Piece of cake," he said.

As he turned to leave, there was the barrel of a shotgun pointed in his face.

"Not so fast ... Brother."

Jimmy wore a full anti-zombie suit and had a shaking gun in his hands.

"So Henry, you think you figured a way out. I don't think so. Drop the dew!"

Henry could smell his brother's rotten teeth and alcohol. He almost gagged. His cranked-up brother was up to something he couldn't begin to imagine. He set down the drinks and held his palms up, praying his fool of a brother wouldn't pull the trigger. The shotgun was different from the one he left behind, jamming the door. Jimmy had come prepared.

He tried to sound calm. "What's going on Jimmy? Why are you doing this?"

"Shut up!"

He saw his friends looking down at him in horror, and he saw Louie coming his way. His brother seemed uncertain and tore off his mask, getting a better look around. Louie had moved on. He looked at his brother's distorted face; dried blood covered the edges of his nose and descended down over his puffy lips. Jimmy's head was greasy and flaked, and his pupils were like black marbles.

"I'll do the talking, Brother! Tell your stooges to come down here, or I'll blow a hole in you!" Jimmy lowered the weapon on his gut.

"Jimmy, listen to me. Louie might attack any minute. We have to leave. Where is Dad?"

His brother's eyes lit up, his face full of panic and regret. Henry knew at that moment Stanley was dead. It made him angry, angrier than he had ever been.

"Ole Stan was shot! It was an accident! Mom did it!" Confusion seemed to mix with fear in Jimmy's eyes, but they regained their wicked intent. "Stan's serum is mine! I'll be saving the world, just like Nate McDaniel, and you won't stop me!" His shrill voice resounded from the hard walls of the room. It caught everyone's attention, including the creepy boy who was coming their way.

"Watch out, Jimmy!"

His brother turned just in time to see the boy clutching at his back.

KA-BOOM!

It sounded as if a cannon went off inside the facility. As it blasted into the floor, Louie ran, wailing like a frightened swine. Henry leaped onto his brother's back and drove him to the floor. Without even realizing it, he had his hands around his brother's neck, squeezing his eyes from the sockets. His brother couldn't muster a sound as his tongue strained from his mouth. The word *please* seemed to escape from Jimmy's lips as reason somehow overcame Henry's animal instinct to kill. He pulled back his arm and punched his brother in the face with a powerful smack, stinging his hand. He did it a few more times, and Jimmy lay out cold.

Henry had forgotten everything at that moment. He fought to regain his breath. Someone was screaming, and someone else was approaching. He dived for the shotgun, whirled around and blasted it in the air. The boy crouched down, moaning like a frightened animal, and then came his way again, nightmarish and unyielding. Henry remembered Louie tearing apart the rubber ball. His legs turned numb.

He let another blast go into one of the television screens. The boy didn't crouch this time as he came on, an angry look in his gothic face. *He doesn't like the sound.* He didn't have a choice now, it was him or Louie. The zombie boy crept forward, hands clutching, as Henry lowered the barrel at the boy's face. *Sorry, Louie.* He pulled the trigger. *Click! — Crap!* He threw the gun at the boy and ran for the drinks. Louie picked up the gun and beat it on the ground, bending the barrel. Henry saw the bottles on the floor. He could hear voices from above telling him to run, and he dared not look back. He jumped over his prone brother, tripped over something, and fell flat as a stone. Someone had his leg. *Louie!* He turned back and saw his brother's pummeled face.

He kicked away, stretching for a bottle of the juice. An open bottle was just inches from his grasp. He looked back and saw Louie coming back their way.

"Jimmy, let go! He's coming!"

His brother looked back, still determined to hold him fast. "I've got a suit, you don't, Brother. He's gonna eat your brains—not mine!"

There was no time. Henry drew his leg back and kicked Jimmy hard in the nose with a loud crack. He was free, low crawling back for the bottle, grabbing it in his hand. He tossed it like a grenade into the charging boy's path. A lanky hand snatched the bottle from the air, his brother's beady red eyes intent to reverse his plan. He watched as his brother drew his arm back, liquid sloshing on his suit. Louie crashed into him with his full weight. The drink spilled all over both of them as they thrashed over the bottle.

"Get off me! Get off me!"

Jimmy screamed and kicked, fighting to free himself from the zombie. The struggle was violent and fast. Henry didn't know what to do. Jimmy faded under the boy's power, trying to crawl away. Louie now clutched the bottle, stuffing it in his throat, sucking the liquid deep inside his belly.

"No! NOOO!" Jimmy screamed, holding a bloody gash where his ear had been bitten off.

Jimmy ran, wailing, from the room and through the security door. Louie was walking listlessly around the room, ignoring several open bottles on the floor. Henry's friends were staring at him in awe from above. Tori stood on weakened legs, supported by his friends.

"Come on, we've got to go!" he said, waving for them to come down.

32

J<small>IMMY'S BLOOD WAS TURNING COLD BUT SWEEPING THROUGH HIM LIKE A</small> fever, and his vision became obscured. Clutching the gash where his ear had been, he screamed all the way down the corridor and ducked into the security room.

The monitors were blurry as he tried to locate his brother. He wanted to shut them back inside, just like before. His fingers were numb, and he couldn't find the keys as he slammed down the keyboard. He grabbed the briefcase, felt for the latches, and tore them open. He had the syringe in hand and jabbed it into one of the corks of the XT Serum. Drawing out every drop he could, he jammed the long needle deep into his neck and plunged the fluid in, screaming in agony. He fell, crushing the flask.

His heart pounded with a rush of adrenaline as he lay on the floor in agony. His veins from head to toe were streams of electricity. He lay still one long moment. His vision began to return, but his limbs became stiff and strong. Rising from the floor, he groaned and shoved everything he needed in the case and latched it. He saw a glimpse of himself reflecting off the stainless steel walls. He was tall and rangy, with a busted nose, bloody chin and rising blue veins. He licked his lips and rubbed his face. If this is what being undead felt like, it felt pretty good. It felt great. But how long would it last? He would worry about that later.

He headed toward the back security door on legs of steel. He scanned his card and went out into the driving rain. He couldn't feel the wind or hail tearing into his face. A tree had fallen nearby, crushing the chain-link fence before him. He could see a swarm of black vehicles blocked by another tree in the distance. Armed men in black were swarming out and heading inside. He had to run and hide. Or did he? He hid in the darkness of the storm as they all passed by. A lone man stood outside in the rain, watching the vehicles, somehow smoking a cigarette. Jimmy fought the urge to eat the man whole as he snuck behind him.

The man turned on him, shotgun leveled at his head. He was small, wearing dark sunglasses, with a black mustache and jutting lower lip. The man's southern voice was deep as a river.

"Whatcha doin', zombie?"

"I'm not a zombie! I'm a man ... Jimmy!" he shouted.

"You sure look like a zombie!"

Something sounded familiar about the man. The voice on the phone—his contact? Was that him? He recalled something.

"I'm Jimmy Bawkula. JB III."

The man gave him a curious look and lowered his gun.

"Is that the XT Serum in the case, Jimmy?"

Jimmy thought he was smiling when he said it.

"Everything you asked for."

The man shouldered his shotgun and held out his hands. He handed over the case and watched the man open it. The notes, videos, and vials were all there.

"Where's the other flask? Weren't there two?"

"The other one is in me. I got bitten"—he pointed at his bloody earhole—"so I injected myself."

The man closed the briefcase.

"Is that so? How do you feel?"

"Like a million dollars! The serum works!"

He knew he was smiling. His reward was on the way.

"That's good to know. Fascinating ... my boss will love that."

"Great!"

The small man had a half smile, half sneer on his face, and his voice changed to ice water.

"Well, Jimmy ... you don't look like a million dollars."

He managed to laugh and shrug. "Well, I guess I don't."

"No, boy ... you look like a zombie."

Jimmy watched in slow motion as the man procured a semi-automatic pistol from thin air and pointed it at his head. He saw the fires of Hell when it exploded in his face.

EPILOGUE

IT WAS A SPECIAL NIGHT AT THE CAMPFIRE AS PEOPLE OF ALL AGES gathered around an older man with an excited face and graying beard. Fathers, sons, mothers, daughters, and cousins shared hotdogs, s'mores, hot cocoa, and beer as the owls hooted and the tree frogs croaked. Everyone at the campsite hung on the man's every word. His deep, melodious voice had drawn them all in over the past few hours. He rubbed his calloused hands together as he continued, while another man dropped another log on the blazing fire.

"When Henry, Tori, Rudy, and Weege finally made it out of the facility, the skies began to clear. The men in the black cars said they were with the World Humanitarian Society, and they took over the place. Henry tried to tell them what was going on inside with the children, but they didn't seem to listen. But Henry never told them about the message Nate McDaniel sent. He was afraid they might kill him right then and there ... but it didn't happen. It was a sad day when he buried Stanley and his mother Linda. He had been given the authority to euthanize her, and he slept better after that."

"What happened to Tori?" a teenage girl with curly auburn hair urged.

"Tori turned out just fine and got her old job back at Fast-Mart."

There was an awkward silence.

"I'm kidding," he said, patting her on the knee. "She and Henry got married not long after that, and he took a job as a school teacher and basketball coach. She stayed home baking cookies and making babies. They had a happier life."

"What about Rudy and Weege?" a boy, about eight, asked.

"Well, they both moved to Las Vegas and became casino dealers."

"That doesn't make any sense," someone said.

"Hey—what about the zombie kids, what happened to all of them?"

The old storyteller didn't say anything at first as he stirred a stick in the ground.

"As far as anyone knew, the WHS took them somewhere else. All but the one they couldn't find ... Louie."

Someone gasped as another young voice said, "You mean he's still out there, Grandpa?" There were uncertain looks and a few cracked smiles on the shadowy faces of the rest of the folks.

"No, boy, he ain't out there ... He's right behind you! Run!"

Half of the camp jumped, while the rest fell over in laughter as the children screamed, scrambling to their parents. Heavy laughs came here and there until they all subsided. Some of the children were crying. The older ones were laughing. One boy, about twelve years old, was lying near the fire, looking up at the dark and distant hilltop called Guthrie. His name was Fergie, and he hated that story, but only because he knew it was true. Things had never been the same in the world since the day he and his grandpa raced away from the facility, home of the Zombie Day Care.

IF you liked Zombie Day Care and would like a free Amazon eBook copy of the next book, Zombie Rehab, send an email to craig@thedarkslayer.com. Put 'Free Zombie' in the Subject line and we'll let you know right away if you win this awesome giveaway!

CRAIG HALLORAN

ZOMBIE
REHAB

1

HE WAS MOVING under a series of bright fluorescent lights. The glare hurt his eyes, but he was determined to keep them open. He had to figure out where he was. His mind fought to regain control of his body, which strained against the leather bonds that had him strapped to the gurney. At least, he thought he was fighting, but his limbs were more like jelly, and his mind was mush. The only thing he recognized was the thump-thump of the gurney wheels rolling over the tiles of the long corridor.

He could have sworn he was hung over and being pushed in a grocery cart over an unpaved parking lot. He retched. His mouth filled with the tang of bile. A blurry figure jerked his head up and was shouting something unintelligible. He was dizzy; the lights above were beginning to blur together like the white dashes on a highway. A sharp pain pierced his arm, causing him to break out into a cold sweat. *What is going on?*

There were several of them, shaped like men but moving like ghosts. He tried to find an outline, recognize a face, let his mind find something that was familiar. Instead, there was nothing, just a corridor that began to swirl and spin into a vortex. He felt euphoria as his frantic eyelids became heavy and he plunged into the darkness.

HIS EYES SNAPPED OPEN. Something was chiseling on his face. His body convulsed and shuddered as a group of faceless people scrambled and screamed.

"He's resisting! He's resisting! Dammit, who prepped him! Get the anesthesiologist."

Bloodied gloves were holding sharp shining objects, and the ghosts began to rush around him. A pair of eyes looked deep into his, large and disturbing.

"Give him more! Give him more ..."

He faded into a bright patch of lilies.

HE WOKE up incapacitated and in pain. His eyes flickered open only to gaze at the darkness of a quiet room. There was a smell of chlorine and ammonia in the air, and urine, too. Inside his sluggish mind he sensed someone else in the room, at his side, gazing with heavy eyes.

"Mrmphh ..." he moaned.

He regretted it. His jaw felt like it was broken, and the rest of his face seemed like a busted vase. *Ah ... I don't understand! Help me someone! Help me!*

A shadow was moving by his side, silent. Perfume. It was nice, like something from heaven. A figure crossed in front of him, this shape more defined than the last, comely, tangible, real. *No, don't leave me!* The figure passed into a dark frame and vanished. His eyes began to water. He wanted to move his arms and legs, but he couldn't feel them. He began to wonder if he even had them. Something soft was obstructing part of his view, like cotton, tape, or gauze. *Hospital? Hospital!*

He tried to remember the last thing that happened to him. His mind was so dreary, exhausted like a car that had run out of gas. Nothing seemed capable of unlocking the vault of knowledge that was within him. It was blocked, either by his own desire or something else. He knew he should be able to remember something, but he couldn't.

There were sounds now. He could hear the hum of an air conditioner and feel the cool air rushing on his eyes.

Beep..Beep..Beep.

It was a steady sound that he found comforting. He was somewhere, and he was alive. That had to be a good thing. He just wished his face didn't hurt so much. What had happened to him? Where in the world was he? As he stared up at the ceiling, he noticed the tiles were loose and water stained, and there was a drip coming from somewhere, landing on the floor and not in a sink. He began to wonder how it was he could understand what these things were but he couldn't remember a thing about who he was. Everything was confusing.

"Mrmphh! MRMRPHH!"

Pain exploded in his face, and the beeping at his bedside began to increase its pace. Two figures in light green scrubs rushed upon him from the darkened doorway. One was a man and the other a woman, he could tell that much, but they were both faceless. As he turned his neck to get a better look it felt like someone was driving a stake in his neck.

"Hrrumph!" he tried to say help.

Tears were filling his eyes as his mind pleaded for them to say something to him ... anything. He felt a delicate hand dabbing the water from his eyes with a soft towel. He felt like his heart was going to burst, the feeling of humanity so close to touching him. He just wanted to reconnect, try to find out if he was still a human. *Why can't I feel my limbs? Why?* He felt the hand pulling away, and he let out an audible sob. *NO! Come back!*

He could make out the pair, huddled at the end of the bed. The man towered over the woman, and even though he was whispering, his voice was as deep as a well and callous as a stone.

"Do not let him revive again, you idiot."

"I'm sorry, Doctor," she said with a quiver in her voice, "I swear I haven't missed a single dose. Not one, and I've checked the other shifts, too."

"Shut up, I don't need your feeble explanation. Give me his chart!"

As he lay in the bed he could see the doctor scribbling something on the clipboard. Then the big man shoved the clipboard into her hand and said, "That dose should take care of it, for another month at least."

What! Another month! I've been under for a month? No. That can't be!

He swore he could feel the bones in his face seeping into his brain, and even though he couldn't remember anything, he could recall despair. Something deep down inside him triggered a small chip of memories, horrible ones, something that had just happened that he'd just as soon forget. The doctor's unpleasant tone interrupted his thoughts.

"Nurse, I don't want to have to remind you that if you screw this up again ... I'll be getting rid of you. And you know what that means, don't you?"

He could hear her sobbing reply, "Y-yes sir, I m mean Doctor Zhan—"

Slap!

He could feel his own cheek stinging from the blow as the nurse crumpled to the ground.

Hey! Why'd you hit her for?

"Mrmmf Fumphnhr!" It hurt so bad to say it he almost blacked out, and his stomach began to churn. He could hear the man walking away on heavy footsteps as the woman struggled to rise from the ground. He watched as her fuzzy outline slowly stepped behind him. He heard the sound of a small plastic wheel grinding and then something ice cold ran in his veins.

"NO!"

The pain was so bad, but he would rather deal with that than be knocked out for another month. Then he saw her face before his: round, sweet, and black. She was whispering something in his ear.

"It's gonna be okay, Honey. It's going to be okay, just hang in there."

Please tell me where I am?

As the pain began to subside, he felt something warm squeezing his hand. It was her hand in his, and it felt wonderful as he drifted away into a dreamless slumber.

2

WASHINGTON, DC

TWO SUITED MEN were seated on a park bench near the Jefferson Memorial, soaking in the sun of a cool fall day. The leaves were turning in some places, but most of them still maintained their rich green colors. Both men sat comfortably, talking back and forth and nodding. The humming of a black Cadillac engine sounded nearby, with one stout man in a navy blue suit sitting on the hood and smoking. A semi-automatic pistol could be seen strapped inside is jacket, but none of the passersby noticed. He seemed to be enjoying the fresh air almost as much as his cigarette. He let out a breath of smoke, flicked his ashes, then took another puff. If he had any interest in what the men were saying, he didn't show it. Instead, he watched and waited.

The taller man, bearded in white, turned, rested his elbow on the back of the bench, and faced the other. The younger man, maybe forty, remained seated with his hands clasped, stooped over with his elbows resting on his knees, eyes gazing at the tip of the Washington Monument in the distance.

"Come on, Jack, it's going to be fine. She'll come back to her senses. She needs you, and she loves you," the older man said in a rich and soothing voice.

Jack shook his head as he ran his fingers back through his thick brown hair. He opened his mouth to speak, but no words came. The older man squeezed his shoulder with a reassuring grip and patted him on the back.

"Jack, women do crazy things. Even before the zombies they were crazy. It's just stress, that's all. Some time at home with her mother will do her some good. I know her mom; she'll talk some sense into her."

Jack took a deep breath as he sat up and then leaned back against the bench. "Her mom seems to be just as testy these days. I keep calling Angie there, but her mom's been pretty nasty. Called me a selfish bastard."

"Geez, Becky said that? That doesn't seem like her at all. She was always so sweet. Hey, let me give Becky a call; I think I can smooth things over."

"Don, I appreciate it, but right now I get the feeling that any more attempted interventions will make them madder."

"Hah ... Jack, they love getting mad. I'd keep it up because you know what will happen if you leave Angie alone too long?"

"What?"

"She'll get even madder," Don said, smiling and patting him on the shoulder.

"Great."

Reaching over, Don grabbed his custom computer and set it on his lap. His aged fingers were as quick as a teen's as he loaded one screen after the other. Whatever he was doing, Jack wasn't paying much attention.

Don's voice took on a dire tone as he asked, "You haven't let Angie in on anything that's going on, have you?"

Jack stiffened.

"No, absolutely not. I swear. That's the problem, Don, we're close, and I'm keeping in all of these secrets."

"Is she still prying into your business?"

"No ... Yes, it depends on the mood she's in, I guess."

"Listen to me, Jack: you can't ever—I mean ever— tell her a thing, or it's over. The WHS has trusted you with a great deal, and if you blow it you'll be deader than a zombie before dawn."

Jack sagged in his chair saying, "I know."

"Angie and Becky will be, too." Don cleared his throat. "I'm sorry, I mean, you're just out of their program, a couple of years, but still new, and you somehow wound up with knowledge you didn't even know existed. But that knowledge gives you power, Jack. It protects you and your family. It protects me, your uncle, and you have to trust me and believe me that you cannot share what you know with anyone. Got it, Jack?"

Jack patted his uncle on his knee and said, "I won't let you down, Don. I haven't said a word, and I won't. Not ever. You know you don't have to worry about that. My mind is like a bank vault; even the most brilliant thieves would have trouble getting in there."

Don laughed and said, "Okay, I know. I just want you to be careful. Extra careful. But you've got to get your household back to normal, else it will arouse suspicion. I figure your mother in-law's house is already bugged."

"Damn. You really think so?"

"Just being a little paranoid for you. Look, you're gonna have to give Angie a convincing lie to get her back home. You're going to have to convince her you were hiding something believable. Tell her you had an after hours encounter with a cocktail waitress or something."

"What? She'll castrate me!"

"Just a close call, nothing overly intimate. It'll work. I mean, you're a good-looking guy. It's not like another woman hitting on you should surprise her."

"Great," Jack sighed, "and if that doesn't work?"

"Then flip it on her, and accuse her of hiding something like an affair. Check her texts and Facebook posts. I'm sure there are plenty of saps out there flirting with her. Use it against her."

"Gee Uncle Don, you sure are cold."

"No, I'm a survivor, a realist. The walls of this world are closing in on us. The waters are rising fast; I'm just trying to keep my head above water. Yours as well. Now, let's get down to business. What's the latest on the XT Formula?"

3

INSTITUTE, WV

"HENRY? HENRY BAWKULA, IS THAT YOU?"

He tried to look away, get into his car and go, but it was too late. She had caught him, and a discomforting feeling churned in his stomach. Still, he pulled his ball cap farther down on his head and hung the gasoline hose back on the pump.

He pressed the "NO" button that was asking him if he wanted a receipt, and when he turned he was face-to-face with Jennifer.

"Henry, seriously, I know you weren't about to blow me off. It's been almost ten years, and I can't believe I'm seeing you again. I'm ... I'm so happy," she said, wrapping her arms around him and giving him a big hug. He tried to pull away, but she was unwilling to let him go. He wasn't so sure he wanted her to let go, either, as there had been a time, not so long ago, when she had been the most normal thing in his life. And there she was, as pretty as she could be.

Jennifer, it's great to see you," he said, managing to break her embrace. "I-I didn't know if you were still around. I mean, I'm sorry to put it that way." He shook his head. "It's just that, well with the apoca-lypse and all I wasn't sure if ... if—"

She put her finger on his lips.

"Shhh Henry, I'm okay. You don't have to worry, me and Mom and Dad and Roger are doing great. We were in Arizona when all of that happened. We were some of the lucky ones."

Just cut it short; you have to go. "I'm glad to hear it. We uh ... well, weren't so fortunate. Look, I have to go."

"Henry! I know you aren't just going to leave me hanging like this. So many people are gone, and now I just happen to run into my last surviving boyfriend, and you want to run off on me? No, Sir. We have some catching up to do."

Jennifer sounded convincing enough. She always had been forward, driven, and desirable. All he had ever wanted to do was please her back then, but that was high school, and the world had changed an awful lot since then.

"I'm sorry, Jennifer, but I can't. Just give me your number and I'll call you, I promise," he said, forcing himself between her and his back bumper.

She pinned him against the car with her body and kissed him. *Oh no. This can't be happening.* But it was happening; a flood of passion began to consume them both underneath the roof of the Go-Mart parking lot. He shoved her away.

"Are you crazy, Jennifer? I'm not alone here. I've got to go. You have to understand that. Just give me your—"

But it was too late. He was caught. She was caught, and the storm was coming. Henry took one last look at Jennifer, noting her sweet smile, silky black hair, bejeweled eyes over top of a rich and bewitching figure.

"What is it, Henry? You look like you just saw a zombie."

He swallowed hard and said, "No, worse, sort of. You're about to meet my girlfriend. My very jealous girlfriend."

Jennifer turned around in time to catch Tori's last few bouncing steps. Henry swore he heard thunder overhead as his butt remained seated on the bumper of his car. Tori's twelve pack of beer bottles rattled as she extended her hand toward Jennifer.

"Hi, I'm Tori ... Henry's girlfriend. And who might you be?"

"Oh, I'm so sorry. I'm Jennifer, Henry's ex-girlfriend."

What? Oh geez! "Uh, that was a long time ago, over a decade."

Tori still held her hand out and slowly Jennifer extended hers as she said, "Well, it seems we both have great taste in brilliant men. It's so nice to meet you—"

Jennifer's eyes glanced down at their shaking hands. Henry watched as her body stiffened and she tried to pull her arm away. Tori held her fast. Jennifer looked over her shoulder at him, eyes pleading for mercy.

"Tori, let go," he said, rising up from the bumper.

Jennifer's knees began to buckle.

"LET GO, TORI!"

Jennifer gasped as she tore her arm away. Without looking back, she jumped into her car, tore out of the parking lot, and didn't wave good-bye. Tori did, however, waving her gnarled half-dead arm like a banner from the 4th of July.

"Tori, put your arm down and get in the car. Now!"

They both slammed their doors as they got in. Henry had the car in drive and had punched it to the floor before she even got her seatbelt buckled.

"Way to go, Tori!"

"What? You can't be mad at me. You're the one sucking face with some woman in the parking lot!"

"I'm sorry—look, I'm sorry. She took me by surprise. I tried to get away, she just—"

Tori laughed, "She just what, over powered you? Give me a break, you cheater!"

"What? I'm not a cheater! You know better than that. Now get a hold of yourself."

Tori didn't say a word; she just stared out of her side window and brushed her hair back from her face with her odd hand.

All Henry could think about was getting back to the complex so he could bury himself back in his work, and Tori would do the same. There had been other highs and lows between them since they departed the Zombie Day Care under the most bizarre circumstances. Normal was no longer an option in his life. Embracing the abnormal to survive was his only option.

"You're sick of being with me, aren't you? Now that I'm deformed and all, you are wanting something better, perfect, like I used to be until you drug me into that day care."

"Don't go down this road, Tori. You said you wouldn't bring it up anymore. I told you to stay outside, but you wouldn't listen. Can't you just be thankful that you're alive?"

"I'm a freak!" she said, slamming her gnarled hand into the dashboard.

"Hey-Hey! Don't do that. Quit acting like a child. You're still beautiful; you know that."

It was true. Tori was every bit as sexy as she ever was. Her auburn hair was lustrous, her buxom figure not as soft as before, but firm. Still, her sweet face was drained, almost haggard some days, but nobody paid her hand any mind as they were too busy looking at the rest of her. As strange as her hand was, it wasn't nearly as bad as she made it out to be.

He glanced over at the appendage, but Tori tucked it under her leg and glared. From the elbow down you could see the flesh was pasty and gray. The fingers remained stiff and bent, the nails dead and black. Henry figured she could have coped with it better if it was her own arm to begin with, but it wasn't. It was someone else's, thicker and stronger like a man's, but they were assured it was a woman's. A woman lumberjack maybe. Henry always wondered about that. At least it worked, and it was better than nothing there at all.

Tori tore open the twelve pack of beer and pulled out a bottle.

"What are you doing now?"

"I'm having a beer," she said, turning the top off of one and tilting it to her lips.

"Tori, quit that. Now you're just being silly. You don't even drink."

"Well, today I'm starting a new diet."

Henry reached and grabbed the bottle saying, "Gimme that."

"Oh Henry, don't take my bottle. Please Henry don't." She said it like she was on a vaudeville stage, exasperated and silly.

Henry tugged at the bottle that was in the vise-like grip of her replaced hand. She was giggling at his futile efforts.

"What's the matter, Henry, can't the big boy take the bottle from the little girl?"

The car almost crashed into the rail as Henry jerked the wheel over and weaved back and forth between the single lanes before getting the car back under control. He let go of the bottle.

"Geez, Tori! You're gonna cause a wreck. Now quit being a baby and put that beer back. It's for the party. Stupid Rudy! And we're on our way to work! Stupid complex! Stupid everything!" he shouted.

The thought of going back to the complex filled him with dread, as each passing hour approached, to the appointed time. He and Tori had been granted three weeks of leave after having been inside the dreadful complex for the prior six months. That's what the World Humanitarian Society had done: given him another job, less than thirty miles from the last one. He had tried to quit, but he wasn't given much choice. He wanted to run, but there wouldn't be any escape. They had made all of that perfectly clear in all the briefings that followed the incident at the Guthrie Facility, home of the Zombie Day Care.

He felt Tori reach out and grab his hand—with her normal one—and squeeze. She scooted closer and said, "I'm sorry, Henry, it's just that, you know it's that time—"

"I know, that time of the month."

"No, Jackhole!" she said, squeezing his hand, "It's the anniversary of the day I lost my parents, Idiot!" She let go and scooted back away.

After he pulled off the highway, the car brakes squealed as he came to a stop. *Idiot would be correct.* Looking through the windshield, his body filled with dread. In the distance, a ten foot high limestone wall stretched over a hundred yards, with a chain-link gate in the center. He could see some of the brick-red building through the gate and some of the many tree tops that jutted over the top of the wall. He wanted to turn around.

"You ready?" he said, looking over at Tori's pouting face.

She shrugged.

"Look, I'm sorry. I didn't realize it was your parents, uh, you know. I'm sorry."

"Forget about it, Henry. Besides, it almost is that time of the month, too. But you're still gonna make things right once we get in there."

Allowing himself a faint smile, he looked over at her and said, "So you forgive me?"

"Of course. You're all I've got, Henry ... all I ever wanted. I just wish things were different. I hate being in there as much as you. But as long as I'm with you, then it doesn't really matter where I am."

He looked into her pretty eyes, held her face in his hands, and kissed her. When he finished, she opened her eyes and said, "You owe me a lot more than that, Henry. Now, let's get this over with."

He nodded his head, put the car in drive, and slowly headed down the road towards the front gate. Once again he would have to make the most of it, but he'd rather turn around. The sun was lowering in the horizon, and a flock of birds burst from the trees behind the wall. He swore he could hear something screaming. Tori grabbed his hand as his stomach began to knot. Six months. Six more months of living among the dead. The complex was a place filled with the unexpected and unnatural. *Forget everything you just left. That was normal. Check your humanity at the gate. Forget your sanity. Embrace the insanity. Think abnormal. Welcome back to the Zombie Rehab.*

4

LOCATION UNKNOWN

THE NEXT TIME he woke up, things were different. The room had changed, and he was starving. The room was illuminated by a blurry light above him, that caused his eyes to ache. He was thirsty. He tried to swallow, but his mouth was raw and sore. He shifted in his bed, and when he heard the steel framework beneath him groan, a thrill raced down his spine. *I'm moving.*

As he turned his head, he noticed a small metal dresser across the room and a heavy wooden door. When he realized he was partially sitting up, he managed to look around some more. No windows, but there was an air conditioning unit rattling along the wall, alongside a padded metal chair and a table. He reached his hand over his stomach as it groaned. *My hand, I can feel my hand!*

He held his hand up to his face and watched it tremble as he opened and closed his fingers. He couldn't feel his legs, but managed to pull his knees up into a bent position. *Thank God, I can move!* He was still weak, hungry, and confused. *What is this place?* The haziness in his mind seemed to be lifting like a fog as he peered around the little room. It looked like an old hospital room, decades old, with the original paint, trim, and checkered floors. The room was stuffy, the air from the air conditioner stale, but for some reason he was still thankful that he was breathing. He just had a hard time remembering the last thing he was doing.

He reached and grabbed a bar that was hanging from the ceiling and pulled himself up. A sharp pain stabbed his belly, and his face ached. He tried to remember if he had been in some kind of accident, then he remembered the gauze, the doctor, and the nurse. There were bandages on his face, or something like that. He rubbed his face, his eyes, nose, and head. No medical tape or gauze, just a beard. He didn't remember ever having a beard. That's when he noticed a small metal sink in the corner and pulled his legs down onto the floor. There was a mirror hanging cock-eyed over the sink, but the surface was dingy and faded. He managed to push himself up onto his feet and stand. His head swam as the floor began to wobble beneath his shaking feet, and he fell. Every bone in his body shuddered with pain as he lay on the floor trembling, tears streaming from his eyes. He wanted to cry for help, but he was too scared. That doctor was frightening. What was his name, *Zhan?*

The floor was cold, and his teeth began to chatter as he fought his way off his back and onto his elbows. His chest was heaving now, and his forehead was beaded with sweat as he shivered. That's when he saw beneath the door: shadows, silent and mysterious, passing by. He couldn't help but wonder what would happen if they came in and saw him on the floor. Would he be in trouble? Would they knock him out again and for how long? A hundred thoughts began rushing through his head as he low crawled towards the sink. His ancestral instincts were urging him on. *Must escape.* Adrenaline was fueling his strenuous effort as he managed to make it to his hands and knees. The hard tiles were painful on his knees as his elbows quaked under the strain to move forward, but he pressed on.By the time he reached the bottom of the sink, he was exhausted and wondering how he would find the energy to pull himself up. His tongue was thick in his dry mouth, and all he wanted more than anything was a drink of something wet. That's when he noticed the shadows underneath the door had stopped. The sound of muffled voices was coming from the other side. What was he going to say when they came in? *Please don't come in. Please, not yet.*

Curled up on the floor, he let his fear begin to overtake reason. He closed his eyes and waited. The sound of the muffled voices faded, and when he opened his eyes again the shadows were gone from underneath the door. Relief washed through him, but something else did as well. A sense—primitive within— had awakened. A bit of anger was rising, too, as the images of the living and the dead began to surface in his mind. *I'm alive.* He reached up and grabbed the lip of the sink, gathered his legs underneath him, and pulled himself up. *Almost there. Come on, I've gotta have more in me than this.*

He gasped and grunted, and the strength in his feeble arms and legs fought the gravity that was holding his big body down.

"No!" he gasped again as he made it up to his knees and began to slip back down. It seemed like the entire earth was against him, pulling him back down into the abyss, but he had been there before. He wasn't going back. He hung on to the sink and squatted down on his feet, then summoned everything he had as his shaking body rose to his feet. *I made it!* He wiped the sweat from his eyes and looked into the blurry mirror. He didn't recognize the man in the mirror, a greasy head of long brown hair and a scruffy beard that hid most of his face. Nothing was right. *All out of place.* His fingers brushed over his cheeks, nose, and chin. Tears formed in his eyes. *I've gone mad.* He touched the image in the mirror, then pulled his fingers back. He was changed, different, no longer who he once was. No longer the man he thought he was. But the eyes were the mirror to the soul, and those brown eyes he saw were still his own. There was no doubt in his mind that the man he was looking at was Nate McDaniel, the Man Who Saved the World. He heard footsteps and twirled around. *I've got to get out of here.*

He licked his hairy lips with his dry tongue. He felt like he could drink a river. The spigot squeaked as he turned it on and let the cold water run over his fingertips. It felt like something from heaven. He grabbed a small cup from the sink's edge and began to fill it. As he brought the liquid to his lips he smiled. *On no!* He blacked out and sank back to the floor.

5

Institute, WV

As Henry and Tori were passing through the gates, he thought about John, the old security guard from the day care. He liked John; the man's soothing demeanor always gave him a sense of security, and his sense of humor was unprecedented as well. Things were different now. The guards were many and their protocol more severe. The guards were a bunch of overzealous thugs, sort of like the TSA at the airports, but entirely redneck.

As they made their way through the second gate, one of the men, brandishing a WHS badge on his uniform, stopped beside Tori and motioned for her to roll the window down.

"I'm gonna need you to step out of the car, Miss.""I don't think so," Tori retorted, pinching her red blouse together at the neckline.

The young man's chin jutted out. He leered inside and said, "I've got my orders. Now you can get out, or you can sit in the car the rest of the day. Don't worry, I won't bite. It'll just take a second.

Henry noticed in his mirrors that more of the guards were gathering around the car. A swagger was in every step as they rubbed on the handles of the guns on their hips. There never was much traffic coming in and out of the complex. It was only natural the bored men would overreact at the sight of a pretty girl. Still, Henry wasn't much for compassion these days. Besides, the look on Tori's face told him she was about to freak out. Something about the man reminded him of his brother, Jimmy, who he hoped he would never see again. He never heard what happened after that night. The leering man was licking his lips like he was about to be fed a barbeque pork chop, and it was more than Henry could stand.

Henry pulled out his phone and texted a message.

"Come on, Lady," the guard urged. "Don't make me use any force, but I will if I have to."

Tori remained rigid and silent. *She's gonna freak out.*

"Looks like she's got something to hide, fellas," the guard said as two other guards began to close in. "Looks like we better pat them both down." He pulled out his night stick and stuck the nose of it inside the window. "You two better get out ... now."

"You're making a mistake ... uh," Henry put on his glasses as he searched for the name tag on the man's shirt " ... Toby. Yes Toby, you're making a big mistake. You see, we've passed all of your little checks, and if you don't let us in you're going to be going home."

"Is that so? Well, Mister, let me tell you something. I could use the day off, but I ain't going anywhere, not until I search you and this pretty little lady right here. Now, you'll do as I say unless you want me to call my uncle, from the local police department, and have you hauled in." The men snickered. "And I'll take her into my personal custody," He licked his lips. " ...and keep a real close eye on her."

"Toby, do you realize how big of an idiot you are?"

"I suggest you keep your big mouth shut, or I'm gonna take this baton upside your head."

Henry sent out another text message.

"Have it your way, Toby, but I tried to warn you."

Toby laughed and said, "Thanks. Now get out of the car—both of you!"

Henry just shook his head and waited. *Come on. What's going on? Is everyone asleep in there?*

There was a loud clicking sound coming from an outdoor speaker overhead.

"TOBY. YOU'RE FIRED. PACK YOUR SHIT AND GO! AND IF THE REST OF YOU MAKE ASSES OUT OF YOURSELVES, YOU'LL BE HEADING BACK TO THE UNEMPLOYMENT OFFICE AS WELL!"

CLICK

Toby looked like someone just shot his dog as the last gate rattled open and Henry drove through.

"You okay?" Henry said to Tori, rubbing her knee.

"Yes, I think. But, poor Toby. Who else on earth is going to give that slob a job?"

"Ha! Ha-Haa! Well, it won't be long before they have the zombies working the gates."

Tori was holding her stomach as she giggled and said, "Oh don't say that, please don't say that. WHS Security guards: Better ... Faster ... Smarter ... than plain ole people."

The jokes were just what they needed before the uneasiness settled in. Henry let the car roll to a stop about thirty yards south of the gate they just left. Ahead was the complex, a roughshod campus of cracked pavement, red brick buildings, and long rows of gray warehouses running along the edge of the interior wall as far as the eye could see. Just ahead was a six story office building that towered over the rest of the campus. The parking lot surrounding the building was vacant except for about a dozen cars.

Henry pushed down on the accelerator and let the car slowly roll over the road towards the back of the complex. He used to come here often, to the complex, back when it was a thriving center for the rehabilitation of many folks in the community. The patients came from all over to be trained by a dutiful staff and refit to function and prosper within society. There was a boarded up entrance to a gymnasium where he used to play basketball games, swim, and even bowl. He remembered the cafeteria, the way it had been, thriving with happy faces and hungry people enjoying a hot meal. They had made the best pizza and homemade biscuits there. Now, the patios where he and his friends used to eat were overgrown with vines creeping up over the walls.

"What a waste," he said.

"What do you mean, Honey?" Tori asked.

"Aw, it's just that I used to come here as a kid, with my mom. It was awesome, like a giant playground. It's just a shame seeing it decaying like this. I mean, you see that rickety gazebo over there?" He pointed up the road to an overgrown patch of grass where a wooden gazebo had collapsed inside on itself.

Tori patted his arm. "I see it, Sugar, I see it just fine. You okay?"

Henry's tongue clove to the roof of his mouth as he fought back his tears.

"I had an uncle; he stayed here. I mean as a patient; he needed help. It was my mom's brother. Anyway, he had some problems, some had ones with drugs and alcohol and Lord knows what else. Well, he and I, we ..." he voice trailed off.

"It's okay, you can tell me. Just let it out."

The warmth of her soft hand gave him the strength he needed.

"We built it. It took two weeks, but we did it. It was one of the best days of my life when we all sat in there and ate. Mom made the best ham salad sandwiches and lemonade. The folks in the cafeteria even brought us some cookies and ice cream." He wiped the tears from his eyes. "It was just a great day ... for all of us."

Jimmy had been there, too, but he didn't want to say it. He could only assume Tori figured so much. It was hard to believe that his life, once so simple and perfect, had turned into what it was now.

"Well Henry, it's a shame," Tori remarked, patting his knee as they stared at the gazebo.

"I know. I guess ... I guess we just didn't do a very good job."

Tori burst out into laughter, and it wasn't long before he followed suit. One thing that the pair had managed to survive on the past few months was a sense of humor. If they couldn't find a way to laugh, at least once a day, they wouldn't have made it this long.

"Funny, why haven't you ever told me that before?"

"I don't know, I guess I just didn't want to think about it. I guess I needed to share that with someone, someone special that is." He squeezed her hand.

"Oh Henry, give me a kiss."

He pressed his lips against hers, and within seconds his sadness was washed away with elation. He didn't care who saw, either, but the complex was like a graveyard, and besides, they were both adults.

HONK! They both jumped as Tori pinned him back against the steering wheel.

"Geez, that scared the poop out of me," Tori said. "Wow Henry, you really surprised me with that kiss, too. It was one of your better ones; I'll say that, but we're gonna have to go."

"Why? I mean, no one will know. I'm trying to be more adventurous here," he said, pulling her back towards him.

"I know, and I appreciate it. I'm sure I'll regret it, too, but I think I just peed myself, so we need to go."

Henry pushed his glasses back up on his face, blushing, and said, "Oh, okay."

He put the car back in gear and took a deep breath. He wasn't even sure what he was doing right now as it was almost like he was having an out of body experience. He needed to get his head back on straight; he was beginning to feel like he was falling apart. *What am I doing?*

Tori was fixing her lipstick in the mirror when she asked, "So, if you don't mind me asking, what ever happened to your uncle?"

"Uh ... well, a few years before the zombies came they released him, and we never saw or heard from him again."

"That's sad. What do you think happened?"

"He used to talk about going to Korea a lot. Maybe he went there. I don't know," he said with a shrug.

"Did you ever try to look him up?"

"Sure, a few times, but no luck."

"Does it bother you?" she asked.

Henry stopped the car.

"Er ... no, but I'll tell you what does."

"What," she said as she checked her lips in the mirror.

"Zombies walking around on the loose like human beings. Roll up your window, Tori. Roll it up!"

Tori gasped as she pressed the window button.

Stupefied, Henry watched two zombies lumbering his way. One was pushing a lawnmower. The other was dragging a rake.

"You've got to be kidding me."

6

Washington, DC

JACK LIFTED his custom laptop and flipped open the screen, bringing the monitor to life. It was one of the perks of the WHS, the latest in computer technology. His busy fingers tapped on the screen as he began loading up data files of information that only a handful of people in the entire world had ever seen.

"What are you doing, Jack? Are you doing to give me a PowerPoint presentation? You know I hate those things. Remember the last time … I think the Senators Grose and Sears were about to die in the middle of your presentation. I still don't know who all of these people are that read and write bills all day long."

Jack laughed at the remark as a spark awakened behind his green eyes. "Yeah right. Those guys don't read or write those bills. Some old man told me that once, not so long ago."

"Ha, ha … you remember that, do you? How old were you, twelve? I could've sworn you weren't listening."

"Oh, I was listening alright. And I was ten."

Don reached over and scruffed up the thick brown hair on his head. The older man was smiling as his gray eyes set themselves on the images on the screen. "I hope you don't want me to read all of that. My glasses are in the car, after all. Speaking of which ... you want some coffee or something? I can have my driver bring over my Thermos. He's really good at that."

Jack gave him a funny look and said, "How many Thermoses do you have in there?"

"As many as I tell him to prepare."

"You really are a piece of work, Uncle Don."

"I am, aren't I? Now show me what you got," he said, waving his arm up in the air. His armed escort made his way over from the car, Thermos in hand. Don closed the black case to his own custom computer, took the canister, twisted off the cup top, and filled it up.

Jack could see the steam rising from the hot beverage from the corner of his eye and said, "Gee, you even filled it yourself. Impressive. You aren't getting soft on me, are you?"

"Some things, a man has to do for himself."

"Huh ... Hey Oliver, you wouldn't happen to have any Mountain Dew in there, would you?"

The man remained stone-faced as he stared out into the horizon, still enjoying his smoke.

Don dismissed the man with a nod saying, "Thanks Oliver, and don't pay my nephew any mind. He doesn't understand war-horses like us. Feel free to help yourself; by the way. It's getting chilly out here." Don took a sip and followed it up with a refreshing sigh. "Okay, get on with it. What's the latest?"

"First, it's not a PowerPoint presentation, even though I do have one, but this isn't that. It's just some data I wanted to pull up to refresh my memory in case you insisted on seeing some numbers for yourself."

"Nope, I'll let you handle the numbers. I stopped keeping track of those little things about ten trillion dollars ago. Just give me the results, the testing, or whatever you geeks refer to it as."

Jack shifted in his seat as he cleared his throat and said, "Since the acquisition of the XT Formula we've opened six new research facilities across the country, all of which are well concealed from the general public ... well, from just about everyone, really. Now these are all separate and apart from the day-care facilities, one focusing on one area, and some on the others. One facility in particular is manu-facturing the formula, while the others are primarily focused on using the formula for zombie rehabilitation."

"Zombie Rehabilitation, hah. Our employers sure come up with awfully clever ways of naming their experiments."

"You don't approve?" Jack asked.

"It doesn't matter if I approve or not. I just think it's silly. I mean, when the WHS was created I thought it was the biggest joke in the world. It was crazy enough that the world was turned upside down by zombies, but now you have a group of people trying to sell it to the public as a good thing. And the people are buying it. I'm even buying it, because I have to. I never believed in any of it to begin with."

Jack gave him a curious look and said, "Any of what, exactly?"

Don's face turned a little bit pale as his eyes darted away. He took another drink of coffee. Don started to cough, and one followed louder than the last until finally the fit stopped.

"You okay?" Jack said, patting his uncle on the back.

"Fine, fine, just getting chilly, I guess. Damn, I spilled my coffee," Don said, pulling out a handkerchief and wiping the liquid off his expensive computer case. "Ah, it'll be fine; it's leather."

Jack had the feeling his uncle was trying to avoid his stare, and had changed the subject as his last question seemed to have struck a nerve. A very sinister feeling rose inside him. He wanted to know everything about the zombies. He had put in his time, and he deserved to know. Had his uncle known about the outbreak before it happened? His gut was telling him yes, but Don's expression was a de facto no. Over the years it had always seemed like there was some-thing dark that hung over his uncle's head after the outbreak. He wanted to know what that was. As a senior advisor in Washington for decades, he knew that his uncle knew things, things that only the world's most powerful men and women may or may not know. He wanted to press the issue. *He's getting old. He's gotta tell me more.*

"Now where were we, Jack?"

"Well, you said 'I never believed in any of it to begin with,' and I asked, 'Any of what?' And you were about to say ..."

Don refilled his cup and said, "Oh, I see what you're hinting at. Easy Jack, what I meant was when they first reported the zombie outbreak in Washington, I didn't believe a word of it. I'm almost eighty. I've seen things happen in my lifetime that I never could have imagined as a child. About ten or twenty years ago, I began to believe that just about anything could happen. Cell phones, computers, the Internet. But zombies?" I said. "You've got to be kidding me. To an old Catholic warrior like me, it might as well have been the apocalypse."

The words seemed sincere enough, but the pitch in his uncle's voice wasn't as convincing as it normally was. Jack paid closer attention.

"Now the both of us work for a company that is a caretaker for zombies. Taking care of my parents before they passed away was one thing, but taking care of over a million zombies ... mindless, useless and dangerous? It's beyond conceivable. It's frightening."

Jack sat at his uncle's side, letting the falling sun warm his face with the last breaths of day. It wasn't so long ago when he wondered if he would ever enjoy another sunset again as he reflected on all of the chaos that struck those many years ago. Now, his life couldn't be any better. He had the zombies to thank for that. *Old people never see the beauty in it.*

"Beautiful evening isn't it?" his uncle said.

"Sure is. You know, this might sound strange, but on days like this I think about Nate McDaniel and how he saved the world."

His uncle nodded and said, "With Zombie Dew of all the ridiculous things."

"Well, if you think that is ridiculous, wait until I tell you what they are using the XT Formula for now!"

"Let me guess, they're going to have zombies counting ballots next."

7

INSTITUTE, WV

HENRY'S first instinct was to jam on the gas pedal and run over the approaching zombies. The pair of undead men moved at less than a mile per hour as they approached, and they were in total oblivion to the danger Henry and his vehicle posed.

"Run em' over, Henry, I hate those damn things!" Tori shouted in his ear.

"Easy Tori, geez, I'm right here," he said, almost pushing her face away.

The zombies' slanted walking gate and slack jaws still turned Henry's blood to ice, despite the fact that he knew he should have nothing to fear. But, here they came, wearing dark green coveralls and hard hats, of all things. He had begun to get used to their presence when he was in the complex before, but after being gone for a while the willies came right back. Now, the last thing he wanted was to have his last remaining prized possession, his classic candy apple red 1968 Mustang, damaged by a zombie pushing a lawn mower.

There wasn't a path to go around them. He was in an alley where the office buildings were boarded up on the left and right.

"Crap, I'm gonna have to back up. Are you going to be okay?" he asked Tori.

Tori sat in her seat, wide-eyed and picking her lip, and he could see the goosebumps on her arms.

"Such a fine welcoming committee. I wonder who is responsible for this mess. It better not be Rudy. That moron's always up to something."

Henry nodded. His friend had never been the most reliable of people and had grown quite fond of walking the grounds with the aimless zombies. To make matters worse, the director of the complex seemed to be enamored with Rudy's bizarre ideas of giving the zombies a life of greater meaning. Henry could have slapped himself when he unintentionally pictured himself rebuilding the gazebo with the zombies.

"All right, this is ridiculous. I'll back it up, and we'll just go around to the other side."

As he dropped his car in gear, he caught a glimpse of three more zombies in the rear-view mirror; they had boxed him in.

"Dammit! There are more of them!"

Tori's head whipped around, and she let out a frightened squeak.

Henry blinked hard as he pushed his glasses back up on his face. They all had on green coveralls, white hard hats, and work boots that were scraping and dragging over the ground. One of them was holding a shovel in both hands as his neck bobbed from side to side. Another one had a pair of metal tree-trimming shears with the tip scraping over the ground, but the third one was the most disturbing of them all.

"Is that a chainsaw?" Tori cried.

He nodded his head. The sound of the small motor in the lethal instrument was very distinct in his ears.

WAHHH! WAHHH! WAHHH! WAHHH!

"Geez, it can use that thing. Lock the door Tori!"

"It is locked!"

Henry began jamming his finger into his iPhone as the zombies closed in, step by dreadful step. He set the phone on his dash board and left it on speaker as it rang.

"Henry, maybe we should get out and run! They can't catch us. Geez, where are their supervisors! Where's Rudy? That idiot never keeps an eye on those things!"

As the sun began to dip behind the mountains on the horizon, darkness began to envelope everything. The alley was no longer a short-cut to his office, but rather a haven for the awakening of evil. Tori clutched at his arm as he tried to swallow down his fears. His heart thundered so loudly in his ears that he almost couldn't hear anything else at all. He looked at his phone on the dashboard, uncertain as to whether or not it was even ringing because the sounds of the roaring chainsaw and the sputtering lawnmower were caving his senses in. He looked at Tori. She seemed to be trying to say something to him, but he couldn't comprehend it. His nerves were jammed, and his mind had frozen.

Closer and closer the zombies came, and they were singing the most horrible song.

"Num-num. Num-Num. Num-num ..."

Henry always figured it was only a matter of time before the WHS had him devoured. Had they finally figured him out? Did they decipher Nate McDaniel's code he had received? *CPWWSZH.* It wouldn't have been that hard to figure out: World Humanitarian Society World Population Control. Maybe this was why they kept the zombies around, and now they didn't need him anymore, other than to be a rat in some kind of experiment. Henry rubbed his temples.

"I'm sorry, Tori! I'm sorry, this is my fault!"

Tori was just shaking her head, speechless in the shadow of death.

The recesses of his mind began to regain their purpose as a plethora of scenarios became a puzzle that needed solved inside his mind. They had sent him away, on a vacation, something that was an odd and unexpected surprise. That must have been the plan: to set the trap, plan his death, and get the entire incident recorded. *I bet they're watching right now.* He remembered going over the scan areas of all the security cameras that they had set up before he left. He wondered if he was going to be the first victim or one of the last. How many others had been snuffed out like this. *Rudy!*

He could hear Rudy's voice on the iPhone, but it was a recording, a stupid one.

"I'm sorry, I'm not here right now, I have leaped back in time to stop NBC from canceling Quantum Leap. Please leave a message after the beep, and I'll have my zombie secretary, Chi-Chi, send me the message."

WAHRAAA! WAHRAAA! WAHRAAA! Went the chainsaw.

"Num-num. Num-Num. Num-Num," went the zombies.

"Dammit, don't you have a shotgun in this thing!" Went Tori, honking the horn and screaming like a woman gone mad.

The car was surrounded now, and the darkening silhouettes of the haunting figures pressed along the doors, pinning them in. Henry couldn't even bear to look at their faces now. He wasn't going to give them the satisfaction. He closed his eyes and tried to block out the kaleidoscope of sounds so he could think.

Drive through them you idiot! he thought.

"Run them over you idiot!" Tori screamed as he slammed the car into gear and revved up the engine.

"Shit! He's gonna run us over!" one of the Zombies cried out, jumping out of the way.

Another zombie was knocking on the window saying, "Hey Henry, did you pick up my beer?" It was Rudy's voice.

The ice in Henry's veins turned into fire. He was furious.

"Get—Away—From— My—Car!

He wanted to kill them, every one of them as he took a special note of each and every one as they removed their zombie masks. All of the horrifying sounds were gone now, replaced with uproarious laughter.

"I gotta get back to the security office and see this on video. Man, Henry you should have seen your face!" a big black fella named Rod said.

Henry wanted to knock his block off, but he was pretty sure Rod could easily prevent that from happening, being an EFC fighter and all. Still, he managed to shake his trembling fist at Rod. The big man and a few others just laughed and walked away, hauling off their stuff.

"We'll make a copy and bring it to the party," a woman named Myrtle said as she limped away.

That's when Henry noticed something else, too. In his terror, he had momentarily forgotten about Tori, but she seemed to be doing fine, even with all of the tears in her eyes that were caused by all of her laughing.

"You—You were in on this?" he stammered.

She was still cackling, and he couldn't believe his ears.

"I'm sorry, Lover. It was Rudy's idea. I didn't figure you'd fall for it hook, line, and sinker."

"Hey, roll down your window, Bawk. It's cool, just a little prank. You know, a little 'welcome you back' party. I figured it'd get you back in the swing of things."

Henry felt like a fool as he rolled down the window, but it didn't stop him from grabbing Rudy by the coveralls and pulling his head in.

"Don't ever do that again," Henry warned as he shoved the man back outside.

Tori started rubbing his arm, still chuckling as she said, "Easy, Lover. I'll make it right. Man, you're still shaking."

"Get out."

"What?"

"Get out ... now."

"Fine then, you big baby," she said as she got out and slammed the door so hard it rocked the car on the springs. "I said I was sorry."

Henry began to drive off as he heard Rudy yell, "Hey, leave the beer, man!"

He stopped the car and tossed the twelve pack onto the ground with a crash.

"Ah, Henry, you didn't have to do that."

But Henry didn't hear him as he peeled away. He hadn't been back for five minutes and he already wanted to get away. *This place is sick.*

8

LOCATION UNKNOWN

THE NEXT TIME Nate McDaniel opened his eyes, he was looking into the face of a pretty black woman with a tiny mole on her chin. She seemed familiar for some reason, possibly the nurse he recalled hearing the first time he woke up. His nose and face were both aching now, and he was still starving as he reached up to rub his eyes. The woman's hands were warm and soft when she grabbed his, pushing them back down.

"Easy now, big fella. All that moving is what landed you face first on the floor, and after all the work that Doctor Z did to you, you almost screwed it up. Oooh ... he was furious," she said as she put a warm coffee mug to his lips.

"What is it?" Nate managed to ask.

"Just some warm milk and honey to start with. If you can keep this down, I'll give you something solid, but you have to be still ... cause if you misbehave I'll have to go."

Nate didn't like the way she said that as the horror of her leaving the last time flashed in his memory. She was the only link to what was going on. The warm porcelain felt good on his chin as he took a slurp. He never remembered milk or honey tasting so good.

"Ah ... you like that, don't you. Here, let me prop you up some more so you can finish it," she said, reaching underneath his bed and winding a crank. In a matter of seconds he was almost in a full upright sitting position, and she lifted the cup to his lips again.

He started to reach for the cup, but his arm felt like it weighed a ton, and her eyes glimmered a warning.

She said, "Go ahead, but you better not make a mess. I'm getting tired of cleaning up after you. It's hard to clean the crack of a big man like you, and Honey, let me tell you, you make a pretty big mess for someone that's hardly had anything to eat the past few months.

"Months?" he blurted, spitting up his milk.

Her chestnut eyes filled with fear as she waved her hand at him and said, "I didn't say that. Take care of me, and I'll take care of you." She wiped his chin off. "Trust me, you and me both don't want to upset Mr. Z. No, no, no. I've seen too many people disappear after they cross him. I'd take a room full of zombies over a room full of him." Nate didn't have anything to say. His sluggish mind was trolling through a whirlpool of thoughts. It was hard to concentrate, and his heavy body was still full of aches and pains. At least the ravenous pangs of hunger were beginning to subside, but he was still tortured with the thought ... *Where the Hell am I?*

She began snapping her fingers in his face.

"Hey, are we good?"

"Huh ... uh, yeah, perfectly."

She tucked the blankets underneath his legs and said as she eyed him, "Perfectly what?"

"Ma'am?"

"Do I look like and old woman to you?"

"Er ... no?" he said as he set the glass on a small table by the bedside.

"Do you think I'm pretty?"

"Well, yes."

"Good, then you can call me Rose."

"I couldn't have named you better myself," he said with a boyish smile.

"Hmmm ... I like that. Keep it up, big fella." She patted his thigh. "Now, you just stay right there while I go and warm you up some more milk and honey. And if you keep talking to me like that, I'll make you a special treat for later," she said with a wink.

He was smiling as he watched her walk away in her white scrubs that seemed to enhance her attractive features, but when she opened the door another wave of fear crashed over him. What if she didn't come back? Had she put something in his drink? *Please hurry back!* When the door closed, he broke out into a cold sweat as only he and the sound of the rattling air conditioner remained. *Where am I? I've got to get out of here.*

He laid his head back, closed his eyes, and rubbed his temples, trying to recall the last thing he remembered. A beautiful woman was dead in his bed. Drugs were everywhere. That evil little man in black and a barrel of a gun pointed in his face—No, put in his hand. There was a loud gun shot. *Oh my!* It was the last thing he remembered before he blacked out.

"Christy Backwater ...," he muttered. He felt an inner victory for just recalling her name. He took a deep breath as he allowed more of the fog to lift from his brain. He wiggled his toes underneath the stiff cotton sheets, and then he realized he had to pee. Over in the corner of the room was a wooden door with a metal handle, either a closet or a bathroom. The pressure in his groin began to burn, and he figured he had recently been attached to a catheter. *Great.* He started to sit all the way up, ignoring the aching fire that was building in his nose, when he heard the door handle moving. *Thank goodness!* He allowed himself to lean back and close his eyes. *Rose will take care of me.* The tension in his neck eased. *I just have to turn on the charm.*

The door closed.

He said, "I missed you, Rose. It seemed like you were gone forever. Now, I've been good and I didn't move a hair, so are you going to give me some more of your delicious milk and honey, Sweetie?"

"No," a man's deep voice belted out, "I was thinking I'd just punch you in the balls, Asshole."

Nate's entire body shuddered at the first syllable of the deep southern drawl from hell.

"I see you remember me," the man in black said. "What's that smell? *Sniff sniff.* Ah, did you just pee yourself? You did that the last time I came to see you, too. Well, I've smelled worse."

This can't be happening! This can't be happening!

But it was, and why wouldn't it be? After all, this was the last man he had seen before he woke up here. Of course, the man in black could only be the reason he survived, who else would have saved him. He assumed the WHS had something to do with it, even though he didn't really have the time or ability to give it much thought.

He closed his eyes again. *Go away! Go away!* He didn't want to open his eyes, but he did. The nightmare was real. Slowly, his lids opened, and there he was: wearing a black ball cap, mirrored glasses, a burning cigarette, a smirk, a black polo shirt with two bean-pole arms, and a sidearm. His lower lip jutted out below a row of yellow teeth and a thin moustache.

Something ignited inside of Nate McDaniel that gave new strength to his limbs.

The little man hitched his foot up on the bedrail as he dropped a load of tobacco in his bottom lip. "So, Butthole that saved the world, how have you been?"

"You killed Christy. You killed Jeanine! You're the asshole, not me!"

The man in black was unfazed, a cold face almost grinning like a fool. The man blew a ring of smoke his way and said, "Is that so?"

"Yeah ... yeah that's so!"

"So you want to fight me now, Lard Ass?"

"What? What is your problem?"

"I don't like you," the man said, flicking his ashes on his sheets.

"Well, I don't like you either! Dickhead!" As Nate pulled his legs over the side of the bed the door opened again, and a large vulture of a man stepped through. Nate froze. *Doctor Z?*

"Get back in that bed, Son," the man said with the authority of a policeman. "Walker, you better not be harassing the patient."

Nate slid his feet back under the sheets, all but forgetting the man in black. The doctor was wearing a white lab coat and jeans, and featured the long haunting face of a seventy-year-old. His droopy gray eyes guarded a calculating mind full of secrets. Nate wanted nothing to do with this man. Something about him wasn't right.

"Did you do this to my face?"

The doctor walked over and leaned over his face with a pen light, causing Nate to flinch.

"Be still," the doctor said, pushing Nate's eyelids back.

The doctor's breath was fresh with peppermint, and his touch seemed squeaky clean as he massaged his fingers all over Nate's face. Nate grimaced. The doctor took a whiff of air and said, "Did you just pee yourself?"

"No ... well, I guess I did when he came in," he said, sliding his eyes over to Walker.

"Hmph ... were you trying to pee on him?"

It was funny how the doctor said it, but he wasn't sure if he was joking or not.

"M-Maybe," Nate replied.

"Walker, get the nurse back in here to clean him up, will you?"

"Yeh Doc," Walker said as he slipped back outside the room.

The doctor sat down on the edge of Nate's bed and folded his long arms across his lap. He rubbed his cheeks and said, "I bet you're ready for some answers, aren't you Nate?"

"Oh, you think?" Nate said, but he held his tone in check. The doctor just didn't seem like someone he would want to upset.

"Okay, I changed your face. Major reconstructive surgery. It wasn't my idea, those were my orders."

Nate started to speak, but the doctor waved him off.

"Why? Well," he paused, "... we couldn't let you exist anymore. It was too dangerous."

Insanity. He was the man who saved the world, so why would anyone not want him to exist? *Harry!* The man had called him every day for years and was the last person he remembered talking to other than Christy. Was he behind this? Did Harry rescue him, or had it been someone else? His mouth was dry, and he had trouble trying to speak as he shifted in his bed. He could feel the spot of damp pee in his pajama pants begin to cool and stick to his leg. He shifted again.

"Don't worry about it, Nate. I'm a doctor; I'm used to it. Come to think of it, I think I nearly pissed myself the first time I met Walker. That gangly little redneck could scare the wings off a bird. He's like a snake made out of ice that slithers up your leg or down your spine. Be glad he's on our side." The strange doctor patted his leg. "I'll tell you a secret, though: I did piss myself the first time I saw zombies. It was early, and I was just starting my shift in the clinic, tending to a comely woman who had a chest cold." The doctor winked. "My kind of patient. Anyway, next thing I know there is all of this screaming and commotion, and I'm running out to see what in the world is going on. The entire lobby was filled with them, eating my patients and nurses. It looked like something you would see on Mutual of Omaha's Wild Kingdom, when the jackals eat a gazelle, except it wasn't natural ... just horrifying." The doctor dazed off, still rubbing his leg, until Nate reached over and brushed his hand aside.

"At least you made it out and lived long enough to screw up my face."

"True, thanks to my SUV. I ran over about twelve of them that day. I never would have survived without it, that's for sure. And to think my wife, my 3rd wife, had almost talked me into buying a Prius a week earlier. Hah! She didn't make it." The doctor stood back up and sauntered over to the door.

"Hey, where are you going? You haven't told me anything."

The man tapped his Rolex watch and said, "It's my lunch time. I'll let Walker catch you up. I think it's time you got better acquainted with him anyway. You two are going to be spending a lot more time together."

It took a moment for Nate to realize that he was all alone again. The air conditioner still rattled, and the air was stuffy. He shook his head, closed his eyes, and opened them again. He was starting to wonder if any of what just happened really happened at all. He reached over for the mug that he had drank from a few minutes earlier, but it was gone. He didn't remember Rose taking it. He shook his head. Was any of this real?

"NO! What's happening to me?" Only the stale air replied.

9

Institute, WV

Henry wasn't in much of a mood to party, but it was hard to ignore all the laughter he could hear roaring down the hall at his expense. If there were a door he would have closed it, but there wasn't. Instead, he was standing inside an open office layout that was filled with outdated desks and cubicles that were actually made out of wood and plaster. There was a large series of plate windows; something like a press box, overlooking another one of the campus's many courtyards that had his attention. He gazed below at a chain-link fence that enclosed an area that looked like an unkempt city park gone wild.

"BWAW-HA-HA-HA!"

It was Rod from the security team roaring with laughter down the hall.

"LOOK AT HIS FACE! LOOK AT HIS FACE! HENRY, YOU GOT TO SEE YOUR FACE! BWAW-HA-HA!"

Rod was so loud that it seemed like he was in the room with him, but he was almost over on the other side of the building. Myrtle was cackling like a hyena somewhere nearby, and about two or three others were guffawing among the throng. He blocked it out and focused on the morbid procession in the courtyard down below.

Six zombies were at work. One was pushing a lawnmower, and another was pulling a made-for-man plow as the other four stood and seemed to be watching in slack-jawed fascination. *Ridiculous.* Two men in black WHS camouflage suits armed with shot guns were in the area, while two other figures, in WHS issue lab-coats similar to his, were watching the zombies. They looked like figurines on a television screen from where Henry was standing. *What are they up to now?*

Henry headed over to the computer station and looked up into the large monitors. Two small joysticks were pinched in his fingertips as he nimbly panned in and out of the images in the courtyard. *What? Weege and Alice?*

"What are those two doing down there?" he muttered to himself.

"Dude, we have a skeleton crew. All of the complex big wigs are gone. Some big conference or something." It was Rudy. *Great.* Henry could hear him gulping down something, but he didn't bother to turn. "The director is still here, though, hiding somewhere in the other quadrant ..."

Henry was panning in on the zombies now. They didn't seem as horrifying in their forest green jumpers and white hardhats. If he didn't know any better, they'd pass for people, from a distance. He zoomed the camera in for a closer look at the zombies that weren't working at the moment. Each sagging gray face had a harness strapped around its mouth. To Henry, it looked more like a retainer, installed by a mad dentist. He could see that the metal brace was hooked inside the rows of rotting teeth, like a bit for a horse, and that it was tethered to a small battery pack that was strapped over the zombie's shoulders.

"... so, are you still mad? We said we were sorry, Henry. You're just so sensitive over the zombies. I mean, they aren't going anywhere, and we have them under control. Come on, have a beer and relax," Rudy said as he edged closer.

Henry didn't even realize Rudy was still talking. His mind was somewhere else. It seemed there was always a surprise of some sort, a breakthrough, whenever he returned. The last time, his brother had been back and intent on killing them all. They had also started testing the XT Formula, without his consent, for what reasons he would never understand. Now, he was certain, and he checked every camera from every angle, certain that something had been done. Something they didn't want to do while he was here, so they sent him away. This time, he was going to figure it out before the big surprise came.

"Hey Henry, quit pouting and get in here and watch this video!" Rod's hulking frame had entered the room and cast a shadow over the top of Henry and Rudy.

He felt obligated to turn around. The two men were just staring at him as if they were waiting for him to say something. Rudy looked like he hadn't shaved since the last time he left, and his Quantum Leap T-shirt had tightened around his belly. Rod on the other hand was a figure that would have made the local fans of John Henry proud. The big man was one of the few people that Henry enjoyed talking with, even though he did have a very boisterous standard of behavior.

"Okay, hold on."

He glanced back over at the screens and almost laughed as he watched the zombie pushing the lawnmower almost run over the little man from India, Weege.

"What's that fool doing now?" Rod sat as he stepped behind Henry.

He could see Weege screaming and smacking his hand on the remote control box. Alice had a similar one; much like the ones you would see at parks where folks would fly remote control airplanes. She was laughing under a pile of wavy black hair and over-sized glasses.

Rudy stuck his pudgy finger on the screen and said, "That tool is going to get himself mowed over by a zombie. It'll be the first death of its kind."

"BWAW-HA-HA-HA!" Rod roared, holding his gut as he did so.

Henry slapped Rudy's fingers away from the screen, saying, "Quit touching it. When are you ever going to learn?" he said as he walked away.

"Hey, where you going?" Rod asked.

"Down there," Henry replied.

"Why?" they both asked.

Henry turned around, pulled off his glasses, and said, "Because I'm going to figure out from them what you're not telling me. Unless you want to tell me now?"

Rod and Rudy looked at each other and then back at him. Something was wrong, but if they actually knew about it, it didn't show. Maybe he was paranoid, but everything in his body told him something was wrong. Where was everybody? This wasn't like the day care. This was a full blown operation with racks of shotguns still mounted along the walls. The ammo was in good supply. Even though the complex was run down and not perfectly ideal for their operations, it was still well equipped for any emergency.

"Bawk, we're all good here. It's not like the daycare, not like last time."

Rod got a funny look in his eye and said to Rudy, "What are you talking about? What day care?"

Henry glared at Rudy.

Rudy reached up and slapped Rod on his back and said, "Sorry, Dude; it's classified."

"Classified my ass. If it's something I should know, ya'll better tell me, because if something bad happens and I live to tell about it ... I'm coming after you."

"It's nothing to do with anything here, Rod." Henry said. "Just a bunch of crap we had to go through at our last WHS assignment. Audits and paperwork up to my chin—"

"Don't bullshit me, Henry. I don't like it. Now, I'm going back to the party," Rod said, punching Rudy in the arm as he went.

"OW! Geez, my arm's going numb."

"Good," Henry said as he walked away.

Bleep. Bleep. Bleep.

Henry pulled his phone out and checked the text message with a sigh.

COME TO OUR ROOM NOW. WE HAVE TO TALK.

It was from Tori. Henry knew that storm was coming, and it clearly had his name on it. Casting his head down as he pushed his way into the stairwell, he made his way down to their quarters with a dozen unanswered questions roving around in his mind. His interrogation of Weege and Alice would have to wait.

10

Washington, DC

"So, you're saying the WHS is trying to contract out the zombies to the federal government to handle grounds keeping services?" Don said, avidly watching the scene on Jack's computer.

The colorful display was a video of over a dozen scientists trying to control the harnesses on the heads of the zombies. One zombie was lurching inside of its stiff joints as it tried to chop up a bush. Obviously fascinated by it all, Jack tapped at the screen and brought up more images.

"Watch this, Uncle Don; isn't it amazing?"

"I'm watching," Don said, covering his mouth as he yawned.

Jack pointed at the screen and said, "See, this is Doctor Milano, and she has the remote control that manages the head and neck. The retainer in the zombie's mouth allows it to respond to signals. A heavy jolt of electricity sent from that battery pack into the bit in the zombie's mouth will cause it to turn left or right, or go forward."

"What? How on Earth can it do that? Are you sure the WHS has approved this? I mean, that seems pretty cruel, running electricity through a dead guy."

Jack smirked and said. "Frankenstein liked it."

"Ho-ho, funny, Boy, funny. And we know how that story ended. Not exactly how I envisioned spending my retirement days, but I see where you are going with this. Seriously though, how does the zombie know where to go? I mean, just because you run some electricity in it, you shouldn't be able to control where it goes. So does this have something to do with the XT Formula?"

"No, not the XT, but I'm glad you asked. Experiments ... Good old fashioned experiments. Once the zombies were subdued, we could strap them down on a table and run tests. As it turns out, there is still a living network of wires er ... well veins ... inside them. We just had to figure out how to manipulate them. Since the zombies are unconscious, so to speak, and they feel no pain, we were able to dig into their brains and rewire them."

Don refilled his coffee and brought it to his mouth as he said, "So, instead of killing them all, were are going spend millions of—"

"Billions."

"Okay ... Billions of dollars so that we can have 24-hour gardeners. Sheesh. So let me picture this: I'm driving to my office, and instead of seeing a human being watering the lawns and planting the flowers, I'm going to see a zombie that thrives off of a steady diet of Zombie Dew. I mean, people need jobs still, don't they? Won't this cost a lot more than just paying regular ole' people?"

Jack hadn't really given it much thought. He only cared about what was going on in his little world in the WHS and not so much what was going on elsewhere. So far as he was concerned, the flowers took care of themselves. It had never occurred to him that people actually did it.

"Well, I guess it's hard to find people to do those types of jobs," Jack replied. "Besides, the zombies can probably work at night, and no one will ever know that they are there. Right?"

Don huffed as he got up off the bench and started pacing around it.

"I like seeing people in the gardens. I like seeing people anywhere, especially since the Zombies almost ate all of us just a few years ago. Why would the WHS think that people want to see zombies doing what normal people could do? What else are you going to train them to do, be lifeguards?"

"Uncle Don, this is just an early phase. I mean, we really have a long way to go before we replace people."

Don's face began to whiten as his jaw dropped.

Whoops. "I mean, the zombies are only going to do so much. The WHS just wants to show the world that the zombies aren't such a big threat anymore."

Don shook his head.

"Oh, I see, they want to put on a good show. A *humanitarian* effort. Put the zombies on display in some type of zoo so the world can see what a positive impact they can have on society. Seriously Jack, is this what the WHS has you doing? I thought they were trying to cure them, not turn them into appliances."

Jack watched his uncle pace back and forth, his face creased in deep thought. He figured it was a generational thing. Jack had grown up with zombies all of his life. There had been video games, festivals, television shows, and movies aplenty even before the zombie outbreak occurred. When the zombies came, it wasn't a surprise for some, so much as it was an expectation. Jack even knew some people who had let the zombies take them, and he'd be lying to himself if he said he didn't wish to encounter one that was someone he once knew. Still, he was more than curious as to where the zombies came from. The more he played along with the WHS and the harder he worked trying get up the ladder, the sooner he was certain that he would get his answer one day.

His uncle sat back down beside him, shaking his head.

"Ah, I'm sorry. It's just that the more I know about what the WHS does, the less I understand what the WHS does. This is science fiction. Apocalyptic. I know history, and nothing, I say nothing compares to this," Don said, rapping his knuckle on the computer screen. "We are talking about the dead walking among the living, and we are trying to act like it's normal. I've been acting like it's normal. It's not normal."

"Big paychecks make a lot of things seem normal," Jack commented.

He could feel his uncle bristle at his side. Perhaps he had crossed the line. *What's going on with him?* His uncle's current rambling was uncharacteristic, and he couldn't ever remember seeing him pace before. Uncle Don was like a mighty dam that held back the flood waters in the most chaotic situations. Now the old man was carrying on like the world was going to end. It was making him a little bit nervous. Why would his uncle care if zombies pushed lawnmowers or not? So what.

"Money doesn't give you peace of mind, just temporary comfort. Jack, I'm in the position I'm in for one reason ... to protect the only thing that is dear to me ... my family. I'm ...," he grabbed Jack by the shoulder, "*We're* lucky ones, to still have our family. But there is no guarantee we'll still have them with us tomorrow."

Jack patted his uncle's hand and said, "Thanks. I appreciate all that you have done for me and Angie. But, really, what's the big deal about using some zombies for cleaning up around here? I mean, we can't just kill them."

His uncle began pulling at his chin hairs and started taking deep breaths through his nose as he watched a flock of ducks heading south. Jack had never been farther south than he was right now, but the stiff winds prompted some thoughts about sunny beaches in Florida.

Don spoke:

"Jack, with government, it always starts as something small; an alleged act of sympathy and compassion in the name of some noble cause. But when you plant an evil seed—and you water it—it grows like a weed and spreads as fast as a forest fire."

"How can a mindless thing be evil?"

Don almost gaped as his statement.

"Anything that takes a human life without fear or remorse is evil,

Jack, especially when it eats them. What did they teach you in college, anyway?"

"I'm just looking at it from the zombie's point of view."

Don laughed out loud as he held his hand to his head and said, "Their point of view? They don't have a point of view. They don't have a mind."

His uncle was becoming winded as he spoke, and he began waving his arm overhead. Jack's heart jumped in his chest.

"Uncle Don!? Uncle Don, are you alright? Is it a heart attack?"

Oliver, the bodyguard, was at his uncle's side and holding out a small plastic canister. Don grabbed the inhaler and sucked the mist into his mouth.

"Is there anything I can do?" Jack said as he scooted over closer. His own heart was thumping behind his temples. He had never seen his uncle in such bad shape before. His uncle took another puff and waved him off. Then a fit of coughing followed. "Do something, Oliver!"

"He's fine. It's just an asthma attack. Just give him a few seconds. What did you say to him, anyway?"

Jack wasn't paying Oliver any mind, though; his thoughts were only on his uncle.

"I'm fine," Don managed to croak out. "I'm okay; it happens. Thanks, Oliver," he said, handing the man back the inhaler.

"Shouldn't you keep that in your pocket?" Jack suggested.

"No," Don grinned, "I like to live dangerously. Now where were we? Oh I remember. Hey Oliver, Jack was just telling me about the zombies' point ... of ... view. Care to listen in?"

Oliver glared at Jack, shook his grim face in disgust, and walked away. Jack began to feel uneasy.

"Ah ... he probably wouldn't understand, seeing how zombies killed his wife and children. You see, it's going to be very hard to convince someone that a zombie had a good reason to do that."

Jack felt himself shrinking underneath the twinkling gaze of his uncle. He was only reiterating what he had learned from the zombie psychology courses he took in college and from the training he had received from the WHS. He felt like a fool at the moment as he looked away from his uncle.

"Sorry, Uncle Don. I didn't mean to upset you. Are you okay now?" he said, finding the courage to look back. *He's getting old, but I've got to be tougher than him. Shake it off. He's weak.*

"Of course, and so is Oliver. Now, honestly Jack, do you really think that zombies can actually do good things? I'm not talking about with our help. I'm talking about doing good things of their own free will?

"I suppose not. But, they're making progress. Maybe. The XT Formula is allowing us to do some amazing things."

Don huffed, coughed a little more, and took another drink of coffee.

"Well, this is what I've been waiting for. I've been hearing about things with the XT and —"

"You have? When?" Jack said, sounding disappointed.

"Easy now, I've only heard that you've been overseeing some breakthroughs. I don't know what they are because I wanted to hear it from you first. That's why we're here. Now show me what you got."

Jack was excited. It was something like the first time he took his favorite toy, Buzz Lightyear, to school for show and tell. His nimble fingers were quick at work when an image emerged. It was a view of a room full of zombies that panned back and forth in a quirky pattern. It seemed as if the person holding the camera wasn't really paying any attention to what they were doing. The picture on the screen slowly rolled to the left or right, up and down, back and forth. The slack-jawed faces of the zombies—men and women of all sizes and colors—filled the hangar-like room, at least a dozen of them, each just as fascinating to Jack as the other.

"This is making me nauseous. You need to fire that camera-man," Don said, taking another slurp of coffee.

"It's not a camera-man; it's a zombie," Jack said with a smile.

"What? Are you telling me the WHS is spending money to create zombie paparazzi?"

Jack bursted out laughing.

"No, no, Uncle Don. The zombie isn't holding the camera. The zombie is the camera. What you are looking at is the view through the eyes of a zombie."

All Jack heard was his uncle's coffee cup clattering on the pavement.

11

HE WAS OKAY, just humiliated, but it was worth it just to see another human being in the room with him again. Nate felt no shame as he sat in a wheel chair, naked, while Rose wiped him down and helped him change his clothes. His hard gaze remained fixed on Walker, who was leaning back in a corner with a lit cigarette dangling from his mouth.

"Aren't there any rules against that?" he said, nodding at Walker.

"Against what?" Walker replied.

Rose rolled her eyes as she stuffed his dirty clothes into a plastic bag and slung them in the corner.

"Smoking, Dickhead."

Walker sucked on his cigarette and laughed as he flicked is ashes in the floor.

Rose said, "Walker, quit that. You know I have to clean that up."

"Ah, I'm sorry Rose, I forgot," he said, rubbing the ashes into the tiled floor with his booted toe.

"I'd hate to see where you live," she said as she helped Nate back into his bed.

His stomach gave a loud growl.

"Oh, I'll be right back with your Milk and Honey," Rose said, pinching his cheek.

Nate sat in the bed and continued his glare into the mirrored eyes of the man in black. He hated the man. One of the most vivid memories he had was of the man taking out a shotgun and blowing away his fiancé Jeanine's face. Instinctively, his hand went to his chest.

"Feeling sentimental, are we?" Walker said, dangling from his hand the necklace that Jeanine had given Nate.

"Hey!"

Walker flung the necklace, hitting him square in the face. The gold metal was warm as he inspected it. It was his, the tiny figurine of Jesus on the cross with every detail in place that he remembered. He let out a relived sigh as he began to realize that he was alive, and everything around him was not some distorted dream. "I suppose I have you to thank for this," he said quietly.

"I suppose so," Walker said as he walked over and sat in the wheel chair.

"Not you, Douche Bag—Jesus!"

"Oh ..." Walker said as he began rolling back and forth in the wheel chair. "My uncle used to ride one of these. Pretty cool."

Nate put the cross back around his neck and shook his head. *Psychotic idiot!*

Rose made her way back into the room, sat along the edge of the bed, and handed Nate the warm cup of milk. It was the same one he remembered from earlier, marked in blue and gold lettering, with a small chip along the rim.

"When did you take this?"

"I didn't," Rose said, "he did."

A memory bulb popped inside Nate's mind as the image of Walker spitting in his favorite coffee cup came to life. He remembered now, like it was just seconds ago. He'd been drugged, paralyzed as a pair of strong hangs held him up like a doll. Walker sat before him, calling him names, mocking him and spitting tobacco juice in his mug. He drew his mug-filled hand back.

"Stop it, Nate; you don't want to do that," Rose warned.

"He's a murderer, Rose! He's a bastard murdering creep!"

Tears were rolling from his eyes and soaking into the wiry hairs of his beard. His arm was quaking, and the liquid began to spill onto the sheets. Rose took the mug from him and rubbed his face like he was a little boy.

"Nate," she said softly, "He's not a murderer, and I shouldn't be the one to tell you this," she cleared her throat as she gave a scornful look at Walker, "but he's the man who brought you to us. He saved your life."

Nate was looking into her eyes, searching for lies and deceit, but he only saw the truth. The truth was something that he had become obsessed with over the past couple of years, but if all of his time representing the WHS taught him anything, it was that truth was hard to find. He looked over at Walker. The man's head was cast down, elbows on his knees, blowing smoke rings at the floor.

"Nah, I don't believe it. He killed Christy. I saw him. Why would he kill Christy?" he said, searching Rose's face for an answer.

She looked over at the man in the wheel chair and cleared her throat.

Walker didn't respond.

She did it again.

"Okay Rose, you don't have to yell," Walker said as he stood back up and faced Nate. "You want to know why Christy was killed? Do you?"

"Yes!"

"Because she was about to kill you, Dumbass! There, I said it, Rose. Happy?"

"No, well yes, but you need to explain."

Nate's mind spun like a blender. Why in the world would Christy kill anyone? Why would anyone want to kill him? It had to be a lie.

"LIAR!" he screamed.

"I told you he was an idiot. How am I supposed to work with an idiot?"

Nate felt Rose take his hand in hers as she said, "I'll explain, Nate. Walker isn't much of a talker, it appears."

"I don't believe you or him!"

Nate was angry and confused. For all he knew, the WHS was behind all of this. Walker was behind all of this. Maybe Harry was on the other side of the door, waiting to surprise him. If he was alive, maybe Christy Backwater was, too. His eyes darted to every nook and cranny of the room, searching for cameras, lenses, anything. He had done the same thing back in his apartment. *This can't be true; it can't be happening.* But, in his heart he knew it was real.

"Nate, I'm going to explain. Just, look at me, and settle down. I have your back, remember."

He nodded. Exhausted, he slumped backward, closed his eyes, and said, "Go ahead. I guess it can't hurt too bad coming from you."

"First, let me tell you about Christy. She was going to kill you. She was a WHS spy of sorts, deep cover. She was going to make it look like an overdose. That's where all the drugs came from. But, being the slut she was, she decided to give you a couple of extra rides, for kicks I guess. You must have been pretty good if she let you live through the night."

A half-smile creased his face as the blood drained from it.

"If it weren't for that, you would've been dead. Our people tipped us off about the plan to have you killed, and we had been watching you. That's where Walker came in. He's the one that came in and took out Christy."

"What about the other guy, the big one that jerked me around like a doll?"

"Oh him. Don't worry about him; he's dead now," Rose said, matter-of-factly.

The room began to feel less like a hospital and more like a morgue as Nate stiffened inside his covers and took another sip of his drink. *I bet that guy's on the other side of the door, just waiting for them to call.*

"You know," Nate said, "it doesn't seem likely that Christy was a spy. I mean, I left her on the bed. She was out cold almost. I find it hard to believe that she was going to take a nap right before she was going to kill me."

"She wasn't asleep, Stupid," Walker said.

"How do you know that?"

"We were in the closet the whole time, you know, the one that was almost as big as your bedroom. It was a great hiding spot." Walker huffed some smoke. "And she was watching you the entire time after you left. Not a minute passed before she was on the move, but I could see the whites of her eyes as I popped her in the head."

Nate shuddered inside at the callousness of the statement. The man was nothing more than a stone cold killer with a heart of coal.

"You enjoy killing, don't you?"

"Only when it's evil."

The statement caught Nate off guard.

"Jeanine wasn't evil," he retorted.

"Jeanine was a zombie, Moron, remember? Did you lock her in that cell because you were scared she'd kiss you, or eat you? Besides … I had my orders."

Nate shook his head and said, "So, you wouldn't have killed her, otherwise?"

As Walker stepped away he said, "It had to be done … eventually."

Something in the man's voice had the sound of a hint of compassion. For all Nate knew, Walker might have had to put his own family down. Even Nate had done that himself, but he had managed to bury those thoughts over the years.

"So, why is my face changed?"

Rose explained to him that Walker and Leo slipped him out of his apartment building in the dark of the storm. It was a lucky thing because the WHS was moving in fast to secure the scene. It wasn't long before the news spread that Nate McDaniel had killed Christy Backwater in a murder suicide.

That's when he retched.

12

Institute, **WV**

HENRY SIGHED JUST OUTSIDE of his and Tori's room. His mind recalled the last time they had a big fight, a little over a week ago. Tori had been upset over her uncooked food in a restaurant and on the very cusp of making a scene when Henry suggested that she 'settle down.' And she had, sitting quietly in her chair, steaming within like a baked potato while he paid the bill. Every footstep he took back to the car left him feeling as if he was closing in on his own grave. She hadn't even given him time to open her door as she jerked it open and slammed it shut. He hated that. Calmly, he entered his vehicle and began to drive out of the parking lot. As soon as they had made their way up the interstate ramp, she had let him have it. Hurricane Tori had arrived with all of the fury of an Italian army. He could swear his ears had been ringing after the chewing out he had taken, but he'd survived.

I'm sorry. I'm sorry. I'm sorry.

Those words would have to be the first ones to cross his lips, as there weren't any flower shops available. He backed away from the door. *I've got more important things to do.* He could always claim he had overlooked her text, or that his phone's battery was dead. He looked at the peephole. *She probably hasn't seen me yet.* He began pacing back and forth in the dormitory hall that once was a thriving living space for many students. His uncle used to live just one floor above. He stopped in front of the door again, pushed his glasses back on his nose, and rubbed his sweaty hands on his slacks.

He hadn't given much thought to what he had done by throwing her out of the car, so to speak. But didn't he have every right to be angry? She was the one that should be begging for his forgiveness, not him, for getting mad, but Tori wasn't the most reasonable person. No, she was a passionate creature whose heart was always exposed. He started to creep away. *Everyone's going to hear her screaming at me.*

"Get in here, Henry! I already saw you through the peephole," she shouted from somewhere inside the room.

There was no turning back now.

"Now!"

As his hand closed around the knob, he took a deep breath and stepped inside. It was dim, but the smell of her sweet perfume hung heavy in the air. His eyes darted all over the room, but Tori was nowhere to be found. The bed was made, the closet doors were closed, and the desk was neat and tidy. Everything was in place, except him. He felt very out of place.

His body shuddered as he heard the sound of a commode flush. From behind the closed bathroom door, he heard her voice.

"Have a seat on the bed, Henry. I'll be out to deal with you in a second, even though you didn't show me the same courtesy, but took your time getting down here."

He sat down on the bed and waited for her to come out. Only a small lamp by the bed was lit, but the room seemed darker than normal somehow. *I'm sorry. I'm sorry. I'm sorry.* It was the only way to diffuse her ... he hoped.

When she emerged from the bathroom, every drop of blood rushed from one head to the other. She stood before him like a dark angel. Her thick locks of auburn hair cascaded down her back, and a long pair of silk black gloves reached up to her elbows. That was all she wore as her voluptuous body came closer to his. He could feel the heat begin to rise between them as she came closer. His mouth watered as his eyes met hers that were so seductive, hungry, and dark.

Her voice was bittersweet as she said, "Take your clothes off."

Henry obliged.

"Lie down on the bed, but leave your glasses on."

Henry was lying back on the pillow, allowing her smooth legs to slowly straddle him. He closed his eyes as she pushed herself down on top of him.

"What—"

"Ssssh ... I'll do the talking."

Then she said as the bed began to rock, "I'm sorry. I'm sorry. I'm sorry. I'm sorry ..."

A ride on the world's fastest roller coaster couldn't have been more exciting, but it would have lasted longer. Still, she was just as sweaty as he was when they both sagged onto the bed and held each other tight. Henry was still trying to catch his breath as he said, "I'm sorry, too."

13

NATE'S HEAD was swimming as he rinsed out his mouth with a bottle of water. *I'm a murderer?* Rose had been trying to explain to him that after the assassination attempt on him failed and he disappeared, the only option the WHS had was to discredit him. It made sense, but still, why did they want to have him killed? He was harmless. He did whatever it was they told him to do. He wiped his mouth off on the washcloth, tossed it to the floor, and said, "Okay Rose, tell me, why did they want to kill me?"

She squeezed his hand and began.

"Nate, almost a year ago you accidentally pried into one of the greatest conspiracies of all time. Before the WHS was formed, they were little more than some government program that did research on Paranormal activities: ghosts, vampires, werewolves, mummies, I mean all kinds of fantasy stuff. As it turns out, that was just a cover for another black operation that did biological and genetic research on people ... living people."

"That's great. Is that where I am now?" Nate asked.

"No, but I'll get to that. This agency created a biochemical weapon —highly contagious—that could be passed from saliva into the blood stream. This organization, along with our powerful leadership here in America—"

"Ah, I haven't been deported; that's good. I know I must be at most ten miles from a Taco Bell."

Rose rolled her eyes.

"As I was saying, America and the UN came up with a brilliant idea for population control. They created zombies and turned them loose in the most populated cities in the world. As you know, it spread like fire, wiping out over a billion people before you sent the Tweet that saved the world."

"Ah the good ole' days," Nate said with a laugh.

"You don't believe me, do you?" she said with a grim look on her face.

"Do you have any proof?"

"Not that I can show you."

"Then I don't believe you, Rose, so moving on, why did they want to wipe out the world? How did they plan on stopping the virus to begin with? Humor me."

Walker stepped into his view and said, "I'll take it from here, Rose. Okay, Turd, I'll tell you why."

Nate stared at the man, hypnotized by his words. Walker's voice drew him in like a moth to a flame as the deep Southern voice rolled from his tongue like honey. The brash tone was gone, replaced by something almost poetic, in a redneck sort of way.

"Okay," Nate said, without realizing he had even spoken.

"Seven billion people and with a billion more, the powers that be won't be able to control them. I mean what are you going to do when you run out of food, water, medicine and the like? The brilliance of the world leaders was to kill people rather than let nature take its course. Think about it. People are living longer and longer. There isn't so much famine or disease, and even the death counts from war are down. It's pretty much up to natural disasters to slow down the population."

Nate shrugged as he finished off his milk and honey, and said, "That was wonderful, Rose. Can I have some more?"

"I'll be right back," she said with a wink.

"But—?"

"Settle down. I won't shoot you, Idiot."

"Why do you keep insulting me?"

He could tell Walker's stone cold face wasn't going to give him an answer to that.

"Okay, Walker, so we have too many people, and they created zombies, and they want to create a new world with less people. Why not have a nuclear war?"

Walker put his booted foot up on the bed, rubbed the toes with the washcloth he'd discarded earlier, and said, "Because of all the fall-out. You can't spend time at the beach in Malibu if there's a nuclear winter ... Idiot."

Nate was smarter than this. As the veil of fog began to lift from his mind, he began trying to put things together. Greed, power, and control. Sure, he could buy that, but someone, somewhere was pulling all of the strings. The question was, who? The whole idea had to start somewhere.

"I'm not buying it. I just don't think anybody could pull it off. Not like you said, anyway."

"You honestly think this is all an accident? Now, think about that. The zombies showed up all over the world, not in just one place."

"So who did it, then? I mean, you say the WHS, but who is really behind the WHS, and where in the hell am I, anyway?"

"You are safe; that's all that matters," Rose said as she re-entered the room.

"What do you mean, I'm 'safe'? Safe from what, zombies? The WHS? Why did you do all this to me?"

Nate could see Rose's light brown eyes reflecting from Walker's mirrored glasses. There was a hint of fear in them. Walker shrugged and continued rubbing spit into his black leather boot.

"Nate, you are a hero."

"So I've been told, but now I'm a murderer, so I don't see how that helps my situation now."

She patted his hand and said, "Just take a second and think about why you are here, right now."

He tugged as the short hairs on his beard. It was a new sensation to him, playing with an unfamiliar face. *I've never had a beard before.*

"I'm here because you guys brought me here," he retorted.

"I told you he wasn't that smart. It took him seven seconds to answer that question," Walker said, switching to polish his other boot.

Nate rolled his eyes and said, "Do that somewhere else, G.I. Scarecrow!"

Walker let out a laugh.

Rose continued saying, "Why do you think we brought you here? We could have let you die. Walker and Leo, God rest his soul, risked their lives for you."

Nate's eyes narrowed.

"So you say."

"Why then, Nate?"

"Because I'm a hero?" he said, with a funny look of uncertainty.

"Bingo, Dickwad," Walker said as he resumed his place back in the wheel chair.

"Nate, you stopped one of the biggest conspiracies of all time and saved millions of lives, maybe billions. People love you. I love you. Walker loves you, even though he won't admit it."

"Hah," Nate said, noticing Walker's face was downcast toward the floor.

"Doctor Z loves you."

"The guy that hit you?"

Rose blanched.

"You saw that?" she asked, rubbing her cheek.

He nodded.

"Well, don't worry about that, Nate. I can take care of myself. He's just different. Just does a lot of things before he realizes he did them.

It's okay." She rubbed his ankle and said, "But it's awful sweet of you to care."

Her touch was as soothing as her honey and milk. He leaned back, and his eyes became heavy. He yawned. His face started to ache.

"Okay, everybody loves me, but what does that have to do with anything?"

"Nate, we're WHS insiders. Some of us work for them, but we don't like them. They're evil."

"Aren't all government entities?" he said.

"No, but this one is. Listen Nate, when some of our insiders figured out you were being terminated, we became furious. There's a lot of people that work in the WHS just because of you, because—"

"I know, they love me."

"They were loyal to you, and because of you they wanted to help the zombies, but they were misled. The WHS couldn't care less about the zombies. They only want to control the people with the zombies. Think about it: they've taken billions in estates to fund their projects. The zombies' property was seized in that bogus zombie bill that stated all properties belonging to the zombies will go towards the cure and prevention of zombies."

"It's bullshit," Walker added.

Rose nodded. "And now they went and pegged you for a murder. You want to know something, Nate?"

"Anything believable would be nice."

"Seventy-five out of one hundred people believe you are still alive and you didn't kill Christy Backwater."

"Now that, I believe ... sort of." The tightness in his chest began to subside. "Why?"

"Conspiracy. The bogus funeral they threw for you, closed coffin and all, didn't settle with the American public very well. Well, most of the world as a matter of fact."

"Except for the Euro-trash. The Norwegians—like me—were pretty sure you did it," Walker laughed as he lit another cigarette. "Most of Scandinavia, too."

"So you think of yourself as trash? Me, too."

Walker blew a smoke ring his way and said, "Well, at least I know who I am when I look in the mirror every day."

Nate looked back at Rose and said, "I thought you said he loved me?"

"Oh he does; he's just got a funny way of showing it."

Rose's voice was like a mother's, telling a child a bedtime story. He felt his energy begin to ebb.

Rose said, "I think you need more rest. We'll come back."

It was hard to say no. He didn't want to fight drowsiness, so he motioned for her to continue on.

"Okay, so you guys saved me. I still have a following, and some of you have risked your lives to protect me. But, now you've changed my face, I guess so you can hide me. I mean, wouldn't it make more sense to let me go out in public and debunk the entire thing?"

"You'd be dead," Walker added.

"True, but we could go viral and expose them."

"You'd be dead, Stupid, and we'd be dead, too."

"Oh," he said, scratching his beard. He was getting used to it. "So, you changed my face to hide me, so other people don't know me."

"Yes," Rose said.

"Kinda like protective custody, huh?"

"Exactly. But they are looking for you, Nate. One slip up and this operation is gone, and it's the only operation that can stop them."

"Stop them from doing what? They have all of the power and control it seems. What else are they going to do with the zombie funds?"

"It's going toward other things, more sinister things."

"We'll what could be more sinister than planning a worldwide genocide with zombies?"

He could feel Walker's mirrored eyes on him, and his blood turned to ice when she said:

"Another zombie outbreak."

14

INSTITUTE, WV

"HENRY, I swear, nothing has happened. Everything is just like it was when you left," Weege said.

Henry and Tori had both made their way down to the field where Weege and Alice were busy rounding up the docile zombies. His good friend from Dubai, Weege, was hiding something, they all were, except Tori. Weege's little eyes were darting back and forth between him and the zombies. Henry kept his eyes focused on the little man as he pressed the issue.

"Have you been here the whole time?" Henry asked.

Weege was fumbling with a remote control that seemed unusually big in his tiny little hands. A zombie woman, clad in the rehab suit and helmet, was slowly spinning around in a circle. Weege banged the remote with his hand and shook it. "Stupid thing."

"Hey, don't call them that," Alice said, glaring at Weege.

"I'm not talking about the zombie; I'm talking about the stupid remote. The zombie's not responding."

Henry had the willies as he stood among a half dozen zombies that walked aimlessly back and forth. One zombie, built like an anvil, pulled a plow the length of the field, only to stall inside the corner of the fence. A couple of others were scraping their boots over the ground, one dragging a rake and the other was biting the end of a small shovel. He felt Tori press her body closer along his side as another woman zombie with a face full of veins and long whispy hair was smacking her lips and groaning "num-num." His stomach recoiled. His hand fell to the .44 magnum revolver at his hip. He didn't take any chances these days. Not with full-grown zombies, anyway.

"Do you really think that's needed," Alice remarked in Henry's direction, with an attitude.

Here we go.

Turning towards her, he replied, "They're always needed when the zombies are around, Alice, and I think it would be wise if you and Weege exercised a bit more caution. Why aren't you two wearing your suits?"

Weege's eyes slid over to Alice and back to him before he turned away.

Alice huffed and said, "The director said we didn't have to wear them if we didn't want to, and I don't think we need to. We haven't ever had a zombie attack inside here, and besides, we have security that will handle any problems. We don't need any cowboys to come to the rescue."

Henry admired Alice's scientific knowledge and appealing looks, but her personality was in need of a major overhaul. He stepped between the two women when he felt Tori stiffen at his side. Tori was very open about her hatred of Alice, and Alice was just as open about her feelings for Tori. He'd better get the train on another course before Alice and Tori collided. He cleared his throat and tried to sound as pleasant as he could.

"Okay, Alice, if the director says you don't have to wear the protection, that is fine. You and Weege can do whatever you want to do with the zombie rehab. As a matter of fact, it looks like you have made an awful lot of progress here. Wow, six zombies, all working towards a common goal," he said, looking around. "This place has never looked better."

Six zombies, millions of dollars spent, and not a single tulip or trimmed tree to show for it. That's the WHS at work.

Alice folded her arms across her chest and said, "My zombies have come a long way, Henry. As a matter of fact, that's the reason I'm going to the WHS Conference—in Aruba—as our facility's top scientist this year, and not you."

"No, it's because you're screwing the director, you four-eyed slut!" Tori yelled.

"You're the one screwing everyone around here, not me," Alice said.

Henry grabbed Tori by the waist and pulled her back, saying, "Let it go."

"Ah, look, the cowboy rescuing the cow pie. How sweet."

Tori pulled away from Henry and pointed her finger in Alice's face.

"I'm going to make you pay, Alice! You zombie-hugger!"

Henry tried to grab Tori as she stormed away. *Best I let her go. Time to straighten this out.*

"Weege, quit screwing with the zombies and get over here," he ordered. "And don't you go anywhere either, Alice. We aren't finished. If you think you can act like a professional for ten minutes and answer my question, I'll be out of your hair in no time. Fair enough?"

Alice was looking at her nails, and Weege was looking at her. It was pretty clear to Henry that Weege was under the woman's spell. Almost every man within the complex was, except for himself. They knew something; Henry was certain of it. *Just wait for it. Weege will bite his nails, and Alice will blow the locks of hair from her eyes.*

"What's new, then? Something is, somewhere."

Neither one of them said anything, but the biting and the blowing began.

"Come on, I've been gone three weeks, and Rudy's already mentioned something classified ..."

Their eyes perked up.

"... so just tell me what it is. I mean, if we've had more zombies dumped on us, you need to let me know. I don't want any more surprises."

Other than the sound of the walking zombies and the words "num-num," the air was dead. Henry rubbed his hands together as a stiff breeze brought him a chill.

"Weege ... Alice, you don't want me to go over the director's head, do you?"

Alice's face darkened as Weege shook his head.

Director Smoot was in charge of the compound, but he answered to Executive Director Galloway, who was over all the compounds, and she didn't like his director. She also just happened to be a former boss of his, as well. She was the one who had bailed Henry, Rudy, Weege, and Tori out in the first place. She didn't like the director, and she didn't like her, either. If anyone knew about any changes in the compound, it would be Linda. She had made it perfectly clear, to him and to Director Smoot, that if he had any trouble all he had to do was call. Maybe now was the time to make that call.

Weege pulled at the hair on the top of his head and said, "Okay Henry, chill out. We got another zombie, that's all."

"Weege!" Alice shot the little man a glance, causing him to cringe.

"Just one?" Henry asked.

Alice looked at Weege and said, "Well, go ahead, Blabbermouth. He's gonna find out as soon as we let them out in the yard, anyway."

"Them?"

"Uh ... well, two actually. They're in the gymnasium. Um ... they're really cool, Henry. I think you're going to like them."

Alice walked away in disgust.

Weege had a fearful look in his eyes as she stormed out of the gate and across the campus. Henry watched her through the chain link fence as her eyes flitted his way and she started talking on her phone. It left him with a very uneasy feeling.

"Man, I'm glad you're back, Henry. It's been crazy around here. She's a freakin' lunatic."

"Settle down, and tell me what's going on. Two more zombies isn't something they need to keep a big secret about. We move zombies in and out all the time."

Weege scurried over the grounds and picked up the discarded remote controls.

"Here, let me help you with that," he said, grabbing one of the remotes. "Man, these things are heavy." He tossed it up in the air.

"Ah ... don't drop that, it's over a 100K!"

"Alice should have checked it back into inventory, then. She signed for it, didn't she?"

Weege had a look of shame on his face as he shook his head.

"Don't worry about it; just take me to see the new zombies."

Weege smiled.

"Hey Weege, you want us to go ahead and round up the zombies?" said one of the security guards who had just walked over from the other side of the courtyard.

The guard looked like an anvil inside his dark gray zombie-proof suit. The material wasn't as heavy as on the suits at the day cares, but the heavy fiber was virtually bite-proof. Henry's toe began to ache at the thought of when Louie had tried to bite his foot off back at the day care. He nodded at the man, who nodded in return. He wasn't very comfortable around the WHS Security team. They seemed to hold an unspoken grudge against the members of the science team. Their manners and professionalism never seemed sincere.

"Thanks, Jake!" Weege said, grabbing Henry's arm and pulling him along. "Let's lock these up in inventory on our way to the gym. I can't wait to show you our newest members. You're gonna love it."

Henry looked over his shoulder. The two men from the security team were shoving a lanky zombie down a chain-link corridor. It always reminded him of the lion cages they used at the circus. The zombies, as dumb as they were, tended to go straight in the direction you pointed them, especially when there was nowhere else to go. He always felt better after the zombies were locked up. He began to breathe easy again.

About fifteen minutes later, Henry followed Weege into the gymnasium. The air was stuffy, and it smelled like mold along with a faint smell of chlorine. Paint was peeling from the walls, and busted pieces of dropped ceiling were scattered everywhere. The fluorescent lights were out in most of the places that led them down one hallway to the other. Henry couldn't believe it was the same place where he had played basketball only a few years ago. He kicked a piece of broken tile, and it echoed down the hall.

"Why aren't they with the rest of the zombies?"

"They're getting fitted."

"How long have they been here?"

"They got here nine days ago," Weege replied as he turned on a light switch.

The lights clicked on to reveal a small basketball court and several rows of pull-out bleachers. Henry thought of all the times he had tried to dunk on those rims, and he swore they were an inch too high.

"It doesn't take that long to put on the head harness. Why are they still here?"

"They needed special fitting, and the director wanted them separated from the others. He thinks they're special."

Nothing was special about zombies; they had all proved that time and time again. *Must be a relative.*

"Is anyone back here with them?"

"Nope, they're under lock up, and the cameras keep tabs on their whereabouts. You know they're all tracked, anyway. Don't be so paranoid."

"How can you not be? They almost took us out, Weege, and that was just one kid. What's going to happen if the adults go wild?"

"Henry, we have armed men everywhere. Plus, the zombies are all doped up on Zombie Dew, and there hasn't been a zombie attack in years. Chill out. I know you just got back, but you'll get used to it."

He shook his head. Nothing was ever going to make him feel comfortable around the zombies. It just wasn't natural. The XT Formula had given him a glimmer of hope, back at the daycare, and the WHS had led him to believe that he would be a part of the solution again, when they asked him to sign the 5-year contract with them. He was wrong to believe, and the XT Formula, for all of his inquires, had slipped from his grasp. His stepfather Stan was gone, and the legacy with him. Thinking about all of his family that had perished left him empty inside.

He stuck his hands inside his lab-coat pockets and said, "Let's get this over with."

Toward the back of the gymnasium was a padded floor filled with weights and exercise equipment that had been modified for testing the strengths and limitations of the zombies. The crew would harness the zombie's arms and legs to the equipment with thick leather straps and observe them trying to push or pull free. Most of the time, the docile creature would just sit there hour after hour, gazing at nothing, but when the hunger came, the weights would begin to jerk up and down. The zombies were stronger than the average man, with the raw power of an athlete but unhindered by fatigue. He remembered one zombie pulling an entire machine over on top of itself and laughing.

Weege's ferret face was lit up with excitement.

"Here we are."

They were standing in front of a window that was as black as night on the other side. Henry knew that the glass was at least three inches thick, but he still felt like it was going to break at any moment. A heavy door with a magnetic security lock glowed with a tiny red light. It didn't give him any comfort. He began to thirst as he wiped the steamed-up lenses of his glasses on his coat and put them back on.

"Okay, let's see it."

Flick

His heart stopped as he stumbled back. It was the two biggest zombies he had ever seen, and they looked hungry. Every fiber of his being told him to run, but his legs wouldn't move. *This is insane!*

15

WASHINGTON, DC

DON BAKER HAD SEEN many mind-blowing things before in his life, but nothing compared to this. His stomach was turning into knots as his nephew, Jack, explained what he was watching. All of the triumphs of mankind, from the automobile to the nuclear bomb to the Internet, seemed minute in comparison to what he was beholding. The zombie point of view was a disturbing thing, but it fascinated him as nothing ever had before. He was hunched over on the bench as Jack explained.

"It's amazing, what we have learned over the past several months, Don. The XT Serum worked miracles of sorts. The brain function of the zombies went from five percent to just around twenty. The entire nervous system was at our disposal. We could explore the brain from the very top, and down to the bottom of the spine. Since the zombies don't feel, we could do just about anything."

"But, if their nerves are firing, won't they feel pain?" Don inquired.

"Nope. No emotions, either. They're like robots made of flesh and bone. Here, let me have your screen."

"Couldn't you have just used little cameras like our military uses? I'm sure it would have been easier and cost much less."

"We can do both. As a matter of fact, those cameras are back-up, seeing as how the zombie eyes are still in an experimental phase. But it's amazing; the zombie's lens is so superior to the smaller camera lenses. We were even able to make a breakthrough on using the eyes to help guide them. It's sweet!"

The excitement in Jack's voice disturbed Don. The younger man over forty years his junior, seemed to have become obsessed with the amazing world of zombies. Don was carrying enough guilt already for having taken part in the outbreak, and now he had drawn his nephew into some psychotic-thriller world that kept morphing into something else. Don never would have believed the zombies could have wrought the amount of damage they had. It was supposed to be just another big government scare tactic, a little something to keep the world in line. He had been certain that even after the intervention of Nate McDaniel, the plug would be pulled and the world would churn back to normal. But now it was clear the WHS had other plans. And the worst thing was they were clearly plans that he wasn't being included in.

Jack handed him back his computer, saying, "Just watch the screen, Uncle Don."

Don's chin dipped down. On the screen, he could see a cavernous room, something like an aircraft hangar, and it looked like he was jogging. The motion was jerky, but realistic.

"How does this work?"

"Hold on," Jack said as he typed messages. "Ah ... the zombie's entire neural network is wired up to people in a simulator, much like they use in video games. We can control them and have them pick up things, run, and jump. But it's not perfected yet. The optic nerve behind the eye has been wired to send signals back to our systems. Some guy said he got the idea from a movie called 'Inner Space'. Turns out it was a good one. It works.

"I guess they don't blink, either?"

"Huh, never thought about that, but I guess not. Here, watch this. I'm going to send them a message to have the zombie jump."

Don held the screen up to his nose. The picture lifted up, came down and headed for the ground. The screen went black. "What happened?"

"I think it fell. It happens; just wait."

Slowly, the concrete floor came into view, and the image panned back to normal.

"See?" Jack said, "now watch this."

The zombie's hands were smacking together, faster, then slower.

"Can they hear, too?" Don asked.

"No, but that's not a problem. We have a microphone in their suit. Just give it a second."

The claps were more like dull smacks, but audible. Another annoying sound filtered into his ears as well.

"Numma-Numma. Numma-Numma."

Don muted the sound. He couldn't take it anymore. All of the senseless deaths over the world had taken a toll on him. He was too old to get involved with another deranged war for the control of mankind, but he was in too deep. Like a good soldier, he had to play along, not just for his sake, but for the sake of what was left of his own family. Maybe even the sake of humanity, itself. Secretly, he wished someone, somewhere, could put an end to all of the madness. He always had hopes that Nate McDaniel would be the one. After all, he had been warning the man for years, but now he was dead. Oliver returned beside the bench and was holding his overcoat. He yawned as he stood up and slipped it on.

"That's fascinating, Jack. They'll make excellent gardeners," he said

"And soldiers."

"What?"

Jack's voice sounded sinister when he said, "Sit back down, Uncle Don, and I'll show you."

Don reached for his computer and sat back down. He flipped open the cover and blanched.

The picture was inside another warehouse that was filled with over a dozen figures. They all were adorned in combat boots, dark green and black jump suits. A dark metal glinted on their faces.

"Are those zombies or men?"

"Zombies."

"What's on their faces? Are those masks?"

Jack snickered.

"This was one of my brain storms. It's a titanium mask and skull cap I designed. I got the idea from something I saw on Warcraft. Pretty badass, huh."

It was horrifying. The zombies looked like metal skulls with snapping mouths, like gladiators raised from the dead. The zombies moved fast as they stumbled and climbed over top of one another. Don pulled his coat tighter over his chest. The chill breeze of the early evening was suddenly cold.

"Why do they need those helmets?"

"So if they get shot in the head they won't die."

Don grabbed his nephew and said, "Who's going to be shooting at them?"

"The people in the complex."

"What complex?"

"Institute, West Virginia."

16

ANOTHER ZOMBIE OUTBREAK?

Nate rubbed his eyes. It was the last thing he remembered Rose saying before he drifted off to sleep as exhaustion took over his weakened body. He didn't want to wake up, though; he still just wanted to sleep ... he felt comfortable. His vision was blurred as he rolled his head to the left and to the right and filled his nose with the musty air. He smacked his lips to keep his tongue from probing the inside of his filmy mouth.

What is that?

He heard a crunching sound, and his mouth began to water. The scent of tortilla shells, cooked beef, and taco sauce filled his nose. His eyes snapped open as he lurched up.

Walker was sitting in the wheel chair, stuffing a hard-shell taco into his mouth. Rose was wiping her mouth with a napkin at his side. His stomach made a sound like a croaking bullfrog. She smiled.

"I told you if you were good I'd give you a treat."

She handed him the Taco Bell box. A new Ferrari couldn't have replaced the treasure he now held inside his hands. Licking his lips, he looked at her.

"Go ahead, just don't eat too fast. And easy on the Dew," she said, tapping the large cup on his food tray.

He didn't hear anything she said. He just ate and ate and ate. *If you can die happy, then take me now, Lord.* For the first time in what seemed to be forever, he felt like a complete human again. He thought of his condo in DC: his toys, games, and DVD's. He assumed all of that was gone, but a small apartment in the middle of nowhere would be just fine, if he could just figure out what he had to do to get out of wherever he was.

Walker wadded up his paper wrappers and tossed them into a metal waste basket. The man sucked the remaining fluid from his cup and it sounded like Nate's brain was being sucked out.

"Do you mind? I think it's empty."

Buu-urp! Walker responded as he lit up another cigarette.

Nate wiped his mouth and asked, "So, when is the doctor coming back? Surely he'll want to do more mutilations to me." He rubbed his face. It felt tight, but it didn't ache as much as before. He sat up on the edge of the bed, fully expecting Rose to push him back down, but was greeted with her supporting arms instead.

"Feeling spry, I see," she said, "Go ahead, see what you can do."

He looked at the gritty floor.

"I hope you didn't do the surgery in here."

"I'll get you some slippers," Rose said.

Walker let out a wicked snicker. Nate watched the man pull off his glasses and wipe the mirrored lenses. Their eyes locked as Walker turned into his stare. Nate's impression of Walker took a sudden turn.

"What're you staring at?" the man said as he put his glasses back on. "What's the matter, Big Mouth, cat got yer tongue?"

Nate's tongue clove to the roof of his mouth. He shook his head.

"I just ... I just thought you were older."

The glimpse Nate just had of the man's eyes told a different story from the cold-blooded soldier the man appeared to be. The man's eyes were soft and round, his skin rosy around the cheeks. The grizzled chin, moustache, and sideburns had thrown him off. Walker didn't look more than thirty years old at the most.

"Well, I thought you were smarter," Walker replied.

"How old are you?"

"I'm old enough."

Nate laughed. He figured that killing zombies for a living and smoking non-filtered cigarettes was bound to age a man a decade or two. Something cold slivered down his spine. He never really got a good look at himself. The floor was cold on his feet as he headed for the mirror.

"Don't you need your slippers?"

"Don't you need to graduate from high school?"

Nate was already at the mirror when Rose returned.

She tossed the slippers on the bed and said, "I see you still haven't found your patience."

"Huh?"

But he wasn't really paying any attention. The eyes and hair were the only things that seemed familiar. His nose was smaller, and his chin bigger. His head slowly turned from side to side. He ran his hand along the back of his head. His ears were smaller, and his long earlobes were almost gone. *Is it still me? Maybe without the beard.*

"No razors here, Nate. It's best you kept the beard for now," Rose said. "I like it though, the new chin, too. Your old chin made you look fat ... at least on TV it did." She patted him on the back. "Don't worry: you're still handsome."

"I still think Doc should have turned him into a woman. No one's gonna pay any attention to an ugly girl," Walker commented.

Nate grimaced as he stared into the mirror. It was going to take some getting used to, that much was for sure. *Yep, it could have been worse.* His legs began to tremble, and his head became woozy. Rose rushed to his side and guided him back to the bed.

"Take it easy," she said.

"I'm ... I'm okay." He cleared his throat.

"Rose, I'm grateful that you guys saved me because you felt obligated, but there has to be more to it than that. Is there?" he said in a pleading voice.

She placed a cold compress on the back of his neck and said, "There is."

"Wow, I wasn't expecting that. A direct answer on my first try. Okay then, what is the other reason, or reasons rather, I am here?"

The door opened, and Doctor Z entered with a clipboard in his hands.

"How are you feeling Mr. McDaniel ... er, rather ... Nate?"

"Better."

The doctor made himself comfortable on his bed.

"Well, your vitals are good. Do you have any questions?"

"I was just asking why I was *really* here. I mean, rather than the fact that I'm an awesome hero. I'm of the impression there's much more behind my reconstruction than that." His eyes slid over to Rose. "Oh, and the fact that I'm a murderer."

Rose gasped when the doctor grabbed her by the collar and jerked her face to his.

"What did you say, woman?"

"Hey! Let go of her," Nate cried.

"Nothing you didn't already discuss, Doctor," she managed to say.

Nate didn't notice the smile in her eyes.

"Hmm. Hmm. Hmm," the doctor laughed as he let her go. "Oh Rose, how you stir the blood in me. Will you be a dear and get me some coffee?"

"Certainly, Doctor."

He slapped her on the rump with his clipboard.

"She loves me. I can see it in her eyes. Can't you?" The doctor's eyes were still following her from the room.

What? This weirdo reconstructed my face.

"So, I see you enjoy *hitting on women?*" Nate said.

"Hmmm—Oh, now don't be silly. I could never harm that endearing woman."

Nate wasn't convinced, but he was getting aggravated.

"Okay, on with it. I'm a hero, I'm a murderer, and I am here because why? The real reason."

Walker made his way over to the edge of the bed.

The doctor spoke matter-of-factly.

"Nate, you are the man that saved the world. We all know that, don't we Walker?"

"Yes sir."

"Now, what we need to find out is: 'Who is the man that wants to destroy the world?'"

Nate was at a loss.

"Why ask me? I don't know. If anyone knows I'd figure it would be you guys."

The doctor tucked his hands under his arms and said, "The WHS has many layers, like an onion or the earth, so to speak. We've only been exposed to the middle, which is deep, but not deep enough. What we haven't been able to do is penetrate the core. That's where the answers are. Now, every once in a while something slips out, and if we are lucky, like we were with you, we can learn more about the enemy. But since you disappeared from their radar, the seal around the core has become tighter." He clenched his fist in front of his face.

"Well, I don't think I can help you. I'm pretty sure I know less than you do."

"I'm pretty sure that you know more than you think you do. The WHS has been squabbling since you disappeared. One faction is blaming the other. Our little rescue has splintered parts of the operation, and many of their operations have gone deeper. I think that you've been exposed to more than you realize, Nate. We think you might even know who is in charge of all of this. You might even be able to point them out."

"That's ridiculous."

"So was the thought of Christy Backwater assassinating you. So are zombies. Nate, what can you tell me about a man named Harry?"

The hairs on the nape of his neck stood up.

17

Institute, WV

HENRY STEPPED backward and stumbled to the ground. Horror. Terror. Fear. Instinctively, his hand clutched at his chest. His breathing was heavy. His heart pounded. *Madness!*

"Henry? Henry! Are you okay?" Weege said. "You look like you're having a heart attack. They're all locked up, Henry. They can't hurt us. They're cool!"

The word 'cool' wasn't something he associated with the zombie vocabulary. He sat on the ground, agape. The silent giants behind the thick glass looked like fiends in an aquarium. Their faces were long and terrifying as they meandered with jagged gaits within the small cell. Their heads would have touched the ceiling tiles if they weren't leaning over. Brain eating monsters on stilts was what Henry saw, and his heart recoiled in his chest.

"Weege! Where did they come from?"

"I don't know. The director got them somehow."

Weege's eyes sparkled like lanterns as he tapped on the glass and waved at them.

"Are those basketball uniforms?" Henry asked, rising to his feet. His legs were weak, but the initial shock had subsided.

"Yep."

He edged closer to the glass, looking up at the men. He whirled toward Weege and said, "That's 'Rifle' Rick Braxton and Sam 'The Slam' Jones!"

"In person." Henry tried to rub his eyes, but his glasses got in the way. He loved the NBA, and *Rifle* and *Slam* were well known all-stars. He felt compelled to ask them for autographs. His step-dad Stan would have loved that. A few moments passed as he and Weege stared at the roaming zombies with awe. *This is absurd.*

"So let me guess: we're starting a zombie basketball league now? Are we going to set up a match against the Harlem Globetrotters? I can't imagine what our infamous Director Smoot has in mind Weege, can you?"

"Take it easy Henry. They just got here, and no one's mentioned a basketball team ... yet." Weege smiled.

Henry could see the wheels turning in the little man's head. Weege and Rudy had become more like pets than men since they'd all been forced into service at the WHS rehab facility. Henry'd previously had control over them, but now he was pretty sure his alliance with them wasn't as strong as before. He'd learned it was best to bite his tongue when discussing serious matters with them anymore.

He noticed Weege was texting.

"Hey, what are you doing?"

"Sending a text."

"About what and to who?"

Weege's thumbs stopped. He put the phone inside his lab coat pocket.

"No one, it can wait."

Little rat.

Ring –Ring!

It was Henry's cell phone.

"Hey."

Rudy was on the other line.

"HENRY! Get up here now! I think we have a zombie breach!"

"What? Where?"

"Avoid Quadrant 14. Where are you, anyway?"

"The gym. Hey—"

"Is Weege showing you Slam and Rifle?"

"Yes but—"

"Quit fooling around, Henry, and get up here!"

"Hey, is Tori with—"

The line went dead.

"What is it, Henry?" Weege said.

"Rudy says we have a zombie breach. Quadrant 14. Let's get to security."

"Ah ... I'm sure it's nothing," Weege turned off the lights inside the zombie room. "Night fellas. Man, I can't believe we have NBA all-stars working with us now!"

Henry was dialing Tori as he rushed back toward security. Weege's footsteps were echoing from behind. Fear rose up inside of him despite his efforts to reassure himself that there was more than enough security to take care of things. Then he remembered they weren't fully staffed because of the zombie conference. He had to hurry back to security to make sure all of the protocols had been followed to secure the zombies.

"Hello Henry," Tori said on the other line.

A wave of relief washed over him.

"Are you with Rudy?"

"Yes, I'm safe. You need to hurry back, Henry. These jackholes don't know what they're doing. Rudy's going bonkers."

"Don't worry, I'm almost back to the doors. Have you seen any zombies on the screen?

"No, they won't let me in there. You need to get back and straighten this out. They're talking about a total lockdown."

Henry scanned his card, made his way into the building, and headed inside the elevator.

"I'm on my way up."

He lost the signal as the doors closed.

"I'm sure it's nothing, Henry. Rudy's probably half in the bag. You know how spooky this place gets at night. It's like a ghost town."

True. The complex was like a graveyard for buildings more than anything else. There was a network of dorms and classrooms, a small hospital, a cafeteria, a church chapel, and even a cemetery. The nearby river was notorious for rolling in fog thicker than soup most of the time, too. It all but negated the security cameras outdoors on some days.

The elevator chimed on the 3rd floor, and Henry and Weege were greeted by Tori.

"That fool is freaking me out. Get in there!"

Henry made his way back to the observation room only to be greeted by two sealed metal doors. He scanned his card. It flared green and the doors parted open.

"Hey!" Rudy shouted. "Get Tori and Weege out of here. They aren't authorized, Henry!"

Rudy's eyes were bloodshot, and his clothes and hair were a mess. Rod was nodding his head, and another guard, Myrtle, had her eyes intently on the wall of monitors. He pushed past Rudy, noting the heavy scent of alcohol on his breath.

"Hey Henry, I'm warning you," Rudy said.

Henry faced the man and said, "You're warning me! I'm warning you, Rudy. You're drunk. One more word and I'll have you locked up."

"That's insubordination," Rudy slurred.

"Everybody, who thinks Rudy isn't fit for duty?"

Everyone raised their hands.

Rudy sat down, slumped on the desk, and mumbled something unintelligible.

"Look! Look here, everyone!" Myrtle shouted and pointed at a screen.

Quadrant 14 was a row of cinder-block warehouses in the WHS lab district. It was a separate operation from their rehab facilities. Top secret times ten. So far as Henry knew, it was just storage. Trucks came in and out every so often, but nothing ever appeared to be out of the ordinary.

A shadowy figure was moving along those grounds. Tori gasped.

"Rod, did you dispatch a team?"

"Yep. A fire team's going in to check it out. Got them on the head phones now."

"Can you put them on speaker?"

Rod looked over at Rudy, who was snoring.

"Looks like you're in charge. A good thing, too. I was about to punch a hole through him."

Rod nodded at Myrtle.

The audio came, and Henry could hear heavy breathing. On one screen he could make out a shadowy figure roaming through incoming fog, and on another he could see three members of a security fire team closing in. Tori was clutching at his back as they all gawped at the screen.

Henry could hear the fire team leader over the speakers.

We got him in our sights. What in the world is that?

The security team had flanked the strange figure in front of one large garage door. Henry could make out all the images on a single screen now. The security lights were doing a good job of cutting through the fog.

"What is that?" Rod said. "Is that a zombie or a man?"

Henry couldn't tell. Its movements were stiff and quick. He could make out a mask of some sort on its head, more like a man. It had on a dark jump suit of some sort.

Halt! Put your hands on you head. This is WHS Security, and we have authorization to use deadly force.

Rod spoke into his radio. "Don't hesitate, Jim. If that thing doesn't stand down, disable it. Don't kill. Just take out the legs."

Roger that, Rod.

"Myrtle, can you zoom the camera in any closer?" Henry asked.

"That's all I can do. There should be another WHS Security team from the warehouse quadrant en route. It's their area. All of our zombies are locked up and accounted for. Maybe it's an intruder."

"I've never seen a man move like that. It's a zombie," Henry said.

He wiped his forehead with his sleeve. *This can't be happening.* He could feel the tension building in the room as they all stood mesmerized by the screen. First giant zombies and now this.

"Has anyone notified the director?"

"Rudy did." Myrtle said.

"And?" Henry inquired.

Rod and Myrtle shrugged.

On the monitor, the security team, clad in full zombie gear, had fanned out in front of the zombie.

"Rod, it's a zombie. It has some kind of skull cap on. Looks like a gladiator helmet or something. It's just acting like a typical walker. Is this some kind of prank or something? It better not be. It's pretty screwed up, and I'm gonna bust someone's ass if it is."

Many eyes fell on Rudy's snoring form.

"Hold on! It's having a spasm of some sort."

Henry watched the zombie arc up like it was shot in the back. It rushed the men. Tori and Weege screamed.

BLAM! BLAM! BLAM!

Henry covered his ears.

Rod ripped off his headset. "Dammit!"

The shotgun blasts tore into the zombie, knocking it from its feet. It was difficult to see underneath the blanket of fog.

"Did you see that? Geez, I never seen a zombie move that fast before. Wooo-Weeee! It's dead as a rock now."

There was a pause.

"Jim, you sure it was a zombie? Are you there?"

As he watched the screen, he could see the men huddle around something. Two of them jumped back, bringing another frightened gasp through the room.

"Yep, it's still moving. Not much left of it, but it's moving. Creepy. The jaws are still snapping like a turtle. Uh ... wait a second. Hey, the garage is opening. Looks like the cavalry's coming ... just a little late is all."

A small wave of zombies burst forth and crashed into the security team.

HELP! GET SOME HELP! HEL ULP—

The sound died. They all stared in horror as the zombies pinned the men under their weight and tore into them with fervor. Henry's worst nightmare had come true. The zombies had been turned loose on them.

"Initiate the lockdown!" He cried. "Secure all floors!"

"No Henry, let's get out of here while there is still time. I don't want to be locked up in here with them," Weege cried.

"We'll be fine in here."

An alarm sounded.

"Just lock this building down. Rod, tell your men to find a bunker and lock down. We don't know what we're dealing with. Weege and Tori, wake up Rudy."

The alarm stopped.

"How'd that happen? Who did that?" he said.

He dialed the director on the desk phone and let it ring on speaker.

"Just let it ring."

The zombies were on the move, like a wave of rioting men.

Chooooooom.

The screens winked out. The lights turned black. The ringing phone went dead.

They stood in the silence of the insecure building with no idea what to do next.

"We're gonna die," Weege said.

18

WASHINGTON, DC

JACK WATCHED IN AWE. The men of the security team couldn't withhold the fear that grew in their faces as the zombie rushed forward. It was almost like playing a video game, except the shotgun blasts and screams were so much more real. Unable to hide his fascination, he giggled as the men fought against the hoard only to be barreled over and pushed down into the fog. They couldn't have made it any better in Hollywood. The zombies were on the men like a pack of jackals, tearing off the suits and sinking their faces into the men. The close view of the zombie eyes was a little too close as the image thrashed and jerked like it was on a roller coaster.

"Good Lord, Jack," Don exclaimed, "What are you doing? Those are our people!"

Jack looked over at the distraught features of his uncle and noticed the man had aged another ten years.

"Ah, you know what you always taught me Uncle Don: Don't mess with the WHS. I've got my orders, and I have no choice but to run this op. It's for the greater good. You always told me that ... remember?"

His wide-eyed uncle looked like he had swallowed a toad. For decades, Jack had thought his uncle was as tough as iron and cunning as a shark. Now his uncle had changed. Don looked old, haggard, and weak. The time had come for a strong young man to pick up the banner and lead the charge to bring order back to humanity. No mercy. Just results. And if turning loose a wild pack of zombies on a bunch of men and women was what they wanted, then that was what they were going to get. A show.

Don was pleading:

"Jack, there comes a time in your life that you're going to make choices that you're going to regret. This will be one of them. I didn't bring you in to become a bigger part of this. I brought you in to protect you. These people that are dying have families. Just like me and you."

"I know that. But, we can't all have the life that we want. I consider myself grateful this is happening to them and not me. Besides, they're all loners."

"They're human beings!"

"They're expendable. Just like that other billion you helped wipe out, so what's a dozen or so more? Isn't that what you wanted to begin with?"

Don was silent.

"That's what I thought. Now keep your eye on the screen, Uncle Don. And just so you know, this isn't my first rodeo," Jack said with a wink. "I'm having them cut the power to everything except the security wall and the interior fence. If anything tries to climb that fence, man or zombie, they'll be fried chicken. The security servers have all been switched under our control. Inside the complex, everything is dead except for the emergency lights. All of the zombie shelters are sealed off with magnetic locks, and if you aren't already inside, you won't be getting in. All communications are off unless they hack into our system, but that's not likely. It's on the other side of the wall."

He cleared his throat as he pointed at his screen.

"And if it makes you feel any better, the humans are still armed. They have shotguns, side arms, and plenty of ammo. They have zombie suits, masks, and helmets, so they aren't fish in a barrel. They're just the fish and the zombies the fishermen."

His uncle was as stone-faced as he'd ever been.

"Come on, Don. Now's not the time to get attached to people. You know what is going on. We're the lucky ones. You might as well make the most of it and enjoy the show. You know they're going to want your opinion on this and that you'll have to play along as if you like it, so go ahead and pretend to like it." He cleared his throat again. "Come on, you're making me uneasy."

"Okay, okay," Don grumbled. The older, bigger man pulled his head and shoulders back and flipped open his computer cover. His fiery gaze returned as he stared Jack back in the eye and said, "You want to make it fun, Boy? Then put your money where your mouth is." Don extended his hand. "I'll put twenty thousand dollars that those men and women beat your zombies."

Jack swallowed hard and said, "Well, I hardly see the poi—"

"TWENTY THOUSAND, NEPHEW! That's what it will cost for me to enjoy this. What's the matter? You're not losing your faith in the dead, are you?"

Jack stiffened at the remark and said, "Fine, you're on!"

"Good, then what are your terms?"

"Easy, just one of them has to live until sunrise."

Don had a calculating look in his eyes as he scratched at his chin. Jack wasn't worried, though. The last complex they turned the zombie soldiers loose on ended up being a slaughter. The humans lasted little longer than three hours, and the next sunrise was over twelve hours away. The zombie soldiers were incredible hunters that could smell blood and brains from a mile away, and even if the men managed to disable them, he still held another ace up his sleeve. He smiled. All of those years of online poker in college were going to finally pay off, big.

Don shook his hand and said, "Let loose the dogs of war ..."

"... and cry havoc."

19

Institute, WV

THE GLOW from the emergency lighting was all they had as they scoured the rooms for weapons on the security deck and loaded up. Everyone was in a zombie suit. Automatic pistols were strapped on every hip, while the black synthetic .12 gauge shotguns were charged. Myrtle seemed calm as she put two belts of ammunition over the top of Rod's massive shoulders. The big man had a fiery look in his eye as he talked on his short wave radio.

"Status report all stations!" he ordered.

"One check."

"Two check."

"Listen up, this is Command One. We have a breach. Zimmerman 23. Zimmerman 23. Over."

"Check."

"What's Zimmerman 23, over?"

"Zombies are on the loose, fellas. Maybe a dozen. But they're fast. We already have men down. Take the high ground. Report any sightings immediately."

"*Roger that.*"

"*Roger.*"

"Henry, we have four guys out there. The gate's not reporting. What's the plan?"

Everything in the security manual depended on the availability of backup power. The zombie panic room on their floor was locked. The computer stations were dead.

"What do we do, Henry?" Tori was shivering at his side.

He had already seen what the zombies had done to a well-armed security fire team, and he didn't have any inclination to take them on. The last thing he wanted to do was put any more lives in jeopardy. They were either going to have to fight, or hide and hope that the cavalry came in time, but deep inside he didn't figure that was going to happen. He had to give his friends hope even though he didn't have any. He was too smart to figure this for some kind of accident.

I can't believe they're doing this again. WHS playing games with men's lives. They must figure we're worthless or that I know too much.

It seemed that the WHS had other plans for the XT serum. The zombies were moving so fast, and the only thing he could think of was that the serum must be a part of that. No, they weren't trying to cure the zombies; they were trying to control them. All he could figure was that his usefulness must have come to an end. *Burn off the loose ends.* It infuriated him. *Lab rats again.*

"Henry! What do we do?" she said again.

"I'm thinking. Just give me a second."

"*Team One to Command One, we've got movement over near your building.*"

"What've you got?" Rod said.

The man's voice on the radio was almost inaudible.

"*Take a look out of your east entrance windows.*"

"Oh my!" Myrtle cried. "There must be twenty of them coming our way. Geez! They move as fast as us!"

Henry tried to remain calm, but the sight of the zombies swarming the building uncoiled his nerves. He counted the heads bobbing through the fog and was relieved that there weren't any more than ten of them.

Weege shouted, "Shoot them before they get here. Shoot them now!"

"Shut up, Idiot," Tori said. "They don't need to hear us, too."

"They can't hear," Weege said.

"We don't know that, so keep it down for now," said Henry.

"What's your location, Team One? Why aren't you in a secure location?" Rod said.

"Sorry Rod, but the nearest bunker was locked down. We've been all over as far as we could stand to go. We're on top of the Municipal Building now. We can't see in your windows, but we're on the ledge facing you. We had a clean shot on them earlier, but not much that a pistol or shotgun can do from this distance."

"Keep it quiet, watch your back, and let me know if you see anything else. Team Two Report."

"We're good. The bunker in the south quadrant is locked up. The fence is hotter than the 4th of July. No zombies though. Over."

Blam! Blam! Blam!

Everyone lurched. The sound of the shots was muffled and distant.

"Disregard! We've got three walkers! Fast ones!

Another procession of gunfire rang out from deep in the complex.

"Get on the buildings, Team Two! Shoot at their legs!"

"We're on the building! Damn things keep moving! Got on some kind of suit, like ours. Who in the hell put the walkers in zombie suits!" Rod's face was dripping with sweat, but Henry thought he was handling the situation quite well.

"You should be safe on the building. Hold your fire and save your ammo until help arrives."

"Rod ..."

"What is it?"

"They can climb."

Henry felt the goosebumps rise on his arms. He'd known in the back of his mind that if the zombies were on the XT Formula that it was a possibility. Now, it was confirmed that the zombies were on the formula, and the evil powers of the WHS were at work again. He grabbed Rod by the arm and said, "Tell them to get as close a shot as they can of the zombie's face. It's the best chance."

"Fire Team Two, aim for the face. Over."

He could see the small flashes of light reflecting off the windows in the distance. The steady popping of gunfire gave him hope that the creatures were about to be stopped. Every face in the room was almost pressed against the window as each critical second passed. Then the silence fell. They all looked at each other then back over to Rod, who held the radio up to his lips.

"Fire Team Two, Over."

Nothing.

"Fire Team Two, Over."

"Rod, it's over."

A collective sigh of relief filled the room along with a few fists pumping in the air.

"They didn't make it. We can see the entire thing. One zombie down. Sorry Rod, but they're gone. Fire Team One. Over."

"Dammit!" Rod said. "Those fiends! I must have heard over fifty shots fired, and they're still moving! We're gonna need some more fire power, Henry! My men ain't gonna die for nothing."

"Hey, what's going on?"

It was Rudy.

"Why are you guys geared up?"

"Tori, get a med kit and give him an oxygen shot."

"Zombies, Rudy. Remember the zombies before you passed out? Well, they're everywhere. Do you know anything about that? Because anything you might know might save all of our lives." He waved his hand across the people in the room. Rudy blanched. "You know something, don't you?"

Tori handed Rudy the oxygen tank and mask. He breathed heavy breaths in and out as his eyes flitted from one face to another. Rudy knew something. Henry was sure of it. Rudy began to stare at Tori's chest as he sucked more into the mask. Henry stepped into his view.

"Rudy, what do you know?"

"I overheard Alice talking to the director about a drill and new zombies. That's all."

"Henry, get over here." Rod was talking from somewhere down the hall. "We've got movement down there."

"Get Rudy in a suit, Myrtle."

He headed down the hall with Tori sticking to his side. Rod had the fire exit door cracked open. The big man said, "Listen."

The voices were haunting and fast.

"Numma-Numma. Numma-Numma."

Tori shrieked. He ran over to the other door and cracked it open.

"Numma-Numma. Numma-Numma."

"They're in both stair wells. Let's get these doors secured."

"We can't lock them without power!" Rod shouted. "We need padlocks and chains!"Rudy had wandered into the hall with his suit half on.

"What's going on?"

"Can you hear that?" Rod said as he charged his shotgun.

The steady sound of Numma-Numma was getting louder in the stairwells.

Rudy looked like he was about to puke when he said, "Yeah."

Rod smiled as he said, "Then grab a weapon, Rudy. The Zombies are coming!"

20

"YEAH, that creep called me every day for years," Nate said.

Rose, Walker, and Doctor Z all looked at one another. It made him uncomfortable. Who was Harry? The man had been like a steady drip of water: calling, calling, and calling. It was never at the same time of day, either, but rather anytime of the day or night. It was odd to feel either hatred or resentment for someone that he had never met. Harry's calls and voice had even awakened him from his sleep. Countless nights he had lain restless in the bed if Harry hadn't called yet.

Doctor Z stood up and asked, "Have you ever met the man?"

"No."

"Do you think you would recognize him if you saw him?"

It was odd, but for some reason he thought that he would. For years he'd had an image in his mind of what Harry looked like, but for all he knew he had probably met the man a dozen times and didn't know it.

"I doubt it."

The doctor's eyes and voice were probing.

"What if you heard him?"

Nate scratched the back of his neck.

"Well, maybe. At least I think I would, but there were many days when I was pretty sure the person I was talking to wasn't him. It was like him, but different. I always figured it was either his mood or it was a voice box of some kind. Still, it was spooky. The man knew everywhere I had been, and then he'd joke about it with me on the phone."

"How so?"

"Oh, I'd be at a bar and he'd call me at the bar and ask me if I was enjoying my martini. Stuff like that. He was like a ghost or something."

"Someone was watching you, but you were just too stupid to notice," Walker said in his matter-of-fact tone.

"Thanks." He directed his attention back to the doctor. "So, why the interest in Harry?"

Doctor Z was staring into space.

Agitated, Nate snapped his fingers in the man's face.

"Hello! What's the deal with Harry?"

The doctor's phone buzzed in his pocket. His eyebrows perched as he read the message.

"Walker, you and Rose finish this up. I've got another patient."

Nate heard the door shut before he even realized the man had left the room.

"Man, he's a strange one. So where were we?"

Rose took the doctor's place at his bed and said, "Our insiders have been gathering information on Harry for the past several months. They are being led to believe that Harry is the man in charge of the WHS. They think he's the brains behind World Population Control."

"Yes, but why would he be calling me?"

"Because you're the man that foiled his plans. You're the man who can foil them again."

"I just love the insanity of all this, but please continue."

"Think about it: every time you went to a WHS function there were always a bunch of lackeys all around, weren't there?" Rose motioned with her hands. "They were jawing back and forth and talking about all the good they were going to do for the world. Remember all of that?"

Did he ever. It had been fun the first few months, but it hadn't taken long before he'd been completely sick of it all.

"Sure I remember. They were all so smug and insincere. Liars, every last one of them."

"If you had to think about it, would any of them make you think of Harry?"

"No. I mean, I really never hit if off of any of them. I'd recognize some faces and names, but they all would have been all over the papers, too."

"Sometimes Nate, the best place to hide is in plain sight."

"Especially when you have a new face," Walker chuckled.

"What are you saying? I can't go around those people."

Rose nodded over at Walker and said, "Let me show you something."

Walker grabbed a computer and handed it over. She turned the display his way.

"Do any of them look familiar?" she asked.

It was a group photo taken at WHS headquarters in Washington DC. Nate was in the picture surrounded by nine other smiling people. Six men and Three women. One just as disingenuous as the next.

"I know them all by name. Do you think one of them is Harry?"

"Maybe. This picture was taken years ago, and at this point in time we know that this group is the highest authority in the WHS. Harry could be one of them, or one of them might know who Harry is. What do you think about this guy?"

She tapped the screen, and a larger picture of an older and distinguished man popped up.

"That's Don Baker." He sucked the rest of his Mountain Dew out with a straw. "He wasn't so bad; he knew some good jokes, at least. But, he seems too old to have been Harry."

"How about her?"

"What is this, a line up? Look, if they're all so bad, why don't you just go send Walker in to kill them all?"

Walker smiled and said, "That's what I said. I think that Taco Bell's making him smarter, Rose."

She shook her head.

"It's been discussed, but the security is too heavy. You know that. But, if we can find the right one and take a shot, we think we can take down the rest of them."

"So you want to cut the head off the snake, huh?"

"No, more like a dragon."

"Then you better hope it only has one head. So what do you want me to do?"

"We're going to reunite you with your old friends. Just get you in the same room. Walker's got it all set up."

"What?" Henry felt his food start to come back up. "I'm not a spy. And they're looking for me? No way, I'm not doing that. Can't you just get me a video or something?"

"We've tried." Rose grabbed his hand and squeezed it. "Nate, the next outbreak is coming soon. We don't have much time. We've run into a bunch of dead ends. As of now, you're Plan C. We are sorry to ask, Nate, but the world needs you again."

Her soft red lips were convincing, and her pretty eyes were pleading. How could he possibly say no?

"Okay," he gave in, "but I have one request before you send me to my next death."

"What is it, Honey?"

He whispered something in her ear.

Rose smiled at Walker and said, "I'll take it from here."

Walker grumbled as he shook his head and left the room.

As soon as the door clicked shut, her lips and his were one.

21

INSTITUTE, WV

WHAM!

Tori screamed. Henry stepped in front of her. He could hear the unceasing chorus of the zombies: ravenous and violent. It was only a matter of time before they made their way through the doors, unless they broke them down first. He cringed at the thought. The zombies were strong enough, but with the XT Serum they would be even stronger than before.

"Fire Team One to Command. What's your status?"

Horrified, Rudy grabbed Rod's radio and screamed, "We're going to die! Get over here! Get over here now! That's an order!"

Whap.

Rod slapped the man and took back his radio.

"We need a way out of here. Any suggestions?"

WHAM!

WHAM!

WHAM!

"Try the fire escapes. We'll give you cover. It's all clear on our side. Over."

Rudy knocked down Weege as he bolted from the group.

Henry yelled after him, "Rudy! Stay with the group!"

As the man's bushy head disappeared down the hall, Henry had a sinking feeling. Everyone's eyes fell to him. Myrtle was picking Weege's shaking form up from the floor. They followed him over and looked down the hall on the opposite end of the main entrance. Rod and Myrtle were standing their ground, shotgun barrels leveled toward the sound of the hungry zombies on the other side of the doors. Everyone's expression was filled with fear.

He heard the door groan somewhere near the elevator's foyer. He expected the zombies to pour through at any second.

"DAMMIT! DAMMIT!" Rudy was yelling, running back down the corridor. "We're trapped. It's sealed! The fire doors are sealed! We're gonna die, Henry! Do something!"

He was afraid of that. The magnetic locks were engaged, making sure nobody was getting in or out. It was his biggest fear. Just like his brother Jimmy, someone, somewhere was calling the shots. He searched for the cameras near the ceilings and noticed a tiny red light burning on the top of each and every one. Someone, somewhere was watching. *Bastards!* But he couldn't say a word. Despair filled him from his chin to his knees.

"Henry," Tori grabbed his face, "Henry, don't you give up. Turn on that brain of yours, and get us out of here. We need you, Henry! I need you. I don't want to die like this!"

At that moment, the pounding stopped, but the moans and the numma-nummas remained. Henry was so sick of that sound that his despair began to melt away and harden like iron.

"Everyone, get your masks on. Just because we don't have a door doesn't mean we can't take the window."

"What! We're three stories up! I ain't jumping. I hate heights," Rod said.

WHAM!

"Look, I'll cover you crazy people, but I'm not jumping out some window."

"I'm with you," Myrtle added. The short woman looked and walked like an Ewok in her zombie suit.

"Let me have your radio, Rod," he said. "Fire Team One, this is Henry. We're gonna have to make our own door. Do we have anything below us to jump on?"

"You've got to say over, Dude?" Rudy slurred.

"Shut up!" Weege said, slapping Rudy in the head. "And put your mask on!"

"Everyone be quiet! Shush!" Myrtle said. "Do you hear that?"

Their necks all tilted. He could hear the sound of the metal doors groaning and popping. The moaning became louder with every creaking sound.

"There's a utility building about 5 feet out from the wing. The jump doesn't look so bad. Better than being zombie chow anyway. Over."

Henry rushed over to the window as the zombies filled the hallway. *Where's that utility building?* The windows were large panes of heavy glass that didn't open or close.

Numma-numma.

Boom! Boom!

A symphony of thunder had entered the room.

Henry's head whipped around just in time to see the first wave of the invading hoard. Four zombies were charging into the room on stiff legs. Rod's and Myrtle's shotguns rang out and knocked a zombie backward onto the floor.

"Get us out of here, Henry!" shouted Rod. "They're getting back up!"

"Reload!" Myrtle shouted, handing the man more shells.

The zombie lurched back up, mouth clutching open and shut. The metal mask seemed to restore a small portion of its humanity, but its intent seemed more deadly.

Henry lowered his shotgun and blasted out the window. He jumped up on top of the desk alongside the window ledge and shouted for Tori.

"Come on!" She reached out, and he pulled her up. She clutched at his chest as she looked over his shoulder. The sound of the shotgun blasts was deafening, and she was shaking her head.

"You've got to jump!"

"I can't! It's too high."

Weege and Rudy were at his side.

Weege looked outside and said, "Just hang over the ledge — like this!" The little man tossed his shotgun out the window and swung his body over the ledge. "The glass can't cut you through the suit!" he yelled, clutching the jagged edge of the window with his gloved fingertips. "Come on, I'll catch you. Better this than being zombie food!" He dropped down, landed on his feet, and fell flat on his back. "See!"

BLAM! BLAM! BLAM!

Rod was shouting.

"GET MOVING, HENRY! We can't reload fast enough! Damn things keep coming!"

Henry grabbed Tori and lowered her to the ledge.

"Hurry up, Dude!" Rudy screamed as he forced himself to the ledge.

Somebody was screaming. Henry looked over his shoulder and saw Myrtle's squat figure ramming the stock of her gun into the face of a zombie. Behind the fray, more zombies were coming.

"LET GO, TORI!" He shouted, rushing to Myrtle's aid, shotgun blasting at everything moving his way.

"Get out of here, Henry!" Rod shoved him back. "I got this!"

Myrtle was pinned under two zombies now, each tearing at her suit. He saw the woman stuff a pistol in one of the creature's mouths and fire away. It slumped over as another bit into her arm. Rod opened up a barrage into the creature's back. Another half dozen zombies were closing in. Some were crawling from the impact of their wounds, but they still came. Myrtle screamed a curse at the zombies, then she screamed no more. Henry felt sick.

"Henry, go! Take care of the others!"

He looked back at the widow, and Tori and Rudy were gone. Rod was the only thing between him and the zombies tearing him to shreds. The big man looked like a super hero in his suit as he fired into the zombies. Henry's fear consumed him as he backpedaled to the window. He could hear Tori screaming for him from down below. He took one last glance at Rod—the bravest man he ever saw—mumbled a prayer, and jumped.

22

WASHINGTON, DC

"So ... Do you have your checkbook with you, Uncle Don?" Jack asked in a mocking tone.

Don laughed. It was a better than revealing what he really wanted to do to his demented nephew. He cleared his throat.

"Don't you worry about the money, Jack. I've got plenty of that."

"I don't suppose you want to increase your wager then, double or nothing?"

Even though Don's stomach was recoiling inside him, he was still enthralled with what he was watching. The zombie vision was much more effective than he ever would have imagined. The views kept changing in order to keep their eyes closer to the action. It reminded him of all the camera angles in sports that seemed to be everywhere at once. The picture on his screen went from one zombie point of view to another, and he couldn't help but wonder what the other people behind all of this were thinking. Were they just as sadistic as his nephew had become?

"I think we can leave things as they are, Jack. I'm not as willing to part with my money as you might be, especially when the deck is stacked against me."

"Okay then." Jack typed a few more commands on his screen. "Watch these things go! They are so relentless."

The zombies had made their way into a stairwell and began pounding at the doors that barred their path. Don still had the sound muted on his machine, but he could hear the zombies pounding and moaning on Jack's.

"Watch this. I'm going to try and get this zombie to open the door. They just need to push that thumb lever down on the handle. Ah, it's not working. They're all too bunched together."

"Won't the people inside just take the fire escape?"

"All of the perimeter doors are sealed."

"Can't you open the interior doors?"

"No. Just good old fashioned fire doors. The kind your generation probably made by hand." Jack chuckled. "The main goal was to keep zombies from getting in or out."

Years ago, Don had plenty of relatives, many of which he hadn't spent much time with, but they had all been amiable folk. Up until today, Jack had been one of his favorites, but the young man's callous behavior had him making mental alterations to his will. *This has got to be stopped.* What could he do, though? His nephew was just executing orders, and he would be obligated to do the same if he was given those same orders. There would be a difference had he been given the same charge though. He wouldn't be enjoying it.

He was holding his screen in both hands when the zombies made their push through.

"Yes!" Jack exclaimed.

Damn! Don had already watched two of the three remaining security fire teams fall into the clutches of the charged-up zombies. He was certain he would have nightmares for the rest of his life after this. It was like watching a horror movie from the monster's point of view.

The sounds of screaming voices and cracks of gunfire now filled the air, along with the sounds of the moaning zombies. Don felt a sliver of hope when he noticed that the men and women in the room were clad in full zombie suits and were fully armed for battle. The image on his screen shook and tumbled downward, only to be switched over to another point of view a moment later. A man had blasted out a window, drawing a curse from his nephew's lips. *Yes!*

"Ah, don't get too excited, Uncle. They won't be going anywhere on broken legs."

"Maybe so, but the sunrise is still getting closer."

"Huh ..."

A stumpy figure in a zombie suit stuffed a pistol in a zombie's face and fired. Don and Jack dropped their screens as they both jumped from their seats. Don's heart was pounding inside his chest as Oliver made his way over to help him back on the bench.

"You okay, Sir?"

Don looked up into the man's stone face and felt relief. Oliver reminded him he was still a part of humanity. He said, "Thanks, Oliver, I'm okay. Whew!"

Oliver handed him a handkerchief. "You're sweating, Sir."

Jack was back in his seat, laughing. "That was awesome! Hey Oliver, you need to go. You can't see this. I'll take care of Uncle Don. You just keep his coffee warm. It'll be over soon."

Don didn't like the condescending tone in his nephew's voice.

"Oliver works for me, not you, Jack. Mind your tongue."

"Yeah, whatever ..."

"I'm alright, Oliver. Best you go."

Oliver frowned as he glanced over at Jack before he walked away.

"I hope you don't treat most people that way," Don said.

Jack didn't respond, his face was intent on his screen.

Don picked his computer up with a sigh. Two more figures were no longer in the room he viewed, leaving only two standing. One was a large man, he figured, based off the view he had of the zombies looking up. A shotgun was blasting into all of them. He heard the large man yell, "Henry, go! Take care of the others!"

Ah ... Henry Bawkula lives. A thrill went through him. He knew enough about Henry to know that he was a capable man. Don had seen all the footage from what happened at WHS Facility III, the

Zombie Day Care. *I wonder if he's still with that Italian girl who lost her arm. She was something.* The big man in the room was holding off the zombies when Henry jumped from the window. The butt of a rifle slammed into his screen, causing his finger tips to tingle. The view was gone.

"Dammit!" Jack cried, shaking his screen like an angry child.

Don chuckled. "Time's ticking."

Another view popped up that was closing in on the big man tossing away his shotgun and reaching for another. Jack was pounding his hand into his screen. "I think we lost sound. Damn. I wanted hear this big man scream!"

Don felt a chill as he watched the throng of zombies rush after the man.

23

Institute, WV

Rod. He had been known as one of the biggest and baddest fighters on the Eastern Seaboard. For over 15 years he had fought in anything from a cage to a parking lot. Never once had he shown fear or shed a tear. He'd been known as the Black Python in the Octagon. He'd kicked like a mule and punched like a heavy weight. He was big, fast, fluid, and feared. He'd had that advantage over his opponents because they were living. This fight was different. His adversaries were dead.

He let off his last round, imploding the face of his latest attacker. It sagged to the ground as another stiff creature took its place, arms clutching at his neck. Two automatic pistols were blazing in his hands. The bullets punched into the bodies of the undead, slowing them a tad. *Head shot! Head shot! Head shot!* The rounds ricocheted from the metal foreheads as the relentless gang surged forward. Rod dove behind a counter and reloaded.

BLAM!

He caught one in the knee, sending it reeling to the ground.

"Yeah baby!"

Ka-Blam! Ka-Blam!

Two more dropped, but they were still crawling. The others were closing in from all directions.

He glanced at the window. Henry was gone. *I've got to get out of here!*

"Ugh!"

Something heavy slammed into him. The stench of the dead filled his nostrils. He fired a series of rounds over his shoulder, every bullet lethal. No effect. A zombie was biting into his suit, and another was pulling him down.

"NO!"

Fear assailed him. If bullets couldn't stop his enemies, then what would?

"NO!"

Rod wasn't going to die like this. He was the Black Python.

"NO!" He flipped the zombie from his back.

Octagon Legend.

"NO!" His boot crushed another's jaw.

As anger coursed through his big body so did the adrenaline. He had started fighting when he was ten. 25 years of training hadn't prepared him for a day like this ... but it would have to do.

The zombies were fast. The zombies were strong ... unyielding. But, the zombies couldn't fight worth a shit.

"Come on, you dead bastards!"

A roundhouse kick sent one staggering to the floor.

"You can't touch me!"

Two more crashed into each other as Rod jumped away. Another clutched at his neck. Rod snapped its wrist. He stuffed its fist inside its own mouth and swept its legs from underneath it. The zombies were writhing all around him now as he jumped, dodged, and dived. The zombies were inferior in size, average men, nowhere close to his height or weight. The death match was becoming a mismatch.

"Let go, you—urk!"

He cracked his head as he was pulled to the ground. Warm blood was seeping into his eyes and the hoard went into a frenzy. The mangled mass became a creeping doom. Rod twisted away from the clutches of two disabled zombies and dashed towards the stairwell. Two zombies cut off his path as they closed in.

"Damn!"

His chest was burning now. He scanned around in the dim light, looking for a weapon of any kind. He bolted into the security room, grabbed a chair, and slung it into the zombies. One toppled over. The other came on. Its fingers tried to tear off his mask. Rod snatched the monster up, hurled it into the others, and yelled.

Now one was hanging on his leg, biting into his ankle. It felt like his leg was in a vice. He screamed. Reaching down, he grabbed the back of its head and tore off its mask. He couldn't see much in the darkness, but there was a skull. He ripped his hunting knife from his belt and plunged it into the back of its skull. He pulled it out just in time to thrust it under the chin of another. He lost his grip

"R-Rah!" he bellowed as he tore through the hoard and headed for the window. The zombie suit was the only thing saving him from being ripped to shreds. There must have been four hundred pounds of zombies tearing into him as he fought for every step. The window was only ten feet away. He could hear voices screaming from down below.

"I'M COMING!"

Like wild animals, the zombies clawed at him and bit into his suit. It held, but the skin and muscles underneath were getting torn. Rod's body was on fire, and the pain was blinding. Sweat and blood seeped into his eyes. *NO! I can't die like this!*

The window was only five feet away from his outstretched grasp.

"Gotta! ... Keep! ... Moving!"

He made another step, dragging a zombie like an angry child. He was so close now, but his body didn't have the energy to make another step. Just one more step. *Please Lord, give me the strength.*

FROM DOWN BELOW they all gasped at the sight. Rod's massive frame appeared in the window, clutching at the ledge. Henry shouted helplessly as the zombies covering the man began pulling him back in. The big man held on, his big gloved hands digging into the metal window pane.

"Come on, Rod!"

Henry thought he heard his friend say *'Run'* as he was pulled back into the darkness.

24

NATE MCDANIEL'S life had been rebooted. New face. New clothes. New Job ... WHS Security Squad. *What a joke.* He scratched his face. His once heavy beard was nice and trim with a touch of gray around the chin. In the mirror he tried making faces. He smiled and frowned. Made an angry face and chuckled at himself. He started to sing.

"Don't talk stupid," Walker said, combing his hair at the mirror by his side.

He still had that at least, the voice. *Smooth as silk and sweeter than honey.* That's what Rose had said after they advanced their relationship several hours ago.

He followed Walker into the parking garage out of the strange building that he assumed had been his home for the past several months. His legs and face ached from the effort. Walking down the stairs winded him. He got into the passenger side of a slate gray sedan with a WHS logo on the side. The moment of eeriness passed as they pulled out of the garage and headed down the road. He thought about Rose's sweet lips the entire car ride over. He still didn't know where he left from for sure, but it wasn't long before he knew exactly where he was. It was a place he had become quite fond of over the years: Washington, DC. Headquarters of the WHS and this year's host of their Zombie Convention.

"Stay close to me. You've got all of the ID and credentials that you need. If someone says something to you, just nod or shake your head. Security is tight here."

Nate wiped his sweaty hands on his pants and said in a gruff voice, "Okay."

"Geez, that's bad. You sound like the Hulk. But, I guess it will do."

"Nate smash Walker," Nate said, imitating the Incredible Hulk.

"Shad-dup."

He rolled down his window and inhaled. The cool air was refreshing. The lights of the city and the nation's Capitol were captivating. He loved it here. Of course, the WHS hadn't given him much choice. Even if he could live somewhere else, he wasn't so certain that he would. The exhilarating feeling of freedom and a new life was soon dimmed as an image of Christy Backwater was etched in his head. She had been gorgeous, seductive, and powerful. He could still feel her sticky blood on his hands. He rubbed his fingertips together. *I can't believe she was going to kill me.* He coughed.

"I'm not putting my cigarette out, if that's what you're hinting at," Walker said.

"Huh ... no, I couldn't care less. As a matter of fact, I wouldn't mind one, myself."

"Is that so? Well, help yourself. Glove box."

He grabbed a box of Camel non-filters.

"They still make these things?"

"In some states."

The smoke burned his lungs as he inhaled. He sighed with a heavy breath of smoke.

"Rose isn't gonna like that. Doctor Z, either."

"I guess they can transplant new lungs to go with my new face, then."

"Yeah, good one."

Solid country gold songs were playing on the radio as Nate watched the street signs he passed by. The music wasn't as offensive as he used to think, more soothing than anything. He didn't figure he should expect much better from a skinny hick like Walker anyway. After a few more songs played and his second cigarette was extinguished, he figured he needed a better idea of what he was getting into.

"Walker ..."

The man came to a stop at a light and said, "I know what you're thinking. What are you going to do when we get there?"

"Well yeah ... What am I going to do when I get there?"

"Follow me. Stay close. Do as I do and say. We're going to be among your old comrades of the WHS. Watch. Listen. Maybe we'll learn something."

It didn't make any sense to him. They wouldn't say anything in front of them. He knew them well enough to know that when they had something important on their minds they would dismiss themselves. Never once did they keep him around for the more important plans. He had tried several times to include himself, but he'd usually been met with a courteous "No."

"I'm not a spy. I'm just some dude that got lucky, is all," he confessed. "You know that, of course, and I'm sure you resent that."

The car was moving again.

"I know that ... but ... man I hate to say this ... the truth is, I believe that everybody is somebody. Even an over-glamorized fornicator like you."

"Hey!"

"Heh-heh. You know it's true. Besides, I'd be lying if I said I wasn't' just like all the other men in the world that wanted to be you just for a day. The star of the century."

"It's a joke."

"Maybe so, but you have a purpose. You stopped the zombies once. You can stop them again. It's probably why you are here."

"Great. So, why are you here, then? Have you figured it out yet?"

"I'm pretty sure I'm here to kill zombies." Walker lit up another cigarette. "And the people that make zombies."

"Sounds pretty simple. I save the world. You kill the zombies. Maybe we should come up with a name for ourselves," Nate suggested.

"Well, the Dynamic Duo is taken. So is the Green Hornet and Kato."

"Hawkman and smoking Hawkman."

"Creampuff and Studman."

"Milk and Honey."

"Better yet, Big Guy and Little Guy."

"The Undertaker ..."

"... and Kane." Nate finished. "I don't even have a real name now, do I?"

Walker tossed him a thin wallet. Inside, there was an I.D. without a picture on it. It had a name, though.

"Rick Jones. Seriously."

"It's all that I could think of. I'm not exactly good with names."

It wasn't so bad. After all, Rick Jones was a hero of sorts. If not for him, there never would have been an Incredible Hulk. The tension between the two men had subsided. Even Walker's stiff talk had loosened up. The man's dry sense of humor had begun to grow on him.

"Nah, it's good. It's not as cool as Bruce Banner, but it's still better than Clark Kent."

"True. I almost used Chuck Jones."

Nate's brows perched as he nodded. He pulled down his vanity mirror and said, "I can see that, too."

Men could easily find common ground with one another if they were willing to speak. Sports, comic books, movies, and video games were all part of their mental playground. The doubt inside his belly about the skinny man in black began to subside. Maybe Walker was on his side. Maybe it wasn't all a hoax. *Keep playing along.*

"We're almost to the convention center. WHS security is going to check you in. Show your ID. They scan it and your face."

"My face?"

"Don't worry. You've already been added into the database. Worst case scenario, we head back to the car ... or die."

"What?"

Walker showed him a thin-lipped smile as they pulled into the garage and said, "It'll be okay. Besides, you've already died once."

25

INSTITUTE, WV

"HENRY! HENRY!"

Someone was screaming as he gawped at the window above.

"Get down here!"

He didn't want to move, but someone was pulling him away. He resisted.

"He's gone, Henry! Come on, Lover, we've got to move on!" Tori said, tears streaming from her eyes.

They both limped towards the ladder. Tori grunted with every step.

"You okay?"

"Just my ankle.

THUMP!

A zombie dropped from the window and crashed on top of the roof.

THUMP!

Another followed.

"Get down, Tori!" he said, looking down the ladder. Rudy and Weege were down below, shouting at him.

"BAWK! COME ON!" Rudy cried.

He spotted two 4-seater utility vehicles and Security Team One. They were all waving him on. The moans behind him became even louder as one zombie rose to its feet in pursuit.

"GERONIMO!"

One of the biggest men he ever knew was jumping from the window. A sickening crunch followed as Rod landed on top of the zombie. Henry rushed over and pulled the man up from the ground. The other zombie was crawling, dragging its busted legs behind it. Henry kicked away its outstretched hand. As the pair of men stumbled to the ladder, the zombies began jumping from the windows like the building was on fire. Henry watched in awe as Rod slid down on the outer rails of the fire escape.

"MOVE, HENRY!"

Rod caught him as he leaped down the last ten feet.

"OW!"

"You'll be okay," Rod said, dragging him towards the awaiting vehicles.

"Thank God you're alive!" Henry exclaimed.

Rod didn't reply as he looked upward. Tori, Weege and Rudy were screaming. The zombies were scrambling off the top of the roof.

Rod shouted, "Get us out of here, Doug!!"

"Where? There's nowhere to go!"

"Just go! We'll think of something on the way."

The Gators sped off.

Doug, Henry, Rod, and another security member were in one Gator. The Weege, Rudy, and Tori were being driven by another member. Everyone had pulled the mesh masks up from their faces. Henry almost enjoyed the cold air on his as they sped through the thick fog.

The complex had the feeling of a haunted village now. The contours of the buildings were distorted, and the blacktopped roads were hidden. All of the lampposts that littered the compound were dark, and most of the emergency lights were dim. Henry tapped Doug the driver on the shoulder.

"Stop. Let's regroup."

The other Gator pulled along their side. Every face was wide-eyed with horror. They were beside a small chapel that was covered in ivy. A small cemetery was nearby. Rudy retched over the side of the ATV as Tori climbed over into the seat beside Henry. Everyone was looking back and forth at one another with heads craning for any sounds of pursuit.

Weege was the first to speak.

"We have to find the director and Alice, Henry. They'll know what to do. Let's go to his quadrant."

Doug was loading shells into his shotgun as he said, "Nope. We checked, or at least the other guys did. They're either sealed up somewhere or on the run. Probably dead."

It didn't seem likely to Henry. Alice had to have been in on something. His gut told him that much. With so many personnel at the Zombie Conference, it didn't seem likely that they'd leave the director behind, unless they wanted him gone as well. As for Alice, she was too much of a suck-up to be black listed. If anyone knew what was going on, he was certain that she would. In the meantime, he had to find a way out of this trap.

"Anybody have any ideas?" he said, looking around.

"More ammo. We couldn't check the munitions depot. They might have heavier stuff in there," one security man said.

"Some armor-piercing rounds would be nice. It's the only thing that'll bust through those metal skulls. Man! What's going on here, Henry? Somebody let those zombies loose ... didn't they?" Rod said, letting out a painful groan.

"You okay?" Tori asked.

"I'm torn up. Busted bones." Rod pulled off his mask and spit blood. "I'm still a man, though."

Henry put his hand on the man's shoulder and said, "Rod ... everyone ... I can't say what's going on, but it looks like the WHS is up to its dirty tricks."

"What do you mean?" one guard asked.

"Without getting into detail, I have knowledge of experiments of theirs. There's a formula that was supposed to cure the zombies, but instead it just sped them up. They were testing it on children, but now they've moved on to adults. I think they are making zombie soldiers." He ran his fingers back through his hair. "And their first war is with us. A bunch of nobodies. Casualties of the greater good, I'd assume."

There was silence. Only the chirping of nature's creatures remained. Henry felt like he had sucked the hope from each and every one of them. Every face was sweaty and drained. Even his own hands were trembling. He started to continue, but Rod's powerful voice cut him off.

"I'm not dying for nothing. I'm not a victim. If it's a fight they want, it's a fight I'll give them." The man was looking at the cross on the roof of the small church. Rod groaned as he left the Gator and said, "Everybody gather around ... I want to say something."

Henry thought he knew what the man was doing, but he didn't think the others would respond. They all gathered in.

"Everyone hold hands and bow your heads."

Henry grabbed Weege on his left and Tori on his right. The small circle was complete. He glanced up at the old metal cross that was illuminated in the pale moonlight.

Rod said, "God ... please help us get the hell out of here alive. Amen."

A few others mumbled the final word as well.

"Henry. Henry," Weege was squeezing his hand.

"Yeah."

The little man's eyes were feverish with excitement.

"I have an idea."

"I'm all ears."

So was everyone else.

"We need blood. Lots of blood."

"What for? We—"

"Ssssh!" Tori said. "Do you hear that?"

The sound was very distinct.

"Numma-numma. Numma-numma ..".

And getting louder.

"Get back in the Gators!"

"Henry, listen to me! Let's head for the gym! I have an idea. We have to get blood!"

Not a second after they started moving, the zombies erupted from the fog like rabid dogs.

"GO!"

The zombies were blocking their path.

26

Now, Don was the one laughing. His nephew Jack was cursing at his custom laptop.

"Impossible!"

Don swore that if that big man in the zombie suit survived, he would put him directly on his payroll and hope the man never learned he had been an associate in his attempted death. At this point, Don was titillated. The massive man slung the zombies around like rag dolls. The WHS team that worked the cameras must have been having a fit. His screen went black on several occasions, only to emerge again with another pummeling scene. He swore he felt his jaws rattle a couple of times.

"Don't get cocky, Uncle. See, the man's out of energy, and the zombies have just begun."

It was a hard thing, watching the valiant man begin to die. The swarm covered the fighter. The screen didn't pick up much of the picture, but it was pretty clear this battle was over. Don's heart was heavy for a moment, and then something amazing happened. His view of the screen changed, and suddenly he was sailing through the air and crashing on top of a gravel roof. After the camera switched, the big man was on the lower roof and hustling over the side. Henry Bawkula was there, too.

"Yes!"

Jack sneered.

"That was just luck. Those people don't have anywhere to run. No escape, and they are running out of ammo."

"True, but it's still getting closer to the dawn. Let me ask you something, Jack. Have you ever taken a moment to ever consider what it might be like if you were in there?"

"No. The only thing that matters is that I'm not in there."

"Suppose that was you. Do you think you could survive? After all, you're smarter than the zombies. What would you do?"

Don waited for the reply, but the only response was the man's fingers moving feverishly over his keyboard.

"Well ... I guess I'll assume you would give up and die, then."

"I'd think of something."

"Ah ... so, don't you think they'll think of something, as well?"

Jack threw his arms out in front of himself and said, "I don't care what they think. It won't matter. They won't survive. No one has, so far."

Wow! Don couldn't help but worry about his status with the WHS. His nephew, someone that he had brought up within that organization, was now privy to information that he was not. His stomach soured as he ran his hand over his face. He became very cold.

Jack continued his gloating.

"How much do you really know about the zombies anyway, Don?"

It was an insult. He knew as much about zombies as anybody. What he knew about the functions of the XT Serum was another matter. Still, the question pissed him off.

"Here's what I know. They are a virus. Man made. An abomination. Something that happens, I believe, when man is saturated by evil. Mindless and hungry with an appetite that cannot be satisfied. And like any other virus, they attack. Infect. Cells and flesh. In this more extreme case, the zombies are hunting blood. They want to infect it. Everyone thinks they are flesh eaters—like cannibals—but if that were the case we wouldn't have any zombies. They would all consume themselves.

"Although I've always enjoyed the headlines ... ZOMBIE EATS MAN'S BRAIN, all of that is bunk. Do you know how much pressure it would take to crack a human skull? How can a man bite into another man's head? Our teeth aren't designed to be can openers. If a zombie ever ate a brain, it was only because it had already been spilled. Besides, what's the best way to kill a zombie? Pierce the brain. Why would a virus kill itself? No brains, no zombies."

Jack was nodding.

"True. But you've got to love all of those old movies. I bet your generation never saw that becoming real."

"We didn't expect to land on the moon, either. Or have a bomb that could destroy an entire country."

"Well, it looks like every generation has its achievements, some good and some bad. Real bad. Still, Uncle, I don't think you are telling me everything you know about the zombies. The 101 segment doesn't help. Can't you at least tell me where they came from? Who created the virus? About the first outbreak?"

Don didn't like the intensity in Jack's voice. For a moment, his nephew looked like a man obsessed with something dark. He looked Jack in the eyes and said, "You seem to already know enough, Jack. You know things that I don't even know. You're doing things that I wouldn't even consider. And now, you want me to share with you everything that I know?" He cleared his throat. "I do what I do because I have to. That doesn't mean that I enjoy it. Look at you. People are dying, and you like it. Don't you?"

Jack tore his eyes away saying, "No."

"It sure seems like it."

"Can't you just tell me who you think is behind the outbreak?"

"No."

"Do you even know?"

Don paused before he shook his head saying, "No."

Jack hissed through his teeth and returned his interest back to his screen. Don checked his. Only the view of the fog remained. He was relieved.

Good

"Looks like they lost them, and the time's still ticking away."

"They'll sniff them out soon enough."

Don hoped not.

"See look! They're already on the trail."

Don looked down at his screen just in time to see his zombie view getting run over by a Gator full of a bunch of shooting people. As exciting as that was, a troubling feeling remained. He was beginning to get a sinking feeling that he wasn't holding the purse strings anymore. He looked over his shoulder. Oliver was still standing outside the car and smoking. *Am I still in charge here?* Maybe his nephew was ... and he might be in trouble.

27

Institute, WV

THEY LIVED. Gators, bullets, zombie suits, and gas propelled the small band of survivors through the latest zombie onslaught. Two zombies were smashed into the payment like roadkill while another got lanced with an 8-foot strip of rebar. No one looked back as they fled through the undead blockade and headed down the road. Now they were stuck, and time was running out. The zombies would be there soon.

Rod and the rest of the security team were slamming the butts of their guns into the gymnasium's door. The magnetic locks weren't giving in.

"Henry, we gotta go! This ain't gonna work," Rod said.

Henry swore he could hear the zombie moans coming.

From behind the wheel of the Gator, Doug shouted, "Get the hell out of the way. I'm making a hole!"

Henry and Tori jumped out of the ATV as the machine barreled toward the heavy metal doors. The sound of bending steel meeting all-wheel drive mayhem crashed into their ears. The Gator plunged inside the darkness.

"Damn. He did it!"

The Gator was still running as they all rushed inside to give thanks to the man. Doug sat unmoving in his seat. A large piece of metal had cut into his head. Henry pulled Tori close as she sobbed.

"Ah man," Rod exclaimed. "I guess it's better dying like this than the other way."

In the distance the moaning became louder.

Weege was yelling, "Come on! Come on! We need the blood. The storage is this way!"

"What the hell is he talking about, Henry?" Tori said. "And I can't see a damn thing!"

A small flashlight beam was glaring in their eyes. It was one of the security team guys. Henry didn't know him.

"Follow you, or follow him?"

"Ow!" Weege screamed from somewhere in the dark.

"Find him," Henry said, "and we'll follow. I think I might know what he's thinking."

"Wherever we're going, let's get there! Those zombies will be here any second," Rod said.

Henry was pulling Tori through the darkness as small beacons of light led the way. Weege was on the gymnasium floor holding his ankle. Rudy stumbled over to the little man and helped him up from the floor.

"What are you doing, you little idiot? What do we want blood for?"

A bright light flashed inside Henry's head. He knew what Weege wanted to do. The zombies wanted blood. The blood bank would give them that.

"Come on, this way everybody," he said, leading the way to a lab room in the back.

Henry knew that the zombie contagion spread through the blood. Testing revealed that living flesh fired the hunting instincts of the zombies, letting them track people for miles. But there was more to it than just the living bodies. There had to be blood inside them as well. Despite what many people figured, brains weren't the object of their ravenous hunger. It was the drive to infect and spread, and only the blood stream could carry that. Still, would stored blood satisfy the zombies' appetites?

Rudy pulled open the door of a walk-in refrigerator and Henry stepped inside. Bags of blood were lit up by the small flashlights.

"What in the world?" Rod gasped. "What's all of this blood for?"

"Transfusions. They try different types to give the zombies new blood. Flush out the corrupted stuff," Weege said.

"Does it work?" Rod asked.

"Er ... testing is inconclusive. Now shut up and grab some bags," Weege ordered.

Rudy began passing them down the line, everyone filling their hands.

"This won't work, you moron. We need to hide," Rudy commented.

"Shut up, you drunkard," Weege fired back. "You hopeless sack of camel dung!"

One of the fire team members spoke up and asked, "What are we supposed to do with it?"

"They'll follow a blood trail," Henry said. "Someone look for a something to carry this stuff in.

"Ssshh!" said a security guard that was watching the door. "I think I hear something."

As everyone shuffled out of the room, all eyes followed the light illuminating the hall. The emergency lights added an additional bit of dim lighting. There was a lot of heavy breathing in the silence and the rattling of weapons being fingered. Henry tried to settle himself down. How many more zombies were out there? How many could they fight off? A dozen bags of blood would only slow them down. They needed a place to hide. But where? *Think Henry! Think.*

"Where to, Henry?" Rod asked.

"Dude, I found some garbage bags," Rudy said. "I've got about ten more pints in here."

"Ssshh!" Tori said.

A distant sound was echoing down the corridor. "Numma-numma. numma-numma ... "

Henry set a pint down on the floor and pulled out the Swiss Army knife that his step-father Stanley had given him for his birthday. He cut the bag open and slung it down the hallway.

"What are you doing, Henry? You'll lead them right to us!"

He could feel their confusion. Every stare was of desperation in the dimness.

He was confident when he spoke.

"No, I'm leading them to the pool."

"The pool?" someone said.

Weege said in an excited voice, "That's right, zombies can't swim!"

They left a trail of blood as they dashed through the hallways and burst into the aquatic center. The smell of chlorine was heavy in the gloom. They sliced open a few more bags, set them near the edge of the pool, and waited.

"I'm burning up."

"Let's find a way out of here."

"We're all going to die," Rudy said.

"Shut up!" They all replied.

Henry scanned the room. There were four exits, and the zombies could burst inside from any one of them. They had come through the door on the east wing, and a there was an opposite one from the west. The north side had two more doors that led back outside, but they were probably locked.

"How are we going to get them in the pool, Henry?" Tori said.

"I guess we're going to have to push them in."

"I'm not doing that!" Weege said.

"Me either!" Rudy agreed.

"We're going to have to make a stand. This is our only chance, unless someone has a better idea?"

Everyone was looking at one another, sweaty and miserable. The heat was unbearable inside the suits and the sweltering building. Henry figured everyone would just as soon die as suffer inside their zombie suits any longer. He was exhausted, too. He checked his weapon. One full clip left. He switched it with the other. Everyone else followed suit except for Weege and Rudy, who were whispering back and forth to each other.

"Rudy, do you care to fill us in?" Henry said.

"Ah ... well, Weege and I have decided that we would rather take our own chances. If you guys want to stay and die by the poolside, that's fine, but we think we can do better on our own."

"Our best chance is to stick together."

"Let them go, Henry," Rod said. "I'm staying."

"There's nowhere to go, unless you know something that you aren't telling us?"

"Good luck, Henry," Weege said as the two men scurried away through the other set of doors.

Henry started to go after him, but Tori held him back. She said, "Those two won't make it very far."

"That's what I'm afraid of."

It was down to him, Tori, Rod, and two security men that he didn't know. Half a dozen zombies would be there any second. Henry knew that they would only get one shot at this, so he had to be sure it worked. They would probably only get one chance. It was time to make a sacrifice.

"Rod, double check those doors over there."

He started to remove his zombie suit.

"What are you doing?" Tori said.

"I'm getting in the water."

"Why?"

"I'm going to draw them in after me, while you guys hide."

Rod yelled over, "These doors won't budge, Henry!"

"You aren't the best swimmer, Henry. Let those guys go."

"No! It's too dangerous. I'll be fine."

Tori stripped down. Henry heard someone gulp in the dark air. She was the perfect figure of sweat and lingerie. Henry grasped after her has she dove into the deep end.

"Ah ... it feels so good in here. Sorry, Henry, but I had to get out of that—"

"We've got company, coming fast!" the guard said, backing away and lowering his barrel.

Henry stripped off his suit and dove in alongside Tori. He said, "We'll suffer the madness together."

The moans of the zombies became a roar.

Over half a dozen figures burst inside the aquatic center, smeared with blood. Henry started shouting.

"In here, zombies!"

Tori was whistling and splashing.

The zombies groaned as they piled into one another, fighting over the pints of blood. Two collided at the pool's edge and fell in with a splash. Rod unloaded his shotgun into another, knocking it into the pool.

Henry felt his heart freeze as more zombies spilled through the door.

"This isn't good. Tori, we've got to get out of here."

The blast of weapons rang out like cannons inside the metal dome. A human voice was screaming out in pain. The zombies became a writhing mass of undead flesh as they found the blood and then rushed after the humans in the pool. The pool lights underneath still glowed, and Henry could see the creatures sinking fast under the weight of their metal helmets. He wondered if zombies could drown. Judging by the looks of things, they didn't. They just kept trying to climb up the sides of the pool, so far, in vain.

He and Tori swam towards the shallow end of the pool and hunkered down.

"We've got to make a dash for that door."

Ahead, Rod was backing towards that very door.

"Come on, you two!"

Henry and Tori scrambled out of the pool and dashed for the doors.

BLAM! BLAM! BLAM! click

Henry shoved down the lever of the metal fire doors and surged down the hallway, pulling Tori behind him. Rod was on their heels, and a pack of zombies was on his.

His lungs were bursting inside his chest as he turned down one corridor and into another. He had to make it back outside. Get the Gator and go. He glanced back over his shoulder. Rod was running with a limp, and the zombies were only another twenty feet behind, jaws opened impossibly wide and snapping shut.

"Henry," Tori moaned, "I can't keep up."

"We're almost there. Hang on."

She slipped on a dark streak of something and fell. He pulled her up and hoisted her over his shoulder. Rod was pulling him along now. The zombies had gotten closer. The gymnasium was just ahead, but he knew they wouldn't have enough time to cross it, start the Gator, and run. The zombies would swarm them before they even sat down.

Rod knocked open the next set of fire exit doors. They were back in the gymnasium. So were the two biggest zombies he had ever seen in the world: Rick the Rifle and Slam Dunk Jones. Rod screamed. They looked hungry, and they were coming their way.

Splat! Splat!

Someone was throwing pints of blood at them. Henry twirled around as he stumbled backward with Tori in his arms. Rudy and Weege were heading for the zombie locker that usually housed the giants.

"What are you doing?"

He saw the trash bag filled with pints of blood on the floor. He snatched a pint up. He had an idea. The shadows of the two giants were closing in.

"Rod, throw these at the zombies!"

"What?!"

The zombies in pursuit burst through the door. As if on instinct, Rod hurled the plastic pint of blood into one's mouth. Its jaws clamped down, making a spray of blood. Henry tore the top from another sack and tossed it onto the giant zombies.

"Come on!" he said, running for the zombie locker where Weege and Rudy had begun to close the door. "NOOOO!" he screamed.

The door closed on his foot. Rod pulled it open and shoved his way inside. One zombie, covered in blood, was almost on top of him as Henry shoved Tori inside the room. The zombie was inches from ripping off his face.

"Close the door!" he screamed. *I'm gonna die a zombie.* A long powerful arm reached out, grabbed the neck of his pursuer and jerked it from its feet. Henry watched in awe as Slam Dunk Jones tried to stuff the zombie soldier in his mouth, which seemed to open as wide as his head. Henry's brain cringed as the giant zombie bit down on the metal skull with a crunch.

Rod pulled his gaping face inside the locker, and Tori sealed the door.

"You tried to kill us!" Rod pointed at Rudy and Weege.

Rudy said, "We thought you were zombies!"

"Really? Then why did you two buttheads try to lock us out?" Rod added, his mighty chest heaving as he fought for breath.

Rudy's eyes were all over Tori, and Weege began to stammer, "There was no time—"

Whack!

Rod dropped Weege with his left.

Whack!

Tori dropped Rudy with her zombie right.

"Nice shot, Honey," Henry said.

Safe behind the glass, they witnessed the zombie fight of the century. The Rifle and Slam Dunk were pulling apart one of the zombie soldiers. It reminded Henry of two dogs fighting over a bone. Henry could hear the fabric tearing on the zombie soldier's suit as it was pulled apart. Slam Dunk pulled the helmet from the zombie and slung it into the glass, causing them to all jump back. Henry checked the lock on the door, held his chest, and slid down along the wall.

"Everyone okay?" he asked.

Rod nodded, "Everyone but these two ass-bags."

Tori curled up beside him, shivering. "What now, Henry?"

"Let's just pray help arrives before we run out of air."

"What?"

"Just kidding." He allowed himself a smile and kissed her on the head. "How's it look out there, Rod?"

"There's a zombie staring in the window."

"Really?" Henry got up and looked.

A skull-faced zombie in full zombie gear was looking right in the window. In the darkness, he swore he could see something glimmer behind its eyes. He was certain the he was being watched. It made him angry. He offered a salute. *Damn World Humanitarian Society.*

The zombie walked away, towards the door. In the background, the giants were still slugging it out with the zombie soldiers. One of the small soldiers was hoisted up and stuffed inside a nearby basketball rim.

"I wish I had my phone to catch that one!"

The outside of the door groaned. The lever was being jostled from the other side.

"It can't get in here, can it?" Tori said.

"No, it's a manual lock, like the Day Care."

Henry wasn't so sure that the zombie wouldn't figure it out.

"Can we get out?"

"These doors lock from the inside or outside. The mechanism is simple enough. We used these pins," Henry pointed to the long rod of metal dropped in the hasp in the door, "to secure them. I've used the pin on the inside. We're safe, so long as no one uses a pin on the outside. If they do that, we're stuck."

28

WASHINGTON, DC

BLOOD WAS COURSING through him like a rushing river, and the WHS security officer told him to step on the scanner. Nate's eyes flitted over to Walker, who had just passed through. The wry man had his back to him as he chatted with other WHS officers. *This isn't going to work. It's not possible.* He was running through scenarios of escape plans. What would they do if they discovered it was him? What about fingerprints? He wiped his palms on his pants as he stepped in front of the screen. What about his eyes? Did they not have records of those, too? He swallowed hard as a neon light illuminated his face. As far as he knew, he had never been fingerprinted before. No retinal scans that he knew of. But certainly the WHS had some way to keep track of him. A micro tag perhaps.

Beep.

He felt like he was about to pee himself as the outline of his skull appeared on the screen. Walker had told him to be calm. The skull-face technology was new, but effective. People could alter many things about themselves, but the entire skull wasn't likely. Hence the reconstructive surgery.

Beep.

Something was wrong. Another officer was viewing the scan on the monitor as a discrepancy was being pointed out. Nate felt like the man was poking him in the eyes as the tall man's slender finger tapped the screen. *They know it's me!*

He could see he skull matching up with another on the monitor. The name Rick Jones appeared, the same as his ID that he had scanned. So what was the problem? He cleared his throat.

"I don't have all day, gentlemen."

They ignored his comments. He could see more members of the heavily armed group move in closer. *Geez I'm dead.*

Beep.

Walker slid back over and said, "What's the hold up, boys? We have to get over to the press room stat."

With a penetrating gaze, the taller man replied, "Colonel, Officer Jones's heart rate is at 120. What happened, did you have him jog over here?"

"It wouldn't be the first time." A small laugh came from the crowd. "Since when are we monitoring heart rates?"

"Sorry, Colonel Walker, but a new regulation came out hours ago. They boost security every year. One nonsensical procedure after the other. I think they're looking for someone, but they won't say."

Walker was rubbing his chin.

"Hmmm ... so does my man check out, other than a jumpy heart rate? It is his first convention rodeo, you know."

"Everything's fine other than a runner's heart rate."

"So, what's the new procedure book say?"

The man opened up a notebook that sat on the counter and ran his finger down the pages. As he read the worst out loud Nate became mortified.

"... irregular heart rates that arouse suspicion can call for a full cavity search with proper authority."

Walker smiled wide under his mirrored glasses as he said, "Well, get the rubber gloves, I've got things to do."

"We'll try to make it quick," the man smiled, "barring any unforeseen objects found in the rectum."

Ten humiliating minutes later, Nate was following Walker through the convention center with a funny walk.

"Gee thanks, that's just what I needed. I'm all loosened up now," he fumed.

"I told you to keep your heart rate down."

"Easier said than done."

"You did fine. I didn't think we'd make it this far. As of an hour ago, our people hadn't hacked the system yet to update your profile. I was sweating bullets, but my heart rate was slow."

"Maybe that's because you don't have a heart."

"Maybe because I don't need one." Walker stopped him in the hall. "Now listen up. We're going in that room." He pointed with his finger. "I'm posting you near the front tables. Keep your hands down. Stand. Observe. Listen. They'll be right in front of you, ready to take some questions after the dinner banquet. I'll check on you. Don't act. Don't respond. If you hear anything, we can cover it after we get out of here. The walls have eyes and ears; they are watching and listening. Go in."

NO!

"Yeah, I got it."

"Let's go."

Less than a minute later, Walker posted him along the wall about thirty feet from the main table. He was one of over two dozen that secured the room. The banquet hall was huge, hosting over 1000 exquisitely dressed guests from all over the world. He remembered being a big part of all of these zombie days, loving it and hating it. He must of posed for over a thousand pictures with people from everywhere inside rooms like this. Now, he stood alone, anonymous, nervous, and free. There was something exhilarating about being nobody. Eyes glanced over and passed him like he was part of the wall. *This is kind of cool.*

Walker was on the other side of the room, seated with a handful of dignitaries, looking like a body guard. A familiar voice from the head table cut through the air in uproarious laughter.

Ben Johannes

Big, old, and bald, the man looked like a white ape with a beak for a nose. He had never liked that man or his rotting cigar-smoking breath. His dirty jokes were vile, and his demeanor was cruel. There was no way that guy could be Harry.

He watched them cut up their food, some right and others left handed. Every man had a blood steak on his plate, and the handfuls of women were eating roast chicken. They were all chatting among themselves, savoring every last bit of gluttony. Nate could picture himself up there as well. He wondered if he realized how barren he seemed. He looked into the sea of tables and wondered if anyone really cared about what these people were doing. How many of them were in on their secrets? Who financed the WHS? Maybe Harry was in the crowd.

By the time dessert was served his legs were aching, and Harry hadn't made himself known. To make matters worse he couldn't make out anything that they were saying. He never heard the word Harry once. Still, he tried to envision one of them being Harry. He went down the line one by one. He knew them all well enough, but the name plates helped.

Julie Edgerd

Clint Raven

Edgar Crawford

Jim Dunahan

Leslie McKinley

Ben Johannes

Rachel Harriet

Edward McMinnis

Anthony Ravenloft

Sally Myers

Pamela Elswick

Missing from the group were himself and Don Baker.

Harriet. Rachel. Ben Johannes was draped over her elegant figure like a cloak. It seemed unlikely that she would be the Harry, but hers was the only name that had any kind of attachment to the name Harry. Certainly, Walker and his crew had made that connection and looked into it. *This is pointless.* He wanted to leave. Start a new life. Go to Vegas and disappear. But there was another zombie apocalypse on the horizon. He didn't want anyone on Earth to go through that again.

"Anything?"

Nate's heart jumped.

"Just nod."

He shook his head a little.

Walker slapped him on the shoulder and said, "Hang in there. It's almost over, but we have to stick around until they leave."

Nate was daydreaming now; trying to take his mind off the pain in his aching legs and feet. He couldn't remember standing so long before, and he would kill a man just to be able to take a seat. At the end of the head table he overheard bits and pieces of Anthony Ravenloft's jovial conversation on his phone. The man had raven black hair, a stout build, and a row of teeth that seemed to be a mile wide. Nate had never talked to that man much. He seemed to keep to himself more so than the others. He excused himself from the table and walked closer to the wall, eyeing the audience and waving at some acquaintances. More uproarious laughter burst from Ben Johannes' throat, which caught his attention and turned Rachel Harriet's cheeks the bright color of roses. *What a pompous jerk.* It seemed like most of the room was laughing at something or another at the time, when his ears picked up something that sent a sliver of ice down his spine.

"... Take it easy, Son. I'm just pulling your leg," Anthony Ravenloft had said. Harry had said that same phrase to him over the years at least a few dozen times.

29

(EPILOGUE)

WASHINGTON, DC

"DON'T TAKE it so bad, Jack. It's only money."

If Don's nephew heard him, he couldn't tell. The young man smashed his computer on the park bench and screamed. The pigeons scattered into the air, leaving Don alone to bask in the moon of the chill night air. He fought the tears and the laughter as the car door slammed shut behind him. Don was getting too old for this. He needed to retire, but for a man in his position, retirement meant death.

The men and women in the West Virginia complex would be safe, for now. Henry Bawkula had proven to be a formidable man. A survivor. A threat to the WHS. Don wanted to be there when the WHS had to explain what had gone wrong. The clean up would be quick and the interrogations ugly, but they would live ... gag order pending.

He took his final swallow of coffee and closed his eyes in a moment of thanks. He was all too happy to close his computer and try to forget the tortuous scenes. *Is this what they have in store for me one day?* His inner core shuddered at the thought. He took another minute to bask in his hollow victory. Maybe he should head over to the Zombie Convention. He needed to pick some brains. The fact that he'd been told it was okay to miss this one seemed awfully strange now. He sighed, picked up his Thermos, and tried to think of some comforting words to say to Jack as he headed for the car.

Oliver sat inside as the engine warmed on the big black Cadillac. His bodyguard started to get out of his car, but Don said, "It's okay, Oliver, I can open my own door."

As he sat down in his seat, he noticed Jack was slumped over, unmoving. Adrenaline surged through him as he heard the sounds of his door locking.

"Oliver, what is this?" he stammered as he lifted his nephew's head back and noticed the bloody bullet hole in his chest.

The barrel of a silencer was pointing in his face in reply. Oliver's voice was ice cold.

"Your nephew had become quite the evil bastard, Don. He had to die."

Don shrunk back in his seat and said, "Why, Oliver? Why?"

"I told you why."

"Are you going to kill me, too?" he stammered.

"Don't you think you deserve to die after being behind the deaths of millions of people?"

"I suppose."

"Then we both agree."

BLAM!

Don felt his breathing thin as all of his strength left his body, and he fell over by his nephew's side. He could hear a song on the radio playing, and Oliver singing. He wondered if he was dead or alive.

"Don't worry, Don, you aren't going to die. But you are going to pay for what you did."

CRAIG HALLORAN

ZOMBIE WARFARE

PROLOGUE

"Look, it's not a setback. Not at all. It was a test run, one of many, and there's more to come," the man said, dabbing the sweat on his bald head. He was older. Portly. He guzzled down a bottle of vitamin water. "You have to trust me. I've never let you down before."

He turned an oscillating fan on and held his face in it a few seconds. Alone aside from the silhouetted image of a man on the computer monitor, he paced around the lab. It was large and private, part of an abandoned hospital in the basement morgue. Another secret lab of the WHS.

When the image over on the monitor said nothing, he rapped his knuckles on one of the metal gurneys and the sound echoed. There were a dozen gurneys: some with bodies, some without. Zombie bodies. He cleared his throat.

"What happened at the Rehab is nothing to worry about," he told the face on the monitor while he strapped a headband with a digital feed on his head and walked over to the laptop to type in a few commands. "Those zombies were serviceable, and they do in a pinch, but now, well ..." He cleared his throat again and gulped down the rest of his water. "I really wish we could get some AC down here. I'm sweating like a pig."

He looked over his shoulder at the monitor but the image hadn't moved. He turned his attention to the zombie harnessed to the table, sitting upright. Its eyes were sunken and the skin pasty, but the jaws and eyes were moving. It moaned a little.

"Can you see what I'm seeing?" he said. "This web cam on my head should give you a bird's eye view." He checked over his shoulder again. Still no reply. "Just shout if I'm too close. Anyway... ahem."

The zombie leaned towards him with its eyes searching. It strained at the leather shackles binding its wrists and they groaned. The zombie had been a fit man, maybe in his twenties. The head was shaved and its chin was strong. One naked arm had a special forces tattoo on it and they were both corded in muscle.

"See this, Boss Man, is a soldier. He got caught up in the middle of the Outbreak where we unleashed the zombies in the Middle East. Probably Afghanistan." He shrugged. "Maybe Iraq, I don't know. Anyway, once the Outbreak was controlled, we discovered an army of them wandering around the desert. This was months after things were figured out, maybe a year. These zombies have stamina, I tell you."

He took off his lab coat, grabbed a notebook and started fanning himself.

"And there wasn't a drop of sweat on them. Not one drop. It's amazing!" He punched the zombie in the arm. "I envy you guys some-times. Ahem. So, we discovered ... correction ... I discovered some-thing helpful. Very helpful indeed. You see, the zombie physiology isn't very difficult to penetrate. As we learned with the harnesses, we can control their movements, but it wasn't fluid. I—" he spread his arms wide as if to bow "—suggested we harness some of these soldiers. Why, you ask?" He looked back at the screen and grinned. "Do you work out, Boss?"

The silhouette remained, but it looked like its hands were folded under its chin. He always wondered how many people were actually watching him. There were cameras everywhere. He assumed he had at least three observers at any given time. At the moment, he guessed on the other side of the monitor was a large office with over a dozen people. The Puppet Masters. One day he'd be seated on the other side of the screen as well.

"I'm just going to assume you work out. After all, folks are really into keeping up appearances." He patted his belly. "At least those of us that have places to appear, that is." He scratched his head. "Where was I?" *Snap!* "Ah yes, muscle memory. Where we had trouble teaching the zombies more complicated things like aiming and pulling a trigger, we've—I've— discovered it can be done. Soldiers have had so much repetition that holding and firing a weapon falls right into place. Well, with some special modifications." He clapped his hands. "It's amazing!"

"Imagine, just imagine if we had them ready during the war on terror. They could cover miles of terrain with no food or water, just a solar battery pack to keep our controls connected to them. Just cover them in Zombie Suits and send them on their way. Sure, the drones are great, but could they fly into those caves?" He pinched the zombie's rugged face. "But this guy can go right in there. Extract data and report. They can do all the searching we can't. They can run and climb. Robots can't do that and we don't have a Six Million Dollar Man. Not even a sixty million dollar man is close to running. No, no, no. This guy just needs weapons and armor. And if we have to remote destruct, no problem. Boom goes the zombie. Boom goes Al Qaeda or whoever."

He patted the zombie on the chest. "Well, not you, Steve. I need you for my experiments." He took off the head gear and made his way back in front of the laptop where the silhouette waited. The silhouette moved a little and he assumed he was muted. He tapped his foot and folded his arms. *They have to like this. Only idiots wouldn't.*

"Dr. Charles, when will this be ready?"

His smile was toothy and broad.

"The first trials are about to begin." He nodded. "I'll have you patched in."

1

-*Washington, D.C.*-
Location Unknown

What's going on here? What's going on?

Don sat on a cot shivering. He'd only been awake a few minutes and everything was foggy, his vision blurry. He rubbed his head and surveyed his new surroundings. It looked like the inside of an office trailer like the ones he'd seen at construction sites. It was rustic and musty, and the windows were blacked out

"Oh ... no" he said, grimacing and rubbing his neck. There was a collar around it. Snug. He could feel a small plastic lump on it and metal prongs touching his neck.

"Damn, a security collar."

He'd seen similar ones on dogs, but this one, he was certain, was meant for humans. Long ago when they were first introduced, they had TNT in them to make a man's head explode. He swallowed hard and the lump was hard to get down. *This can't be happening.*

He stood up on shaking legs. It felt like he hadn't walked in months. "Jack, oh no, Jack." He sat back down, holding his stomach.

He wanted to retch. The recollection of his nephew's death hit him like a metal sled.

Oliver, his personal body guard, had shot his nephew in the chest. Don was mortified. Things like that didn't happen to a guy like him. It was unimaginable. It was a nightmare. His lungs thinned and he started to wheeze a little. He reached into his suit pockets one at a time and patted himself down. "Dammit." He rummaged through the small drawers alongside the kitchen sink and found only napkins, ketchup and mustard packets. There was some Taco Bell sauce in there too that read, "Ah ... we meet again." The cabinets above the sink were empty and the spigot squeaked when he turned it, but no water came.

"Oliver," he said. Shaking his head, he took three short steps to the door and jiggled the handle. "Locked, of course. What did you think, Don, that it would be unlocked? That they went to all this trouble just to let you walk out of here? Wherever this flea trap is."

A bright red dot caught his eye. A small black security camera was mounted in the ceiling corner left of the door.

"Ah," Don said, wheezing. He resumed his seat and waved. "Probably gonna be awhile."

He closed his eyes and began some breathing exercises, but they weren't helping. He thought about Jack being killed right before him. *His family. I wonder if they know already. I hope he took out that life insurance policy I told him to take out years ago. Those things always lessen the grieving. Besides, she was about to divorce him anyway.*

An image of his own wife formed in his head.

"Aw shit, Becky! She's crawling the walls by now." He pointed at the camera. "Oliver, you bastards are going to pay for this. My colleagues from the WHS will be here any moment." He made a gun with his finger. "They'll shoot you in the head. They'll shoot you all in the head." He wheezed and coughed a little. "I'm Don Baker, dammit. And no one messes with Don Baker!"

A key was jammed in the lock outside the door and the knob twisted open.

A small man in mirrored sunglasses stepped inside.

"Aw shaddup, you old asshole."

Don sat up.

"Excuse me?" He shook his head and squinted his eyes at the man. "Say, you're WHS security aren't you? You're Walker."

The man closed the door behind him, took a seat in a folding chair and pulled a pack of cigarettes from his shirt pocket.

"What are you doing, Walker? It's time to get out of here." Don craned his neck. "And get this damn collar off me. Whoever did this is going to die if they aren't dead already."

Walker clicked open a burnished Zippo and torched the end of his cigarette.

"Give it a minute, Chief." Walker spoke with a heavy Southern accent. "We have to wait for the all clear, you know." He blew smoke in the air. "It'll be a few moments."

Don eyed the .44 Magnum semis on Walker's slender hips.

"Two of them. Is there a hoard of zombies out there?"

Walker looked at him. Silent.

Don got glimpse of himself in Walker's glasses.

"Geez, I look like Hell," he said, rubbing his bearded chin. "How long did it take you guys to find me, anyway?"

"Not long."

"Fools," Don said. "Only an idiot would think they could capture a high ranking WHS member. I just can't believe Oliver is one of those rebels. He was a good man. I liked Oliver." He coughed and wheezed. "Is he dead?"

Walker reached into his pocket and tossed Don his inhaler.

Don exhaled and then squeezed the pumper into his mouth. He held his breath several seconds and blew out a pale mist. He slipped the inhaler back in his pocket.

"Thanks, Walker," he said. "Once you get me out of here, I'm taking you out for the finest steak you ever had. How much longer do you think it will be, anyway?" He rubbed his stomach. "I'm starving."

"Not too long."

"So, how long have I been out? A day? Two?"

"Nah," Walker said, blowing smoke Don's way. "More like two weeks."

"What! Two weeks!" Don jumped to his feet.

Walker shoved him back down.

"Hey," Don said. "Don't be insubordinate, Walker. Remember who you're dealing with. I'm Don Baker."

Someone else outside jiggled the handle.

"Looks like the rest of the cavalry is here," Walker said with a smile, "Asshole."

2

"IT'S BEEN TWO WEEKS, Henry! Two!" Tori stuffed her face in the bed pillow and screamed.

Henry loaded up his tooth brush and started scrubbing. Since the last incident they'd been treated like prisoners, confined to their room until the WHS guards escorted them to eat in the cafeteria.

"Geez, Henry," Tori said, "How many times are you going to brush your teeth in a day? That must be the sixth time already."

It was the seventh time actually, and he'd probably brush ten times before the day was over. He scrubbed harder. *You're driving me nuts, Woman.* The first few days cooped up together had been pure ecstasy. Tori had the most fascinating way of showing how happy she was to be alive. Henry had never felt so alive before either.

"Are you ignoring me, Henry? You know I hate that."

The room seemed to shrink. Henry's skin got thin as Tori's clingy personality took

over. She was breaking down. Tears started to flow.

"Do you still love me, Henry? Henry?"

He rinsed his mouth out, put on his glasses, and smiled his best smile.

Say cheese.

He peered outside the bathroom door, looked right at her and holding his smile.

She lay on the bed like a goddess in a black tank top and pink panties. Her auburn hair was frizzy and her bottom lip jutted out. She glanced at Henry and said, "No, you don't."

Not this again.

He fought back a sigh, took a seat at the end of the bed and gently rubbed her sensuous legs.

"Sure I do," he said. "You know that."

"Liar."

"Tori, I..."

He didn't want to have this conversation again. It always ended up with him apologizing for something he hadn't started.

I have to try something different. I can't handle Tori the Tornado again.

"You what?" she snapped.

He cleared his throat. "I was going to say, 'I think you need your feet rubbed.' Would you like that?"

She eyed him. "Are you trying to avoid this conversation, Henry? Huh? Are you?"

"No, I'm just trying to rub your feet." He stared right into her eyes. "I know these interviews have been hard on you."

"Interviews?" She sat upright. "Interrogations is more like it! Those zombies tried to kill us, and they're blaming us for killing them. Mother—"

"Keep your voice down, Tori! Remember last time."

She fell silent, glared at him, and fell back on the pillow.

"Get some lotion."

"For what?" he asked.

"For rubbing my feet, you idiot. Sheesh!"

HENRY RUBBED her feet until his thumbs were sore. About fifteen minutes into it, Tori was snoring. He sighed, but kept rubbing.

Yes! I hope this works as well the next time I try it.

The hard lines on Tori's face eased and Henry eased his rubbing. *Thank goodness!* He released her feet and shifted up from the bed. Tori stirred and her eyes started to open. *Ah!* He grabbed her feet and started rubbing again. She blinked a couple times, showed him an angry look, and then drifted back into her pillow. *That was close.*

He pushed his glasses up on his nose and rolled his neck. The past week had been miserable. Every day, the WHS grilled them with questions. No, the same questions after the same questions. It was as if they wanted to see if one of them changed their story. It was madness.

Henry started rubbing Tori's foot harder. *Fools.* He glanced at Tori's zombie arm. It was dark and a little pasty and corded in skin-tight muscle. When one of the WHS 'interviewers' had pushed her too hard, she had grabbed the man by the neck with that zombie arm and slung him over the table. It was the scariest and sexiest thing Henry had ever seen. He patted her thigh.

"I sure know how to pick them."

At this point, their lives as WHS employees had become ridiculous. He wasn't a fool and neither was Tori. Someone had tried to kill them. With zombies in Skull Helmets. He and Tori had been just lab rats in an experiment. A sick trial of sorts. Henry had won and the zombies had failed. Score one for mankind. The good side that is.

He replayed his memories of everything that happened a thousand times, trying to piece it together. He assumed it all went back to the Day Care incident. Too much had happened there and he had become a liability. So had Tori, Weege and Rudy. His brother, Jimmy, and his step father Stanley had been pawns in a bigger scheme. What had been made to look like an accident was anything but that, more like a test. Henry had concluded that months ago.

He stopped rubbing and moved over to the chair at the desk, turned off the light and peered out the window. It was a moon filled night and there wasn't a soul moving outside of the rehab courtyard.

The place was closed down and abandoned other than the guards and the interviewers.

He hadn't seen anyone else since the incident either. Not Weege, Rudy, Rob, or any of the other security guards. There was always a possibility Weege and Rudy could be manipulated. They'd changed since they started working in the Rehab. They'd gotten greedy or something.

He removed his glasses, leaned back and rubbed his temples. His neck was tight as a spring. Something big was brewing. He could feel it. And he couldn't help but think that his stepfather's XT Formula was being used as a weapon and not a cure. The way those zombies moved—so fast and almost fluid—ate at his soul. *Stop thinking about it, Henry. Stop thinking.* He dozed off.

Knock. Knock. Knock.

Henry's head popped off his chest and his glasses clattered on the floor.

He blinked and rubbed his blurry eyes.

Did I just hear that?

Reaching down, he grabbed his glasses and checked on Tori. She was curled up in a ball. He walked over and covered her with the blanket at the foot of the bed. Wiping the drool from his mouth, he headed for the door, checking his watch. 10:31pm. *Who'd be here this late?*

He pressed his eye to the peep hole.

It was the last person he wanted to see.

Damn!

It was Alice.

3

"OLIVER!" Don said, jumping from his bed. "You killed my nephew, you sonuva—*oof*!"

Walker socked him in the gut. Don sagged back onto his bed.

Oliver made his way inside. He wore a turtleneck sweater and jeans that were both packed with muscle. Just as stony faced as ever, he was sitting down when a third man entered. Don didn't recognize him. He was taller and a bit heavy set. His beard was neatly trimmed and he had softer eyes. He closed the door and leaned back on it.

Don glared at Oliver though and shook his head. "Why, Oliver? I was good to you." He wheezed and straightened himself up in the bed. "You didn't have to kill my nephew."

Oliver smirked and folded his thick arms over his chest. "I didn't have to. I wanted to."

"Did you want to kill me, too?" Don asked.

"Every day for the last several years."

Don grumbled a long sigh and rubbed his beard. Things were clearly not what they seemed. *I'm in trouble. I'm in my seventies. I don't need this kind of trouble.* He popped his head up and clapped his hands.

"Alright, gentlemen, you got me. What is it you want?"

Walker puffed on his cigarette. Oliver didn't budge, but his eyes bore right into Don.

"Well?"

"World Peace," Walker said with a laugh.

"Ah," Don said, wagging his finger at Walker, "that's a good one. But I don't think that will ever happen. And gentlemen, I don't think what you've done here is very smart either." He slapped his knees. "Nope, not very smart at all." He looked at Oliver and Walker. "Now you both know that nothing in this world, and I mean nothing, gets by WHS. Oh, you may have me now, but it won't be long. You'll see. So, whatever you want to get from me you better make it quick. I wouldn't be surprised if they arrived here any minute."

Walker and Oliver chuckled.

The trailer filled with a layer of smoke and Don started coughing a little.

"Do you mind?" he said, fanning it from his face.

Walker reached into his shirt pocket and withdrew a small hunk of metal. He set it on the table.

Don cocked his head. He started rolling his tongue around his mouth, feeling his teeth. A tooth was missing. He shook his head.

"That's right," Walker said. "That's your filling, or should I say, your tracer." Walker picked it up and pinched it between his fingers. "Pretty dated, but still effective. When did they put that thing in, the sixties?"

Don nodded. "About right," he said, voice sagging. "But they'll still find me."

"They haven't yet," Oliver said. "We've been plenty careful."

"Well, it hasn't been that long now, has it?" Don said, eyeing Oliver.

"Two weeks is a pretty long time," Oliver said, bobbing his head, "and they haven't found you yet."

Don's eyes widened. "No," he said in disbelief, "it can't be."

The stranger at the door showed a smart phone display to him. It was the front page of USA Today, with a date two weeks from the last date Don remembered.

"It is," Walker said. "And I'm pretty sure they've given you up for dead. At least, that's what they're saying back at the office. The search is over, Bub."

Aw, Becky. She must be a complete mess by now.

Don fought the urge to collapse his face into his hands. This wasn't his first interrogation. He'd been down that road many times before. OK, a few times on this side of things, but mostly on the other. He could handle these overachievers. They were amateurs.

He looked up at the man standing in front of the door.

"So, who do we have here?"

The man stared right back in his eyes without blinking. He seemed familiar.

"Is this the mastermind behind it all? The team leader of my kidnapping?" He huffed. "No offense, but you don't look like much of a mastermind. Maybe you're one of those hackers. Eh? Is that it?"

The man shook his head.

"Not much of a talker," Don said. He looked at Walker. "Did you cut his tongue out? Maybe a zombie ate it?"

The man smirked and stuck out his tongue.

Don's stomach groaned again.

"Alright, this is getting old. Out with the questions. What do you guys want?"

Walker finished his cigarette and flicked it at him.

"Hey," Don said, brushing it off, "respect your elders."

"Don't piss me off, Old Man," Walker said. He busted open his zippo and fired another Camel up. "Anthony Ravenloft."

Don stiffened for a split second then resumed his lax posture.

"Ravenloft? Pfft. What would you want him for? He's a strange bird."

"How strange?" Walker said.

"Well," Don started, clearing his throat, "I don't think he's a cross dresser or anything. He's just weird, is all. One of those paranormal geeks. Say, if I've been down for two weeks, can I please get some-thing to eat? I'm not much of a conversationalist when I'm starving."

Walker nodded to the man at the door. He excited quickly.

Don didn't get a glimpse of anything beyond. It was dim outside, wherever they were. *Damn.*

"So, is that a fellow foot soldier? A WHS insider like you, Walker?"

"Nope."

He turned his attention to Oliver.

"How'd you get sucked into all this, Oliver?"

Oliver had been his personal guard for fifteen years. A former Secret Service agent he'd recruited. The man didn't have much. No wife or children. His parents died when he was young and he was bounced around in foster homes until he graduated high school and joined the Air Force. Liked girls and gambling a little. Simple, rugged and kept to himself. He had been an ideal henchmen for Don. Now he'd betrayed him.

"When I'm not driving you around or fixing your coffee, I like to read. I like to read a lot. Not those best sellers either. No, the other stuff. You know, the stuff they don't want people to read." Oliver leaned forward with his elbows on his knees. "You know, conspiracies and such."

"Ah," Don said. "Got you thinking, did it? Did you read the ones about Kennedy and Lincoln?" He rolled his eyes. "How exciting for you, Oliver. Are you going to write a conspiracy book of your own?"

"No," Oliver said, "I'm just going to do my part."

"Oh, and what part is that?"

"Making sure that scum like you don't get what they want."

"And what do we want, Oliver?" Don said, looking bored.

"Another Zombie Outbreak. You bastards want to finish what you started."

"You flatter me, Oliver. You really do," Don said, holding his stom-ach. "But you've got the wrong man for that. But my nephew, well, he might have been able to help. He knew more than I do."

The door opened up and the bearded man slipped in. He had a

cooler in one hand and tossed Don an object with the other. He caught it with his chest. It was a small can with a blue label. He read it out loud.

"Vienna Sausages."

"Don't worry, Don," Walker said. "After all this time, I'm sure it'll taste like a steak dinner."

4

-INSTITUTE, WV-

"ALICE," Henry whispered, wedging his mouth into the crack between the door and the jamb, "what do you want?"

Her arms were folded over her lab coat and her high-heeled foot tapped the floor. She was pretty with a dark ponytail. Round glasses. Arrogant.

"What's the matter? Did I interrupt you and your little hussy?" she said with a smirk. Loudly at that.

"Ssshh," Henry said, slipping outside and closing the door behind him. "She's asleep and if she heard you say that, she'd tear you in half."

Alice laughed.

"Whatever, Henry."

There were three security men in the old dormitory hallway. They wore flack vests and carried M-16 assault rifles. Their helmets had shaded face shields. Two must have escorted Alice and the third was always stationed in the hall near their door. There were cameras in the halls too.

Henry brushed his hands over his clothes and blushed a little. He was in the white Scooby Doo T-Shirt Tori had bought him on their last outing. His pajama pants were navy blue. Alice looked him up and down and the guards snickered at him. He folded his arms over his chest and stepped right up to Alice.

"What do you want?"

"I just wanted to personally let you know that the interviews are over."

"And what?" he glanced at security and back to her. "We face the firing squad tomorrow?"

Alice reached over and brushed some lint off his chest. She smelled really good and her nails were painted now.

"Not you," she said, "just Tori. She is part zombie, after all."

"Ha, ha," Henry said.

"Well, be thankful. I talked Rudy out of pressing charges against her."

"What?" Henry's face flushed. "For what?"

"Assault," she said. "She broke his jaw, you know. That fellow Rod put Weege in the hospital."

And they so deserved it. Henry didn't know what to make of it, but the pair of them had almost gotten him and Tori killed. He couldn't help but think Alice had something to do with it. Possibly Director Smoot too.

"So are we free to go back to work? What is the situation, Alice?"

"You're being reassigned," she said.

"To do what?" Henry said.

"You'll find out soon enough. Pack your bags. *You* leave first thing tomorrow."

"What?" Henry scratched his head. "What do you mean by *you*, Alice?"

"Oh, you're worried about your little freaky girlfriend." Alice leaned forward and spoke in his ear. "Your little pet isn't coming. She can go back to Go-Mart where you found her."

Henry's door popped open and out came Tori. She jerked him back behind her.

"What's going on out here?" Tori said, getting in Alice's face.

Tori was still in her black top, pink panties and nothing else. The guards shifted and craned their necks. One's mouth fell open.

"Nice hair," Alice said.

Slap!

Tori slapped Alice's glasses off her face.

Alice's eyes turned into daggers of ice.

"You bitch!"

She drew back her fist. Tori jumped on her.

"Tori! Stop!" Henry said, stretching his arms out.

Both women rolled on the floor. They punched, bit, cursed and clawed at each other.

The guards looked at Henry, then back at the women.

Henry couldn't care less if Tori ripped Alice's head off, but he didn't want Tori getting in any more trouble.

"Want me to get a water hose?" one guard said.

"Good idea," said another.

"Geez," Henry said, "Do I have to handle this?"

Tori and Alice had each other by the hair and were screaming in each other's faces. Henry wrapped his arms around Tori's waist and pulled. One guard did the same to Alice. Both of them still had handfuls of hair, which tried to keep them attached to each other.

"I'm going to kill you!" Alice screamed.

"I'm going to kill you!" Tori fired back.

"That's enough, Tori!" Henry yelled. "Let her go!"

"NO!"

"Now, I said!"

They pulled them apart. Both women screeched. They had clumps of hair in their hands. Alice's hair was all over her face.

"Shoot her!" Alice said, trying to grab the guard's rifle. He turned Alice around and shoved her down the hallway. Another guard picked up her glasses, grinned and said, "Thanks."

"You'll never see her again, Henry!" Alice yelled back down the hallway. "Never!"

The guards got her to the elevator and disappeared.

Henry put his arm around Tori's waist to lead her to their room. She jerked away.

"Let go of me!"

She dashed into the room.

Bam!

The door slammed in his face.

"Great," he sighed.

He gave it a moment, then tried the handle. It opened. He slipped inside and closed the door behind him.

Tori sat on the bed, shaking and sobbing.

"Are you alright?"

Her face was miserable when she said, "Do I look alright?"

Stupid question.

He sat down beside her and rubbed her back.

"Don't," she said, getting up, snatching some tissues and blowing her nose. She sat down in the desk chair. "What did she want anyway?"

"She came to tell me the interviews are over. She says I'm being reassigned."

"What about me?"

Henry shrugged.

Tears started rolling down Tori's cheeks.

"Hey, hey, hey ... I'm not going anywhere without you. Alice is just saying that. We'll figure it all out tomorrow."

Tori continued to sob. Henry's chest ached. They should be happy the interviews were over. They should be celebrating. Alice had gone awfully far out of her way to tell him the news and now he didn't have any more answers than he had before. Thanks to Tori he'd have to wait until tomorrow. *Can't she ever control herself?*

"You're mad at me, aren't you?" she said.

"No. I'm just mad." He went into the bathroom and grabbed his toothbrush. "They say it's a reassignment. To do what, I don't know."

"When will you find out?" Tori said.

"Tomorrow." He squeezed his toothpaste onto his brush.

"When does it start?" Tori said, getting up and leaning on the bathroom doorway.

He turned and looked at her. "Tomorrow. She said to pack my things. I—well, I assume we—leave tomorrow." He wet his brush and started scrubbing.

"You want to leave me, don't you Henry?"

He could see her distraught face in the mirror. Her eyes caught his. Her limp trembled.

"You don't love me, do you?"

5

-Location Unknown-

"A<small>H</small>, Steven, let's take a closer look at you," Charles said. He held a pen light in his mouth and pushed the zombie's eyelids open with his thumb. The pupils didn't dilate one bit. The eyes glanced side to side. "Hmmm," Charles said to himself. He grabbed a clipboard and made some notes on a chart.

Steve strained against his shackles. Charles kept writing.

The zombie snapped his teeth, inches from Charles's face. He jumped back. His clipboard clattered on the floor.

"Cripes, Steve!" he said, "You almost bit my ear off. Don't be a Tyson."

The zombie groaned at him.

"Alright, alright. I guess it's Mountain Dew time." He checked his watch. "Huh, I'm about an hour late. Guess I better be more careful." He waddled over to a two-door commercial fridge and popped open one door. "What will it be, 'Voltage' or 'Super Nova'?"

Steve's jaw clamped open and shut a few times.

"No, we're out of the original. Pardon me, Steve, but I drank it all. Just hold on."

He twisted the cap off, stood on a stool, and held the bottle over Steve's head. Steve tilted his head back and his jaw opened and closed.

Glug. Glug. Glug.

"I hate that sound. Gives me the chills." He shivered. "Bottoms up, Steve." He poured the reddish liquid down the zombie's throat. It gulped every drop down. Charles shook his head. "I'll never, ever understand how that works." With the briskness of a routine he practiced twice a day, he stepped off the stool, scooted it back against the wall with his foot, and tossed the bottle away, all in one motion. The trashcan was almost full of bottles again. He groaned.

"Better check the others." He looked at Steve. "Feeling better, Mister Cranky?"

Steve grunted. His head started rolling left and right.

Charles opened up a cabinet on the wall and twisted the lid off a blue jar. Sticking his finger inside, he rubbed Noxzema under his nose. He twisted the lid back on and put it up.

"I wish you dead people didn't smell so much." Charles had figured on getting used to the smell by now, but for some reason he never did. "Stinkers."

Charles headed to the next zombie-filled table. It was another man, not so different than Steve except lying down. An IV marked DEW hung from a hanger like a blood sack. Its eyes were closed and the liter-sack of Dew was over half filled.

"Heh, heh, hew, Zombie Dew." He grabbed a handkerchief and patted the sweat on his head. "I'll never get over it. Frickin Nate McDaniel. What a putz!"

There were three others he tended to, one by one. The last one's Dew bag was empty. "My, you are a thirsty little lady, aren't you?"

It was a large woman with long hair. She was the biggest one of them all. He grabbed another liter of Dew from the refrigerator and switched it out. He checked her bonds. Her eyes were still closed. "Irene, you used to be the funniest woman on TV. Made me laugh all the time when I was a kid. 'Nobody Messes with Momma' was my favorite show. And now, here you are, strapped to a gurney. But don't you worry." He pinched her cheeks. "I'm pretty close to getting you back on your feet one day." He showed a gap between his fingers. "This close."

He sauntered over to the wall of cold chambers that held all the other bodies. There was a temperature gauge on it. He tapped it with his finger. "Damn thing should be digital. It's always fogging up." He wiped the moisture away. It read 30F. "Good."

There were twelve of them stacked in three rows of four. He opened up the first one.

"Ah," he said, basking in the cool mist. He slid the table out. A zombie lay there, bald, frosted and sort of blue. Charles knocked on its chest, making a hollow sound like wood. He smiled. "Another part of my genius. You can freeze zombies and make them easier to transport. Then just thaw then out in the sun." He patted himself on the back. "I got this job because of that one. Heh. Heh."

The watch on his wrist started buzzing.

"Oh! Oh yes! It's time." He tapped the screen on his smart watch, shoved the zombie back inside its sarcophagus and slammed the door shut. "It's zombie time!"

On tip toes, he dashed over to a computer console, clicked the mouse and fired up several larger monitors. The fans whirled to life. "Oh, hold on." He dashed over to the microwave and tossed in a sack of popcorn. Over near his desk he opened the door of a waist-high fridge and withdrew a green bottle of Mountain Dew. He made the mistake of looking over at Steve. The zombie's head was tilted at him and its crooked jaw was chewing at its lip. Charles shrugged. "Sorry, Steve. Zombies can't be choosers."

Ding.

He snagged the popcorn and practically jumped into his seat, fingers already moving like Mozart's over the keyboard. Screens 1 thru 6 fired up about a foot above his head. The high definition burst to life with the moving scenes of a painted desert. He opened up the audio.

"Charles? Charles? Are you there?"

The voice had a deep drawl, Texan like, but they weren't in Texas. It was Arizona.

"This is your rodeo, Cowboy," the voice said again. "Where in Sam Hill are you?"

"I'm here," Charles said, "just hold your horses."

"Bout time. Where ya' been? We got us a coyote on the loose!"

"Just one?" he said, stuffing popcorn in his mouth.

"I didn't think you needed any more. Besides, this is a big one. Been causing Uncle Sam lots of problems. Dealing with another Cartel. We'll get gold plated spurs for our boots with this one."

"Great," he said. "But I'm not seeing anything." His eyes darted from screen to screen. "Well, not really anything. I can see cacti, tumbleweeds and rocks, but that's not why I'm looking."

"Hold on, the drones are about to circle."

"Vultures, Rancho. Vultures," Charles fired back.

"Whatever rings yer bell, Cowboy. Just give it a second. The vultures are almost there."

Charles propped his glasses up on his head and sipped his Dew. The images on Screen 2 and Screen 3 were a little fuzzy.

"You need to focus better, Rancho. I can't see a thing."

"You wearing your glasses?" the voice fired back.

"Funny," Charles said. The screen cleared again. "Better." The image on Screen 2 to his left zoomed towards the ground. Four moving images appeared. His veins ignited. He clapped his hands together. "That's beautiful! Absolutely beautiful."

"If you say so," Rancho said in a funny kind of way.

The drones weren't the typical kind commonly used in the Middle East and at the Mexican border. These were different. Newer. Quieter. The kind that could hover. Charles had insisted on them.

"Closer, Vulture 2," he said, "closer."

The image zoomed right in.

"Better?"

"Perfect," he said. I can see their pupils now."

There were four of them. Two men covered head to toe in desert camo with M-16s strapped on their backs. Both strained to hold the other two figures on the leashes. Zombies.

Charles drummed his desk.

"I love it! Zombie Blood Hounds!"

The zombies wore desert-colored zombie suits with metal skull caps that left their mouths uncovered. Each had a black collar on its neck that pinched into the skin. Nostrils flared. Their jaws snapped open and closed, practically towing the men behind them.

"Where's the perp?" Charles asked.

"Vulture 3 is swinging around. Hold on," Rancho said. "He snuck into a ravine. Hard to get a good shot. Hold on."

The image dropped through the sky. Stopped maybe a dozen feet above the ground in a dry ravine. Slowly it panned around. A man stood in the shade of some rocks, sucking for breath and clutching his sides. He was big, tan and tawny haired. He had desert camo on like the others. He leaned on a rifle.

"Say," Charles said, "who is that guy? And why's he got a rifle?"

"You said you wanted it to be more of a challenge," Rancho said. "Not really sure who the guy is."

"He looks like one of our guys." Charles said.

"Yup."

"Well ..." he didn't finish. His eyes were fixed on the man hoisting the rifle onto his shoulder. "Tell me he doesn't have any bullets?"

"It's a carbine. Small load. You said you wanted them to have a fighting chance, didn't you?"

To Charles it looked like the man pointed the rifle right at him. His tongue clove to the roof of his mouth. The man closed one eye and took aim. He couldn't speak. *Get that drone out of there!*

He saw a tiny flash. His heart jumped. The screen went black. He fell backward out of his chair.

"Charles? Charles? Are you there?" Someone snickered. "I don't think that fella was close enough to hit you." There was more laughing. "Woooo Howdy, that was something!"

Charles kicked his chair away and bounced back to his feet.

"Did we just lose a drone!"

"You mean Vulture?"

"You know what I mean, dammit!" He slammed his fist on the console. Knocked his drink on the floor.

"It's just technology. We can fix it. Not like it's people."

Red faced, Charles picked up his chair and sat down. He also had to deal with Rancho and his twisted cowboy ways. He always screwed with Charles's plans. Treated everything like toys. Played games. He'd never met the man and he didn't like him. But, he trusted him to get the job done.

He typed a command into the computer. His finger hovered above enter.

"Alright Rancho, you've had your fun. Now it's my turn. Get me a view of this man and keep your distance," Charles said. "Those cameras can identify a flea in the sand from a mile away."

Screen 4 moved over the landscape and spotted the man. He was moving.

Good. Good.

"I'm turning the hounds loose," Charles said.

"You sure they won't turn on our men?" Rancho said.

"I've gone over this. As long as they keep the suits on and don't bleed anywhere, they'll be fine."

"Well the last time—"

"A miscalculation."

On Screen 2 the soldiers unhooked their leashes. The zombies lumbered onward, towards the man that was less than a mile distant.

Charles smiled. *Time to test the new XT Formula.* He pressed enter. The zombies lurched where they stood, stutter stepped a few times, and took off at a half run, half walk.

"That's new," Rancho said, "what's that on their gloves?"

"Hooks."

6

Don finished off the sausages and wiped his mouth with a paper napkin. They weren't so bad. If anything they were tasty. He had eaten something similar to them in his Meals Ready to Eat back when he served in Vietnam. It brought back memories.

"It's been awhile since I've eaten with my fingers," he said, wiping them off, "other than the occasional éclair." He took a drink from a green soda bottle. The tall one had left and brought it back when he complained about his thirst. "This Mountain Dew is pretty good. Funny thing, unlike almost everyone in the world, I've never even tried it before. I see why zombies like it."

No one said a word, but the one at the door had a smirk on his face. There was something about him. He stretched his limbs and yawned. He was still groggy and hungry. His mind raced. *Somebody has to be coming.*

"Well, thanks for the food." He rubbed his knees. "So where were we? Ah yes. You wanted me to tell you all about the next Zombie Apocalypse."

"Outbreak," Walker said, putting out his cigarette on the table. He didn't light another one. "Just tell us the best way to get to Ravenloft."

"Well, Colonel Walker, you're the one who is privy to all the security details, aren't you?"

"Not Ravenloft," Walker said. "He's special. All the rest of you have the same clearance, but not him. He's on another level. I've done my homework. You check in with him and so do the others. All of you have a special one on one with him."

Don leaned back against the wall. He'd always figured he had a relationship with Ravenloft that the others didn't have.

"Well I'll be," Walker said, "you didn't know that, did you? Huh-huh, seems Mister Ravenloft has you all tied around his fingers."

Don shrugged.

"We all have our own blend of uses. That's hardly surprising."

"True," Walker said, "but you all figured you were on the same footing. The WHS leaders. All reporting to another Commander in Chief, not realizing all along you all reported to Ravenloft."

Don hid his irritation. The truth was after all these years, he wasn't really sure who he worked for. He kept his eye on things. Made the rounds. He was a face to the public that would comment and report. But now that role had been reduced. A great deal lately.

Walker snapped his fingers in his face.

"You still there?"

Don lifted his brows.

"Seems I've nowhere else to be."

Oliver grabbed the cooler, pulled out a can of beer, and cracked it open.

Don's mouth watered.

"You didn't tell me beer was an option."

"It wasn't," Oliver said. He gulped down about half the can. "Ah ..."

"Oliver's been keeping a close eye on you, Don. And he's picked up a few things." He extended his hand to Oliver, who gave him two cans of beer.

Don licked his lips. His thirst was building.

Oliver handed the other can to the man at the door.

"Seems you were on the outs with the WHS," Walker said. "They wanted rid of you."

"What?" Don said. "I don't think so."

"You're getting old, Don. It's a younger man's game, killing billions of people. You don't have the stomach for it anymore."

"You don't know what you're talking about." He said. "Now give me a beer."

Oliver finished his first and cracked another open.

"It's your favorite brand. Extra stout and milky."

"Screw you, Oliver," Don said. "And you made lousy coffee."

"Whoa, someone is pretty cranky. It's that old thing, Don. You're brittle. They didn't need you anymore," Walker said. He put the can to his lips and took a swig. "I like your taste in beer though. That's one thing old farts know. My granddad drank this too. Too bad a zombie ate him. He'd probably have one with you."

I'm going to kill them all.

Don felt the anger swell in his chest. He was in good health, but he was rattled. He *was* old. And the WHS was cutting him out. Or so it seemed. He'd been denying it for quite some time too. But now these three men had confirmed everything he didn't want to admit. He could see it in their faces. But the WHS still needed him. He hadn't told them everything. He had a chip to play and they knew it.

"What makes you so certain they aren't coming after me?" Don said. "They need me. And even if they didn't, they'd make sure I was dead before I fell into enemy hands."

Walker shifted in his seat and Oliver stopped drinking.

The trailer became quiet. Still.

That's it. Roll it back on them. They aren't so certain.

Walker grabbed a can of chew from his back pocket and tapped in on his hand. He stuck a big pinch of rub in. Stuffing it in his lips with his tongue, he grinned. There were some tobacco flakes on his lips.

"Show him the paper," Walker said.

Oliver opened one of the desk drawers at the bottom and tossed a newspaper over. A headline jumped out at him.

WHS EXECS KILLED IN FIERY CRASH

Don skimmed the article. It said there'd been a freak accident. Three men burned to death, the result of vehicle malfunction. One was Jack Baker. Another was Oliver. It all happened two weeks ago.

Don went cold. The paper trembled in his fingers.

"How did ..."

He glanced at the obituaries stapled to the front page. He saw his face. It was a younger picture of him in his Air Force uniform with a stern smile on his face. Jack Baker, his nephew, was on the other column and so was a picture of Oliver.

"Becky," he said, in a whisper. "Can you tell me anything about her?"

Walker spit in his beer can.

"She looked fine last time I saw her. Ben Johannes is looking after her. She's taken quite a shine to him," Walker shrugged. "As the story goes."

Don's brows buckled. He crushed up the papers and tossed them aside.

"That bastard's as old as me. Damn suck up! He should be here, not me!" The thought of that man with his wife ran right through his veins. "I'll kill him."

He started to wheeze.

"Better get your puffer out, Don," Oliver said.

"Oh shut up!"

Everyone chuckled but him.

"They really did bury me," Don said. "How'd you pull it off?"

"It wasn't too hard, considering I was the lead investigator."

"Who were the other bodies?"

"Ah, just a couple of leftover zombies. Not anyone you knew."

Don's head sunk into his hands. He was a tough guy. Dangerous. Feared. The articles in the paper confirmed everything. The WHS had abandoned him. He rubbed his eyes in his palms. *I'm too old for this.*

"So, how's it feel to be dead?"

"Huh?" Don said, looking up.

"Dead?" the man in front of the door said. "How does it feel?"

Don's face perked up. The man behind the voice seemed familiar. Very familiar.

"Say again," he said. He took a closer look at the man. Stared right into his eyes.

The man leaned closer.

"How does it feel to be dead, Don?"

He knew that voice. Not the face but the voice. Everyone in the world knew that voice.

"Nate?" Don said.

"Damn straight."

7

THE KNOCK at the door came later than expected. Henry couldn't have been happier when it finally did come. Tori had kept him up all night. Fighting. Crying. Complaining. Nothing he said was right. He was exhausted when he opened the door.

A black man filled the doorway with a big grin on his face.

"You two love birds ready to go?"

It was Rod.

Henry wanted to hug him.

"Hey man, I mean Rod, it's great to see you."

"You too," Rod said. "Hi, Tori."

She flipped up her hand.

"Did I come at a bad time?" Rod said. He clapped his hands. "Come on now. Let's move it, the both of you. I can't wait to get out of this place, and they're waiting on you."

"So Tori's good?" Henry said.

"Of course she is. Why, what did Alice say? She messed with your heads last night, didn't she. She's crazy."

"Well," Henry started. He turned back to Tori. "I told you it would be alright."

Tori pushed her way through the doorway and headed down the hall. She had a duffle bag strapped over her shoulder. She clopped down the hall in a white tank top, tight jeans and high heels.

Rod squeezed Henry's shoulders. "I like you, Henry, but you don't deserve that. I'd fight a dozen zombies for her."

"I know, Rod."

"Hey, wait up at the elevator. I've got the key code." He started up the hallway and looked back. "Shake a leg, Henry! It's Mo-Time!"

"Rod, will you at least tell me where we're going?"

"How should I know? Come on now, let's go!"

The three of them waited in the courtyard. It was cold out. A little damp. Henry wore beige trousers and had his hands inside his navy blue hoodie. Rod was chatting with the security guards. There were six of them and they were looked over at them, laughing.

Looks like last night's cat fight made the rounds.

Tori stood silently, shivering.

"Why don't you wear my hoodie?" he said.

"No."

"I have an extra jacket."

"I can dress myself, thank you," she said. "Maybe Alice will need it."

A long black van pulled through the security gate, full size. Its tires crunched over the pavement as it rolled towards them. The wheels squeaked as it came to a stop. Rod walked over and opened the door.

"Ladies first."

"Thanks, Rod," Tori said, smiling up at him. "Can you sit with me? I haven't talked with anyone but Henry for the past two weeks and I could use a change."

"Sure," Rod said. "I feel you. You don't mind, do you, Henry?"

"Whatever makes her happy," he said.

Rod and Tori filled the first row and tossed their things in the second. Henry squeezed his way into the seat in the back. Tori was already giggling. Rod's gusty laughs were like a roar.

Great. Just great.

The van's windows were tinted, but he could see out just fine. Two WHS Security guards sat in the front, with shotguns locked up in the center console. Rod started to pull the door shut just as another person entered. He was fuzzy bearded and wore an orange Quantum Leap T-Shirt with stains on it. It was Rudy.

"Hey guys!"

"Damn!" Rod said, "I'm not riding with this fool!"

"Me either," Tori said.

"Listen," Rudy said. "I'm sorry. It was a crazy night. Let's just let bygones be bygones. I've really missed you guys."

Tori stuck her zombie fist in his face.

"No."

"Come on, guys, really?" Rudy whined. "I was blasted out of my mind. You can't hold me accountable for that. Seriously?" He looked at Henry. "Bawk? Come on. Forgive me."

"What about Weege?" Henry said. "Where's that weasel?"

"Probably with Alice. Who knows." Rudy extended his hand towards Henry.

Henry rubbed his eyes. It was bad enough he barely got enough sleep last night, but now this. He didn't even know where he was going.

Screw it.

He took Rudy's hand in his.

"Welcome aboard."

8

-*ARIZONA*-
Location Unknown

CHAD BLASTED the drone and watched it fall from the sky. He wiped the sweat from his eyes and jogged to the next outcropping to duck into the shade.

"Damn! How'd I get into this?"

He checked his rifle clip. Five bullets. He slammed the magazine in and charged the handle.

Seventeen years Chad had been a Border Patrol agent. He never imagined his career would end like this. Even after the Outbreak. He'd chased down drug runners, smugglers, illegals and zombies. The hunter, never the hunted. Now it was him. The desert. Rifle. Buck knife. And nowhere to go.

He peeked from under the rocks and checked the sky. The clouds puffed in long lines over the pale blue sky and nothing else. He knew there were more drones. They'd been using them for years. But there was something else out there. After him.

Hours ago he'd been a prisoner. He meddled too much. Got too nosey. Being a good scout. His boss told him there were people that didn't like that. To keep his nose inside the window. He stuck it out. Got caught.

The drug trade was busted up for years after the Outbreak. Most all of the cartels were wiped out. South America was one of the places hit hard. But the drugs had started moving again. New cartels had cropped up. All were bad except the ones funded by his own government. He'd caught them red handed. They'd tried to explain. Reel him in. Offered him a chip in the game. Piss off, he'd said. He hadn't gotten a chance to follow up after that. Hours later he'd woken up, wrists bound behind his back with a sack over his head.

When they took off the sack, there was nothing but desert and sky. Two soldiers. A van. And something that horrified him. Zombies. Their faces were horrific. They were big too. Mouths snapping. Eyes wandering. Hands clutching. There were strange hooks on the gloves they wore. Chad had never felt cold in desert heat before.

They'd given him an hour. Supplies were straight ahead. A box in the sand. Good luck they said. He thought he knew those guys. He'd cursed them and started running. That was two hours ago. At least his watch still worked.

He took off the wristband and read the engraving.

Happy 10th, Love Monica

He sobbed. Hit the rocks. He'd never see his wife again. Or his children. All four of them.

Life isn't fair. That's what his father said. *Don't be surprised when it swallows you.* Fitting words.

He took the final sip from his canteen and tossed it away. Double checked the safety on his rifle. He stepped away from the rocks and scoured the land. Just sunlight, desert and him. He could run south and maybe find the border wall and some friendlies, but that was probably twenty miles away. He'd never make it. Whenever the zombies caught up with him he'd be exhausted.

I'm not going down without a fight.

He crawled up on the rocks. Faced the direction he came from and rubbed his chin. Sweat dripped in his eyes. His mouth was already dry. Two specks moved across the desert. Coming his way. His heart jumped.

"I don't care what happens to me, Lord, just look after my wife and boys."

He lay over the rocks. Wet his sight. The sun was setting in his eyes.

Not going to get any easier, is it.

He squinted. The zombies were maybe a quarter mile away. They ran with a jagged gate and zigzagged over the sand. Chad never figured zombies for trackers. It was uncanny. But they came right after him.

Can't be possible. Did they spray something on me?

The zombies scrambled over the dust and dirt, stumbled, clawed their way back to their feet. Chad's heart pounded in his ears. His legs trembled. He wanted to run. He was a soldier though. Running wasn't an option.

Pull it together, Chad. They're zombies. You're smarter than them. Fill their heads with lead.

They were less than a hundred yards away. Moving fast. He took aim. Finger trembling on the trigger. He could make out their faces. The heads were covered in a matte finished metal. Only their gaping mouths were exposed.

"Never easy ..."

He took aim. *Go for the eyes.*

50 yards.

Their voices were heard. Chills raced through his spine.

Numma-numma.

25.

Numma-numma.

Crack!

One zombie head recoiled back. It stumbled and fell.

Chad slung the bolt back. Aimed for the next.

Crack!

It's head snapped back. It stumbled backward. Then forward. It ran right at him.

Crack!

Ten yards away Chad hit it square in the nose. The bullet zinged off. The zombie kept coming like it went right through him. The other zombie was up and running. The nearest clawed at the rock he stood up on.

"Damn!"

The zombies' eyelets were slits. A bullet was stuck in one of them.

Chad rocked the bolt back again. Stuck the barrel in the zombie's eyelet and fired again.

Click!

He rocked the bolt back again and fired.

Click!

"Son of a bitch! Those were dummies. Dirty Bastards!"

The zombies clawed at the rocks. Teeth gnashed.

Swinging his rifle like an axe, Chad busted one in the head. He beat it. Beat it and beat it again. It tore the rifle from his hand. He slipped. His arms flailed and backward he fell on the other side of the rock. He jumped to his feet. Clipped his head on the rock. Blood dripped from the side of his eye.

Chad spit in the dirt. The jitters were gone. His blood churned. Temper boiled. He slid the Bowie knife out when the first zombie came around the rock. He ran at it full throttle.

Glitch!

He shoved six inches of steel in its throat. Ripped it out and stabbed again. Again.

The zombie tore at him. The tiny hooks in its gloves snagged Chad's shirt and tore skin off. It went wild. Snapping and licking at the blood.

"No you don't!"

Chad was bigger. Strong. It was smaller. Stronger. He stuck his leg behind it and slung it to the ground. The back of its neck was exposed. Wild eyed and bloody, Chad pounced. The blade sliced through the Zombie Suit and slid between its neck and out the other side. He raised the knife again.

"Die, Monster!"

The second zombie plowed into him.

The knife slipped from his fingers.

9

-*Washington, D.C.*-

"I'll be damned," Don said, gaping, "The Man Who Saved the World lives."

Nate offered a little shrug and showed some teeth. The look on Don's haggard face was priceless. Almost joyful.

"It's me, alright. A different kind of zombie."

Don huffed. Leaned forward in his seat, eyes squinting.

"So they reconstructed your face?"

Nate rubbed his hairy jaw. It still irritated him. It clicked when he chewed sometimes too.

"They did about everything they could do."

Don's eyes slid over to Walker. They narrowed then returned back to Nate.

"I have to admit. You guys have really pulled off something. Kidnapping me was one thing, but resurrecting you," Don's white brows lifted, "that's impressive. I feel I've underestimated my captors."

Nate dragged a metal seat across the floor and sat in front of Don.

He'd talked to Don more than a few times during his tour of being the Man Who Saved the World. The older man was hard, but alright. He said enough, but not too much.

"Tell us about Ravenloft."

"Are you an interrogator now, Nate? Huh."

Nate looked him dead in the eye. Pushed up his sleeves up. Leaned in.

"No. But I'll tell you what I am. I've been murdered. Revived. My face reconfigured. Thanks to guys like Walker and Oliver I've been rebooted. Both lives that I had? They've come and gone. It doesn't leave me much to live for. And I have you and the likes of you to thank for it."

"Alright," Don said, wheezing a little. "So your life's been bad. At least you still have it. So now what, Nate? Do you plan to save the world again? From who, me? Ravenloft? Pfft." Don leaned forward until their heads almost touched. "You'll never get close."

"We will if you join us."

Don's eyes popped open. He chuckled.

"Are you kidding me? You're recruiting me? Hah!"

Nate leaned back and folded his arms across his chest.

"Think of it as getting a second chance. Everyone deserves a second chance. Even you, Don."

Don swallowed hard. Took a sip from his Dew. Nate saw his eyes water. *The old man's still got a piece of heart left.* Nate had spent plenty of time with Don and his colleagues at the WHS Zombie Conferences. He'd joked with them from time to time, calling them the Magnificent Twelve. They were all polished and cold. They'd still buttered Nate's behind though. He'd made them. He knew they didn't like him. He could feel it, but he could never quite touch it. But now he understood. He was the man that had foiled all their plans.

"Ha," Don grumbled, shaking his head. "There'll be no second chances for me and no third chances for you." He shifted in his seat and eyed them all. "None of you stand a chance. You might as well try to kill the President."

"Come on, Don. You don't really want to protect them, do you?"

Nate said. "Think about it. They tried to kill me. They were ready to kill you. Take a shot at them. Save millions in the process."

Don patted Nate's knee.

"You know, I liked you, but the others. They really hated you. The way you screwed things up for them. Everything was going according to their plans, when all of a sudden," Don spread his arms out in the air and flicked his fingers. "Boom—The Tweet that saved the world. Ha. Ha. Ha. Nate, I wish you could have been there to see their faces." He bobbed his head. "It was like all the blood left their bodies. Then the cursing started. I laughed. Huh. I think that might have caught up with me." He shook his head at Nate. "Man, you really screwed up everything for a while."

Nate leaned back in his chair.

Walker said, "Huh."

Oliver was shaking his head.

Don had confirmed the entire conspiracy. He'd been there when it all happened. He knew all the plans.

"I bet you want to punch me," Don said, lifting his chin. "Don't you? Go ahead."

No blood rushed. No anger swelled in his chest. Nate felt empty. Smaller than he ever had.

Walker slugged Don in the jaw.

Smack!

Don's head cracked against the back wall. His lip was bleeding.

"That was stupid," Don said.

"Why?" Nate said.

Don rubbed the blood on his jacket sleeve.

"Why what?" His brows lifted. "Oh. Well, I'll give you seven billion reasons why."

Nate's cheeks warmed. "So some people think there's too many people and decide to wipe out billions of them?"

Don's face hardened. "There's too many people to control. They consider it a threat."

Electricity raced up and down Nate' spine. Walker and Oliver had been filling him in on some of the conspiracies he'd been looking into before all this started. Weeks before Christy Backwater was killed.

Don continued.

"They considered you a threat too, Nate. You started snooping around. Digging into those theories. They panic. You foiled them once. Now, if you came out, vocalized your doubts, you might have blown all their covers." He clapped his hands. "It was time to snuff you out. Not my call though. I liked you, Nate. You were entertaining. Human. Nothing like those blood suckers. They're cold. Malicious."

Nate got up. "You seem pretty talkative all of a sudden. Are you sure you aren't having second thoughts?"

"No, I'm certain I'm not. I'm just entertaining you fools. You must have watched too much X-Files when you were kids. All of your eyes light up at the mention of the word conspiracy. Like children at Christmas. If you're smart, you'll just walk away from all this. But if you're stupid—which you've already proven you're committed to—just know this. It's not going to end well. They'll find you. They'll torture you. And maybe, maybe they'll kill you." He gazed at Walker. "You know what I'm talking about."

Walker took a slurp of beer and set the empty can on the table.

"Tell us everything you know, Don. Or it' s you the end won't go well for."

"I might be old, but I'm not brittle. I'll die first. I know they're coming. They might be late, but I know they're coming."

Nate shifted in his chair. Walker and Oliver had covered their tracks. But that wouldn't last. They wouldn't stay hidden forever. They'd be caught soon enough. He rubbed his sweaty hands on his pants. Nodded at Oliver.

"It's time. Bring in the interrogator."

Oliver departed.

Don's eyes lifted. They were hard. Tired.

"You guys aren't capable of this," he said. "It's not in you."

"It's not too late to change your mind, Don. Make all your wrongs right and help us."

"Huh. One last noble act? No. I'll take my chances."

Walker's Zippo clacked open. A flame burst. A puff of smoke rolled. A long silence fell.

Nate reflected. *What am I doing? Why am I doing it?* He rubbed the gold cross of Jesus under his shirt. The one Jeanine gave him. She was a gorgeous woman turned into a hideous monster. A life taken, one of millions, because of guys like Don. Part of a bunch of men and women who thought it was up to them what was best for the world. It was unfathomable. Sadistic. Evil. Unbearable.

"Having doubts?" Don said with a smirk. "Perhaps you should ..."

The stairs outside creaked. The door opened. Oliver stepped inside. He had a leash in one hand. He was tugging someone behind him.

Nate watched Don's eyes enlarge. Chill bumps popped up on the man's arms.

"What is that?" he said, recoiling in his chair.

A heavyset boy about five feet tall lumbered in. His brown hair was thick and his face veiny. He had thick forearms bulging underneath s short sleeved striped shirt. His tennis shoelaces were untied.

Nate smiled.

"Don, meet Louie. Louie, eat Don."

"Num num," the boy said.

10

-INSTITUTE, WV-

THE VAN RUMBLED over the parking lot and made its final stop by the gate. The driver signed off on a clipboard and they were on their way. Henry glanced over his shoulder and he wasn't the only one. He wondered what would happen to the zombies in the rehab. Who would replace him? *Did I even accomplish anything?*

He turned back. Tori was staring at him. He smiled. She looked away.

"Bawk," Rudy said, grabbing his shoulder. "How've you been?"

"Not now, Rudy," he said, looking away. "Give me a minute."

Rudy jammed earphones on his head.

"M'kay."

A few miles later they hit the main road, cruised by Go-Mart and circled onto the interstate. Henry's hands rested on the seat in front of him, clutching in and out. He hated not knowing where he was going. The van cruised down the interstate, over the Kanawha River and past Charleston. Henry didn't see many boats on the river. Still, he thought of Stanley and his brother, Jimmy. They'd done plenty of fishing back when they were young. Before the Zombie Outbreak. Before the madness.

He dipped his head and closed his eyes. Tried to meditate. Tori and Rod started talking again in low voices. He opened his eyes just as they passed Exit #1 Mink Shoals on Interstate 79. They were headed north.

"Rod," he said, leaning forward, "Are you sure you don't know where we're going?"

"What?" Rod's brows lifted under his shaved head. "Ah, no. No idea."

"Ask them," he said.

"Phfft ... they ain't telling," Rod said. He put his arm over the seat where Tori was sitting. "And I ain't asking."

"Well, can you ask them how long it's going to be? Hours? Days?"

"Why, you need a potty break?"

Tori giggled.

"No," Henry said. He slid back into his seat.

The next sixty minutes was torture. He'd been up and down this road at least a hundred times. Outside, the leaves were turning on the tall hilltops. Bright reds and oranges mixed with whites and yellows. There was a little purple in there too. His mother had loved traveling this time of year. She'd talk the whole time about how pretty it was.

He laid his head back and tried to rest his eyes. It had been a long enough night. He needed some rest. There was no idea what to expect. He was trapped. Trapped in a world of the living dead.

All he'd wanted to do was help the zombies. Or help his stepfather, Stanley rather, find a cure. But somehow everything he did was turned inside out. The zombies needed to be put in the grave. Keeping them alive was the sickest thing. But what he thought didn't matter.

He cozied up by the window.

CPWWSZH. That had been Nate McDaniel's last text to him. His college friend was dead. The most famous man in the world a murderer. Henry hadn't given it much thought lately, but a crappy world had gotten crappier ever since. At least in his world it had. No, he was pretty sure Nate had been on to something. His friend had been as sharp as he was lucky. Henry unjumbled it in his mind. WHSWPCZ. World Humanitarian Society World Population Control ... Zombies.

He shuddered in his hoodie and drifted off.

A rough hand shook him.

"Hey Bawk."

He was half asleep.

Rudy shook him again.

"Hey, Bawk," Rudy said in a quiet voice.

"What?" he said, blinking his eyes.

Rudy had a silly look on his fuzzy face. He glanced over at Tori.

"So," he grinned, "tell me."

"Tell you what?"

"You know. About last night." Rudy made claws with his hands and mewed. "The kitty cat fight. Was it hot?"

Henry jammed his foot on Rudy's hip and shoved him off the bench seat.

"Hey!" the driver yelled. "What's going on back there?"

"Nothing." Rudy popped back into his seat. "I just slipped off the bench is all."

"That man's a fool," Rod said.

Henry could feel Tori's eyes on him. He didn't give in. Instead he gazed through the window. There were cattle in the hills. Maybe there were some zombies too. A few minutes later he fell back asleep.

He dreamed. About zombies. Labs and zombies. She was screaming. He was running but couldn't catch her. Zombies stumbled his way, knocking over racks of basketballs and bubble gum machines. They turned to shoot at them with a pistol. *Click. Click. Click.* The zombies were on top of him. Their mouths seemed to hang to the floor and their teeth were made of sharp metal.

Scrreeeeeeeeeeech!

He jerked in his seat. Eyes wide open.

Rudy was staring at him.

"Bad dream, Bawk?"

Henry wiped the drool from his mouth, straightened his glasses and faced front. They were stopped at a light.

"I know this intersection," he said. "Are we—"

Rudy stuck his arms in the air. "We're in Mo-Town baby!"

The light turned green and the van accelerated and turned left. They passed a few more lights, all green, and headed down a twisting hill. There wasn't as much traffic on the road, at least not as much as he was used to seeing. Henry hadn't been back to Morgantown since college. The van turned right at the next light and headed up a driveway on a winding hill. At the entrance, a weathered sign in an overgrown garden read Mountaineer Mall.

The van traveled another quarter mile and stopped again. There was a chain link gate and a guard shack. The setup was very similar to the one at the Zombie Day Care. Henry's breath quickened. Two guards stepped out of the shack armed with shotguns. One came out, checked the manifest of the driver and peered in the back seat. His eyes stopped on Tori. He smiled and a couple of teeth were missing. She scooted closer to Rod.

"Alright," the guard said, stepping back out of the window. He waved to the guard behind the fence and the gate rattled open. "Enjoy your stay." The driver accelerated through the gate.

Everyone in the van was quiet. This trip to Morgantown wasn't as thrilling as they used to be. Henry remembered the days of tailgates and football games. Cars filling the streets bumper to bumper in gold and blue. Now it felt like a one-car funeral procession.

A closed grocery store was to the left and at the top of the hill an empty parking lot loomed, with grass growing through the cracks of the blacktop. A drizzling rain splattered on the boarded-up windows.

"Looks like the mall's closed," Rudy said. "No shopping for you, Tori."

"Funny," she said, not looking around.

The abandoned mall wasn't huge. It was encircled by an outdoor parking lot with maybe a few thousand spaces. Henry remembered coming to it as a kid, and the malls weren't all so big back then. It was just a couple of department stories like Elder-Beerman and J.C.

Penny and maybe a couple dozen other stores. This one looked like it had been closed since the Outbreak. With all the entrances and windows sealed up, it looked more like a bunker now.

The van wheeled around to the far side and pulled down a loading dock ramp. A couple of empty truck trailers were parked nearby. Nothing else moved. Just the rain that pattered on the van's roof.

The WHS driver honked the horn three times.

Henry's fingers started to tingle. A sense of dread filled him. It looked like his home was going to be another abandoned building, but this one didn't have many unboarded windows except a few skylights in the ceiling. He rubbed his shoulders. *My Life Among the Zombies: From Chaos to Madness. The Autobiography of Henry Bawkula. Deceased.* He sighed.

Rudy slapped him on the back.

"Don't be so glum, Bawk," Rudy said. "I'm sure it's not as bad as it looks. Besides, it's Morgantown. Lots of college chicks."

Tori shot him a look over her shoulder.

"For me, that is."

"I have a feeling we won't get much of an opportunity to mix with the locals," Henry said, looking out his window. There were black cameras everywhere. He'd counted at least fifty of them on the way up the road.

The side door alongside the docking garage opened up and a WIIS Security guard stepped outside. He was a big man. Bigger than Rod, heavyset and white. His gray mustache and beard were neatly trimmed. A pistol was on each hip. Automatics by the looks of them. Nickel plated .44 Magnums, Henry guessed. It took a big man to wield those.

"Come on in," the man said, waving. His voice was loud and heavy. "It's pouring rain less than a mile away."

Rod shoved the side van doors open and burst outside.

"You got any food?"

"Yep, but maybe not enough to fill you." The man chuckled. "We have good coffee and all the donuts you can eat."

Rudy tripped over his bag trying to get out.

"Watch it," Rod said, glowering at him, grabbing his own bags.

Henry waited for Tori. She took her time without looking back.

Great.

Henry was the last one out. He grabbed his bag and shut the door behind him. The van started backing away. Seconds later they were all alone with a big burly stranger. The man's eyes smiled and he tipped his hat at Tori. "Ma'am," he said.

The raindrops started to pour down.

Everyone hussled for the door. The man stopped them under the overhang.

"My name's Jake." He pointed to the sewn-on name tag of his WHS uniform. "I'm the boss around here." He stepped aside. "Go on, get in there."

One by one they crossed the threshold into a corridor. Drywall. White. Lit up by fluorescent lights. It was clear to Henry the place had gone through some major renovation, but nothing expensive. Not all the bulbs were lit. Twenty feet down the hall was a Security Door. Heavy duty. All steel. A green and red light panel showed red. A camera was mounted above the threshold.

Jake jostled Henry as he passed.

"I'll get that."

Jake pressed his thumb above the key pad. The door slid open and in they went.

There was an old conference table and a mishmash of office chairs on rollers around it. A coffee urn, juice boxes, and a spread of donuts in boxes. It looked like a large break room. Cabinets and a refrigerator. The room was cold and the air filters rattled in the high ceiling above. There were two Security Doors near the other corners of the rectangular room.

Rudy took a seat and started eating.

Jake hitched his knee up on the chair and tightened up his bootlace.

"Eat up and relax, everyone," Jake said. "They'll be here to brief you soon enough. And the shitter, er, pardon me Ma'am, the ladies is over there."

"Who's coming to brief us?" Henry asked.

"Them," Jake said. He scanned his thumb. The door slid open. Jake stepped through and it closed behind him.

"I don't like how he said that," Tori said, rubbing the goosebumps on her arms.

Rod agreed.

"Me either."

11

-Arizona-

Location Unknown

"Argh!" Chad screamed out.

The zombie pinned him down. The tiny hooks on its gloved hands tore into his shoulders, ripping cloth and flesh. Its jaw snapped at his face. Teeth chomping and clattering. The zombie was ravenous.

Chad locked his fingers around its throat. Shoved it back.

"No!"

It was strong like a wild animal. Relentless. He gasped for breath. Kicked. Pushed. Squirmed. He'd seen zombies eat people before. The horror. Dead men eating the flesh of the living. *Don't panic*, a voice in his head said. *Don't stop fighting. Kill it!*

He pulled his knees to his chest. Squeezed its neck. Its teeth chomped and snapped. Its fingers dug deeper into his flesh. It pulled him closer. Its tongue brushed his cheek. Licked his ear.

"Numma-numma. Numma-numma!"

Chad groaned. Wriggled. His shoulders burned. He heard his skin tear. His lungs were flames. He'd wrestled his way into college, but he'd never wrestled anything like this. An opponent with super-human vitality and hunger. The match of his life.

One move! One move!

Its hands ripped up his arms. It tore hunks of shirt and skin. Blood dripped in tiny pools on the sand. Chad squeezed its neck and glared into its dead eyes.

"I'm not going down to you," he spit. "Dead Devil."

He summoned everything he had left. Let out a roar.

He flipped to his belly. Pulled his knees under him. Hooked the zombie's arm under his elbow. Burst up and twisted the zombie's arms behind its back. Drove it face first into the ground. He screamed again.

"Take that!"

He shoved its arm towards the back of its head, snorting like a bull.

Snap!

Its arm popped at the shoulder and no longer flailed.

Chad jumped on the other arm, grabbed the wrist and twisted it behind its back.

"Take that!"

Pop!

The zombie writhed on the ground. Snapped its jaws and kicked.

Chad rolled away, gulping for air. Clutching at his chest. Blood dripped all over his arms and down his face. On shaking hands and knees he crawled for his knife. The zombie pushed its head over the sand with its legs right after him.

"Numma-Numma," it said, with mouthfuls of dirt.

Chad wrapped his bloodstained fingers around the buck knife's handle. Staggered to his feet, swaying. The zombie nipped at his toes. One eye in the dirt. One eye on him. Chad sucked in all the hot air he could handle. His dry throat tried to swallow. He felt things hurt he'd never felt before. Other things he knew well. Anger. Hatred.

He stepped onto the zombie's back and jumped up and down.

"Die!"

"Die!"

"Die!"

He ripped its mask off

Its neck crackled and snapped to the left and right.

"Numma-numma."

"I'll give you some Numma-Numma!"

Chad jammed the knife in its skull. Wrenched it to the left with a sickening crack.

The zombie juttered. Limps twitched and then twitched no more.

Chap rolled off its back and stared into the setting sun.

"Numma dumma damn dead ..."

"Now that's a real cowboy," Rancho said.

Charles slung his popcorn over the room.

"Dammit!"

"What's the matter?" Rancho said in his deep Texan voice. "You didn't put too much money on the zombies did you? Woo Hoo."

"Shut up," Charles said. He banged his fist on the table. He'd wanted to make the man die. Tear him asunder. Eat him. His damn zombies hadn't been up to it. He slung his chair across the room.

"Say, are you alright in there? The man wasn't some soft bellied civilian. And you said to arm him."

Charles picked up his chair and slammed it back down in front of his work station.

"Didn't I tell you to shut up?"

"I think your expectations of the zombies are a little high. They don't have the best reflexes, you know," Rancho said. "And what brains those ones did have, well, they've got big holes in them now. But, me and the boys enjoyed the show. It was better than what we saw at The Octagon last night. I say we keep this guy around for another fight."

Charles punched a key on his board with his pudgy finger. The sound was muted. The drone showed a clear shot of the man, lying in the sand, eyes to the sky, closed, and bleeding all over. He winced. His mouth curled.

"I hate people like that," he said. His forehead dripped sweat on the table. "Bloody survivors." He grabbed a handkerchief from his back pocket and wiped his brow. It made him think of Nate McDaniel, the Man Who Saved the World. "Cost us time and money, those guys do."

The man on the screen crawled into the shade and hunkered down. What happened wasn't a failure. Just an experiment. It just would have been more fun if the man had lost. It was no reason for Charles to lose his head.

"Oh well," he said to himself, "I can always send more zombies. We have plenty of them." He tapped his keyboard. "Rancho?"

"You finished with yer little fit?"

"What's it to you?"

"So, Cowboy, do you want my men to waste this guy or let him bleed and bake to death?"

CHAD SAT in the shade with his bloody back against the rock.

If I live till tomorrow, it's gonna be the sorest I've ever been.

Eyeing the sky, he could see a drone hovering about thirty feet in the air. It was silent. Like a Flying Saucer or something. He raised his arm, turned his hand and gave it the finger. What kind of men was he dealing with? They couldn't just kill him. They had to watch him being killed by zombies. A lab rat in a carnivorous cage.

He shifted his seat and winced.

"Ah."

His shoulders were raw meat. Blood, sand and cloth were mixed in with his muscles. He flipped a dangling piece of skin back into place. It fell over again.

"What to do," he said, wiping his arm across his mouth. His throat was parched. He lived, but what for.

A sound caught his ear. Boots crunching over the sand and rock.

It made him think of the little girl in Poltergeist. "They're here." A sliver of fear went through him. It could be more zombies. He only remembered two, but they didn't get the job done. Maybe they sent more. If it were him chasing them, that's what he would do.

His neck rolled over on his shoulders toward the sound. A black silhouette stepped into the sunlight. Tall and lean. Assault rifle in the ready position.

"Hoy Mate," the man said, "looks like you put on quite a show."

The soldier stepped over one of the zombies and kicked it in the head.

Chad got a better look at the man. Desert camo from head to toe and topped off with a jungle hat. Two canteens were on his side. The man's chin was narrow and jutted out. The other one appeared. Shorter and thicker. Close set eyes. Chinless with hairy black arms.

"Damn," the other one said. He looked at Chad and the zombies. "He did this?"

"No, a giant scorpion did it."

"I'm just talking."

"Yes, you Americans do a lot of that. Yak, yak, yak about nothing. Too much television."

"Better than being a Kangaroo poker."

Chad cracked a smile.

The taller one walked over and knelt down in front of him.

"Not feeling so bad are you, Mate? Aye?"

Chad lifted the knife. It felt like a brick of lead. He gently jabbed it at the man.

"Ho, Ho, this mate's still got some fight in him. He must not be a product of TV Land." The man's gray eyes lifted. "A good hard boned American. Like the old ones."

"So," the other man said, "what's the plan? Do we kill him?"

"Probably. I'm still waiting for orders."

The soldier slipped his cell phone from his pocket and eyed the screen.

Chad leaned forward.

"Aye now," the man said, turning his barrel towards him. "Lean back, and go ahead and let the knife go."

Chad shook his head.

"Come on, Mate. I'll switch my canteen for it." He pulled it off his belt and wiggled it. The sloshing sound made Chad's mouth water. "You deserve it, Mate. I'd give you a can of lager if I had it. What you did to those zombies, now that was impressive."

Chad chucked the knife. He caught the canteen. Fired roared through his shoulders. He twisted off the cap and gulped it down.

"I bet I could have killed those zombies," the other soldier said, bobbing his head. "I wouldn't look like he looks either."

"Shaddup, you moron," the soldier said. "I can't think of many men that could survive that and you sure ain't one of them." He turned back to Chad. "Shame. We could use more men like you. Most of my men are like Shit for Brains over there. Are you sure you don't want to make a deal?"

Chad kept drinking.

"Ah, it probably don't make a difference now anyway." He checked his phone again. "Any day now. Ew," the man grimaced, looking at Chad. "Looks like a zombie chewed off your ear." The man backed off. Started texting.

Damn!

Chad didn't want to reach up and give the man any satisfaction. He reached up and felt his left ear. Most of it was missing.

"Not good, Mate, not good at all. You've been bitten." The soldier shook his head and lowered his barrel to Chad's forehead.

"Great fighting, Mate, but this is a better end for you." He huffed a sigh. "If you got any last thoughts, go ahead and say them."

I'm not going to be a zombie. God help me, not a zombie. Shoot me! Please, shoot me!

12

-MORGANTOWN, WV-

"HEY!" Henry whacked the Security Door with his fist. "It's been two hours already!" He shook his hand and rubbed it. He shook his fist at one of the cameras mounted in the corner ceiling.

"Don't hurt yourself, Henry," Rod said. He was sitting by Tori. They both had sour looks on their faces. "Try not to lose your patience. It's not like you."

He eyed Rod.

"Really?"

Ever since Jake departed, his skin had been tingling. The man seemed friendly, honest, but there was something cold about him.

"You know," Rod started. His swivel chair groaned when he moved. "I'm pretty sure Jake used to played football up here. Pretty badass back in the day."

Henry took off his glasses and rubbed his eyes. *Great. This place is probably full of more zombies like Rod the Rifle and Slam Dunk Jones.* He whirled and kicked the door hard with his toe. "Ah!"

"Henry!" Tori said. She started up from her chair and sat back down again. "Settle down, will you? You're making me nervous."

He glared at her. *Fine one she is to talk!*

She hadn't said hardly a thing to him since they left, and he still had no idea what he did. How was he supposed to avoid a conversation with Alice? He couldn't ever avoid her getting mad over just about anything it seemed lately. First the interrogations and now this. His nerves were thinned.

"Are you glaring at me?" she said, folding her arms across her chest. "Stop it, Henry."

"Oh, speaking to me now, are we?"

"No."

"Good!" He half hobbled over to the table. Took a seat far away. Filled up a cup of coffee and looked in the corner.

"Bawk, I've never seen you like this," Rudy said. He had donut powder on his shirt and mouth. "Makes me nervous too. But listen." He dug his heels into the floor and wheeled his chair over. "You know these big government gigs take a lot of time. Think about it. Remember the Day Care? It took days to get set up in there. The Rehab wasn't much different." He dusted his Quantum Leap shirt off. "Come on, Bawk. You're the calm one."

Rudy had a point. His fuzzy pie face seemed concerned as well. Still, Henry couldn't shake the feeling. The Red and Green lights like the Day Care had a chilling effect. It made him think of Jimmy and his stepfather Stanley. It made him wonder what he was doing exactly. What his purpose was—if he even had any. He took a deep breath and let it out slowly. Leaned back in his chair. *Accept the madness. Accept the despair. Life just isn't fair.*

"Henry," a soft voice said.

He turned in his swivel chair towards the table. Tori was on the opposite side.

Now what? Am I talking too much to Rudy now?

"Yes?"

She got out of her chair and walked to the far side of the room.

"Would you come over here?"

He hesitated.

"Please?" she added.

He met her at the spot.

"Yeah?" he said.

She whispered in his ear, "I'm sorry."

He put his hands on her shoulders and gently rubbed them up and down. He didn't know why he said it, but he did. "So am I."

She wrapped her arms around him and held him tight.

"I'm so tired of this."

"What," he said, "us fighting?"

She shook her head no in his chest.

"No, this zombie crap. I'm sick of all of it." She sobbed. "I want to go home, and I don't even know where that is."

He felt guilty. Torn. Tori was there because of him. He wished he'd gotten out long ago. But the pay was great. Stan had been there, and Tori. He'd had everything. Sort of. Assuming the Living Dead didn't bother you. The study. The experiments. The Power. It was all fascinating. But the price for knowledge was taking its toll. He felt cold. More dead than alive. He tilted her chin up and held her sweet face. "Maybe this one won't be so bad."

"I hope not." She dug her nails into his back. "But it's always bad.
Ding.

A different door's light turned from red to green. All eyes fell on Henry.

He shrugged

"Let's go, then."

Everyone moved towards the door. Henry was the first one there and reached for the handle.

The door popped open.

Tori gasped.

Rudy's soda splashed on the floor.

Jake filled the doorway.

"Don't worry about that," he said. He pushed the door aside with his back and stepped out of the way. "Come on in, but leave your stuff here for inspection. Sorry for the wait."

Henry's breath eased. The next room was huge. One of the old department stores. Gutted and white washed. The high ceiling was missing some tiles and the air handlers rattled above. It was cold. The old carpet and tiled floors were still there, leading from department to department. The door snapped shut behind them and Jake walked by.

"Follow me," Jake said, walking along with a slight limp in his step.

"Jake," Henry said, stopping, "We never got any clarification on what happened at the Rehab. You do know that we almost died in there. And someone needs to be held accountable."

Jake stopped and turned like a grizzly. Thick chested, his shoulders rolled a bit.

"Listen, Henry, I only know what they tell me. And what they told me is that it's been *Dealt With. Won't happen again.* I'm not one to argue with the ones that sign my paycheck, and life's pretty good around here." He offered a tight smile. "And it'll be pretty good for you around here too. Trust me."

"That's what they said the last time," Tori said. "Do you know about the Day Care? About what happened there?"

"Like I said, I know what they tell me. You're here now, and I think it's a good assignment. Personally, I'd like to say I'm glad to have you." He started walking again. "I think what we're doing is really exciting. Creepy, yes, but exciting. I think you'll like it here too."

Rudy clapped his hands.

"Sounds good to me. College towns have always been fun."

"Sure," Rod added, "Assuming we'll be able to leave here from time to time."

"You'll have more off-campus time than at those other facilities," Jake said, "at least more than at the Rehab, that is. That's always been a bad assignment. They keep people cooped up too long in there."

Jake approached the entrance from the department store to the inside of the mall and stopped at the gate. It was one of those grids made of tubes of metal that lifted up. Henry found the key lock in the center. The mall was dim and black on the other side. The area looked like the old Food Court. He squinted but couldn't read the signs.

Tori wrapped her arm around his

"Is someone walking around in there?"

Henry rubbed her hand and squinted harder. Something or someone was moving.

Jake lifted a small black radio off his belt.

"Showtime, ladies and gentlemen."

He keyed the mic with his thumb.

"Fire up the lights," Jake said.

Henry crept closer to the gate. He could feel Tori breathing on his neck.

The lights popped and flickered overhead. They made an eerie hum.

Rudy had his bearded face pressed against the gate. Rod stood tall at his side.

"What the ..."

The muscles tightened between Henry's shoulders at the next distinct sound.

"Num-num. Num-num. Num-num..."

A half dozen zombies staggered through the food court. Mumbling. Gaping.

"You gotta be shitting me," Rod said, eye cocked. "That is creepy."

Henry could see men and women wearing clean clothes. Polo shirts. Blue jeans. A zombie woman hobbled up and bumped right into the gate. Her sunken eyes wandered.

"Num-num."

"Are those Buckle jeans?" Tori said, exasperated. "She's got five hundred dollar pumps on. That's more than mine!" Tori's cheeks flushed. "Henry, she's got makeup on too."

Henry and the others moved backward. He could see the horror on everyone's faces. It made him think of his mother, Brenda, and what Stan had done with her, dressing her up like that.

"What's going on here?" Henry said.

"I'll let the others explain that," Jake said. He put his hand on

Henry's shoulder. "You'll get used to it. It's a good thing. Rod, you come with me. You'll be assigned to security."

"Huh," Rod said, tearing his eyes away from the food court. "What are they supposed to do?"

"They'll be fine," an unfamiliar woman's voice said.

Henry turned.

Two women stood on the other side of the gate with the zombies. A short brunette and a tall dirty blonde. Casual in dress. Pretty. The zombie woman wandered off. They both smiled.

"I take it you're not zombies," Henry said.

"No," the brunette said. She smirked a little. "We're your WHS tour guides." She stuffed a key in the lock and twisted. "Welcome to the Zombie Outlet."

The dirty blonde pushed the gate up with a grunt.

"Come on in. Don't worry, the zombies don't bite. Just make sure you don't cut in line."

Rudy was the first one to step through. He extended his hand to the blonde.

"Hi, I'm Rudy."

"Hi, I'm married."

Rudy turned to the brunette.

"Me too," she said. She slammed the gate down behind Henry and Tori and locked it tight.

"Henry," Tori said, scanning the wandering zombies, "this gives 'shop till you drop' a whole new meaning."

"More like 'shop till you drop dead,'" Henry said.

"So Rod, how long have you been doing security?" Jake asked.

The pair of men had made their way back to the large break room and gone into another door. The corridor led to a set of stairs and up into another room. Rod breathed easy. It was all security. Big screen monitors. The hum of computers. Living bodies at work. He caught a glimpse of the images on the screen. Zombies wandered throughout the mall in everyday clothes. One even pushed a stroller.

"Rod?" Jake said, tapping him on the shoulder.

"Oh," Rod said. "Fifteen years, on and off. Well, I've got another gig."

"I know, Rod. Anyone that watches the Octagon knows who you are. I've seen you fight. You're something."

Rod smiled. Nodded his chin.

"Well, I remember watching you play, back in the day, Jake. You were something else yourself."

Jake slapped him on the shoulder. "Still am!" He let out a gusty laugh. "Come on, I'll make introductions later. Let me show you where you'll be working. Give you a feel for the place. I'll take you to your quarters next." He shrugged. "Not much, but comfortable. Private."

Rod followed along, eyeing everything. He saw three others in a room that was like the dispatch office of a large police station. Men. Casual in dress with headsets on. One nodded. Another tipped his ball cap. Seconds later he was inside an armory. Big. Racks of rifles. Shotguns. Automatics. Zombie Suits. Flack vests and helmets. A few things he'd never seen, and he'd seen a lot of things.

"You guys don't play," Rod said, bobbing his chin. "I like it."

"They've got over a hundred of them out there."

Rod turned to him.

"Zombies? You serious?"

Jake's voice was low.

"They're nuts. I know. And that's why you're here. They're bringing more of the damn things."

"For what?"

"Assimilation into society or something." Jake grabbed a long black stick off the wall. It had a metal tip on one end. Buttons on a grooved out handle. "Our employers really think they can save the zombies."

"No, no, they can't."

"I know that, and you know that. Hell, even the zombies know that." Jake depressed the button on the handle. The end charged with blue sparks. *Zap. Zap.*

"Nice," Rod said. "What's that for?"

"Kinda like herding cattle." He shrugged. "We have to lead them back to the Dew Trough to feed them, you know."

"Is that what I'll be doing?" Rod stepped deeper into the armory, looking upward. "Herding zombies?" Something caught his eyes. "Say, that's one of those—" He spun around.

Jake jabbed the stick straight in his chest.

Zap!

Rod hit the ground hard.

Jake shook his head. He reached up and grabbed one of the metal zombie masks from the shelf Rod was looking at.

"No, you won't be herding zombies. A crying shame too. They've got something else in mind for you."

13

-Washington, D.C.-

It was a warehouse. Huge. One of many in an abandoned depot miles north of Washington D.C. At one time it was the hub of a thriving business, now just one of thousands gone belly up since the Outbreak. The roads were overgrown and full of potholes. The perfect place to hide an elite prisoner. Assuming you didn't do anything stupid.

Nate sipped his coffee. Checked his watch. Stared back out the dirty glass window.

"Any minute now," a voice said. She sounded like she was a mile away. A chair groaned. "Any minute."

Nate turned. Made the long trip over.

The warehouse was fifty yards long and twenty yards high. Metal frame skeleton and rafters supporting a metal roof and walls. There were wood crates, broken, empty. Some pipes and conduit lay on racks for storage. Large bins decorated some of the walls, filled with nuts, bolts, nails and other rusting junk. There were machine tools.

Industrial drill presses, planers, jigs and routers. A car lift and two cars. A minivan, white, and a four-door sedan, dark blue.

He made his way over to the haphazard office in the middle of the room, two dozen yards from the trailer. Walker was leaned up against the trailer, foot hitched up on the wall, smoking. Oliver sat on the trailer steps, whittling a piece of wood.

Nate sat down in the nearest chair with a grunt. Raised his foot on another, wincing. He wanted to take his shoe off, but didn't.

"You should try Vitamin C and B3 for that," the woman said. She eyed some empty bags on the desk. "And lay off the Taco Bell. Eat better; feel better." She sucked on a large Taco Bell cup filled with soda.

Nate shook his head.

"Hey, I'm younger," she shrugged.

Her name was Ashely. Auburn hair up in a bun. Electric blue eyes. Sweet. Friendly. Smart. Dressed in black from her boots to her neck. A shotgun, .45 automatic, and a revolver lay on her desk. Her office, what there was of it, was more desks and chairs, some laptops, ThinkPads and filing cabinets. Typical office gear. A jug of spring water on the cooler and cases of Mountain Dew stacked in the corner.

"Did you get anything off that laptop yet?" Nate said. "It hasn't moved since I got here."

"Hey, I've only been back a day." She grabbed a ThinkPad off the desk. It was the one that Don's nephew Jack had used. Her fingers danced on the screen. "It's got really good encryption."

"Ugh," Nate said, rolling his eyes.

Ashley laughed.

"Well, it had really good encryption," she winked at him. "It's all taken care of, Nate. Now let me see if I can find anything interesting."

"Just don't connect."

"I'm not ... any minute now."

Nate looked back at the trailer. Walker shrugged. Don had been in there almost two hours, alone with Louie. It wouldn't be long before the Dew wore off. Not long at all. He turned his attention to Ashley.

She was one of Walker's people. Zombie Rebels, she and the others liked to call themselves. Ones that searched for the truth. There were only a handful of them. Quiet types. Effective. They used the old ways to find information. Avoided the Internet when they could. Didn't hack from the same location. Folks that nibbled at bits and pieces. Putting together the larger puzzle without drawing suspicion. Old school, just not old.

"Nate," she said with her head down, typing, "I remember seeing you on an interview talking about your fiancé Jeanine. I thought that was horrible. Sorry for that."

An image of Jeanine popped into his mind. In the cell, drinking Dew. Crawling on the parking lot. Pressing her face through the glass of the convenience store. It was hard, so hard to remember the woman he had loved and lost without those things coming to mind.

"I don't think about it much, but thanks."

"I just wanted to say something. I didn't mean to ... pry, you know. You're a hero though. Saved a lot of people."

He nodded.

"Hmmm, this is interesting." Her fingers drummed the screen. "He's got some awesome video stored right on here. A good thing." Her mouth formed an 'O'. "Holy Shit, what are those things? Who are those people?"

Rap! Rap! Rap!

Nate jumped. Don was pounding on the door from the inside of the trailer. Nate moved to another chair and looked at the screen linked to the video camera inside with Don.

Nate turned the mic and speakers on.

Louie's jaws were clamped down on Don's belt. Grunting. Growling. The zombie's meaty fingers were digging into Don's sides. Don was screaming at the camera. Pounding at the door. "Get me out of here!"

Nate spoke into the mic by the keyboard on the desk.

"You going to tell us what we want?"

"Hell yes!" Don cried out.

"Let him out," Nate yelled down to Walker.

Oliver was already up and unlocking the door. He swung it open. Don burst through.

"Get it off me! Get it off me!"

Oliver grabbed Don by the waist belt. "Be still!" he said, "It's just a little zombie." He unclasped the belt.

Louie tore the belt free with his teeth.

Don stumbled down the stairs and crashed face first into the ground.

"Bet that hurt," Walker said.

Louie staggered down the steps. Piled on Don's feet.

"No!" Don screamed. His face was bleeding. "I said I'd talk! Get it off me!"

"Where's the noose, Oliver?" Walker said.

"Aw Crap, it's under the trailer. Hold on a sec."

Louie chomped down on Don's foot.

Don cried out, "YEEOUCH! It bit me!" He kicked Louie in the face.

"Just give him some Dew," Nate yelled. He hobbled towards them with a bottle in his hand. "Bloody gout." It felt like there were a thousand needles in his foot. He cranked his arm back. "Catch."

Walker snatched the bottle from the air. Twisted the cap off. He waved it under Louie's nose.

Louie's head snapped over. Pupils enlarged. He spit Don's shoe from his mouth.

"Num num."

"That's right, Dum-Dum. Time for num-num."

"Give me that, Idiot," Ashley said. She snatched the bottle from Walker's hand and stuffed it inside Louie's lips. He wrapped his fingers around it and sucked in. *Slurp!* The bottle collapsed. Louie was still sucking. "Toss me another," she yelled at Nate.

"Damn," he said, hobbling back with a grimace on his face.

"Hurry!"

Oliver dangled the zombie noose over Louie's neck.

"Don't you dare," Ashley said, her bright blue eyes cold as iron.

Nate flung another bottle down.

"*Urk!*"

It bounced off Louie's head.

Ashley clenched her teeth. Glared at Walker.

"I'll get that."

He twisted off the cap and handed the bottle to her.

"Here, Buddy," she said, stepping backward. "Come and get it."

Louie's jaw slacked. The crushed plastic bottle clattered to the floor. His eyes locked on the new bottle. Fingers stretched out.

"That's it. Grab it."

"Num num."

Slowly his fingers wrapped around the bottle.

"Num num."

His mouth stretched open like a python's. He stuffed it in his mouth ... backwards. The soda spilled all over his shirt.

"Aw, Louie," Ashley said.

"You people are sick," Don said. He jumped up and dashed for the first exit he could see.

Nate jammed his foot into the ground to trip Don. It exploded like fire.

"Agh!"

"I got this," Ashley said, pulling a black box off her belt clip and pressing the button.

Don lurched up, arms wide, and crashed face first into the floor.

"Idiot."

14

-*ARIZONA*-
Location Unknown

CHAD CLOSED HIS EYES. Made his peace with God. Muttered the Serenity Prayer his mother taught him as a boy. At least what he remembered.

"I'll be," the soldier with the Australian accent said.

Chad opened his eyes.

The gritty man's eyes narrowed on his smartphone screen. He lifted the barrel of his gun along his shoulder. Stood back up.

"What?" Chad croaked.

"What is it?" the other soldier said. He walked over to look at the screen over his comrade's shoulder.

The first soldier shoved him backward.

"Booger off." The soldier shook his head. "Well, Yank, I just don't think it's your day today. My orders are not what I expected. Tsk. Not at all." He squatted back down. "I bet you have family, don't you?"

"What's it to you, Abbo?"

"Eh ... not friendly I see. Well, can't say I blame you." He reached over and grabbed his canteen. Slid Chad's knife in his belt. "So long now."

"We're just leaving him here?" the other soldier said.

"Come on. Orders are orders and I need a cold one."

Both men walked away until their shadows disappeared behind the rocks. Their footsteps grew faint. A group of voices were talking and car doors slammed shut. An engine fired. Rubber rolled over the rocks until only the sound of the breeze in the cracks of the rocks remained.

Chad's watch read 4:15pm. He wondered how much longer he had. Minutes? Seconds? Hours? He crawled out of the shade. Stood up. Limped over to the dead zombies. Fought the pain of every step. He wanted to live. He kicked a zombie corpse in the head.

"Damn dirty creepers!"

He stomped on its back. Again. Again. And again. Drove his steel-toed boots into its ribs.

"I'm not dying like this!" he croaked. His throat was parched. "I won't be some undead devil!" He kicked it again.

A dark spot flickered in the sky. A drone hovered in the sunlight, twenty feet away and above his head. He grabbed a rock and chucked it.

"Argh," he said. He bit his lip and held his sides. "Bastards are watching this still. Sick freaks. I won't give them the satisfaction." He fought the pain. Picked up his knees and started running. Maybe he'd get lucky. Maybe a Sidewinder or Rattlesnake would bite him. Maybe he'd fall and break his neck. Maybe he'd have a heart attack. Worst case, he hoped he would die from dehydration.

On he went. A hundred yards. Then two. A quarter mile. Behind him the drone hovered, but he didn't look back. He thought of his wife, Monica. His sons. His Mother. Father. Friends. It ached that he'd never see them again. It angered him they'd never know what happened to him.

He puffed for breath. His heart was fire in his chest.

Keep running. Keep running. What am I doing? Killing yourself. Not right. Do it. Don't do it.

His legs were leaden after a mile. Bad cramps set in shortly after. *God, I don't know what to do.*

On he went, one heavy step after the other. His joints ached. Stiffened. His vision blurred. Darkened. The white sunlight turned gray.

What's happening?

Pins and needles pushed from the inside and out all over is body. He wanted to scream. Nothing came out. No sound. Pain. Motion. Agony. The world shook before him. Dark spots burst in his eyes. He moved. He didn't know how, where or why. There was nothing but a gray landscape bouncing before his eyes.

Who?

"Looks like this mission's over, Cowboy." Rancho said.

Charles stood, hands pressed on the table, peering at the screen. The man, Chad, had run for a few minutes, only to slow into a staggering zombie trot.

"That's different," he muttered, drumming his pasty fingers on the table.

"What's that?" Rancho said.

"You ever seen a zombie move like that?"

"No, why?"

Charles felt a little flutter behind the walls of his big belly. The Zombie Soldiers had been injected with a new version of the XT Serum. It was modified in hopes of giving the Zombie Soldiers more human-like responses. The older serum sped them up and quickened their reflexes, but the newer version had more promise. It just hadn't been tested much yet. And when it was, there were side effects.

"Just keep an eye on this one. I have other matters to attend to." He dusted the popcorn dust off his fingers. Grabbed some paper towels and finished it up. Chad, the zombie, was making a staggered line through the sand. "Just don't lose him."

"How long? He'll walk for days."

Charles glanced at his watch.

"A few hours at least. If things look good, we'll pick him up and freeze him."

"The drones don't have enough juice to follow him that long." Rancho's voice sounded irritated.

"Just—" Charles started, glanced at the screen. The zombie dropped to its knees. Crashed face first into the dirt. It twitched. Lurched. Moved no more. "Never mind. Let the carrion have him. He's gone."

There was a moment of silence.

"We done here, Cowboy?"

"We are."

"Alright, we're bringing the vultures back in. Rancho out."

The audio went silent. The fan rattled and Steve made raspy sounds with his breath behind him. Charles watched the image of the painted desert and the man turned zombie fade away.

"Damn."

The modified XT Formula had been tested on several subjects, but it never turned out. It didn't even turn the people into zombies. They just wound up dead. He walked by Steve and patted him on the cheek.

"I'm not giving that one to you, Big Fella. Not until I know it works right."

"Numma."

"You really should try some new words. Hmm." Charles picked up a TV remote that sat on a nearby table and turned it on. He wheeled Steve around on his metal gurney to face it.

"Might as well give it another go."

An episode of Baby Einstein came on. The classic music sprinkled the metal room with life. Little pig puppets were sliding down into the mud.

Steve jogged his head and jaw a little. His mouth was all grey teeth.

"Numma numma."

"Are you smiling, Steve? You like that one, don't you?"

Charles proceeded towards the back of another refrigerator. The doors were glass. The racks were filled with vials and colorful liquids. He slid one open. Grabbed a large beaker marked XT10. He swirled the light blue liquid around.

"Can't have any mix-ups," he said. Made his way over to the sink and poured it out. He spent the next several minutes motoring around the lab, destroying old XT10 notes and securing the rest. He emailed. Texted. Notified the only lab he'd sent the XT10 to in Arizona. *XT10 bad. Destroy at once.* Sweating, he took a seat by the fan. Listened to a little Mozart with Steve and closed his eyes. Dozed off.

Brrnnng! Brrnnng!

Charles jolted in his seat. Wiped his mouth on his sleeve. The ringing that woke him was so loud.

Brrnng! Brrnng!

His iPhone rattled on the console on the other side of the room. He got up out of his seat with a groan. Held his lower back and shuffled over.

"Oooh," he sighed. "I really should exercise."

Brrnng! Brrnng!

"I'm coming," he said. He banged his thigh on the corner of a gurney table. "Ow!"

Steve gaped at him.

"What are you looking at?" Charles said, hobbling.

Brrnng!

The phone fell silent just as he snatched it up. Missed Call, it read. The number was listed as unknown. He checked the time.

"Seriously! I've been out two hours."

A text popped up.

New Entrants Ready. Facility 105. Login ASAP.

Charles licked his teeth and rubbed his hands together. A crooked smile crossed his lips.

"I've been waiting for this."

15

-Morgantown, WV-

There were dozens, maybe hundreds of zombies sauntering around the abandoned mall. Each and every one had on new clothes. Shoes. Hat. Even handbags and back packs. The Day Care was one thing. This was another. A herd. Herds of dead people bumping into clothes racks, counters and knee high walls. They passed in and out of storefronts.

Not so much different than the mall used to be, Henry thought. He huffed a disappointed laugh.

"Nice," Rudy said. He stuffed a quarter in a candy machine. Twisted the handle. A large orange Sweet Tart ball fell out. He stuffed it in his mouth. "I haven't had one of these in years. I used to love these." He stuffed another quarter in. Grinned.

The black haired tour guide who had introduced herself as Jo Ann rolled her eyes.

"Come on, please," she said. "We have places to go."

Rudy stuffed the other Sweet Tart ball inside his other cheek.

"You're kinda mean, aren't you?"

"Depends on who you are." She offered a quick smile and walked on. "Come on."

Tori held Henry's hand, squeezing it tight. He could see a deep crease between her eyes.

"It'll be alright," he said.

She just shook her head. Her eyes were everywhere.

"They almost seem like real people. But that smell," she said. "Zombie flesh. Can't ever get used to that."

The tall blonde with long frizzy hair turned. Jo Ann had introduced her earlier as Karen.

"I know, I know. They tried spraying them with perfume and cologne, but that just made it worse." She tossed her hair. "Then the place really reeked. Blak!"

"So," Henry said, "how long have you guys been doing this?"

"We came on about this same time a couple of years ago," Karen said. "Not exactly what I had in mind for my career path, but things changed."

"We know how that goes."

"Henry," Tori said, hugging his arm. "Look."

Over a dozen zombies were coming straight for them. Some spoke. Num num. Others were silent. Jo Ann stepped in front of them, saying, "Just keep going. Don't let them shove you around. Think of them as Christmas shoppers, or Black Friday ones."

The hairs on Henry's neck rose. Their faces were haunting. Their jaws clicked and clacked.

"They sometimes move in herds. Not sure why, but they do," Jo Ann said, once they passed. "But, I'm not a scientist. I'm just a highly paid zombie social worker." She smiled.

"Is it worth it? Being around dead people all day long?" Tori asked.

Jo Ann shrugged.

"I used to work for the state. At least these zombies have some character."

Karen chuckled.

Henry didn't know about that, but many of them did seem

awfully real. Living that is. Walking by the store fronts he caught glimpses of movement behind the clothes racks. Some of them seemed too quick. Others stood still as mannequins. Maybe they were. There was a Build-A-Bear. Zombies stuffed baubles and stuffing into their mouths. A book store with books all over the floor. Henry cocked an eyebrow. A zombie held a book open in front of its eyes. A second later it dropped it.

"Did you see that?" he said to Tori.

She gave her head a quick shake no.

Rudy jogged up beside Jo Ann.

"Uh, what are you doing?" she said.

"Easy now," he said. "I don't bite."

"You kinda look like you do, with the furry face and all. Like that Muppet, Animal. Uglier and fatter though." She looked at his shirt. Shook her head. "They've got to make me a recruiter."

"Sheesh," Rudy said. "I'm not that bad. Cut me some slack. We're going to be working together, after all."

Jo Ann stepped on the other side of Karen.

Rudy walked backward in front of both of them.

"Well, are we going to be doing what you guys are doing?"

"We don't know," Karen said. "And, we don't care."

"Watch out, Rudy," Henry said.

Another herd of zombies was coming. Num. Num. They shuffled. Staggered. Grunted.

"How do you keep track of all of them to feed them?" Henry asked. He pressed through them. "There's so many."

"Ah," Jo Ann poked her finger up. "Glad you asked, and good question." She pointed at the walls and ceiling. "First off, there are cameras everywhere. If a zombie gets fidgeting we know how to feed them. Second, they all have trackers."

Henry looked up. He saw the cameras, all right. He also saw black sky and rain pelting on a lone pane of exposed glass, way up high.

Jo Ann and Karen veered from the mall's main hallway into another concourse. Henry heard the familiar sound of water trickling. A large fountain waited at the end of the hall. A waterfall of green liquid burbled over the stones. Six zombies knelt over the fountain's ledge, sucking on strange tubes.

Jo Ann took a seat on the wall alongside one of the zombies. Crossed her legs.

"This fountain's always full. The falls attract the zombies and stir the smell. Draws them here when they hunger. The tubes stay filled. I don't know how that works." She rapped on the Plexiglas that covered the surface of the fountain. "And this keeps the zombies from swimming in it and getting all sticky. It works great. No glitches the whole time I've been here."

"Wow," Rudy said. We walked over to one of the tubes that was higher along the wall. "Can I take a drink?"

"You really are a moron," Jo Ann said. She got up. "Alright, let's go."

Henry and Tori looked at each other. Shook their heads.

"Are you thinking what I'm thinking?" he said.

"Yes," she sneered, "the ridiculousness never ends."

"Oh, looky there," Karen said. "Looks like the zombie herd is hungry."

Henry stopped. There must have been twenty of them coming their way. Jaws snapped and popped.

Num. Num. Num. Num. Num.

"Wait a minute," Henry said, pulling Tori aside. "If they're hungry, won't they bite?"

"Two hundred and twenty days without an incident," Jo Ann said. "Better step aside. But probably only one of them is hungry. Herd mentality, remember. It actually makes our job easier."

Henry and Tori pressed along the columns between stores. Rudy did the same on the other side, while Jo Ann and Karen stood among the throng, having a normal conversation.

"I don't know about this, Henry," Tori said. "Seems too risky."

"I know—"

Jo Ann and Karen screamed.

Zombies had a hold of both of them.

Tori's scream followed. It was blood curdling.

16

-*WASHINGTON, D.C.*-

"YOU CAN'T STOP THEM," Don said. He held a pack of ice over his eye. "You don't want this."

Walker poked him in the chest.

"You said you'd talk, so talk, Bub."

Don took a long swallow. His eye was blinking around, following Louie.

The zombie boy teetered in a chair that Ashley had harnessed him to nearby. She was glaring at Don.

"Be glad you didn't hurt him," she said.

Don looked at Nate.

"She's kidding, right?"

Nate shook his head no.

"How did ... where did you get him?" Don said.

It was a good question. Things had been happening so fast over the past few weeks, Nate hadn't even bothered to ask. He'd been doing his best to accept things the way they were, seeing how the life he'd formally known didn't exist anymore.

"He's from one of the Day Cares. The one where they tested the XT Formula, remember?"

"In Guthrie?" Don said.

"That's the one." Walker fired up a smoke. "I found a lot of helpful notes in there. A lot of notes the WHS didn't get a hold of."

Don's brows lifted.

Nate's chair groaned when he took a seat. Something was eating at him. Guthrie sounded familiar. It was important. He was sharp. Bright. An effortless straight A student. But lately things had been so nuts he didn't have his focus. He should know this. Simple trivia. Everything he heard was trivia to him. The problem wasn't in what he heard, but in what he didn't hear. The WHS. The Magnificent Twelve. They kept things from him. He hadn't let that bother him back then though. He hadn't wanted to know. He should have paid more attention.

Don switched the pack of ice from his black eye to the bruise on his chin.

"I'd be lying if I said I didn't want to know what you learned."

Oliver kicked the back of Don's chair.

"Out with it, Don," he said. "You play too much chess with the lips. That always irked me. You're little battle of wits. Let's just stick him back in the trailer."

"No, no, Geez, Oliver. Don't be so sensitive." Don stretched his neck. Tugged the collar with his finger, eyeing Ashley. "Can we take this thing off at least? I'm in. You guys win. My word, I'm in."

There was something in the way Don said it that tickled Nate's ears. He leaned forward.

"What do you mean, *You're in*?"

"Anthony Ravenloft," Don started. "I can't believe I'm telling you this. Huh. Well, He's secure. He has his guards. But he can take care of himself too. A fighter. Seen him do it before. Quick and strong. I'm not for sure, but I think he used to be Special Forces or something."

Oliver kicked his chair.

"Quit bullshitting, Don."

"Well, he could be."

Walker held his cigarette under Don's eye.

"You're beginning to annoy me."

Don drummed his feet on the floor.

"Well, I'm sorry, but being honest doesn't come easy for me. I'm a liar. That's how I live. That's how I survive."

Zap!

Don't lurched in his chair. Sagged to the floor.

"What'd you do that for?" Nate said, alarmed.

"I hate liars," Ashley said.

"Well shit," Walker said. "I hope he didn't piss himself again. Come on, Oliver. Let's get him up." He turned to Ashley. Held out his palm. "Toss it over."

"Toss what over?"

"You know what."

"Say please?" she said, toying with the remote.

"Puh-leaze," Walker said, puffing out smoke.

She tossed it over.

He stuck it in his belt.

"Henry!" Nate said.

"What?" Ashley said.

"My friend Henry was in the Guthrie Facility."

Walker's cigarette fell from his mouth. He grinded it out.

"Walker," Nate said, getting up. "What do you know about Henry Bawkula? What happened to him? I got him a job there with his step-father, Stanley."

Walker helped Oliver lift Don back into his chair. He had his back to Nate when he answered.

"Who?"

It felt like nails in his foot when Nate stepped over and grabbed Walker by the shoulder.

"You know who. Exactly who. Don't you."

Walker gently shoved him off.

"Yea, but I don't know what's happened to him now. He moved on. Transferred after the debacle at the Day Care."

"What debacle?" Nate asked.

"It's over now," Walker said. "Doesn't matter. Just have a seat. We can talk about it later."

"Sure we can," Nate said, plopping back in his chair. "Sure we can."

He bit his nails. Walker was an insider. A double spy of sorts, but Nate still didn't feel he could trust the man. Or any of them, for that matter. He just didn't have any choice right now. There was nowhere else to go and he had to help people. *Henry.* The last Jumble he'd sent Henry popped into his mind. CPWWSZH. *Crap!*

"When did this incident happen exactly?" Nate said. "Did it happen near the time I was assassinated, so to speak?"

Ashley's chair squeaked when she turned away.

Oliver shrugged his broad shoulders.

Walker nodded.

"Yes."

Nate's temperature jumped.

"And you knew? And people died?"

"I've seen lots of people die. Just be glad your friend wasn't one of them." He puffed on his cigarette. "And I was part of the clean-up, not the execution, so to speak." Walker turned his attention back to Don. The man's chin sagged on his chest. "Shit Oliver, splash him with some water or something. Pronto."

"Great," Nate muttered.

Guilt set in. His text must have endangered his friend. Henry was bright. A loose end. It would hurt if anything happened to Henry because of him. They'd been best friends in college. Rivals too in a friendly sort of way. Henry worked hard for knowledge. To Nate it came easy. Too easy. He envied Henry's drive though. He lacked that ethic. He wished he had Henry around now. Henry gave him good guidance, but Nate didn't often listen. He scratched his chin. *I'm not that guy anymore. Am I still a bullshitter? Charmer? Who the Hell am I?*

He wheeled his chair over to Ashley and scooted alongside her.

"Uh ... excuse me?" She glared at him.

"Say," he smiled, "you mind pulling up what you were about to show me earlier? That sure would be nice." He glanced at her nails.

They were black, white tipped with gold designs and beads on them. "Those are pretty sweet. When did you get those done?"

She stopped typing.

"Oh, well, thanks," she said, her face flushed a little. "I get them done once a week. It's one of my things."

Nate nodded, still smiling.

"It's a nice thing."

Her bright eyes locked on his.

"Okay."

He petted her arm. *I've still got it. Must be the voice. Maybe the eyes.* He leaned closer to the screen.

"What was that thing that startled you before?"

"Uh," she shook her head. Blinked hard. "That's right."

Her lacquered fingernails danced on the keys. An image popped up. Zombies suited up in the heavy canvas Z-Suits. The image bobbled. Dropped up and down.

"Oh that's not the one," she said. "There's dozens of them saved on here."

"No, leave it," he said, squeezing her arm.

She looked at him.

He released his fingers.

"Sorry, didn't mean to crowd your space." Nate's eyes widened. "Are they wearing helmets? What are those? Skull faces?"

"Kinda cool," Ashley said.

"Who's holding the camera?" Nate said. The image remained unsteady. "A zombie?"

The body suits covered the bodies from neck to toe. The skull masks covered everything but the mouth. The jaws chomped and bit. The zombies scurried around the room in quick jerky motions. They were fast. Their motions ravenous.

He looked at Ashley.

"Pull up another?"

"Okay."

She clicked a file and another window popped open on the screen.

The image was dark. Shaky. Bodies in motion. A swarm of bodies fighting for their lives. Zombies gnawed on flesh. Ripped flesh from limps. Blasts of light burst everywhere.

"Ew!" Ashley said.

Blood flowed. Spurted. Faces screamed. Leg's kicked.

"Where is this?" Nate said.

A big man stepped into the frame. Black. Fast. Arms like Hercules.

"Who's that?"

Nate's heart pumped in his ears. His stomach knotted. His fists clenched.

The big man tossed a zombie through a window. Slammed another one down. The images were bits and pieces. Black and bloody.

"Get him!" Ashley yelled.

"What are you guys watching?" Walker said, leaning over Nate's shoulder.

Nate's eyes flitted over the screens. He saw somebody in the background.

"Stop, go back!"

"No," Ashley said, "I want to see the fight." The big fighter went down in a heap of zombies. "Maybe not." She paused the image on the screen.

"Go back two seconds," Nate said.

She did.

There was an image of a man standing in front of a large series of windows.

Nate's heart jumped.

"That's Henry!"

"Damned if it isn't," Walker said.

"Oliver," Nate said, turning around and pointing at Don. "Get him up!"

17

"YOU GOT THOSE ZOMBIES THAWED YET?" Charles said, sitting at the console chair. "The last shipment got up there three days ago. They should be moving now."

"We got all of them warmed up but two that some knucklehead left in the ice truck. But we've got the others fitted and ready to go."

"Idiots," Charles said, adjusting his headset, mind racing. He couldn't wait to unleash the next experiment.

Fingers working the keyboard, he sat back at his semicircular console, checking the monitors. One by one he logged into the cameras in the labs of Facility 105 in Morgantown, WV. The 1st screen on his left was broken down into twelve picture-in-picture screens, all currently blank. Screen two showed a lab. Screen 3 monitored the WHS personnel watching monitors. Screens 4 and 5 had shots from inside the mall. He could toggle through all of them. Hundreds. But that's what he relied on the other WHS Monitors for.

"You want us to put them in the sauna?" a man said, stepping into his screen at the lab. He had a headset on too. WHS Security Team leader Jake.

"No," Charles said. "I don't like thawing them out too fast. And don't you do it either. You guys would microwave them if you could. We've waited this long. Don't rush it."

"We just followed orders the last time."

"Sure, but not mine, and without my consultation. Next time someone tells you to do that, tell me."

"Seems like a good plan when we need them field ready."

"Seems like a good plan when we need them field ready," Charles shot back. "Don't be such a pinhead."

"Alright, Charles. Alright."

Charles rose from his chair and touched Screen 2, panning through the lab. Stopped and zoomed in on the man strapped to the table with his big chest gently rising up and down.

"So, is this our next candidate?"

Jake's big frame lumbered into view by the table.

"Sure is. Trained soldier. Excellent reflexes. Prime candidate for a Zombie Soldier."

Charles folded one arm under his elbow and rubbed his chin with the other, nodding. Sweat dripped down his cheek.

"Maybe a Zombie Super Soldier, by the looks of him. A much better fit than those NBA players. Who is this guy anyway?"

"Rod the Black Python or something. Octagon fighter. Champion."

Charles rubbed his hands together. Licked his lips.

"Strong heart, sounds like. He should survive the process then. It's a toss-up. Go ahead and bring the machines in."

Jake dropped out of the picture. Charles sat down in his seat, grabbed a handkerchief and wiped the sweat off his face. He hated sweating. He always sweated, even when it was cold outside. He craned his neck towards Steve.

"I wouldn't mind being one of you sweatless morons for a day. Just not feel a thing. Not itching. No excreting. No flu. No nothing."

Jake pushed a cart back onto the screen. Two other people accompanied him. A man and woman. They went to work sticking Rod with needles. Hanging sacks of liquid. Hooking up monitors. Jake held a mask with an oxygen type of tank on it. Placed it over Rod's mouth.

"Will this keep him out?" Jake asked.

"For hours," Charles said.

He tapped on the keyboard and altered Screen 3. A digital graphic of Rod's vital signs came up. Blood Pressure. Pulse. So on.

"Everything's a go. Now bring in the saliva."

The woman departed and quickly returned with a plastic sack in her hand. The liquid was grey and milky. She hung it up on the metal IV stand.

Charles adjusted his wireless headset and kicked himself around in the chair.

"Grab the XT Formula too."

"What?" Jake said, glaring up at the camera, stepping forward. "" We've barely got enough in supply for the soldiers we've got."

"It's all cleared, Jake," Charles said. "Feel free to check it out. Shit, it's synthetic, man. It's not like you have to dive to the bottom of the Atlantic to fetch it."

Charles was lying, but Jake wouldn't know that. *Stupid Jock. I ought to make a zombie out of you.* The ingredients for the XT Formula were ninety-nine percent synthetic, but a few were natural. Grown. Rare. Science hadn't been able to replicate synthetic options yet, but he hoped it was possible. Without them, so far as he could tell, the XT Formula wouldn't work at all. But in the last few months it had taken him leaps and bounds, not only offering the slimmest possibility for a cure, but turning the zombies into monsters greater than even he had hoped for.

"I'm back," Jake said, hooking the liter sack on the hanger and attaching it to the IV. He faced the camera and dropped his big hands, rubbed the muzzle of his .45 auto. "Are you sure this is alright?"

"Nervous, Big Jake?" Charles chuckled. "Afraid the Black Python might bust his bonds and eat you?" *Oh, that would be great! I can dream.*

Jake shrugged his heavy shoulders.

"The unknown makes me antsy. You, Charles, make me antsy."

Good.

"Then why don't you and the two lab coats get your butts out of the room then. You do know now to lock it from the other side, don't you? Or do I need to do that too?"

Jake shooed the others away.

"I'll stay."

"How noble."

I ought to be there. He wiped the sweat off his face. *If only it were zombies running the place.* Charles liked isolation. Not people. People bothered him. They talked. Smelled. Wanted to get to know you. He wanted privacy. Control. He got that from his father. Didn't know his mother. Came home from school. Went to his room. Did his homework. Ate. Went to bed. Never went fishing. Never watched sports. Study. Study. Study. His father either prepared him for great things or didn't want to deal with him at all. *Damn people. Don't need them all.*

"Check those IVs again, Jake. Those straps too. He's gonna flinch when the saliva pipes through."

Jake sauntered around the table, checking the tubes and cords.

"Make sure nothing can get pinched or jerked."

"I know."

Saliva glands. Charles couldn't take credit for that one. No, it was in the notes from Stanley Logan, top scientist at the Zombie Day Care. Deceased. Charles would have loved to talk to the man. His files and advances in zombiology were incredible. Even to Charlie. He didn't know what happened to Stanley. He wasn't a part of that. But at least he got something out of it. Stanley's notes. Not all, which infuriated him. But some. And they revealed a deep, dark secret about the zombies. It had taken him weeks to decode it from what he had, but now he saw it. Simple. Brilliant. Untested until he'd gotten it. Extract fluid from the saliva glands of the zombie, the dead, and inject into the humans, the living. *Yes! Uneaten zombies.*

It had opened up an entire new world of possibilities. If he could figure out how to synthesize it, the WHS could spread it through vaccines and immunizations.

"We ready?" Jake said, fingering his pistol grips.

"I'll inject remotely."

Charles pulled up the commands on the computer. His finger hovered over enter.

"One ... Two ... Three ..."

18

"EEK!"

"Get off me!"

"Aaaaaaah!"

It was a frenzy.

Rudy ran.

Tori kept screaming.

Jo Ann and Karen slapped at the zombies.

Henry, frozen to the wall, watched on with horror.

"Easy! Easy!" One of the zombies said. "It's just us, Jo Ann!"

"Paul," she screamed. "You idiot!" She shoved the zombie back. Pointed her finger at him. "I'm going to get you for that."

Karen slugged the other zombie in the gut.

"Oof," it said, going down with a groan.

"Payback, Craig. Payback."

She and Jo Ann took deep breaths, smiled, and laughed a little.

"What is going on here?" Henry said, holding his heart.

"Sorry," Jo Ann said, "I hadn't gotten to that part yet."

"What part?" Tori said.

The two zombies popped forward, eyes on Tori.

"Hi, I'm Paul," one said, sticking his hand out.

"And I'm Craig," said the other, giving his head a quick bow and rubbing his stomach.

They were young, college age, medium height and build. Blond hair, light eyes. Dabbed with grey make-up of some sort. Twins. Paul wore a sweat shirt with the letters KA on the front. Craig's shirt had the logo from The Darkslayer movie on it.

"Sorry," Paul said. "We just got carried away."

"Yes, very sorry," Craig said. He presented his hand to Tori again. "And your name is?"

Tori smiled, took his hand in her zombie hand.

"My name's Tori."

Craig's eyes popped open. He sagged to his knees.

"And don't you ever do that again. Do you understand me?"

Craig's tongue clove to the roof of his mouth. Eyes watered. Head nodded quickly up and down.

"I can break it, you know," Tori finished, letting go.

Paul pulled Craig up from the floor.

"I told you this was a stupid idea."

"Really, Paul," Jo Ann said. "You listened to your brother? I always expected better from you. I'm going to have to write this up, you know."

Paul's face turned long. Blue eyes pleading.

"No, please," he said. "It won't happen again. And Craig's already on probation. We need this job."

Jo Ann shooed them away with her hand.

"Just get out of here and don't let me see you for the rest of the day. Got it?"

They both nodded their heads yes.

"Sorry," they both said, and darted away.

"Shoot," Karen said. "We need to find the other one. What was his name?"

"Rudy," Henry said back. His spine still tingled. "Will you tell me what that was all about?"

"Let's walk and find your friend, not that I really want to."

"Well, he can cause trouble too, if we don't find him."

They walked. Karen called out for Rudy as they passed the zombies. Henry walked alongside Jo Ann.

"I've a feeling I'm not going to be surprised by what you're about to tell me, but I should be, right?"

"Hey, nothing should surprise you anymore. Not in this world. But here's the deal. The WHS, our employers, mind you, have a lot of college interns on the payroll."

"Here?"

"Yes."

"And they what," Henry said, taking off his glasses and cleaning the lenses on his shirt, "take the zombies shopping? Out to dinner? The movies?"

"Well, sort of. The idea is to assimilate the zombies into a common lifestyle. Recode them. Modify their genetic imprint with environment." She grabbed his arm and squeezed it. "I know it's crazy, but it might be working." She let go. "And the interns love the job. They like the clothes. Putting the zombie make-up on. You just have to have fun with it."

"Fun with zombies?" Henry smirked. "Sounds like a good book title."

"Huh, funny you should say that. One of the twins said he was writing a book about it. I forget which one."

"How many of these interns are there?"

"Maybe thirty."

"And they're here all day and night?"

"We have shifts. Maybe ten at a time. They're pretty good at what they do, so you probably won't even notice them."

Henry shook his head. His voice rose.

"This is Top Secret, isn't it? The highest level clearance? How can you make sure they keep their mouths shut about what's going on?

Especially with Facebook, Twitter, Snapchat and all that? There's no way you can keep a lid on it."

"That have so far," Jo Ann said. "Not my department though. Yours either." She stopped in front of a sporting goods store. A couple of zombies were bumping around inside. One had a Gold and Blue #9 jersey on. "They're top students. Well rounded. Signed off on confidentiality agreements. No tech is brought in with them. And besides, they won't risk losing a full scholarship ... all the way through med school if that's the path they're taking."

Henry wanted to choke something. It was absurd. Stupid. Ridiculous. He stuck his glasses on his head.

"This earns a full scholarship to higher education these days? Picking out shoes with zombies? Wandering around doing absolutely nothing?"

"Don't knock it. It's a dream come true for these kids. They grew up with the zombies. We didn't."

"Yeah, well if our generation was as smart as our parents' generation, we would have terminated them. All of them."

"Sssh," Jo Ann said, whipping her head around. "Don't let them hear that. They'll get upset about it."

"Good," Henry said, walking away. *Disgusting.* He made his way up to Tori and Karen. "Here, let me yell for him." He cupped his hands over his mouth. "Rudy! Ziggy gave the all clear!"

"What?" Karen said, making a funny look at him.

"It's a safe word. A nerd thing."

"Obviously."

Ten seconds later Rudy appeared, flushed and disheveled.

"Way to go, Coward," Tori said.

"Well, what did you do?"

"Alright," Jo Ann said, "the tour's over. Let's get you guys into headquarters. We're almost there."

They came to a walled off store space with a Security Door in the middle. A small red LED light glowed below the green one. It gave Henry chills every time he saw one.

"We'll get your security set up first," Jo Ann said, placing her thumb on the scanner.

Nothing happened.

She pressed her thumb on it again. Nothing.

"Great," she said. "Must be updating the system again. Karen, do you mind?"

Karen pressed her thumb on it. Nothing. The lights in the mall flickered.

"Was it storming when you guys came in?" Jo Ann said.

"No, but the rain was steady," Henry said.

Something popped, like a transformer. The lights flickered and went out.

Num-num. Num-num. Num-num.

19

-*WASHINGTON, D.C.*-

HE HURT. He wheezed. Coughed and sputtered. Don Baker hadn't felt this bad in a long time. Not since the training. Decades ago. He used to be one tough SOB. Now he was old. Shaky. Scared. *Suck it up.*

Everyone faced him. Walker fingered the pistol on his hip. Oliver glowered with his arms folded over his chest. The woman rubbed the shot gun on her lap. And the zombie boy's tongue rolled around in its mouth as it said Num-Num. It made him want to vomit.

"Can you at least take this collar off?" Don asked. "Let me feel like a human for one more day."

Nate pushed Louie a little closer.

"I bet he would've liked more days as a human too. Ever wonder what being a zombie feels like? I've read reports that they're in pain all the time. What do you think, Don?"

He turned his head away from Louie. He didn't think about such things. He couldn't afford to have compassion. Compassion made you weak in his business. A minnow among the sharks. He'd been a shark until they left him in the box with Louie. The undead child frightened the Hell out of him. Dark dead eyes. Strong pasty hands brushing against him. Jaws clicking and snapping. It wasn't natural. He'd vomited in there. The thought of turning into one of them was horrifying. *Did men like me really enable this madness?*

"I'll talk, I said. My word. Just don't put me back in with that thing."

"His name's Louie," Ashley said. She pumped the handle on her shot gun. "Got it?"

Don pushed his hand out.

"Yes, Little Lady. I've got it."

Nate nodded to Oliver, who reached over and unlocked the collar.

"Oh," Don said, rolling and rubbing his neck. "Thank you." He sighed. "I'm seeing this in a new light now. Would you mind scooting him away?"

Ashley rolled Louie back and turned him away.

"Num num."

Nate held the laptop in front of Don's eyes. Started one of the videos.

"Where is this?" Nate asked Don. "And what is Henry Bawkula doing there?"

Walker kicked his chair. Don flinched.

"And don't forget about Ravenloft." He poked him in the tender area below his swelling eye.

Don sucked through his teeth. Wincing.

"I didn't even know about that. My nephew showed me those soldiers for the first time. I was only up to speed with the rehab centers. This was entirely new." He huffed a laugh. "And I know you won't believe me, but I'm not on board with the zombies. I swear it. But they aren't going to stop with those things."

"What about Henry?" Nate said.

"Huh, yeah. Well, he survived ... again."

"What do you mean, again?"

"He's a loose end. His father, or stepfather I think, Stanley Logan, invented a serum in hopes of curing or helping the zombies maybe live some sort of life. It was silly. Souls, assuming they exist, don't come back. They're either in Heaven or trapped in the abyss." He shrugged. "That's what my priest said." He swallowed. "Long ago."

"Just get on with it," Walker said.

"There's not that much to get on with. They want to use the zombies as super soldiers of sorts. The serum Stanley Logan created sped their metabolism up. Reflexes. They can climb. Run faster. Their bodies are remote controlled now. WHS wired up their nervous systems to control them. This picture, all shaky, but clear," he poked the screen. "That's the zombie's eyes you're seeing through. Jack played it like some sick video game."

Walker backed off. Stood by Nate. "Shit."

NATE BALLED UP HIS FIST. Got up. Sat back down.

Dammit!

The old man started talking again.

"Yea, and you guys want to go up against this. Stop this. You're crazy."

"So, no one is supposed to do anything?" Nate said, "Sit around and wait and hope you're one of the ones chosen to die in some dick-head's video game?"

Don's eyes, always bright and vibrant, were dull. Guilty even.

"It was never supposed to be this way. When I started, it was all about National Security."

Walker and Oliver laughed.

"Or Human Rights Violations," Oliver said. "Peace Keeping missions. Ha! Different names, same M.O."

"Well we kept plenty of people safe. Got our hands dirty and saved a lot of lives."

"By turning them into zombies," Nate said.

"That never was the plan," Don argued.

"Did you ever stop to think that maybe that was *always* the plan?"

Don turned a little green. He wanted to say no, Nate could feel it. The old man just curled his lips instead. Nate could see it in the man's eyes. The truth Don believed in came full circle now. Layers of lies covering the dark and dirty truth. The people behind all of this weren't humanitarians. They were evil. Plain and simple.

"Where'd they take Henry Bawkula?" Nate said.

"There are facilities everywhere. He could be at any of them. Probably still at the Rehab." Don sat up in his chair. Draped his arm over the backrest. "You guys should make a clean break. We all should. Listen, they won't trust me anymore. I'm as good as dead, just like you. I know places. We can go there. Live our lives out in peace."

"Or pieces," Walker said. "Ash, I think he wants to play with Louie again."

"Look, I'm just trying to save us all a lot of pain. This won't end well. Honestly. How big is your little network of rebels," Don said, "a couple dozen? You're going up against thousands with unlimited resources."

"We have plenty," Walker said.

Nate nodded. He didn't know much about the help they had. Walker told him bits and pieces but there was plenty left to discuss. He said the less he knew the better. The fewer of them, the more likely they could surprise someone. But how could such a small operation take on a global organization?

"Plenty?" Don shook his head. "Well, I hope you're paying them well. The more you have, the less you can trust. Someone is always going to spill the beans. Rat you out. Tell their wife, mistress or best friend."

Nate wiped his clammy hands on his pants. Looked at Ashley and the others. Could he really trust them? Maybe the WHS was behind all of this. Setting him up. *Play it through, Nate. Play it through. Stay focused.*

"Where's Henry Bawkula?"

"Might still be at the Rehab—"

"No," Walker interrupted. "We want Ravenloft."

"Hey!" Nate said.

"Sorry about your friend, Nate. But he's not the mission. Ravenloft is. Capiche?"

Nate eyed him. Took a breath. He couldn't abandon all his plans on account of his friend.

"Well," Don said, "I can't tell you much about either of them. Really. Ravenloft does like to oversee some of the operations first hand. If they're doing some new testing with the zombies, and you found out where, there's always a chance he might be there. The only other option is to wait him out at his home or attack him at one of the zombie meetings. You'd need an army for that though. And I don't think killing him will stop any of this."

"But he'd make the call?" Nate said. "He'd order the next Zombie Outbreak?"

"Yes, he would. But if it's not him, then one of us will. Or one of them? Don't you see how juvenile your plan is? Killing or interrogating Ravenloft won't stop this thing. It might slow it, but it won't stop it."

"Exposing it. Exposing him," Nate said. "That should be more than enough to do it. When the people find out that the WHS is behind this, they'll shut it down."

Don leaned forward in his chair.

"Suppose you get it all out there. Who do you think they'll believe? The WHS or a bunch of nobody renegades?"

Nate felt himself being painted into the corner. How many times had he seen the truth crushed by lies, money and power? The plan was thin. He felt stupid. He felt compelled, too. He loved sports. There were upsets in sports. Plenty of stories of David beating Goliath. Immaculate Receptions and Seventy Yard Field Goals. The unknown philosopher had said, 'Only the ridiculous achieve the impossible.' Besides, they were all going to die one day anyway. Might as well try to do something meaningful.

"You know what, Don?" Nate said, getting up, "I think we're just going to try and kill him and let the chips fall where they may." He looked at Oliver and pointed to the trailer door. Nodded at Walker.

Walker snapped the collar back on Don's neck.

"Hey, what are you doing?"

Oliver jerked Don out of his chair and dragged him over to the trailer. Shoved him up the stairs and in the door.

"Ashley, our guest needs more time with Louie."

"Well, he'll be hungry again soon," she said, unbuckling Louis's restraints. "Those Dew bottles were watered down. They won't hold him more than an hour."

"Good."

20

One. Two. Three ... Charles pressed enter.

The liter's murky grey saliva and the blue XT Formula pumped into Rod's veins. The sacks emptied. His body jerked on the table. Chest heaved up and bucked.

"Shit!" Jake said, jumping back.

Charles checked the vital sign monitor. The heart rate spiked over 300 BMP. The blood pressure didn't register. Rod's body jumped all over the table. Fingers stretched and curled. Biceps bulged and strained. Metal groaned with every jerk and flinch.

Jake pulled out his .45 Auto.

"Put that up!" Charles yelled. "He won't break loose!"

"Yeah? Well I'm not taking any chances in case he does."

Charles's eyes were intent on the vitals monitor.

The BMP spiked. *370.390.415.*

He could feel his own heart beat inside his ears. *Don't die, dammit.* He'd tried this before on others. Many hearts ruptured, leaving the zombies useless or completely dead. So he had altered the formula.

Altered the doses. The process was still new, however. *Come on. Needs to work. Needs to work.* He ran his sleeve across his brow.

395.330.273.

The convulsing body went still. Fingers slack. Head sagged onto the table.

185.130.88

Charles crossed his fingers.

Jake holstered his weapon.

75.68.59.58.

"Oh, he's stabilizing!" Charles jumped. "He's steady!"

32.20.12.

"Noooo!" He screamed at the monitor, clutching at the hairs on his head. "Come on, Jake! Shoot him with more XT."

"Why?"

"Just do it!"

Brrrrrrnnnnnnnnnnnnnnnnnnnnnn...

The heart monitor flat lined.

The blood pressure monitors fell to zero just as Jake hooked the other IV in.

"Too late now," Jake said. "But I can try the paddles."

Charles pounded his fists on the table.

"No! No! No!"

He fell back into his seat.

"Just leave it," he sighed. "Don't need to waste any more of it."

He'd wasted enough already and his superiors would notice. He'd already abused his allotment and he didn't have any results to show for it. None. All he needed was a little bit of movement. Some promise. Brain activity. He eyed the screen. In the upper right corner was a diagram of brain activity. A rainbow of colors still resided in the middle.

"What have we here?"

Bip. Bip.

The heart monitor spiked.

BPM started moving. Charles sat and gawped.

12.20.32.32.32.32

He checked the other monitor and watched the man on the table. His fingers moved gently. The head rolled side to side.

"He's breathing," Jake said. "Blood pressure shows 59 over 30. Are you seeing this?"

32.30.32.30.30.30.32.32.32 ...

"Yes! Yes, Jake! The Black Python lives!"

Charles covered his chest with his hand. His heart pounded. This was the breakthrough he needed. This was what he'd been sweating his ass off in a wretched basement filled with rotting zombies for. This was his ticket to a seat at the table. The Table. He watched the diagnostic monitor. Blood pressure, steady. Pulse, steady. Brain function, active. He took a deep breath and let it out through his nose. *Now everyone will know my name.*

"Let's give it a few more minutes, Jake. As you hillbillies like to say, 'Let's not count our chickens before they hatch.'"

"Fine by me," Jake said. The big man holstered his pistol and took a spot leaning against the wall.

Charles's wildest fantasies began to run wild. If all went well this would mean more funding. More staff. More power. They'd give Charles everything he wanted. He spun around in his chair once. Circled again and stopped. Steve still sat with his head tilted, watching the TV screen.

"There just might be some hope for you yet, Steve. Well, maybe not among the living, but I see a bright future for you as a parking attendant." He held his belly and laughed. "No, seriously. You might be the ultimate weapon out in the field one day." He clapped his hands. "Damn, I'm good. We just might have to celebrate." He turned his attention back to the monitors. Jotted down some notes on some papers.

He could see the big man on the table struggle with his bonds. His jaws started snapping.

Hmmm. He rubbed his chin. *Vitals still steady.* He zoomed the camera in for a closer look. The skin on the black man's face grew taut. Its luster began to dry. Darting eyes started to sink.

"Helluva way to murder a man," Charles heard Jake say.

"Well, he doesn't look dead to me. He looks amazing."

The purple veins began to bulge beneath Rod's skin. The Black Python flexed, stretching the leather straps that bound him. The gurney groaned.

"Shit," Jake said. "I think he's hungry."

"Wait!" Charles said, "Just give it a few seconds. Those straps are wired. They monitor his strength." He fingered the keys and pulled up another diagnostic that measured the zombie's power. On average, zombies were twice as strong as a typical human. A good deal stronger than the fittest man. Rod was reading double the strongest zombies. "Beautiful!"

"What?"

The gurney groaned again.

"What?" Jake said again. "Geez, we need to feed him!"

"Alright, hold on," Charles said. He punched a few more keys. The Zombie Dew formula injected. "Try not to wet your pants, Jock for Brains. He should calm down any moment."

Jake gave him the finger.

Charles huffed a laugh. Locked his fingers over his belly.

"Great comeback."

Thirty seconds later, Rod, The Black Python, was still. Listless.

Charles kept his eye on the diagnostic monitors for a few more minutes. *Wow. Steady as she goes. It's going to be a wonderful life, Charles.*

"Alright, Jake. Let's roll him into recovery and have them prep him for Phase 2. Start getting the other soldiers ready." He stretched his arms and yawned. Brought up a new image on Monitor 3. A small group of people huddled by a door inside the mall with worried looks on their faces. "The new lab rats have arrived. Heh, heh, heh."

21

-Morgantown, WV-

THE GROUP of zombies filtered by, dragging their feet over the floor. Jo Ann and Karen still worked at the lock. Failure after failure.

"I don't like this, Henry," Tori said.

"Me either."

There was always something. The modified facilities never worked the way they should have. The elevators stalled. The Security Doors failed. The computers glitched. It almost seemed as if everything was set up to fail. Old buildings remodeled and reconfigured on limited budgets in compressed time frames. That's how the WHS was. They didn't want these things right. They wanted them right now.

"What's the plan in case of an emergency, Jo Ann?" Henry asked, eyeing the zombies. He was trying to figure out which ones were real and which ones were fake. "Suppose a zombie goes on a frenzy or there's an accident and the cameras are out? Are there any emergency exits?"

She kicked the door with her toe.

"Nope. We have back-up generators for that sort of thing. You know, you don't have to be a scientist to figure out you need a back-up generator." She shook her head.

"So," Rudy interrupted, "You're telling me that this place is filled with students. College girls? In zombie makeup?" He bobbed his head. "That's sexy."

Henry punched him in the arm.

"Ow!" Rudy said, rubbing it. "What did you—"

Tori socked him in the same arm with her zombie fist. Rudy stumbled into the wall.

"Ow!"

"Shut up," Tori said.

Jo Ann and Karen's eyes got real wide.

"Uh," Karen said, backing away, "I'll see if I can flag a camera down."

Rudy followed her.

"Don't you have radios?" Henry said.

"Yes, but we never use them. And we can't have our cell phones in here either." She patted Henry's arm. "This happens. It'll be alright. Just give it a few minutes." She looked at Tori. "Sorry."

"It's alright."

Henry backed against the wall and squatted down. Took off his glasses, yawned and rubbed his eyes. He tried to block out all the echoing num-num's in the corridor. He'd do anything to check into a motel for a few days and forget about all of this. He just wanted to get away. Start all over. The WHS wouldn't allow that. They'd made that indirectly clear. Several times. They owned him. All of them. Play and live. Rebel and die. A dirty Game of Life, where little peg-like zombies ride in the car with you until you retire in the Adams Family Mansion at the end.

"You look so tired," Tori said, sliding down beside him. "I'm sorry." She leaned her head on his shoulder.

He patted her knee.

"It's alright." He looked up at Jo Ann. "So, as long as we're waiting, do you care to share what is going on behind this door?" He pounded it with his fist.

"We call it The HUB. There's another door that leads to Zombie Central, but you'll learn about that later. That's where the zombies come in and out. The HUB's for us. It makes me think of an abandoned space station but it used to be a JC Penny's once. The bottom level is full of work stations, vendeteria, makeup and wardrobe stations. The upper level's been modified into apartments, bathrooms and such. It's not much, but the students seem to like it."

"How long do you and Karen stay here?"

"We do a week on. Week off. 7 day stretches."

"That doesn't sound too bad, Henry," Tori said.

"Well," Jo Ann said, "You'll stay here for the first thirty days, for orientation. And it'll make you stir crazy." She smiled. "It goes fast though. Lots of work to do."

Henry nodded. Jo Ann seemed nice. Karen too. They weren't uptight like the other employees at the Rehab. Their attitude was positive and not weird. It was refreshing.

"Now if we could just get this door open, we could get you guys settled in. Let you breathe a little. I know this is a big place, but it always feels stuffy."

Like a tomb filled with moving dead people.

Three zombies shuffled by. One in a green ballcap, a woman, was looking at him. Henry swore it winked.

"Did you see—"

Pop!

Tori jerked and Jo Ann jumped back. The door swung open. A small man popped out with black hair, scraggily chin hair and a lab coat.

"Hey Guys!" he said.

It was Weege.

Henry had mixed feelings. He helped Tori up from the floor.

"Hi Weege," he said, extending his hand.

"What? We don't shake. We hug, Henry!" The little man

embraced him, then Tori. "I'm so happy to see you guys. I didn't think you'd ever get here."

"How long have you been here?" Henry said.

"A few hours. Come on. Come on in. I'll show you around. Where's Rudy?"

"Weeeeege!" Rudy roared, jogging their way.

They high fived.

"Man, I'm glad to see you. Is this place full of college chicks?"

"The best and brightest. Sometimes they're even friendly."

Weege started back inside. Jo Ann jerked him back by the collar.

"Are these doors working now or not?"

"Oh, oh yeah." He shoved the door closed, locking them all back inside the mall.

"Weege!" Tori said.

"It's okay, it's okay. Just doing an upgrade."

Jo Ann shooed him aside. Pressed her thumb on the pad. The red light flipped to green. The latch popped in. She pulled the door open.

"Go on in, guys," she said.

"Weege," a voice shouted from down the hall.

Henry heard Tori suck her breath in through her teeth. He looked back at Jo Ann. "Aren't you guys coming?"

Karen was shaking her head.

"Uh, we'll catch up with you later," Jo Ann whispered, "We'd rather bathe the zombies than listen to Alice. Bye now."

Henry felt his own tomb close when she shut the door behind them.

"Oh no."

PAUL HUNCHED over the urinals inside one of the Zombie Mall's restrooms. They were the same as they had always been: white plaster walls with blue, white and yellow tiles on the floor, except they needed security pad access. Craig checked underneath the stalls and pushed open the doors.

"I'm not listening to this," Paul said, zipping his pants. He headed for the sink.

Craig hopped up on the counter beside him. "You need to fix your makeup. You don't look enough like a zombie. More like a college nerd with gray skin and ruddy hair."

"My hair's not ruddy. It's the same as yours, Stupid."

They were the same. Identical. Thick tawny hair. Blue eyes. Athletic. Closing in on six feet in height.

"Listen, Paul," Craig said, slapping his brother on the shoulder. "It will be legendary!"

Paul shoved his hand away. Turned on the water in the sink.

"Shut up, will you?" he whispered. "I'm not losing everything I've worked for because of you. Mom and Dad will kill you. Then they'll kill me for letting you do it. Try it. Just shut up about it."

Craig turned to face the mirror. Checked his face and smiled.

"Don't you wish you were as handsome as me?"

"What?"

"On the inside I mean. I've got *the glow* and you've got a cloud."

Paul shut off the sink and snatched some paper towels. Craig had his merits and Paul had his own. True, Craig was more fun and open. Knew more jokes. Drank more beer. Dated more women. Had a nicer car. Talked really loud. Made his presence known in the bars. Tended to push things to the limit. And when he got in trouble, Paul got in trouble with him. He tossed his towels away and headed for the door. Craig cut him off.

"Listen to me, just listen to what I have in mind."

"You don't have a mind, at least not in a positive sense, but rather a demented one."

Paul was the babysitter. Liked the fun and the quiet. Dated the same girl for the past two years. Had an old truck he took everywhere, particularly where he'd hunt and fish a lot. They were the same, in the sense they liked the same things, but very different in how they went about it.

"Paul, no one will notice. It's just one night. Reco night. It'll totally freak out the pledges."

"We, er you rather, will get caught."

"I've got it all figured out. And besides I never get caught. Remember the time we stole that Camry from the car lot and took Debbie and Terri out? I didn't get caught then, and I had the car back the next day."

"It was Lisa and Kim. And no you didn't get caught because you parked the car by a crack house and called it in."

Craig was laughing.

"Oh yeah, I totally forgot I pinned it on those crackheads. See? I did a good thing. Got that crackhouse shut down."

"This is different. You're talking about biohazardous materials now. A contagion. A virus."

"Pfft! There won't be another Outbreak with all the Dew around. You know that."

"But they can still turn people. Kill people. How can you be so stupid? Geez, I can't believe I'm still listening to this."

Craig was hard to deal with. When he made up his mind, there was little you could do to change it. Paul had to talk him through it until he saw the shortcomings of his plan. Problem was, Craig was as short sighted as he was determined.

"We'll just take one of the little ones. That tiny fella, the jockey that everyone loses. I can slip him out with the garbage. We'll toss him into the truck and have an Awesome Reco night."

"It's a felony, you idiot! Someone will tell. We'll get caught."

"No one in the Manor will say anything. They're sworn to secrecy."

"You can't be that naive. What happens when you blackball a pledge? He'll rat us out."

"No one's getting 'balled."

"You ball pledges all the time. You 'balled my little brother!"

"He was a dork."

Paul poked him in the chest.

"I'm warning you, don't try this."

Craig's eyes narrowed.

"You don't think I can do it, do you?"

"Oh, I know you can do it. But you'll get busted on this one. Trust me. And besides, the zombies have trackers on them."

"No they don't. You're just saying that."

Paul didn't know, but he wasn't asking either. Ask questions you get fired.

"Well, wouldn't you put trackers on them?"

Craig shrugged.

"And just think, someone is bound to video you making a zombie do a beer bong."

Craig's face lit up.

"That's a great idea. A drunk zombie. Can they get drunk?"

"Sure, and you can teach it to do push-ups with the pledges too. Maybe you can make the pledges sing the KA rose to it."

"Alright, alright. I'll let go. Man, Brother, you'd be a lot more fun if you just acted on your ideas. They're good ones."

"Glad you came to your senses," Paul said, following Craig out. He bent his neck and started his zombie gate. Craig limped away. "Where you going?"

"I'm after that new dental school gal, Leslie."

"Good luck with that, and it's Lisa, stupid."

Craig grinned and shuffled away.

He's lying. He gave up on that too easily. There's no Leslie or Lisa.

22

It had been hours. Nate watched the monitor image of Don Baker curled up inside the trailer. Louie, the zombie, bumped around the interior of the trailer, back and forth, his sluggard pace becoming quicker.

Walker and Oliver sat just outside the trailer, talking quietly and smoking.

"He has to know more," Nate said, rubbing his neck. He sighed. *Interrogation is not what I'm made for.* He'd laid out all his cards. Creating doubt. Causing fear. He'd done everything, but Don still hadn't offered anything helpful. The old man had been burying the truth for decades. Any helpful fragment wouldn't come willingly.

Ashley sat nearby, eyeing a television screen. The news showed a throng of protesters picketing all over downtown D.C. They held a variety of colorful signs.

Free the zombies. Zombies have rights. Killing zombies is murder.

Ashley huffed a silent laugh. Nate felt her eyes glancing over him from time to time.

"What are you thinking?" he finally asked.

"Let me see if I can find your friend, Henry. He has to be somewhere in the system. It shouldn't be that hard for me or Walker to locate him." She offered a smile and wriggled her fingers. "I can do it all quiet-like."

Nate shook his head. Chewed on his fingernails. The WHS had a net too big. Leaving digital signatures was out. Walker was smart. He handled everything by word of mouth. He said you could still get things done the old fashioned way. That it was how countless wars in history were won. Others lost. It took patience in an impatient world though.

"Let me make one call," Ashley urged. She pulled open a metal desk drawer filled with packages of unopened burner phones. "They're good, but they aren't that good. And the landlines are still safe too. ZR gets all kinds of classified information. Someone will know something about Henry Bawkula. The WHS keeps logs, digital and on paper. That's how our operation works."

ZR. Zombie Rebels. That's what they called themselves. An odd movement that showed up spray painted on overpasses here and there. Nate wasn't sure if what she was talking about was the same thing or not.

"Maybe," he said, looking back at the monitor. "Let's just give it some more time."

She shoved the drawer shut and said, "Alright, but if you're too paranoid, we aren't going to stop anything. At some point we're just going to have to do what we have to do."

Nate felt odd. For some strange reason he was being groomed to assume the role of leader, but he'd never felt like much of a leader. He was bright, but a goof off. Never took things very seriously. He accidently saved the world once and now, actual living and breathing people expected him to do it again. Was the leadership in this world that severely lacking? Did people have to count on a guy like him?

Ashley started feeding bullets into a 15 round pistol clip.

"You been using those things long?" Nate said.

"It's called a weapon. And no, no training until the zombies came.

Of course, I was pretty young then. Not a lot of kids getting heavy weapons training, aside from the video games, which I've always been awesome at." She jammed the clip in the pistol. Started loading another.

"Have you killed many zombies?"

"That's the only way you can become a rebel. You've got to hate them. You have to want to kill them. It's us or them."

"Why do you hate them?"

She looked up at him.

"Hate too strong a word for your tender ears?"

"No," Nate said, offering a slight smile, "It's just that so many people are infatuated with them these days. Especially young people. It's just surprising."

"Well, that's only because they haven't seen their friends and family eaten ... alive. And those gory scenes are all but banned from television and Youtube. Even during the anniversary of the Outbreak, you don't even see a nugget of anything." Her bright blue eyes darkened. "But I remember. And I blast a tunnel in one of their heads every chance I get. Twenty one and counting."

"Damn," Nate said, leaning back. "Well, that's certainly the most effective way to stop them. Do you think they'll ever find a real cure for them?"

She got out of her chair and twirled her pistol on her finger. "They say there is no cure for evil." She stuffed it in her holster. "Death is the only cure for evil."

"Well, what about Louie? You seem to care for him."

"I do, but I also know that if the time comes, I'll have to do what I have to do. But for now, he's cool. He's not trying to eat me. Plus, I've never wasted a kid. Not even a zombie kid."

"Well, if we go anywhere, I'm riding with you."

The trailer started to thump from the inside.

"Hey! Hey! Let me out of here!" Don screamed from inside.

Nate turned towards the trailer. Fists were pounding at the walls from the inside. Walker and Oliver were on their feet.

Don was screaming at the top of his lungs. Right at the camera. Louie pawed all over the man. Pushy.

"Tell us something useful, Bub!" Walker yelled at the door. "Or you aren't getting out of anywhere."

"I'll talk! I'll talk!"

Nate switched the audio on to the camera inside the trailer. Louie's grunts were getting hungry. Heavy. Biting teeth were clacking.

"Then start talking!" Walker yelled again.

Don was shoving Louie in the face, his expression horrified.

"There's a key WHS Facility that Ravenloft likes! Lots of tests. Advances. He gets off on the stuff." He shoved Louie away. "Get away from me! It's like Christmas to him there. Most of the top scientists are there too. Never been, but he talks about it. Brags about it even, but never shares."

"Where is it?" Walker shouted.

"Facilty 105. Morgantown." Don punched Louie in the head. "Ow!"

"Hey!" Ashley yelled at the monitor.

"Ask him about Henry!" Nate yelled over.

Walker shook his head.

"Do it!"

"What about Bawkula?" Walker yelled.

"They'll kill him. Probably sent him to Morgantown to run the zombies against him. That's what they did at the Daycare and the Rehab. That's it. That's all I can offer! Please let me out of here!"

"I can make a call," Ashley said. "We've got good people there. Won't even take a minute."

"Ow! Ow!" Don screamed. "It's biting me! Noooo!"

Louie's teeth were latched onto Don's arm. His jaws were sunk deep.

"Let him out!" Nate said, running over with a bottle of Dew.

Oliver took the bottle and jumped into the trailer.

Walker led Don back out seconds later. His arm was bleeding through his shirt. His face ashen and eyes watering. He was mumbling. "I-I can't believe this." He started shaking and wheezing.

Walker stuffed him in a chair. Checked his listless eyes.

"He's a goner. Any final requests, Jackass?"

"Please, please, just kill me. I don't want to be a zombie."

Walker pulled out is pistol and pressed it on Don's forehead.

"I can do that. But first, it there anything else you'd like to add?"

"No, no, I swear, I have nothing."

"Wait a minute," Nate said, "let me ask him something."

Walker pulled his gun back with a shrug.

Nate kneeled in front of Don.

"If you could do it all over again, would you do the same thing again?"

Don's head slumped over Nate's way.

"I suppose not. Like it matters now." He rolled his neck back towards Walker. "Go ahead, make my day."

Nate backed off and turned away.

"Say your prayers then, Rabbit," Walker said, "this might sting a little."

Don closed his eyes.

Ka-Blam!

23

-LOCATION UNKNOWN-

CHARLES BROUGHT five new images up on his monitors, overlooking various angles of another lab. Zombies, ten of them, filled the room. They stood solemnly with wires and small hoses running in and out of their arms and necks. WHS workers, dressed in casual clothing and lab coats, zipped their stiff forms into the Z-Suits one at a time. A backpack was harnessed to each zombie's back and connected to the straps and hoses around their necks. They looked formidable. Frightening. Even without the skull helmets.

"I should be there," he said to himself. And he would be if they insisted, but here, he was protected. The top dog in the science department. A man protected inside his abandoned fortress. "Remember, it's only a test run. Just needs to be a successful one." He panned through the zombies.

They were all above average in height. Men with sturdy builds. The gray and camo Zombie Suits made them look big and dangerous. The helmets, the metal skull faces, were dropped over their heads and latched to their backpacks. A modification Charles had added so they wouldn't fall off. No, he wanted his soldiers to be unstoppable.

He adjusted his headset and took the mute off his mic.

"Jake, get one of them weapons ready."

"Alright."

"And take him to the range." He pulled up another image on Monitor 4. A dark-complected man sat at a desk, his straight dark hair pulled back in a ponytail. "Are the Mall Creepers ready?"

"Two dozen of them are prepped and ready."

"Good," Charles said, "I'll let you know when." He switched Monitor 4 to a scene in the mall. Creepers traipsed everywhere. Many of them now time bombs. A large tablet with condensed XT Serum waited to be released inside each of their stomachs via radio signal. It would make them ravenous. That was the first capsule, but there was another that would null the effects of the Dew formula by spreading a virus that killed the sugar loving antibodies and endorphins in their bodies. No, these zombies would be different. There wouldn't be any Zombie Dew to save mankind this time. At least that was Charles's hope, but the zombie chemistry was still unpredictable.

"Ah, it'll still be fun to torment those college kids. Spoiled brats." He turned his attention back to Monitor 4. Jake and some others had led a Z-Soldier into a small shooting range inside the mall. "Be a shame to accidentally shoot some of them. Hee-Ilee."

He watched with intrigue. The Zombie Soldier walked over to the table and picked up a loaded pistol. *Blam. Blam. Blam. Blam...* Started blasting into the ground. Jake and the assistants started running.

"Who's operating that zombie!" Charles cried.

...*Blam! Blam! Blam! Blam! Click. Click. Click.*

"Sorry," a voice fired back. "Not on me. That's the zombie. He's got in itchy trigger finger. Ah, there, I think I've got it."

Charles turned to Monitor 5. A man stood on a treadmill in a blue body suit with small yellow balls all over it. It was the same technology they used in video games and for making live movie animation. It was good, just a little catchy getting it synced into the zombie's nervous system.

"Can you load another clip?" Charles said.

On Monitor 5 the man started walking slowly on the treadmill. On Monitor 2 the zombie bumped into the weapons table. Its hand fumbled around with the pistol until the clip fell out. It grabbed another clip and tried to feed it in. It was ugly. Finally it slipped in and locked tight.

"Charge it," Charles said.

It took half a minute.

"Damn! This is not good."

"It'll get better," the man on the treadmill said. "How about some more shooting?"

"Fine," Charles said.

The zombie raised its arm and aimed it at the silhouette.

Blam! Blam! Blam! Blam! Blam! Blam! Blam! Blam! ...

The zombie popped the clip out when it was finished. Jake appeared and reeled in the target. The bullet holes were all over the black silhouette and not all fifteen shots were there either.

"I've seen worse from people," Jake said.

Charles grunted. They'd made great strides with the Zombie Soldiers but they were far from military ready yet. Months away, maybe longer. He wasn't so sure the top brass in the WHS would be happy with that, but he'd give it a go anyway. Besides, so far as he could tell, the zombie was probably a better shot than him.

"I want five soldiers with pistols. 2 each with full fifteen round magazines. The other five need assault rifles. 30 round magazines. And make sure those rifles don't have safeties and aren't set on auto. Else they'll blow all their ammo in seconds."

"We doing this now?" Jake said, turning to face the camera. "We still have to get the lockers in the mall set. And what about the new guy? The Python. What are we doing with him?"

"Don't worry, Jock Head," Charles said, typing on the keys. "Just get the Z-Soldiers ready. This drill shouldn't take too long once the hunt begins. Just make sure everyone, and I mean everyone, is ready. This is going to be huge."

Bzzz. Bzzz.

His cell phone vibrated on the table. He snatched it up. Read it.

Report in.

His heart jumped. It was WHS Headquarters.

"I'll check back," he said to Jake, jerking off his head set. "What do they want?" he said to himself. He logged off his computers. Screen savers of zombies came up.

They called him at the oddest times. Every time something exciting happened. He updated them on all his progress, but they always seemed to be one step ahead of him. He swore his place wasn't bugged. At the same time, there was no reason to believe they wouldn't see everything that he did. His network was only as secure as his employers. Still, he'd like to have some privacy to himself.

He punched the keys into the remote computer from earlier. The silhouette of a man came into view.

"Yes?" Charles said. He wiped his sleeve over his sweaty lip. "I'm here."

"Report to Facility 105."

"Uh, me?"

"Helicopter is on the way. Sixty minutes. Have security escort you to the pad."

"But ... what about ... Who's going to—"

The screen went blank.

A chill went through him.

No. No. No.

He sauntered through his lab. He didn't want to leave. He wasn't ready for people. And who'd take care of his zombies? He unshackled Steve.

"Sorry, Bud. Orders are orders."

He led him through the lab and into a large walk-in freezer. One by one he shoved the rest of the zombies that lay on their gurneys inside as well. He waved at Steve.

"Num. Num."

He closed and locked the door behind him. Sagged against the door. He didn't want to leave. He did want a seat at the table, but not literally speaking. He reached into his pocket and pulled out a prescription bottle. He twisted off the cap, popped two small capsules and took a deep breath.

Damn.

24

TWO HOURS after the tour of their new accommodations, tensions subsided, slightly. Tori kept away from Alice and Alice stayed away from Tori. Henry's chest felt tight, but he could breathe easier. He sat inside the commissary, elbows on the table, yawning. The room had a checkered floor and orange wall with vending machines all around that were free.

Rudy sat at another table with Weege, crunching chips, talking and laughing. Alice sat with her arms folded over her chest, frowning and rolling her eyes. Henry ignored what they were saying. He was concerned with other things. The interns. They were a quiet bunch. About ten of them were in the room, in three small groups, huddled together. Some were in zombie makeup, others were without, or not finished yet.

"Doesn't this give you the willies?" he said to Tori.

"I don't know," she said, sipping her soda, "I'm not sure I can even get them anymore, since I've been creeped out so many times."

Henry yawned again. Took a sip of his coffee.

"It's like a zombie college dormitory. But the food's a little better."

"It's always better when it's free."

He heard some snickers and eyed the table of zombies. A bunch of guys were gawking at Tori.

"I wish they'd let us in our room. It's taking too long for them to brief us."

"Well, they probably have zombie maids dressing the room."

Henry picked the brownish lettuce off his sandwich and chuckled.

"They're probably fixing this commissary food too."

"You're smiling," Tori said, thoughtfully. "I haven't seen that in a while. You know, you're a lot more handsome when you smile."

Henry bobbed his head and his face flushed a little.

"Really?"

She leaned over and whispered in his ear, "Really." She placed her hand on his thigh. "And when we get our room I'm going to make you smile some more. Make this lousy world melt away from your mind."

"Uh ..." Goosebumps popped up all over him. "If you say—"

"Who's Bawkula?" A gruff voice interrupted.

A tall woman built like an ostrich stood in the doorway. She reminded Henry of the girls' gym teacher back in middle school, minus the grey sweat suit and whistle.

"You inturds," she said, "Get in makeup and get the hell out of here. We don't pay you to snack and peek at the newcomers. This isn't a rest home for jackasses. Move it!"

The interns, all ten of them, cleared off their tables and dumped the mess in the trashcans. In seconds it was as if they'd never been there.

"What are you gawking at, Fuzzy Face?" the woman said to Rudy. "You Bawkula?"

Rudy shook his head. Pointed at Henry.

"You're a big help, Flounder."

She walked over to Henry and extended her hand.

He got out of his chair and took it.

"I'm Dr. Deidre. But you can call me Dana."

She was taller than Henry, long necked, strong gripped and with short frosty hair. Not ugly. Not pretty. An open lab coat revealed her blue blouse and her black slacks.

"Nice to meet you. This is Tori."

Dana nodded at her.

"Alright, come on now. All of you. That means you too, Prissy," she said to Alice.

"What for?" Alice said, remaining seated.

Weege's eyes widened. He whispered in Alice's ear. Worry filled her eyes. She popped out of her seat and followed along.

"Up here with me, Bawkula," Dana said.

He fell in step beside her.

"You'll be supervising them," she said, jutting her thumb backward. "I'll be supervising you."

"Alright," Henry agreed. It was pretty clear by her tone that these arrangements weren't optional.

The room she led them to had been another department store. Modular furniture with low walls built into offices. Each office was big, computerized with large monitors on the desks. A few heads popped in and out of their cubicles. Fingers tapped gently on the keyboards. The overhead lights were many but dim.

"These will be your hidy holes, for now. We'll start you out in Observation. It's not fun work, but it's a paycheck. Then we'll ease you, Bawkula, into the labs where they do all the stuff I don't understand. Not that I couldn't. I'm more or less a sports freak. You ever play ball, Bawkula?"

"Sure, basketball."

She raised her brows, slapped him on the shoulder and squeezed it.

"Great. Perhaps we'll have a little one on one later. We got a half court in the other quadrant."

He looked back at Tori. She was hiding a laugh behind her hand.

Henry's mind started doing a rotation. *I'm here to watch zombies shop in the mall. My boss is an Amazon. My co-workers are college students dressed up for Halloween. I feel like I haven't slept for a week.* He wanted to ask more questions, but he feared they might offend her.

"Uh," Henry said, "so who's in charge when you're not here?"

She pointed at Alice.

"Not my call, but I've got orders too." She looked at Henry. "You might have already figured it out, but I used to be a soldier. Got shrapnel in my leg from a peacekeeping mission in Afghanistan. I'll tell you more about that some time."

She turned, backed up and faced everyone.

"Listen up. I run the show here. I make sure these interns do their thing, don't get silly, and go home. We don't fraternize with them." She eyed Rudy. "They do twelves and go home. You don't walk, talk, eat or drink with them. Back there, in the commissary, won't happen again. They know the rules. They fool with you or you them, they're out a good job and a scholarship."

Henry wanted to rip his hair out. How much more money would they pour into these monsters? Why didn't they just kill the damn things? *The world has gone mad.*

"I'm sure it's been a long day," Dana said, rolling her neck. "But there's one more thing I want to show you before we let you take a load off in your rooms and prepare for a fresh start tomorrow. Follow me."

She led them into a large conference room where a large illuminated floor plan of the mall was built into a long rectangular table. Several areas in the mall were lit up in red, yellow, green, purple and blue.

"Green – lavatories. Red – exits. Yellow –food stations. And purple," Dana said. "Care to guess what purple is?"

"Ice cream station?" Rudy said.

"No, Flounder. Not Ice Cream. Ammo. Weapons. You didn't think we'd host zombies without adequate back-up, did you?"

Henry felt an inward sigh. No one wore any weapons, aside from Jake. At the rehab he was used to having a six gun on his hip at all times. Shot guns were everywhere too. But it felt good knowing they took precautions inside the mall.

"Can you handle a weapon, Bawkula?"

Singled out, he shrugged and said, "Sure."

"I bet," Dana grinned. "Anyway, the interns are dark on this. Most of these Zombie Hipsters haven't even touched a weapon. Probably rather be eaten than shoot a zombie anyway. Bunch of pusses." She cleared her throat. "Anyway, the lockers only respond to thumb scans, in case there's a breakout. That said, we have WHS Security here. Plenty of them. Good men. You met Jake when you came in here. Good man and there's never been an incident. Never will be either."

Everyone shook their heads. At Henry's side Tori yawned. Everyone's eyes seemed blurry. The pressure started to ease.

"Any questions? Alright," Dana said, "Let's get you to your rooms then."

The followed her out, through the offices and past an unmoving escalator.

"I thought the rooms were upstairs," Henry said to Dana.

"They are, Bawkula. What's the matter? You got something against elevators?"

"No," he said, letting her lead the way.

She stopped at another Security Door, scanned her thumb and watched it pop open. Another security door with a red / green light was at the end.

"After you," Dana said, holding the door open. "The elevator's up ahead."

They filed in.

"Ah," Tori sighed, "I can't wait to get out of these heels and lie down in bed. Say, we'll need our stuff by the way."

"Oh yeah," Henry said, turning back to Dana. "What about our—"

Dana disappeared behind the door that was closing shut. She tossed a metal canister inside. It clanked over the floor to a stop.

"What is that, Henry?" Tori said.

"Huh?"

White smoke started billowing out of it.

Everyone but Henry screamed.

Choking and coughing, everyone scrambled. Henry pounded on the door. His vision blurred and the world turned to white roses as he fell.

25

Don jerked in his seat so hard he fell over in his chair. Ears ringing, his eyes fluttered open. Walker stood over him with his gun barrel smoking. A smirk was on his face.

"Am I dead?" he sputtered through his heavy mustache.

"The dead can't talk," Walker said. He shoved his pistol into the holster. "And zombies can't either."

Don pushed himself to his knees and crawled back into the chair. Wincing, he checked the nasty bite mark on his arm.

"Patch that up," Walker said to Ashley.

Don's heart pounded in his chest.

"Patch it up? That won't help. I'll still turn. Just kill me, man, kill me," he pleaded.

"You aren't going to turn into a zombie," Walker said.

"Hold still," Ashley said. She ripped his sleeve off. "Ew, it is a nasty bite though. It wouldn't be so bad, but that sagging skin and those wrinkles." With nimble fingers, she cleaned the wound and then wrapped him up and taped him off. She looked Don in the eye. "Don't ever hit Louie again."

Don swallowed.

"Okay, Miss. Can someone tell me what's going on? Look, I'm broken. I can't take any more of these games. You win. Am I going to die today or not?"

Nate shook his head. Rubbed his beard.

"No. You see, Don, we know a little something about zombies the WHS doesn't know. At least we don't think they know."

"What's that?"

"If you remove the saliva glands of the zombies, they aren't infectious anymore."

Don's mouth fell open. His wheezing stopped for a moment.

"You mean, the boy, Louie, isn't contagious?"

"He's as harmless as a bumble bee," Walker said. "Well, he still has his teeth. But he can't spread the virus."

Don wanted to hug them. Praise them. He felt more alive than he'd ever been. His mouth opened to a smile, then returned to a frown.

"What are you going to do with me if you aren't going to kill me? I'm just a liability."

"Would you rather be an asset?" Nate said.

"Asset? Ha, you know you can't trust me," he said.

"No, and we can't kill you either. It's not the way we do things."

"You killed Jack," Don said.

"No," Oliver said, walking up behind him. "I killed Jack. There was no good in him, Don. But there's good in you." He patted Don on the shoulder. "And I won't kill you unless I have to. Don't make me have to."

One of the burner phones buzzed on the desk table. Ashley snatched it up.

"Ash here," she said. Her eyes widened. Her head nodded. "Stand by." She flipped the phone shut.

"What'd they say?" Walker said, puffing on his cigarette.

"Something big is happening at Facility 105. A chopper landed.

Cargo trucks have rolled in. A passenger van came in earlier. One of them was Henry Bawkula. He's been scheduled."

"Scheduled for what?" Nate asked.

She shrugged.

"WHAT DO you know about this, Don?" Nate said.

"I assume they're going to pull the same stunts they did at the Daycare and Rehab," he said.

"We need to stop them," Nate said.

"Just hold your horses," Walker said.

"There's no time," Nate said.

He could feel it. Something bad was about to happen. He had to try and do something. If nothing else, maybe he could save Henry.

"Walker, you know about all the security at these facilities. You're one of the top brass. You can get us in there. I bet you've even been to Morgantown, haven't you?"

"I'm one of many, Nate. They have facilities all over and I've been to dozens of them. And those are the ones I know about. I've been to Morgantown one time. They never seemed to be doing much of anything up there." Walker shrugged. "That said, hell I don't know. If our people say something's going on and your friend's there, then I suppose we check it out. Suit up, everybody."

"What about me?" Don said.

Walker looked to Ashley.

"I'm not babysitting," she said. She headed over to a set of lockers, popped open a door and grabbed a uniform shirt. "I'm going where the action is."

"Fine," Walker said, "I guess will just take him with us. Oliver, grab the van. Ash, get the warehouse secured."

"What about Louie?" she said.

"We're not taking him," Walker said. "Just have Dr. Z's gang pick him up."

"But—"

"It's either that or you stay here and babysit.

THE BLACK VAN blasted through traffic like rolling thunder at eighty miles per hour. Oliver drove. Walker rode shot gun. Don sat strapped in the middle row and Nate was in the rear seat with Ashley. Through the back window he could see two more black vans. It was a small convoy of Zombie Rebels. Nate wondered if this was what being deployed to war felt like.

Up front, Walker rolled down his window and chucked a burner phone outside, where it shattered on the interstate pavement. That was the fourth one in three hours. Walker's conversations were brief. To the point. And coded.

"Listen up," Walker said. "We're posing as extra WHS security. Our back story—that they'll discover when we arrive—is there was a mix up. A bad call was made and they overreacted. This bullshit should fly enough to get some of us in. Maybe all of us. Might be able to get a peek at what's going on. So keep quiet. Act a little stupid and we might just pull this off." He popped his zippo open and lit a cigarette. "If they sniff us out, well, just plan on getting your butthole filled with bullets. Capiche?"

Everyone nodded, except Don. The man sat head down, quiet. Nate was bothered. It didn't make much sense to bring him along. He spoke up.

"What about Don?"

"I've got a rendezvous scheduled for him. Rest stop twenty. They'll hold him until this is over," Walker said. There seemed to be some finality about it.

Nate rubbed the synthetic stock of his shotgun. He hadn't used one since the day of the outbreak. The day his friends and family were torn to shreds and devoured. He had fired. He had lived. Life had been a psycho circus ever since. Now he felt like a new recruit going off to war. He stomach turned inside his belly. Sweat beaded his forehead.

"You alright?" Ashley said.

"Yeah, just a little uncertain about the future is all."

"You should be used to that by now," she said, jokingly, "you'd think."

He slunk back in his seat.

"You never get used to almost dying—because one of these times is going to be the last time."

THE VAN'S wheels squeaked to a stop. Nate rubbed his face and combed his fingers through his hair. *Ow!* His foot was burning like fire. *Today of all days.*

"Head to the pissers," Walker said. "Make it quick. Life's going to move really fast after this."

Nate watched Don being moved from one van to another. The old man took a long glance at him, made a causal wave with his hand-cuffed wrists and showed a grim smile. Nate had a feeling Don was going to fare better than him. A moment later the van door slammed shut. It backed out of its space and sped away. He hobbled out of the van and headed towards the rest station. Outside, the air was fresh. The sun bright. He could smell the dew on the honeysuckles that blossomed on the green backdrop. Men, women and children bustled in and out of the rest station, more smiles than hurried faces. *At least some life is still normal.* He made it inside, did his business and headed out. Took one last look at his surroundings.

"Come on, Rick Jones, get the lead out," Walker said, his mirrored glasses reflecting in the sun. "It's time to save the world."

"Again," Ashley added, opening up the door.

Nate rubbed Jeanine's crucifix under his shirt. Took a breath, looked up above and hobbled forward. With stabbing pain in his foot he stepped into the van, sat down and buckled himself in. Ashley shut the door. Oliver fired the ignition. Seconds later they were rolling.

"Say," Walker said, "How about some music?"

26

CHARLES HUNCHED over a Zombie Soldier lying on a gurney. His feet splashed on the floor when he moved. His stomach was queasy, his handkerchief soaked with sweat from his forehead. His breath was quick. Rapid. *Settle down, Charles. Settle down. Damn, feels like my first day of school all over again.* He had hated every grade, kindergarten through twelfth. He slid an IV into the zombie's arm. Let out a short cough.

"You need anything?" a deep voice said.

Charles half looked over his shoulder.

Jake was behind him. Tall and heavy shouldered. A gorilla in the room compared to the others that doddled about in a rush.

"A scalpel," he said.

"I mean like a drink or something. Maybe a towel. Maybe a mop to clean your sweat off the floor."

Damn ogre! I'll turn your ass into a zombie if you're not careful. Dime a dozen, you brutes.

"No thanks, Jock Head." He took a pen light and studied the zombie's eye. "But I appreciate your humor."

"Huh. Careful then, might slip on your own sweat and crack that egghead of yours. Maybe you should invent a deodorant for that."

Charles reached over and grabbed a scalpel off a shiny metal plate of medical instruments. Turned and faced Jake. "Do you know how many living people I've operated on? Hmmm?"

Jake's dull eyes brightened a little before he shrugged.

"Some of the people that died could have lived, you see," Charles continued. "Imagine what would happen if you ended up on my table after an accident, hmmm? If I still didn't like you?"

Jake's Adam's apple rolled in his thick neck. Then he let out a short laugh.

"I'll take my chances, because I'm pretty sure you don't like anybody."

"Hmmph," Charles said, "Well that's one thing we agree on. Now, if you'd be so kind, I could use a coffee."

"Sal," Jake barked, causing Charles to flinch. "Bring two Joes. Pronto!"

Charles shook his head and turned his attention back to the zombie.

"Idiots," he muttered, cutting the zombie deep in the thigh. He grabbed some metal tongs and spread the pasty gray skin open. "Water on the floor's not because of me. This zombie's still thawing." He chiseled at the frozen muscle over the bone. The zombie didn't move or flinch, but its sunken eyes rolled in its head. He sighed. "He won't be worth a lick for hours."

"I don't think we'll need him," Jake said. "It'll be like fishing with dynamite today."

"Pah, you think it's all so easy, don't you, Jock Head. Let me ask you something. Did you ever lose a game that you were sure you'd win?"

Jake nodded. "Good point."

"And, in case you haven't noticed because you've been so preoccupied with entertaining me, your staff is rolling out." He wiped his forehead. "Not all hands are on deck. Did you ever go play a game with half a team?"

Jake dropped his big paw on Charles's shoulder, jolting him. He offered a broad smile behind his trimmed goatee.

"The team we have, I'll have ready."

Charles pushed Jake's hand away.

"That's not reassuring."

In all truth, Charles wasn't worried. He was excited. These lab rats had as much chance of surviving as a fish had of getting out of its tank and into the ocean. No, this would be fun. This would be brilliant. Everything he'd worked on for years was falling into place. Zombie Soldiers. Modified XT Formulas. A new zombie virus. The keys to the kingdom would be his.

The man named Sal, a big black bearded middle easterner, returned with two coffees. Jake's phone buzzed on his hip. He checked the message.

"Hmm, seems like they're ready for you, Doctor."

Charles felt his spine freeze.

"Looks like you're gonna have to wait on the coffee."

Jake looked him in the eye and chuckled.

"Let's go. It's time to show the Magnificent 12 what you got."

"Twelve?" Charles swallowed.

CHARLES ENTERED the room first and Jake right after. It was a Board Room of sorts. A large oval table made from black modular furniture was in the middle, surrounded by over a dozen four-legged chairs. The ceiling was a grid of drop tiles and incandescent lights, and the windowless walls were stark white. A man sat at the end of the table. Two attractive women on either side. Business types. Back against the wall were two guards, dark blue suits and mirrored glasses. Uzi's at the ready on their chests.

"Charles," said the man at the end of the table, brightly. He stood.

Clapped his hands. "Doctor Charles Sikes. The man of the hour. So good to meet you."

Charles nodded. Swallowed.

"Thank you," he said. "Thank you kindly, Mister Ravenloft."

Fists on hips, the man tossed his thick black hair back and chuckled. Ravenloft was average size. Well put together in his dark gray suit. Piercing dark eyes.

Ravenloft walked over and shook his hand. His grip was strong like a construction worker's.

Ouch!

"Come sit," Ravenloft said, "the both of you. This is Julie Edgerd and Leslie Mckinley."

"A pleasure," he nodded. He extended his hand.

They nodded, smiled.

He withdrew. Feeling embarrassed, he sat down. *A lady offers her hand, you idiot. Not you. It's bad enough I'm sweating like a pig.* He knew both women. Both a part of the Magnificent Twelve. Top of the order in the WHS world. *Be smart. Don't look stupid.*

Ravenloft resumed his seat.

"I tell you, Charles, I'm excited. Very excited about all of this. Looks like all your hard work is about to pay off." He picked up a glass filled with water and drank. "Ah. We have a lot of facilities. Many. But no one has made the strides with the zombies what you have. Zombie Soldiers. Brilliant. An anti-dew vaccine." He slapped the table. "Marvelous! And you've even got something else brewing too. What would we call that? Zombies without blemishes?" He laughed a little. Smiled. "I'm having them get that big man ready. Let's test him."

Charles shifted in his seat. *What? That's my experiment.* How did Ravenloft already know all of this? He knew every detail. Every bit. He'd only done the testing on Rod a few hours ago and now—zoom —here he was with Ravenloft himself.

"I'm not sure what to call it, yet?"

"Don't you worry, Charles. You'll get plenty of credit for whatever we choose to call it." He shot his fists at him. Excited. "It's wonderful how all of a sudden so many breakthroughs fall into place. Perseverance, Charles. Perseverance. Have you ever noticed that the zombies have amazing perseverance? Hmmm. So do you."

"Thank you, Sir."

"Please, you flatter me. Call me Anthony."

"Alright, Anthony."

"So," Ravenloft said, "I'm eager to get started. We are just waiting on a few more guests to arrive."

Charles eyed the empty seats. Eyed Jake, who sat across from him. The big man had a little grin on his face. *Bloody Hell, they're all coming.* He rubbed his hands on his pants. *I'll probably sweat to death before they arrive.*

27

"Hey."

Henry felt someone shoving him.

"Hey."

Henry flinched. Popped up into sitting position from the floor. "What the hell?" he started to say.

"What's going on?" the same voice said again. It was a young woman's.

Henry felt his face. His glasses were gone. His heart jumped.

"Anyone see any glasses?"

"No," the unfamiliar voice said.

Henry's vision wasn't horrible, but it wasn't good either. He squinted. Peered around. A group of people had formed a circle around him. Other forms lay stirring on the ground beside him.

"Tori," he said. He crawled over and shook her shoulders. "Tori, wake up."

"What's going on?" she said, rubbing her head. "Ow! Did someone hit me with a pipe or something?"

"I think you fell. We were gassed. Remember?"

"Uh-huh," she responded.

They were inside the mall. The people surrounding them looked like zombies. Num-num sounds rattled farther down the main corridor.

"Who are you guys?" one of the interns said.

"We're the new help," Henry said, getting up. He helped Tori.

"What's going on?" said another face in the crowd. "We were just making our rounds, and, well, we tripped over you. Why are you sleeping here?"

"Did you see anyone bring us in?" Henry said. He checked his shirt pocket. Felt his glasses. *Ah.* He slipped them on his head. "That's better." The zombie interns didn't look good, but they didn't look bad either. It was more like a group from a Halloween party. Younger men and women. Five in all. They all started talking.

"I didn't see anything."

"Something weird is going on. I can't get access to the Cove. And my shift is up."

"Mine too."

"No! No! No!" a woman said. She seemed hysterical. It was Alice. "They can't do this to me! They can't! I've been loyal!"

"What are you talking about?" Weege said.

"Yeah," Rudy added. "Do what to us?"

Alice ran to the nearest Security Door. It was the one they had entered earlier. She scanned her thumb. Red.

"No!" She pounded at the door. "No!"

Weege tried his. Red.

"What are they doing? What are they doing?" he said. "They can't do this. Henry?"

"Told you they didn't work," one of the zombie interns said. He had a football jersey on. "We're locked in here."

"It's just a malfunction," said another in a DTD sweatshirt. "Don't wet your pants over it. They told us these things would happen. I'm not panicking."

"I'm scared," one mousy girl said.

"Look, you old people need to tell us what's going on."

"Hey," Tori objected. "I'm thirty one."

"Look, everyone just calm down. Stick together. We'll figure a way out of this," Henry said.

Alice was yelling up at the camera mounted high on the wall, waving.

"Don't do this! Don't do this! I'm loyal! I'm not like them."

"What is she freaking out about?" a zombie intern said, horrified. "What does she mean?"

"We're bait, Man! We're bait!" Rudy said, digging his fingers into his hair. "Damn, I thought this gig was going to be so good."

"Shut up, Rudy!" Tori said. "You might be zombie food, but I'm not. They didn't—"

Henry grabbed her. "Let it go, Tori."

"What?"

He looked at the zombie interns. Two of them were crying, their dark makeup smearing.

"Everyone, just stick together."

Why not just kill us? Henry thought. *What does the WHS need us for?* He didn't know what was going on. What to expect. He couldn't trust anyone except Tori. He checked his watch. Over six hours had passed. *We've been out that long?* The num nums seemed to be growing in numbers. Shivering, he grabbed Tori's hand and addressed the zombie interns.

"Have any of you noticed anything else strange the past few hours?"

"I just got on shift a few hours ago. Lots of staff were heading out. Seemed weird at the time. Bird Lady said they were running drills. They do that sometimes."

"The Zombie Dew fountain drained a few hours ago."

"There was a black helicopter outside."

"There was?" said another. "I didn't see it."

"I saw the prop on the backside of the building. Saw some suits coming out too."

"Yeah," added another. "It was weird how they were rushing us around. Normally it's really casual. I hope nothing bad's going to happen to the zombies." She sniffed. "Are they going to take them away? I saw one of them fall over dead the other day. Poor thing."

"You're kidding me," the guy in the frat shirt said. "You're worried about them? I'm worried about me. We've got to get out of here."

"There is no way out of here," Alice said, distraught. "We're all dead."

"Shut up, Alice!" Tori said.

"Someone has to know another way." Rudy suggested. "There's always a way, right Bawk?"

"Craig would know," one intern said. "That schemer tricked Bird Lady a half a dozen times. Comes in for twelves and works six. Changes his makeup. She still hasn't figured it out."

"He told me he's got a master passcode," another one said.

"Yeah, to you pants," chuckled another.

"Hey!"

"He's a dickhead," the guy in the frat shirt said. "Just a bullshitter. You can't believe anything that creep says."

"Well, he and his brother, Paul, were here a few hours ago. Let's find them."

"And if they aren't here? And we're locked in here?"

"Then we'll just have to make another way out," Henry said, thinking of that one skylight that had escaped being boarded up. But it was a long way up. Another way out would be preferable.

"Let's split up. Meet back here," Rudy suggested.

"This mall's not so big. No, we better stick together and round up any others," Henry said. He took a head count. Alice and Weege were already moving. "Hey, were are you going?"

"Screw you, Bawkula," Alice said and kept going.

Weege didn't even turn his mousy little head around.

"Maybe I should follow them," Rudy said.

"Sure, Rudy. Go right on ahead."

"Henry!"

"I'm not fighting it," Henry said with a sigh. "It's their lives, they've got to live them."

"But what if they find a way out?" an intern said.

"Look, you guys can do what you want. You're big boys and girls. But I think it's best you stay with me."

No one argued. They followed. Henry planned. In all truth, he didn't think they stood a chance. With the Zombie Dew fountain drained, the zombies would be getting aggressive in a few more hours. They had to get out before that happened.

"Come on," one of the girl interns said. "Craig likes to hang around at the food court."

On the way, Henry noticed a small kiosk near the wall with a small green and red indicator on it. He pulled Tori towards it.

"Remember what Dana said? About the weapons for emergencies?"

Tori nodded.

"Kinda odd, isn't it?"

It didn't seem likely that the woman who had gassed and trapped them would be an ally. But maybe she'd been trying to warn them. Help them.

"Here goes," Henry said, pressing his thumb on the pad.

The kiosk popped open.

A shotgun and handgun were inside. Ammo too.

"I'll be."

Henry grabbed the shotgun and stuffed in the shells. Stuck the others in his pocket. He handed it to Tori and held the pistol ready.

"You know I'm not very good with these things," she said. "But I'll hold it for you."

"Say," an intern said, "How'd you get those things?"

"They're called weapons, Dumbass," the frat guy said. "Give me one."

"That's all there is," Henry said.

"What's it there for?" another said.

"Dana, or the Bird Lady, said they were for emergencies."

"Never told us that."

"Well, you better not be shooting any zombies," said the mousy one. "That's murder."

"No, it's self defense."

"That's not what they're teaching me in law school."

"Ayeeiii!"

Someone screamed at the empty fountain.

"It bit me! It bit me!"

A commotion started. A zombie had an intern pinned to the ground.

Pop! Pop! Pop!

Shots rang out in the mall. Voices screamed from everywhere.

Rudy appeared in the main hallway waving his hands.

"They're back! Run!"

Pop! Pop!

Rudy's big body spun around and collapsed on the ground.

"Rudy!" Henry yelled. He started to run.

Tori snatched his arm. Yanked him back.

A dangerous figure rounded the corner.

A metal skull masked the zombie's face. Its sagging jaw snapped. It was just like the ones at the Rehab. In a zombie suit for the toe to the neck, its movements stiff. Fast. No, it was different. It had a pistol in each hand. Pointed right at them.

Duck!

He pushed Tori to the ground. Covered her with him.

Pop! Pop!

28

-*Morgantown, WV*-

Nate felt like he had a thousand butterflies inside his stomach when they squeaked to a halt at the gate to Facility 105. *What am I doing? Why am I doing this?* For some reason people were counting on him. They wanted him to lead them into the belly of the beast and back out again.

Oliver and Walker stuck their badges in the faces of the men on either side of the van. A third guard popped the side door open.

Nate and Ashley handed over their ID's.

"Getting a lot of visitors today," the guard said. "Seems pretty strange."

"So?" Ashley said.

Nate shrugged.

"Just making conversation," the man said. He handed back their ID's and slammed the door shut.

"I'll have to phone it in, Colonel," the guard at Walker's window said. "Be a couple of minutes."

The other two guards checked the two vans behind them.

Walker looked back at Nate.

"It'll be alright. Just don't say anything stupid." He fired up a smoke. "Remember, I do all the talking."

Nate could barely breathe. He ran his finger under his collar.

"You okay?" Ashley said. Her pale face was calm, almost serene.

"No. And you are?"

"Sure, every day is a life or death situation. You should be—"

"I know," he huffed, "used to it by now."

No, this wasn't normal. Life wasn't normal. It was a mess. And now Nate felt like he was about to storm the beaches of Normandy. Ashley sat there all prim and proper, like she was going to a wedding. Up front, Oliver and Walker, normally stone-faced, grinned and chuckled a little.

A few minutes later the guard emerged from the gate shack. Saluted.

"You're all clear, Colonel. Just swing up the hill," he pointed, "take the back entrance where the depot is. They'll clear things up there."

"What do you mean, clear things up?" Walker said.

"Hey, people coming in and out all of a sudden. I don't know, but something's going on. Probably closing us down."

"Why you say that?"

"Black Chopper. Bad Omen. When they show up, bases start closing."

"I'm sure it'll be fine."

The guard motioned to the other men. They stepped out of the way and the gate opened.

Oliver put the van in drive and eased his foot on the pedal.

Up the hill they went, rounded the corner and there it was. An old mall. All the store entrances were sealed up with block and mortar. Like a bunker. It made Nate think of a Mausoleum. Oliver pulled around to the loading dock. A dozen men in black flack vests and helmets stood along the dock, M-16's at the ready on their chests.

Nate's chest tightened

"What the—Walker, I don't like this."

"It's alright," Walker said. "We've got friends. Allies. I'll do the talking."

"Should I keep it running?" Oliver said.

WHS security didn't move. They were all still as statues in the rain.

Walker slipped on his ballcap. Popped open his door.

"What are you doing?" Nate said.

"I said, keep it closed. I can handle this." Walker hopped out. Closed the door.

"He's going to get himself killed," Nate said. His foot was burning. Fingers tingling. Nothing was right about this. He rubbed his hands on his thighs.

"Are you going to vomit?" Ashley said.

"Maybe."

She scooted away.

"Where's your leader?" Walker said.

One of the garage doors juttered open. A big man with salt & pepper hair and a neatly trimmed goatee emerged. He had two cannons on his hips, as big as Walker's one.

"Walker," he bellowed, "When you going to stop smoking those damn things?"

"Soon as you stop eating at the Eat-N-Puke," he said, flicking away his cigarette.

The man sauntered down the ramp with a big smile on his face.

"You keep dropping those butts on the ground I'll have you and your men policing this lot later."

"I don't think so, Jake." Walker shook his hand. "Remember who you're speaking with."

"Sorry, Colonel," Jake said, releasing his hand. "Just funning around." He eyed the vans. "You sure brought the cavalry up today, didn't you?"

Nate sat quietly, neck craned towards the window. Walker said they had allies, but who was who? He hoped Jake was one of them. He felt Ashley's hand touch his. Her hand fell to the pistol on her hip. "Feeling it now?" he said.

"Uh huh," she nodded. She popped the strap over the hammer. "I don't like the way those dudes are looking at us."

"Me either," Nate said. He checked his pistol. *I couldn't hit the mall with this.* He grabbed the shotgun. Jake and Walker were walking farther away. "Where are they going? Oliver, roll down the window. I can't hear them."

Walker lit up another cigarette. Pointed towards the vans.

"What's he saying?" Nate said.

"I can't read lips," Ashley replied.

Walker and Jake's exchange got heated. The big man's ears reddened. Walker was on his tiptoes poking him in the chest.

"We need to get out of here," Nate said. "This is bad. Real bad. They're on to us."

Walker punched Jake in the arm. Laughed. He waved at the van.

"Come on out. We're gonna stay for a while."

Oliver shut off the engine.

"Let's go."

Nate looked at Ashley.

"You first," she said.

Nate opened the door, winced as he hit the ground.

Walker dipped his glasses on his nose and pushed them up.

Be ready.

Behind Walker, Jake waved to his men on the dock. Then he looked up at the mall roof. Pointed. Dropped his hands.

Two men were hunkered behind the low roof up there. A long green tube was hoisted on their shoulders.

"It's a trap!" Oliver yelled.

Two blasts of fire burst from the roof. White hot missiles shot through the windows of the other black vans.

Ashley shoved Nate to the ground.

"Cover your—"

Two muffled explosions blasted the van's windows out. Gunfire crackled.

Kaboom! Kaboom!

The vans were burning. Black smoke rolled out. Men screamed and dove out. Rolled and patted the flames out.

Nate felt a rifle barrel in his nose. Ashley had a knee in her back. Walker had his hands behind his head. Oliver lay with his blood spilling on the blacktop.

The Zombie Rebellion was over.

"AH," Ravenloft said, "I see our guests have arrived."

Arms flexicuffed behind his back, Nate was shoved into a chair alongside Walker and Ashley. He was in a conference room with oversized blank LCD screens lining the walls. Ravenloft, Julie Edgerd and Leslie Mckinley were the only familiar faces. Two security guards stood along the wall behind Ravenloft.

A stumpy bald man in a white lab coat sat near the head of the table. His dark eyes were intelligent. Beady. Two other men in lab coats sat staring at fancy laptops like the one Don Baker had. Everyone else was dressed to the nines.

"Colonel Walker," Ravenloft continued, resuming his chair at the head, "it's taken months to snuff you out. So full of dirty little tricks. The WHS's chief assassin and betrayer. Scandalous."

"Thanks," Walker said.

Jake popped him in the back of the head. Knocked his mirrored glasses off.

"Yer gonna pay for what you did to my men, Asshole," Walker said.

"Every war has casualties," Jake said, shoving his head.

"Oh don't stress, Walker. The men who survived will make excellent zombies. Hmm. Hmm. Hmm."

Nate kept his chin and eyes down. Keep quiet. That's what Walker had said. Maybe this was all part of the plan. After all, they were right here in front of Ravenloft. The very head of the WHS.

"Excuse me, Mr. McDaniel?" Ravenloft said.

Nate kept his head down.

"Come now, Nate, surely you aren't going to continue to play the game. Please, Man Who Saved the World. Engage me. Engage us. It's fascinating."

Nate rolled his head back and stared Ravenloft in the eye.

"Oh, what a fine job they did, don't you think so ladies?"

"I like the beard, Nate," Julie Edgerd said.

"And your eyes are still soft as a puppy dog's," said Leslie Mckinley.

"Thanks," he muttered. There wasn't much of anything else to say.

"No, thank you," Ravenloft said. He drummed the table. "Not only have you risen from the dead, but you're even bold enough to try and save the world again. Brave. Admirable." His smiled turned downward. "Stupid. You see—Nate, Walker—this world, you should know by now it's not worth saving."

A fire lit inside him.

"Who are you to determine that?" Nate said. He struggled with his cords. *What am I doing? I'm not a superhero.*

"Ah, Nate, if you only saw it our way. You see, the world is overpopulated—"

"Just shut up!" Nate said. "I don't care if it's over or under. Killing people is murder. You, all of you are mass murderers. You'd make a Nazi blush."

Ravenloft giggled.

"Don't be so serious, Nate. Listen, you're alive. I like you. I like Walker too. I can use good men like you. I'm giving you a chance here."

"What about Ashley?" Nate said. "Do you like her, or does she fall in the category of the overpopulated unwanted people?"

Ravenloft raised a brow. Smiled.

"Quite the contrary. Young, bright, energetic. The WHS always has openings for people like that. Especially when they're ..." He eyed Ashley. "... loyal."

Jake walked over and unbound her wrists. She rubbed them and smiled. Shrugged.

"Sorry guys, I caved. I'm too young to die, and your plan was a pretty stupid one to begin with."

"But," Nate blurted out. He wanted to choke her. He wanted to ask why, but he knew the answer to that. The WHS paid better.

"Oh, the look on your faces. It's one of the reasons I brought you up here." He huffed a laugh. "For my entertainment. Oh, I wish I had a picture of that. Priceless."

"You might as well be the one to shoot us too, Ashley," Walker said with a sneer. "An awful lot of people will have died today because of you."

"Everyone dies anyway. It's the price we pay for living."

"Alright," Ravenloft said, "let's get on with this, shall we? Begin the show, Charles."

This is really happening. Nate felt helpless. Angry. The last moments of his life were closing in.

"You had it right, Walker," Ravenloft said. "Another Outbreak is coming. And that's not all." He turned in his chair and faced the screen. The others followed suit. The men in lab coats' fingers went to work on the computers, and images took form on the LCD's. "That look is outstanding. Terrifying. Almost gives me a chill."

Several images popped up on the screens. An overhead camera image of zombies like the ones from Don Baker's computer caught his eye. The same metal skulls and chomping jaws. Their suits were dark gray camouflage. One thing was different this time. They had guns. Bright flashes burst from their guns.

They can shoot! Nate leaned back in horror. The interior of the mall was a madhouse. Zombies were fighting zombies. Zombie faces were screaming, yelling, shouting. *Those aren't zombies.* A pair of zombies latched arms with a man in a fraternity shirt and ripped the man's arms off.

"Oh!" Julie Edgerd said, turning away. "That's horrible."

A Zombie Soldier blasted a woman in the back.

"Good shot!" Ravenloft said, swinging his arm. "Now, get those cameras on Bawkula." Ravenloft looked over at Nate. "Let's see how that buddy of yours fares. He's quite formidable."

One screen was at eye level. The motion of someone running, gun barrel forward. Darting figures dashed left and right. A gun barrel raised in the line of sights. The face of a man with glasses was in the cross hairs.

"Henry!"

29

"GET THAT SUIT ZIPPED UP."

"I'm trying, but it's tight. This guy's bigger than the others."

"Boo hoo. Now hurry up."

Ziiiiip Ziiiiiip Ziiiiiiip Ziiiiiiip.

"He doesn't look like the others. Look at his eyes. They're blinking. Zombies don't blink, do they?"

"Just shove a helmet on him and get him to the treadmills. Let the eggheads figure that out."

"Well, I'd hate to be the one facing this guy. What he doesn't shoot—"

"What he doesn't shoot, he'll eat. Just be glad it's not you. Now get the lead out."

WHAT?

The lights were bright. The images blurry.

What?

The lights moved. Stretched out like clouds overhead. Something was squeaking.

What?

He tried to speak. No words could be found. A sugary taste hung in his mouth.

The squeaking stopped. Fuzzy faces formed over him.

"Get those IV's out. He's full. Strap the pack on him. They want him pronto. Seems they want to show him off or something."

Pop. Click. Zip. Pop.

"Avatar synchronization ready. Man, we're really getting the hang of this. Give me a hand sitting him up. Damn he's heavy."

What?

"Sync complete. Get him out there. The show's started. Need the finisher."

What?

He moved. He walked. He touched his head, fingers, knees and toes.

"This one's a keeper. Fluid. A real killer."

"Duck, Tori!"

A zombie stumbled over, jaws clicking and mouth bloody.

Kablam!

Henry shot its brain across the food court.

There was screaming. Twisted and mangled limbs. Flesh being torn from the bone. The Zombie Mall had become a Chamber of Horrors.

Henry grabbed Tori by the arm and tugged her up.

"Stay with me!"

Pop! Pop!

Bullets zinged past Henry's head, blasting the plaster off the walls behind him. He dashed behind a metal trash can.

Pop!

A voice screamed behind him. He checked over his shoulder. An intern in zombie makeup collapsed to the floor. Two zombies piled on top of her.

"Henry, what about Rudy!"

Rudy was crawling over the floor. The Zombie Soldier stepped on his leg. Pointed the gun at his face. Rudy covered his face, screaming. "No man! No, man, not in the face! Bawk!"

Pop!

Tori choked a heavy sob.

Henry felt a fire ignite inside him.

"Give me that shotgun!" He snatched it from Tori.

"Don't leave me!" she cried.

He pumped the handle, charged, yelled at the top of his lungs. The shotgun rocked the hallways.

Boom!

He caught the zombie in the back. It whirled.

Boom! Boom!

He blasted it off its feet.

"Damn, Henry," Rudy said, rolling over to his side. "That was brutal."

Dumbfounded, Henry said, "You're alive!"

"It missed. Point blank, it missed!"

"Can you walk?"

"No," Rudy said, dejected. "I'm done for. I'm done for!"

The zombie soldier rolled from side to side on the floor. Henry jumped over and jammed the shotgun into its neck. Pulled the trigger.

Ka-pow!

"Henry!"

It was Tori, pointing.

More Zombie Soldiers were coming, walking down the hallway. Pistols pointed at them. Henry snatched the gun from the Zombie Soldier. He handed it to Rudy. Helped him to his feet.

"Argh!" Rudy shouted. "Just go, Bawk! You and Tori go! I'll hold them off!" He looked at Tori. "Good-bye, Sweet—"

"Oh shut up!" Tori grabbed one arm. Henry grabbed the other. They dragged him down the hall. "We're getting the Hell out of here!"

Pop! Pop!

"WILL SOMEBODY HIT SOMETHING! You missed a man point blank! You're wasting ammo!" Dana said. She pointed at the LCD screen. "See those people? They're the targets! Hit them!"

There were twelve treadmill like contraptions with real men on them. They wore suits with small balls all over them and heavy helmets covered their heads. They were moving, walking, trotting. What they saw through the Zombie Soldiers' eyes was on the screen. Most of the screen showed a man and woman dragging a man. The others were taking aim everywhere.

A door opened in the back of the room. Jake entered.

"What's going on in here? We're supposed to be killing them, not them us!"

"Oh, shut up!" Dana said, marching up to his face. "It was decided to arm the subjects. Did you really think they wouldn't fight back, Fathead!"

"Get it under control, Dana! Ravenloft is here!"

She turned her back. Eyed the screens, shaking her head.

"It's just a matter of time."

"The way they're shooting they'll run out of bullets. Then what?"

"It won't come to that, Idiot. They don't have anywhere to go or hide. We have plenty of cavalry to send in for clean-up. I'll do it myself if I have to."

"You better hope it doesn't come to that," Jake said. He slammed the door behind him.

"Jerk!" She kicked the wall. "Alright, men! Listen up. Quit wasting ammo, you trigger happy bastards! The next one of you that misses a point blank shot is going in. As a zombie!"

"WHERE ARE WE GOING, HENRY?" Tori said.

The first priority was Rudy. He was dead weight, just not dead yet. There was no way he could climb up to that skylight.

"In here!"

He turned into a small women's clothing store. They dragged Rudy clear to the back. Headed into a dressing room. Henry tied a shirt he'd grabbed around Rudy's leg.

"Just lock yourself in," he said. "We'll lead them away."

"But, Bawk?"

"I've got to find a way out of this. I'll come back." He squeezed Rudy's shoulder. "Survive."

"Ziggy says that's not likely."

"Just keep quiet. We've made it out before." He grabbed Tori's hand. Closed the door. "Keep down," he whispered.

Numma Numma.

Jaws clicked and clacked. Bodies of Zombie Soldiers pushed through the clothes racks.

Henry'd figured one thing out so far: the zombies weren't good shots. He kept crawling towards the front. The booted feet of zombies were all around him. He could see out into the main hall. More Zombie Soldiers waited. Skull Faces scanning all around. *Trapped. What's the plan now, Henry?*

Numma. Numma. Numma. Numma.

The moaning was worse than the sound of gunfire. Tori shuddered behind him. He reached back and grabbed her hand. *I should have hidden her with Rudy.* He knew she wouldn't leave his side. Not now. Worst case, they would fight and die together. He took a breath, summoned his courage.

"I don't think they can hear us," he whispered back.

The Zombie Soldiers started pushing over the racks.

Tori squeaked.

He and Tori would have to make a run for the skylight. Climb up and out somehow. With zombies and Zombie Soldiers everywhere. He had to lead them away from Rudy first. He lowered the shotgun barrel towards the nearest zombie's foot.

"Cover your ears. Get ready to run."

Ka-Pow!

The zombie teetered. Crashed to the ground.

Henry made a dash at the Zombie Soldiers in the hallway.

Ka-Pow!

He blasted one in the chest. Surged between the others.

Pop! Pop! Pop!

The zombies' shots were erratic. He kept sprinting. Handguns were only good at close range. The more distance the better.

Pop! Pop! Pop! Pop! Pop!

"Agh!"

His shoulder caught fire. The shotgun clattered on the shiny floor. He stumbled. Fell.

"Henry!" Tori huddled over him. "Get up!"

"I can't! Run, Tori, run!"

The Zombie Soldiers closed in.

"I'm not leaving you."

They were surrounded. Barrels all around.

Henry grimaced. Struggled to rise.

Numma. Numma. Numma. Numma.

The moaning was worse than the pain.

"You sick bastards going eat us or shoot us!" Tori screamed.

Pop! Pop!

30

NATE'S HEAD SAGGED INTO HIS CHEST. HIS STOMACH TURNED. HE'D seen many die, but not like this. He couldn't stand the thought of his friend being blown away on the TV screen.

"We could fund all our projects if we could just televise this," Leslie Mckinley said. "Reality TV at its finest —with zombies!"

"You people are sick," Walker said. He spat on the floor. "Demented."

"Depends on your perspective," Julie Edgerd said, checking her nails. "When you're rich and powerful, you can be all the demented you want."

Ravenloft threw his head back and laughed.

"Excellent, point. Excellent." He placed his finger over his mouth and under his nose. "This reminds me of the days of Caesar. At the arena. The days when they had gladiators. What the Romans would do—give the fallen warriors the thumbs up or thumbs down."

Charles and the other technicians were typing commands on their stations.

"Charles," Ravenloft said, "don't kill them just yet."

Nate's eyes went back to the screens. Henry emerged from the clothing store blasting away. A charge went through his legs. *Go Henry!* A moment later Henry fell.

Ravenloft and his people let out a cheer.

"Excellent shooting, Charles! Well done." He clapped. "Everything I'd hoped for. Now we have them, so let me see a show of thumbs. Do we shoot them or let the zombies eat them? Thumbs up for mercy. Thumbs down for mutilation."

"Oh, that gal has some potential. She'd make a great candidate for the catwalks," Leslie Mckinley said.

"Interesting," Ravenloft said, rubbing his chin. "And look at that arm of hers. She'd be a star. Hmmm. Well, how about the man then. Bawkula. Mercy or mutilation?"

Nate wanted to scream. People were dying right in front of him. Others were turning into zombies. All he could do was sit there, cheeks flushed, sweating.

"We need to be quick now. The flesh eaters will be on them soon," Charles added, eyes shifting back and forth.

"Mercy!" Nate blurted out. "Mercy, for God's sake! He's been a WHS employee for years, and I don't think he's ever not done what he's been told."

"Noted," Ravenloft said. "Seems you're a bit overwhelmed, Nate. So how about I show you and Walker some mercy. Put them against the wall."

The two security guards pulled them out of their chairs and shoved them against the wall.

"On your knees," one security member said, shoving him down.

"Ow," Nate said, grimacing.

It was over. He lifted his chin. He'd heard a preacher say once that death in all its forms was ugly. Inevitable.

"I'll spare you the horror of your friend's demise. But now it's your time to go." Ravenloft was on his feet and made his way over. He took a machine gun and handed it to Ashley. "Time to prove your loyalty."

Her eyes widened like moons.

"Can you do this?" Ravenloft said in her ear.

She took a breath. Nodded.

"Then make it quick and soon you'll be having dinner with the rest of us."

She leveled the weapon, aiming uncertainly.

"Pick one or the other," Ravenloft said, stepping aside. "You don't have to do them both."

"Just shoot me, Ashley," Walker said. "Don't miss."

She flipped the safety off. Took aim.

"I won't."

31

HE WAS MOVING. HIS NECK ITCHED. BURNED. HE HEARD ... RUSTLES. Screaming. Snarls. Wails.

Where?

Images changed. Shifted. He was one with others.

Pop. Pop. Pop.

Guns?

He saw his hands. Weapons filled them. There were men. Familiar. He didn't think but he followed.

Two figures lay on the floor. Blood on their clothes. On the floor. Chests heaving. Mouths panting. Skull faces loomed over them. Pointing weapons.

Henry?

The woman was screaming.

His back burned. Itched. He wanted to scratch. He couldn't move. He should move.

Who am I?

Pop. Pop.

Memories appeared. Snapshots. Family. Friends. An eight sided arena. A sign in the crowd.

The Black Python.

H<small>ENRY JERKED HIS PISTOL OUT</small>. *Screw em!* Aimed for the biggest one. Squeezed the trigger.

Blam! Blam!

The bullets ricocheted.

This was it. The end. Filled with screams and moans all over. The world was in for it. All over again. The madness would never stop.

He grabbed Tori's hand and squeezed it.

"I love you," he said.

"I love you too," she replied.

The big Zombie Soldier's arms started to shake. The weapons remained locked in its palms.

"W<small>HAT'S THE PROBLEM</small>?" Dana said to the man on the treadmill. "They want the big guy to waste him. Squeeze the trigger."

"I am," the man said, pulling his finger back and forth. "He's not responding. Use another one."

Dana slapped a man at the computer terminal in the back of the head.

"Get it working."

T<small>HE BIG</small> Z<small>OMBIE</small> Soldier raised his arms up and jammed his barrels under the Metal Skulls to either side. Squeezed the triggers.

KaBlam!

The zombies crumbled to the ground.

"*Henry ... run*," it said.

It dropped one pistol and tore the cords from its neck.

"Aaaag!"

Another Zombie Soldier started blasting into its chest.

Pop! Pop! Pop!

The big zombie grabbed it by the eyelets and ripped the helmet off its head.

KaBlam!

Tori shot it in the skull.

"Henry, go!"

"Rod!" Henry Exclaimed.

Rod stuck his pistol in another zombie's mouth.

Kablam!

"Black Python..."

Kablam!

"Let's go!" Henry said. In agony, he got to his feet, grabbed Tori's hand, and started running for the skylight.

A pair of zombies wandered into their path. It was Alice and Weege.

"Num. Num."

Henry and Tori opened fire.

Blam. Blam. Blam. Blam. Blam. Blam. Blam.

"That was long overdue," Tori said.

"Over here! Over here!"

A man was waving at them. He was with two women. It was Paul or Craig, with Jo Ann and Karen. They all held baseball bats with zombie ooze all over them. Two zombies lay twitching at their feet.

Tugging Tori behind him, Henry made a run for it.

Two Zombie Soldiers cut them off.

They opened fire.

Blam. Blam. Blam. Blam. Blam. Click. Click.

The soldiers took aim and fired back.

BULLETS RIDDLED HIS BODY. Bones cracked. Rod fired back. He jerked helmets off heads. Put bullets in them until there were no more.

He could think. He could fight.

He ripped a soldier's pack off. Grabbed its head. Twisted till it snapped.

Bullets ricocheted off his face. Punched into his body.

He didn't feel them. He only felt one thing. Strong. Fast.

He picked a zombie up and tossed it into the others. Two more tackled him. Drove him to the ground. He tried to laugh, but couldn't.

I'm awesome!

He broke their necks. Got up. Looked for Henry. Tori.

32

"WHAT JUST HAPPENED?" RAVENLOFT SAID, GAWPING AT THE SCREENS. "Charles, what happened! One of the zombies just shot the others!"

Charles' fingers drummed on the keypad.

"I-I don't know."

"YOU BETTER KNOW!"

All eyes were glued to the screens.

Screw it! Nate thought. *I'm not going down like this. Hail Mary, full of grace!*

He hopped up on his feet, lowered his shoulder and barreled into the security guard.

"Oof!" the man said.

Nate drove him into the table. Gunfire went off. The guard elbowed him in the nose. He stumbled backwards. Got slugged in the gut. Then the chin. His face was bleeding. A machine gun blarred.

Takka-Takka-Takka- Takka

"Walker," Nate said, looking back at the wall. Walker was gone.

Takka-Takka-Takka- Takka

Takka-Takka-Takka- Takka

Ashley blasted away. The target. Ravenloft. His chest filled with holes and lead.

The guard swung his weapon around at Ashley's back.

"Ulp!"

Walker jumped on his back. Gun blasts went into the ceiling.

Ashley whirled. Shot a burst into the guard's chest.

The man sagged to the ground.

Jake burst through the door, big guns blazing.

Ka-Choom! Ka-Choom! Ka-Choom!

Everyone dove to the floor.

Takka-Takka-Takka- Takka

Takka-Takka-Takka- Takka

Jake's body sagged to the floor.

Walker lay on the ground with the guard's gun barrel smoking.

"Take care of them," Walker said. He slammed the door shut. Locked it. Grabbed Jake's knife. "Cut this off, Nate."

Numb, Nate did as he was told. Walker cut his hands loose.

"What just happened?" he asked.

"Vengeance," said Walker.

"Justice," said Ashley, checking the bodies on the floor.

"Did you kill all of them?" Walker said.

Charles' bloody face was on his laptop. Unmoving. The other lab coats were dead too.

Julie and Leslie were goners.

Ravenloft lay pressed against the wall, chuckling a mouthful of blood.

"You can't stop this," he sputtered. "Nothing can stop the evil."

Blam!

"Unless you got a bullet," Walker said to Ashley. "Great plan, Girl. Secure the room."

Ashley smiled. Walker grabbed a laptop and started typing. "Find some smartphones, will you, Nate?"

"Seriously, what just happened?"

"You saved the world again, Bub."

"I didn't do anything. Nothing!"

"Sure you did. We used you to draw out Ravenloft. We never would've gotten close on our own, so Ash and I devised a plan."

"Did anyone else know about it?"

"Nope."

"So, what was going to happen if Ravenloft hadn't given Ash a gun?"

"We would've died. She'd have taken him out later."

Nate sagged down in the seat. Touched his bleeding nose. "Ow." So much had happened so fast he felt like he was forgetting something. "Henry!"

THE ZOMBIE SOLDIERS had the drop on him. He hugged Tori and turned his back to them.

"Numma. Numma. Numma. Numma"

No shots came.

"Come on! Come on!" voices yelled.

Henry turned. The Zombie Soldiers' gun arms were down.

ABORT! ABORT! ABORT!

"What?" Dana said, looking over the computer tech's shoulder. "What the Hell is going on?"

EVACUATE! EVACUATE!

Something crawled up her spine. She grabbed her radio. Charged the mic.

"Jake. Jake, come in, over."

Nothing.

"Jake, come in, over."

"Jake's dead. You're next, over."

One of the men on the treadmill took his helmet off. The others followed suit.

"I'm out of here."

"Get back on there!"

"You get on there, Ostrich Face!"

"Run! Run!" they yelled and pointed.

Another Zombie Soldier approached Henry and Tori. The big one.

Henry blocked Tori. Stood his ground at it approached.

"Rod?"

"*Yes*," he said. His voice was eerie. Garbled.

Rod took off his helmet.

Tori gasped.

It was Rod. His dark face smoky and veiny. Eyes sunken in.

"Is it bad?" he said. "Am I dead?"

"I-I don't know, Big Guy, but you're talking. That's living, I'd say."

A zombie stumbled down the hallway.

Num. Num.

Rod picked the zombie up with one arm and slammed it on its head.

"*I can't be that, Henry.*"

Henry could have sworn Rod's eyes watered.

"*I can't be that.*"

Nate sat in wild eyed disbelief. Henry was fine. The cavalry was coming. He lived. As he sat in his chair, Walker debriefed him.

"We've got insiders. It only takes one to get the message out. Soon as we got captured, Plan 2 went into action." He puffed on his cigarette. "Plan 1 was to get in here and do it on our own. Plan 2, call in reinforcements if captured. Even if we wound up dead, at least the WHS's cage would've been rattled. Another Outbreak might've been stopped. I think we've done it by getting Ravenloft. Just have to make sure the world knows what they were up to."

He pointed to Charles.

"That man there, well, it'd probably been better if Ash hadn't killed him, but hopefully his secrets will die with him. We're already pouring over his notes. We'll try and bury the evil within."

"So," Nate said, "who's in charge now?"

"Well, with the Magnificent Twelve whittled down, and Ravenloft dead, I'd say no one is in charge until after the investigation. I just hope they'll take my word over one of these knuckleheaded drones. That'll give us plenty of time to figure out everything they were up to. You on board?"

"What? Me?" Nate said, pointing to himself.

"No, the Other Man Who Saved the World in the room," Walker said.

"I didn't save it today." He frowned.

"You stuck your neck out, Nate. Pile drove that sack of meat over there." Walker nodded. "Not many men have the guts to finish on their feet. Most in your situation would've lain down and died." Walker couched. "I thank you for it, but you aren't getting any medals.

"No, I got more than my share the last time." Nate toyed with the crucifix of Christ on his neck. Looked around. Shrugged. "I don't think I have anywhere else to go." He looked at the LCD screens. WHS soldiers were hard at work herding the zombies. Shooting others. He didn't see Henry. "Where'd Henry go?"

HENRY TRIED NOT to shout when the medic pulled the bullet out. It felt like his entire shoulder was being ripped from his body.

"Henry," Tori said, "bite on this, Baby." She shoved a wooden shower curtain holder in his face. It still had an expensive-looking shower curtain on it.

"No," he said. "I can take it."

"Okay." Tori wiped his head with a damp washcloth that matched the shower curtain. "You're a brave man, you know."

"You're a brave woman. Ow!" he winced. "Numb it, will you!"

"Sorry," the medic said.

Henry wasn't certain what was going on, but someone had saved the day. Minutes after he and Rod had spoken, the cavalry had come. They'd shot the turned zombies but left the others alone. He wished they'd shot them all. *Evil things.* Now, he was under the bright lights in the vendeteria where they'd been hours ago, trying to sort it out.

"Look," Tori said, pointing.

Dana the Bird Lady walked by with her hands cuffed behind her back. She sneered at them. There were over a dozen being walked out. Others were stuffed in body bags. Henry remembered hearing another gunfight going on. His mind was at work. This Facility was a place of amazing breakthroughs. He could feel it. But they were doing it for all the wrong reasons.

"Henry, do you think we're ever going to get out?" Tori whispered, rubbing his leg.

"I'm not going to even think about it," he said, looking around. "Say, where's Rod?"

"Quarantined," a guard said.

"I need to see him," Henry demanded.

"Got to get clearance."

Two men and a woman entered the room.

"Attention."

The guards saluted.

"At ease," the small one with mirrored glasses said.

"Henry!" the big guy with the beard said. "Henry, thank God you survived!"

Henry looked at Tori. She shrugged. Turned back to the man.

"Do I know you?"

The man extended his hands. Looked into his eyes with a smile.

"Come on, Henry. It's me."

Henry lurched up in his seat.

"Ow!"

"Easy, Son," the medic said.

Henry leaned forward.

"Nate?"

"The one and only."

"I, I thought you were dead. I thought you killed that ... woman."

"No," Nate said, shaking his head. "Hard to tell the lie from the truth these days, but I'll be glad to tell you."

"I'm looking forward to it already."

Rod sat in a cell, unmoving. He'd been shot a dozen times. It didn't hurt. He didn't feel tired, but alert and strong. He thirsted. For what, he did not know. He could wait in the meantime. Forever and a day. When he got out, he smiled, he'd do whatever he wanted.

Ashley made her way over to a handful of people sitting along the wall.

"You guys alright? You need anything?"

Jo Ann shook her head. Karen was trembling.

Paul was wiping off zombie makeup. He asked, "Have you found my brother Craig yet?"

"Uh," Ashley said, stalling. She felt bad for the young man. All of them. *Sheltered people.* "They're still looking."

"I'm sure he's okay," Jo Ann said, rubbing his shoulder. "He's a slippery one."

"Yeah," Karen said, nodding.

"They just went in there and started wasting the zombies. I didn't even get to see. Mom and Dad are gonna kill me."

High Street. Morgantown. A minivan pulled into the parking lot of the KA Manor.

Craig hopped out and slid the side door open. He grabbed a squirming black sack and hoisted it over his shoulder. He smiled as he looked up the stairs. "It's going to be the best Reco night ever!"

EPILOGUE

CHAD PUSHED his face out of the sand. Faced the moonlight.

"*Ah,*" he said. "*I live.*" He smacked his lips. Surveyed his surroundings. Everything seemed black and white. In the distance, a pack of coyotes howled. He could see them. Clearly. Not covered by the night.

That's strange.

He retraced his steps to where the zombies he'd killed lay dead. *Hmmm.* He felt fine and wrong at the same time. His limbs felt chill. An urge to kill consumed him. Images of those mercenaries formed in his mind, the Aussie and the putz. His throat growled. He had an idea.

He tugged the zombie suit off one corpse and put it on. He placed the Skull Face helmet on his head. He needed a car. He knew where to get one. He followed the car tracks in the dirt, mile after mile, into the morning. He wandered into camp. A man was seated in a folding chair with three others, all eating breakfast.

The pudgy one saw him first. Jerked and fell backward over his chair.

"Whoa!" the Aussie said. "What have we here? It followed us all the way back here? Amazing."

"That-That-That's not p-possible," the pudgy one said. "It's cursed."

"Aw, shaddup. It's probably hungry. Get it some Dew. And get on the horn. They're gonna want to hear about this."

A merc tossed the Aussie a bottle. He waggled it in front of Chad's face.

"Here, Boy. Drinky drink."

"*No thanks,*" Chad said.

The Aussie's eyes exploded open.

"Wha—"

Chad snatched the man's wrist. Grabbed his neck. Crushed the man's throat.

Blam! Blam Blam!

Bullets tore into him. The Zombie Suit held. Lead zinged off his helmet. He wanted to laugh. Instead, he killed. He busted two men's skulls together. Pounced on the pudgy one's back. Stuffed his face in the dirt until he kicked no more. He looked up at the sun beating down on him. *I'm not even hot or tired.* He eyed his gray-skinned hands. *Am I still a man? Or am I a zombie?*

PLEASE DON'T FORGET to leave a review, they are a HUGE HELP! LINK!

Learn more about my books below, over 100, and if you like my zombie series check out The Supernatural Bounty Hunter Files or The Henchmen Chronicles. See more details below.

AFTERWORD

From the Author

First off, thanks for reading. In all truth, I didn't have any intention of doing a 3rd book, but enough people contacted me saying they wanted to read more. I wanted to try my best to make them happy. Now, I've left things open for a possible 4th book. That will all depend on how this 3rd book does. I write fantasy, and those books do much better, but I do enjoy having fun toying with all the possibilities with zombies. I hope you like some of the ideas I came up with. And maybe I'll expand upon them later.

As for where this book ends, just assume for now that Nate and Henry are teaming up with Walker to unravel all the things the WHS had planned for the zombies. They started putting Dr. Charles Whitmore's notes together. They pay a visit to Charlie's lab and meet Steve. Play cards. Watch Baby Einstein and have a few beers with him. Who knows? Maybe I'll write about Chad adapting to his new zombie-type life. Rod too. Maybe a breakout in Morgantown is unloosed. Honestly, I don't know what makes for a good zombie book. I just try not to do what I've seen in movies and TV. But as of

February 2014 I'm giving this series a rest. I'm always glad to hear your thoughts on this topic.

Don't Stop,

Craig Halloran

ABOUT THE AUTHOR

Check me out on Bookbub and follow: Craig Halloran

I'd love it if you would subscribe to my newsletter and download my free books: www.craighalloran.com/email

On Facebook, you can find me at The Darkslayer Report by Craig Halloran.

Twitter, Twitter, Twitter. I am there, too: www.twitter.com/Craig-Halloran

And of course, you can always email me anytime at craig@thedarkslayer.com

CRAIG'S COMPLETE BOOK LIST

OVER 100 TITLES! PURE ADRENALINE!

5 MILLION WORDS IN PUBLICATION!

EPIC FANTASY, SWORD AND SORCERY URBAN FANTASY, SCI-FI, POST-APOC! LINKS BELOW!

FREE BOOKS

The Darkslayer: Brutal Beginnings

Nath Dragon – Quest for the Thunderstone

The Henchmen Chronicles Intro

Dragon Wars Prequel

The Odyssey of Nath Dragon Series (Prequel to Chronicles of Dragon)

Exiled: Book 1 of 5

The Odyssey of Nath Dragon Boxset (Best Deal)

The Chronicles of Dragon Series 1 (10 Books)

The Hero, the Sword and the Dragons (Book 1)

Boxset 1-5

Boxset 6-10

Collector's Edition 1-10 (Best Deal)

Tail of the Dragon, The Chronicles of Dragon, Series 2 (10 book series)

Tail of the Dragon Book #1

Boxset 1-5

Boxset 6-10

Collector's Edition 1-10 (Best Deal)

The Darkslayer Series 1 – 6 books

Wrath of the Royals (Book 1)

Boxset 1-3

Boxset 4-6

Omnibus 1-6 (Best Deal)

The Darkslayer: Bish and Bone, Series 2 (10 Book series)

Bish and Bone (Book 1 of 10)

Boxset 1-5

Boxset 6-10

Bish and Bone Omnibus (Books 1-10) (Best Deal)

Dragon Wars: 20-Book Series

Blood Brothers: Book 1 of 20

Boxset 1-5

Boxset 6-10

Boxset 11-15

Boxset 16-20

CLASH OF HEROES: Nath Dragon meets The Darkslayer

Book 1 of 3

Special Edition - Books 1-3 (Best Deal)

The Supernatural Bounty Hunter Files (10 book series)

Smoke Rising: Book 1 of 10

Boxset 1-5

Boxset 6-10

Collector's Edition 1-10 (Best Deal)

The Henchmen Chronicles 5-Book Series

The King's Henchmen - Book 1 of 5

The Henchmen Chronicles Collection: Books 1-5

Zombie Impact Series

Zombie Day Care: Book 1

Zombie Rehab: Book 2

Zombie Warfare: Book 3

Boxset: Books 1-3 (Best Deal)

The Gamma Earth Cycle

Escape from the Dominion

Flight from the Dominion

Prison of the Dominion

The Sorcerer's Power Series

The Sorcerer's Curse: Book 1 of 5

The Red Citadel and the Sorcerer's Power (All 5 Books)

The Misadventures of Dan - Drama/Comedy

Gorgon Thunder-Bot Incinerator of Worlds (1 book, childrens)